Advance Praise for *The Third Hill North of Town*

"This is an eerie, haunting, beautifully realized novel populated by charming misfits and eccentrics."
—Joseph Olshan, author of *Cloudland*

"Once *The Third Hill North of Town* turns over its engine, readers will do well to secure their grip on themselves, their loved ones, and any notions they have about guilt and innocence, truth and trust, convenience and blame. By its end, Bly's whirlwind challenges much of what we believe without necessarily meaning to, including those comfortable views on the infinite gradations we lump under the banner of mental illness, including racism. A hell of a journey."
—Kyle Beachy, author of *The Slide*

"What a wild ride this novel is! *The Third Hill North of Town* grabs hold and doesn't let go. A story of the tragedy and beauty of coincidence and circumstance, this novel is one that brings the unlikeliest characters together in a way that is somehow both surprising and meaningful."
—T. Greenwood, author of *Bodies of Water*

"Noah Bly takes readers on an unforgettable ride through America. Well written, page-turning, and hard to put down!"
—Jim Kokoris, author of *The Pursuit of Other Interests*

"A glorious, madcap American road novel in the picaresque tradition, *The Third Hill North of Town* explores a dark uncharted territory where vengefulness and desire and coincidence and consequence blow wild through human hearts, tossing people together and tearing them apart. Think *On the Road* written by Flannery O'Connor. A profound meditation on the sanctity of improvised friendships."
—Stephen Lovely, author of *Irreplaceable*

The
Third Hill
North
of Town

NOAH BLY

KENSINGTON BOOKS
www.kensingtonbooks.com

KENSINGTON BOOKS are published by

Kensington Publishing Corp.
119 West 40th Street
New York, NY 10018

All Kensington titles, imprints, and distributed lines are available at special quantity discounts for bulk purchases for sales promotion, premiums, fund-raising, educational, or institutional use.

Special book excerpts or customized printings can also be created to fit specific needs. For details, write or phone the office of the Kensington Special Sales Manager: Kensington Publishing Corp., 119 West 40th Street, New York, NY 10018. Attn. Special Sales Department. Phone: 1-800-221-2647.

Kensington and the K logo Reg. U.S. Pat. & TM Off.

ISBN-13: 978-0-7582-9077-9
ISBN-10: 0-7582-9077-2
First Kensington Trade Paperback Printing: March 2014

eISBN-13: 978-0-7582-9078-6
eISBN-10: 0-7582-9078-0
First Kensington Electronic Edition: March 2014

10 9 8 7 6 5 4 3 2 1

Printed in the United States of America

For Nellie Josephine Nixson:
Beloved citizen of Pawnee

ACKNOWLEDGMENTS

Heartfelt thanks to:

Gordon Mennenga, for his brilliant, exhaustive, and blisteringly honest feedback on the first draft of this novel. I don't even want to think about how much I owe him.

Sergeant Jeff Yates (retired) of the Bettendorf Police Department, Bettendorf, Iowa, for answering endless "what-if" questions about everything from forensics to federal manhunts. Any mistakes regarding police procedure in this book are mine, not his.

John Scognamiglio, my talented, long-suffering editor at Kensington, for his utter decency, kindness, insight, support, generosity, and passion.

Dr. Abraham Assad, for helping me figure out the best way to shoot somebody in the torso without really hurting him too much.

John Talbot, my agent, for his expertise, patience, and common sense.

Larry and Shirley Forari, for sharing their experience of working in a small-town sheriff's department in the 1960s.

Steve Kennevan, for alleviating my ignorance about the engine of an Edsel.

Scott Nelson, the Mac Doctor of Iowa City, for miraculously resurrecting the only electronic version I had of this novel after my computer died. I have now learned how to back up my writing. . . .

Sarah and Willie, for their love.

Much Madness is divinest Sense —
To a discerning Eye —

EMILY DICKINSON

Chapter 1

As far as Julianna was concerned, the boy she kidnapped on the street that morning in Prescott, Maine, was Ben Taylor, her closest friend in the world, and the two of them were teenagers from the same town, both lost and far from home. That she was actually fifty-four years old and he was fifteen never occurred to her, nor did it trouble her much when the boy insisted they were strangers. After all, Julianna was nobody's fool. Ben had always been a clown, and she knew better than to listen when he said ridiculous things.

A lot of things seemed ridiculous lately to Julianna Dapper. Topping her list on this particular morning, however, was the date of the newspaper beside her on the seat of the car. The paper stated it was Saturday, June 23, 1962, but she knew for a fact the *real* date was Saturday, June 23, 1923. Somebody at the newspaper office had obviously made a ridiculous typographical error, and she shook her head and laughed every time she glanced down at the paper. It was hard to understand how such a thing could happen, but the world was a funny place.

The car she was driving was a cream and brown Edsel Ranger, with four doors, a tan Naugahyde interior, and child-safety locks on the rear doors. It belonged to a psychiatrist named Edgar Reilly, who'd accidentally left his keys in the ignition earlier that day at the state mental hospital in Bangor, Maine. When Julianna slipped out of the dementia wing of the hospital, shortly after breakfast, the car was sitting in the sunlit parking lot, a few steps away from the fire door. She remembered parking it there—though she had done no such thing—and she scolded herself for being so scatterbrained as to leave the keys in it.

"For heaven's sake," she muttered as she opened the door and got in. She tossed the sweater she was carrying onto the backseat and removed her headscarf, too. "I might as well have posted a sign saying *please steal my car.*"

Cities, as she knew all too well, were full of thieves, and she was thrilled to be going home, where she never had to worry about such things. She started the engine and drove off, still puzzled as to how she could have done something so careless. She shook her head in dismay, thinking how furious her father would be if he knew how irresponsible she'd been.

Julianna was a tall, slender woman with a long nose, short brown hair, and high, sharp cheekbones. She wasn't pretty, necessarily, but she was graceful and strong, with an appealing, crooked smile, a no-nonsense handshake, and enormous green eyes that studied, with intense curiosity, everyone she passed on the street.

It was these eyes of hers, more than anything, that allowed her to abduct Elijah Hunter two hours later in the sleepy town of Prescott, Maine. When she pulled up to the curb where Elijah was standing and leaned across the seat to talk to him through the open passenger window, he gazed into those inquisitive, intelligent eyes and saw nothing to fear.

Prescott was an isolated little community surrounded by woods and fields, about ninety miles west of Bangor. Elijah's parents were Samuel and Mary Hunter, and the Hunter family was one of only a handful of black families living in that part of Maine. Because of this, Elijah was used to people gawking at him, and he was also used to cars slowing down as they passed him on the road. It wasn't the first time somebody had pulled up to the curb to address him, either, though this was less common. Most people who had something to say to him from a car window chose to do so while speeding past, and seemed to be more interested in shouting obscenities than in talking.

Elijah's eyes—soulful and brown—were almost as large as Julianna's. He had a lean, finely boned face and a small, pert nose, and though most people he knew considered him handsome, they also believed his good looks were marred slightly by a chronic look of anxiety that wrinkled his forehead and drew the corners of his mouth into a more or less permanent frown. What was causing his anxiety on *this* particular day was an article he'd just read in *Life* magazine, in which he'd learned that forty-nine million people in the world died each year. Not content with the level of horror this aroused in him, he had taken the statistical nightmare a step further, and had calculated humanity's daily death toll at roughly 138,000. This had nearly paralyzed him with despair, yet as he emerged from the drugstore that morning (where he'd picked up the magazine), he was hard at work estimating the hourly death rate, as well, even though he knew that doing so would likely ruin his whole day.

Such was the way Elijah's mind worked, and the reason his parents had forbidden him to read magazines and newspapers. He ignored this prohibition all the time, though, because he couldn't help himself.

He had been engrossed the day before with a *Reader's Digest* article about overpopulation, and the day before that he had gagged and nearly vomited in front of the town librarian soon after scanning a *Newsweek* story about the likelihood of a coming global famine. In fact, his preoccupation with dire news tidbits had gotten so bad recently that his mother, in a fit of concerned temper—after she found a dog-eared copy of *U.S. News and World Report* squirreled away under his mattress—had compared Elijah to "a thick-headed, morbid little moth, in search of the biggest, baddest flame it can find."

Elijah had small ears, and big hands and feet, and long legs. He was slender and almost six feet tall, but he wasn't used to being this height. (Nor was his mother, who kept referring to him as "little.") He'd grown five inches in the last eight months, and he was prone to knocking over glasses and bottles on dinner tables, and tripping over things on the sidewalk. His limbs seemed to get longer every day, and refused to do what he asked of them.

He'd walked into town that day to mail a letter to his grandfather—and to spend a few stomach-churning minutes thumbing through magazines in the rack by the drugstore window—and had exited the drugstore only moments before Julianna pulled up to the intersection in front of him.

"Hello, dear!" she called from the car. "Would you like a ride? It's an awfully long walk to your house."

Elijah was dressed in a white button-down shirt, new blue jeans, and clean white sneakers. His shirt was flawlessly pressed, as were his jeans; Mary Hunter never let her son leave the house looking less than respectable. It was a point of pride to her that Elijah should always appear as well cared for as any of the white boys in town. She believed, with some justification, that people would judge him more harshly than they would other children, and she wasn't about to let anybody think Mary Hunter's son wasn't up to snuff.

But Julianna Dapper was oblivious to Mary's efforts on Elijah's behalf. She didn't see the attractive, presentable boy he actually was; what she saw instead was a thin and rather ragged young man, with no shirt or shoes. In fact, he looked as if he needed a bath rather badly, and it broke her heart, as always, to see him running around in nothing but a pair of worn overalls. She knew, of course, that nobody from their little corner of the world had much money, but Ben Taylor's family was dirt poor, and everybody knew it and poked fun at them. She looked at his filthy bare feet and tried not to show the pity she was feeling.

Elijah had never seen Julianna before, but he felt no surprise that she seemed to know who he was and where he lived. There were only twelve hundred people in Prescott, and every single white person in town would know he was Samuel and Mary Hunter's son just by looking at him, and would also know their farm was on Temple Road, two miles north of the old meat-packing plant. Nor was it particularly strange that he didn't recognize her. He may have been born and raised in Prescott, but he paid no heed to the older people in town and knew very few of them by sight. He kept to himself most of the time; the bulk of his days were spent on the farm with his parents, or in school, or in a quiet corner of the library.

He leaned over to get a better look at her. He noticed her startling green eyes immediately, and also her pretty green dress, but he became self-conscious under her scrutiny and transferred his attention to the carpeted floor in front of the passenger seat. It was full of groceries. He saw bags of potato chips and bottles of Pepsi sticking out of brown paper sacks, and there was also a generous supply of Chips Ahoy! cookies and a dozen or so Butterfinger candy bars. On closer study, there looked to be nothing nutritious in the bags at all; the only thing he saw besides the junk food was a carton of Marlboro cigarettes. Elijah wondered how the woman remained so thin if this was the kind of stuff she ate all the time.

"Hi," he said. His voice was polite, but wary. "You know my mom?"

Elijah had already concluded that Julianna was probably one of the twenty or so middle-aged ladies from the Methodist church up the road who congregated every Saturday morning to play bingo. He'd heard about several of these "bingo ladies" from his mother—who cleaned house for many of the white families in town—but he had met none of them.

Julianna looked taken aback at first, but then she laughed. "Very funny, silly. Everybody knows Mary," she said. "Stop being ridiculous and hop in."

It was an unfortunate coincidence that Julianna's old friend Ben from Missouri had a mother named Mary, as did Elijah.

Elijah wouldn't normally have gotten in the car with a stranger, but the woman seemed harmless, and since she knew his mom he decided accepting a ride from her would be fine. He might have been more cautious if he'd noticed the plastic hospital wristband Julianna was wearing on her left arm, but he was still extrapolating the hourly death toll of the human race, and so was distracted. He also wasn't looking forward to the long walk back to the farm. He'd tripped on the gravel road on the way into town and torn a small hole in the knee of his blue jeans, and the likelihood of tripping again on the way home was worrying him, too.

"Okay," he agreed. "Thanks, that would be nice."

"You'll have to sit in back." Julianna gestured at the bags on the floor of the front seat. "I hope you don't mind."

"That's fine." Elijah took hold of the rear door and found it locked. She reached over the seat to unlock it and became flustered when the knob wouldn't budge, no matter how she pulled on it.

"I don't know what the trouble is," she huffed. "The silly old thing is stuck."

Elijah hid a smile. He could almost hear his mother muttering something caustic in his head. Mary Hunter had zero patience in general, but became especially irritable with people who were flummoxed by simple mechanical things, as this woman seemed to be.

"It's probably just a safety lock," he said quietly. He poked his head into the car to get a better look at her control panel and she sat up to give him room. He pointed at her door. "Yep. Just push that little button above your armrest."

"Oh!" Julianna exclaimed. "Daddy didn't tell me about that." She punched the button and the locks on the rear doors sprang up with a pop. "As you know, I'm far more comfortable on a horse."

Elijah thought this an odd comment from a stranger, but he wasn't really paying attention. Now that Julianna was sitting upright again he could see the newspaper on the seat beside her, and he was trying to conceal his agitation. The headline announced: PLANE CRASH IN WEST INDIES KILLS 113, and the lurid picture beneath it showed the smoldering wreck of an Air France airplane. His stomach lurched and his throat went dry, and he got into the backseat as quickly as he could and closed the door behind him. He was wondering if she had already read the paper and what the chances were that she might let him have it when she dropped him off at his house.

Julianna hit the button on her armrest again, locking him in. "Better hold on tight, Ben," she said over her shoulder, putting the car in gear. "The road may be a little bumpy."

Back at the state mental hospital in Bangor, the deputy who came to question Edgar Reilly about Julianna's escape was a young man named Vernon Oakley, who (in Edgar's professional opinion) was suffering from a blatant father complex. He seemed all too eager to pin the blame on Edgar for everything, no matter what, simply because Edgar was an older male, and an authority figure.

"Let me get this straight, Dr. Reilly." Deputy Oakley didn't even bother to conceal the disdain on his mustached, bulldog face. "Not only did your staff somehow neglect to watch the fire door after letting the painters in this morning, but then you also left your keys in your car in the parking lot, so this Julianna Tapper—"

"Dapper," Edgar corrected, fidgeting. He had just celebrated his sixty-first birthday a month ago, and he was is in no mood to be chastised by someone half his age. He gave the deputy a sour smile. "With a *D*, as in 'Dementia.' "

They were sitting in Edgar's office, facing each other across his desk. On the wall behind Edgar were several framed diplomas (one from Princeton and two from Duke) and a photograph of a younger, less chunky Edgar, dressed in fishing gear and holding up a large carp.

Deputy Oakley wasn't placated by Edgar's attempt at humor. "So this Julianna Dapper was able to just waltz out of here, free as a bird?"

Edgar hated people who insisted on speaking in clichés. A lack of imagination in speech patterns was a clear sign of low intelligence. Edgar reminded himself that few people were blessed with an IQ as high as his own, but the rude young man before him was making it difficult to keep this forgiving thought in mind.

"As I told you, it's not that simple," he grated. "In spite of her condition, Julianna is an extremely bright woman, who took advantage of unusual circumstances. No one could have foreseen her escape."

He said this with as much certainty as he could muster, but in truth he was furious with his staff, and himself, for allowing something like this to happen.

What a brainless fiasco, he was thinking. *What a stupid, careless, miserable fuckup!*

The Bangor State Hospital had recently hired a local remodeling company to spruce up the smudged white walls of the dementia ward. Painters had arrived mid-morning and requested permission to wedge open the fire door for a brief time, to allow them access to their truck and their materials. Two hospital orderlies had been posted—one at the entrance to the corridor that led to the fire door, the other next to the open door itself—to ensure that none of the patients would be able to slip out as the painters unloaded their supplies. The door was open for barely five minutes, and was guarded, and nothing untoward should have happened.

But it had.

Deputy Oakley flipped a page in his pocket notebook and scribbled something in it. "So what exactly is this condition of hers?"

Edgar sighed. "She's suffering from a severe schizophrenic disorder of some kind, but I fear we haven't progressed much beyond that in our diagnosis. She's only been with us for less than a month."

Oakley's pen hovered over the page. "She's been here for a month and you still don't know what's wrong with her?"

Edgar bridled. "The human psyche isn't a car engine, Deputy," he said curtly. "We can't just pop the hood and poke around with a screwdriver to figure out why things aren't working." He settled back in his chair and moderated his tone. "Suffice it to say, though, this is quite serious, and she shouldn't be out among the general population."

He rummaged through his desk drawer for a pack of cigarettes and offered one to Oakley before helping himself. He was running low on cigarettes; the full carton he'd just purchased that morning was now in Julianna's possession, along with Edgar's Edsel and several full bags of junk food—the loss of which, incidentally, upset him almost as much as the theft of his car.

Edgar was a bald, portly man with heavy jowls and a big, bristling mustache; his brown eyes were watery and he had a large mole on his left cheek that looked like a teardrop. His hands were short-fingered and pudgy, but his fingernails were impeccably manicured and the silver cufflinks on his shirtsleeves were polished and elegant.

Oakley shook his head, declining the offer of a cigarette. "Is she dangerous? What did she do to get put in here?"

Edgar lit his cigarette before answering. "A few weeks ago she set fire to her neighbor's garage."

The police had found Julianna perched on a log near the twenty-foot-high blaze, her hands held toward the flames as if she were sitting beside a campfire. A box of matches and a can of kerosene were at her feet, and she was humming "Kumbaya."

Oakley raised his eyebrows. "On purpose? Why'd she do it?"

Edgar shrugged. "We don't know yet. She's never done anything remotely like that before, and what set her off is a mystery." He rubbed his ear. "By all reports, Julianna is a lovely person, Deputy. And until a month ago, she was as normal as you or I. But something traumatic appears to have happened to her, and she's now experiencing a variety of complicated delusions we haven't been able to control or lessen whatsoever."

Even with extremely high doses of Thorazine, he added somberly to himself.

He lifted a folder from a stack on his desk and opened it. Julianna's picture smiled up at him from the commitment order signed by her son.

"For instance," Edgar continued, "she now believes it's 1923, and that she's a fifteen-year-old girl living on a farm in northern Missouri. She has absolutely no recollection of anything that's happened since she actually *was* fifteen years old, and if you try to tell her that she's now a middle-aged grammar school teacher with a grown son and a charming little two-story house in Bangor, Maine, she thinks you're teasing her, or that you've gone crazy yourself." He took a long, satisfying drag on his cigarette and continued speaking with his lungs full. "She also sees things that aren't there."

Oakley smirked. "Like little green men and flying saucers?"

Edgar blew a plume of smoke at the ceiling in irritation. "Certainly not. Her delusions are entirely non-bizarre. But she doesn't really see what's in front of her. She superimposes images from her past on almost everything and everybody she encounters." He picked a piece of tobacco from his tongue. "For instance, she thinks I'm her family doctor from the Missouri town where she was raised, and her son is a blacksmith named Lars Olsen."

Gabriel Dapper had come to visit his mother every weekend since she'd been a patient at the hospital. He was a big, gentle man who was devastated by Julianna's break with reality. She kept asking him about the metal buggy he was building for a mule called Floppers, and whenever he addressed her as "Mom," she would blush and giggle, and beg him to stop being silly.

Oakley made a sour face. "Wonderful. So she's not only a firebug, she's also a lunatic." His expression made it clear he believed psychological disturbances only happened to people who lacked moral fiber. "How in God's name did somebody like *that* sneak past your orderlies?"

Edgar's temper flared again. "This isn't a homicidal maniac we're discussing," he snapped. "Julianna is neither violent nor suicidal, which is why she's in the dementia ward instead of the insane asylum." He jabbed a thumb toward the window, indicating the maximum-security wing of the hospital, which was reserved for criminally insane patients. "She needs to be institutionalized, but I assure you she doesn't require an armed guard and a straitjacket."

He knew he sounded defensive, but he couldn't help it.

Oakley snorted. "Yeah, she sounds like a real princess." He jotted something else in his notebook and his voice dropped to a mutter. "I just hope to hell she doesn't find any fucking matches in your glove box."

Edgar glared at the top of Oakley's head. "As I said before, Deputy . . ."

Oakley interrupted, still writing. "I believe you were getting ready to tell me how this firebug of yours got past your orderlies."

Edgar fell silent. He needed to regain control of this interview, but he wasn't sure how to do it. He stared out the window at the blue sky and chewed on his lip in frustration.

"I'm told they thought she was someone else," he muttered at last.

Oakley looked up, instantly suspicious. "Come again?" He narrowed his eyes. "Do your orderlies have schizophrenia, too?"

Edgar took another drag on his cigarette to stall for time. He didn't want to go into detail about Julianna's escape with Oakley, because he was quite sure the man would just use it as ammunition against him. Besides, how Julianna had gotten away wasn't really pertinent to the police investigation; he believed the deputy's only interest should be in catching and returning her to the hospital.

Oakley was waiting for an answer.

Edgar rested his cigarette on the lip of an overflowing ashtray, then opened another drawer of his desk and dug through it until he unearthed a bag of butterscotch drops. A bite or two of something sweet always made him feel calmer when he was under stress, but he only kept a small stash of candy in his office, for fear his staff might suspect him of an eating disorder if they knew how much he craved such things. With a pang he remembered the heaping bags of goodies sitting on the floor of his missing car, and knew if Julianna wasn't captured soon he would have to return to the grocery store to replenish his dwindling home supply.

Oakley cleared his throat impatiently.

Edgar sighed in surrender. He supposed there was nothing else for it but to attempt an explanation.

What a miserable fuckup, he thought again.

*   *   *

Coincidence loves insanity.

Several hours earlier that same morning, Julianna Dapper had risen and breakfasted, then proceeded under supervision to the nurses' station to get a caplet of Thorazine, just as she'd done each day since her arrival in the dementia unit. A prune-faced intern handed her the medication and a small paper cup with water, then watched as Julianna popped the caplet in her mouth and swallowed. Julianna stopped on her way out the door afterward to admire a potted African violet on the windowsill, just as she had done each morning since being committed to the hospital.

"Oh, my, you're a pretty little thing," she cooed, stroking its leaves and glancing over her shoulder at the intern, who was ignoring her. Julianna continued to caress the plant and her fingers drifted casually to the soil of the pot. "Momma would just love to get her hands on a pretty little thing like you!"

In truth, the African violet was a marvelous representative of its variety: It had recently nearly doubled in size, seeming to very much appreciate the daily dose of anti-psychotic medicine Julianna had been administering to it for the past twenty-six mornings. Julianna had no idea what the big orange pills they kept giving her were for, but she didn't feel even the teensiest bit sick and thought it was ridiculous to take something she clearly didn't need. This being the case, she had just palmed her medication and pretended to swallow it—yet again—in front of the negligent intern, and was now busy planting, with considerable stealth, Thorazine caplet number 27 in the violet's soil.

"Ta-ta for now!" Julianna sang to the plant as she successfully finished her morning ritual and departed the nurses' station. The attendant in charge of escorting patients was at that moment trying to prevent an elderly gentleman from urinating in an ashtray in the waiting room outside the nurses' station, and Julianna—considered by the hospital staff to be both "high functioning" and "highly cooperative"—was ordered to proceed by herself back to the common room of the dementia unit. Julianna agreed without complaint, skipping out of the waiting room and humming to herself as she entered an empty hallway, delighted to be left to her own devices.

Finding herself truly alone for the first time in weeks, she slowed to a walk and gazed about her with a puzzled expression. She didn't know where she was, but she knew she didn't like it; the plain white walls on each side of her made her feel depressed and the reek of ammonia everywhere she turned gave her a headache. An office door that had been left ajar caught her attention, and Julianna ambled over to look into the office thus revealed, noticing at once a bright-green dress, a checkered headscarf, and a white sweater hanging on the coatrack; on the floor next to the rack was a lovely pair of black pumps. She then glanced over at the desk by the door, and happened to see a daily calendar, open to the day's date. The lettering was large and easy to read (though upside-down from her perspective), and her eyes lingered on the page for nearly a minute.

"June twenty-third," she whispered at last, and the quiet syllables seemed to echo off the sterile, cold walls surrounding her. A sudden, imperative desire gripped her.

Time to go home.

Without hesitation she stepped into the office, shut the door, and changed into the dress, headscarf, and pumps, believing them to be hers. The pumps were a bit too small, as was the dress, but not terribly so. She exited the office immediately after dressing with the sweater draped over her forearm, hiding her wristband, and she glided smartly down the corridor and vanished around the corner at the precise moment the bathroom door across from the office opened and Nurse Helen Gable appeared.

This was a bit of good timing for Julianna, but she would not have made it much farther than that were it not for the fact that Nurse Gable wasn't feeling well that morning. The previous evening she had sought solace in a bottle of tequila, and was dealing with a ferocious margarita hangover. (Binge-drinking was out of character for Nurse Gable, but her nerves had needed calming after a vicious fight with her husband over whose fault it was that Sparky, their beloved guinea pig, had been eviscerated by Plummy, their equally beloved Siamese cat.) No sooner had she emerged from the bathroom than her stomach rebelled again, and she spun around on the spot to scurry back to the toilet.

Thus occupied, it would be another fifteen minutes before she discovered the formal clothes she had intended to wear to a conciliatory dinner that night with her husband were missing from her office, replaced by a patient's gown and a pair of institutional white slippers. The gown was folded on a chair, the slippers lined up next to each other on the floor.

Meanwhile, Julianna rounded the corner to find herself faced with a choice. The hallway to her left was empty and led back to the common area for the dementia ward; the hallway to her right had two orderlies in it, standing guard at each end as three painters laid plastic down on the floor between them. The orderly at the far end of the corridor was next to an open door, with sunlight streaming in behind him.

Home is that way, Julianna thought.

She spun toward the sunlight and marched up to the first orderly in her path. She recognized him at once as Clyde Rayburn, her next-door neighbor from Missouri. Clyde could be ill-tempered and bossy, but she knew from experience that if she was pleasant and direct with him—and didn't allow him to bully her—he could also be quite decent.

"Good morning," she sang out, presenting him with her warmest smile. "How are you today?"

The slouching orderly she had mistaken for Clyde nervously returned her smile, said hello, and told her he was fine.

Jeptha Morgan was freckled, pimply, and very new to the ward, having started a mere twenty-six hours prior to this encounter. Two weeks earlier—and only a day after dropping out of junior college—he had been fired for lipping off to a supervisor at the Happy Valley Nursing Home (his exact words to his former employer were *"Oh yeah? Why don't you suck my balls?"*), and soon thereafter his parents, whom he still lived with, had threatened to expel him from their house if he dared to pull the same kind of stunt here. (His choleric father's exact words were *"Your skinny ass will be out on the street so fast it will make your pointed little head spin around like a fucking Frisbee!"*) This being the case, Jeptha had concluded he should play it safe at this new job at all costs, since he had no intention of paying any kind of rent for years to come.

Jeptha was still meeting the patients in his care, and had not yet been introduced to Julianna. He also didn't know the administrators in the ward any better than he did the patients, and what he saw as she stood before him was a tall, elegant woman in a stylish green dress who looked nothing like what he believed a resident of a dementia ward should look like. Her manner, too, was purposeful and assured, and he assumed she was somebody important. He straightened up and did his best to appear alert and earnest.

She indicated the open door at the end of the hall with a nod of her head. "Will I be in the way of these painters if I go out that way?" she asked.

"Nah, you should be fine," he said politely. "It's too bad it's not open all the time, ain't it? It's way closer to the parking lot than the front door is."

Jeptha hoped she noticed how well he already knew his way around the place. The best way to climb the hospital food chain ladder, he believed—and to keep his parents off his back—was to kiss the right people's asses. And this imposing woman, who was now beaming at him in appreciation, was clearly one of the right people.

Like hell I'll pay for some shitty little apartment, he thought.

"Thanks very much," Julianna said. She stepped past him, keeping close to the wall so as not to disturb the plastic sheet the painters were fussing with. She teased the painters as she passed, inviting them to come put a new coat or two on her house when they'd finished there, and one of them chuckled and said that sounded like a fine idea, if she'd agree to provide the beer. She laughed and promised to do just that.

And then she was face-to-face with the second orderly, and what should have been the end of her excursion.

Connor Lipkin was both smarter and more experienced than

Jeptha Morgan. In May he had graduated (summa cum laude) from the University of Maine with a bachelor's degree in psychology, and the next fall he had been accepted at Yale to begin his master's. Connor had worked at the state hospital in Bangor every summer for the past three years, and his life's ambition was to be a famous psychologist, just like his hero, Carl Jung. (He even fancied he bore a physical resemblance to Jung, and he cultivated this resemblance as much as he could. The balding head and stocky body came naturally to him, but the thin black mustache and distinctive wire-rim eyeglasses like those Jung had worn as a young man were recent additions to Connor's developing persona.)

Julianna's luck was now bordering on the miraculous, however, because that very morning Connor, who was nearsighted, had gotten his new, Jung-like glasses knocked off and rendered unwearable in a scuffle with an unruly patient. Thus impaired, he was forced to squint in an attempt to get a clear look at her features as she approached.

Connor had seen Julianna Dapper many times over the last month, but he had never seen her in a formal dress, and from a few feet away her face was still a blur. The ease with which she had passed Jeptha and the painters made him relax his guard, though, more than he would otherwise have done, and gave him no reason to believe she was a patient. After taking into account her height and her checkered headscarf, which he was sure he recognized, he decided this woman coming toward him must be none other than Nurse Gable.

This initial impression shouldn't have lasted longer than a moment, of course. And when Julianna finally drew close enough for him to see who she really was, there should have been, by all rights, a much different outcome to the day's events. But in the split second before Connor's straining eyes could detect her true identity, yet another quirk of fate came galloping to her aid.

"Morning, miss," he said, ducking his head.

It just so happened that Nurse Gable figured into all of Connor Lipkin's private sexual fantasies. She was a torment to him, and had been for years. Most of his fantasies were a variation on the same theme: Nurse Gable, in her uniform, massaging his back with her naked feet. He had never seen her naked feet, of course, but he was quite sure they would be large, perhaps even a bit mannish, and high-arched, with finely painted toenails. This secret desire of his made it impossible for him to look the woman in the eye, and so he always ducked his head when he was around her. He was convinced she would see right through him unless he were to keep his head averted in her presence.

For her part, Julianna thought Connor Lipkin was a man named Tom Putnam, who had been a mild, shy janitor from her school days in Missouri.

"Good morning," she responded sweetly to Connor's greeting.

Her voice was low and husky, much like Nurse Gable's.

Connor, flushing, stepped out of her way, almost tripping over his feet in his haste to allow Julianna access to the outside world. She patted his arm in thanks, but he kept his head down even then, noticing only her long fingers and the feel of her cool skin on his wrist. His heart almost exploded at her touch, and he found himself wishing ardently for twenty-twenty vision, so as she walked away from him he could get a better look at the backs of her ankles, and the black pumps she was wearing.

If there were any remaining doubt that Julianna was absurdly blessed with good fortune that morning, it would be banished by what occurred at this juncture. As she glided down the sidewalk and emerged at last from the shadow of the hospital, she was granted the biggest boon of her journey: Squarely in front of her, as if waiting for just this one special moment in its dull mechanical existence, was an unlocked automobile, with the key in its ignition.

Edgar Reilly had never once, before that day, left his key in the car. The only reason he had done so that morning was because as he pulled into his designated space in the hospital parking lot, a bee had flown through his open window and attempted to land on the crown of his bald head. Edgar was allergic to bee stings, and deathly afraid of bees. He had leapt from the car, slammed the door, and dashed for the safety of the hospital, waving his arms about his head and swearing under his breath. Once inside, he realized he had left his key in his car, but as he kept his office key on a separate keychain and intended to only be inside for a short while, he decided not to risk another encounter with the bee until it was time to leave.

Thus it came to pass that Connor Lipkin watched—and did nothing—as Julianna's blurred, graceful figure climbed into the Edsel. He knew it was Edgar's car she was taking, but he also knew Nurse Gable and Dr. Reilly were friends, and since the woman he had mistaken for Nurse Gable obviously had the key to the automobile, he didn't bat a nearsighted eye as she drove away from him, waving. He assumed she was borrowing Edgar's car on hospital business, which explained why she was dressed so formally. (Connor preferred her nurse's uniform, of course, but he thought her dress was nice, too.) He placed a hand over the spot on his wrist where she had touched him, and he turned back to the hallway with an aroused smile.

Edgar's staff wouldn't notice anything amiss until Nurse Gable returned to her office and went looking for her dress. By this time, though, the door Connor had been guarding was closed and locked again, and the painters were hard at work, and Connor and Jeptha were in another part of the ward, attempting to calm a patient named Phyllis Farmer, who was having a bad day. Phyllis believed Connor and Jeptha were trying to steal her "golden egg," which was actually half an orange she had snatched from the breakfast table and promptly shoved, for safekeeping, under her ample buttocks. She put up a spirited fight, which ended up lasting the better part of an hour.

This being the case, Nurse Gable wasn't able to piece together what had occurred for some time. When Julianna's absence was at length confirmed, there was a mad, unproductive search of the premises (leading, incidentally, to the discovery of the hugely overmedicated African violet in the nurses' station), followed by a heated argument among Nurse Gable, Jeptha Morgan, and Connor Lipkin about whom to blame. This all took far more time than it should have, primarily because none of them wanted to be the one to give Edgar Reilly the bad news.

Edgar was a more-or-less understanding employer, but when mistakes happened he had a baleful way of looking at the responsible party that they all dreaded—his displeasure underscored by the crisp, almost violent manner with which he would unwrap a Tootsie Roll or a caramel before popping it into his mouth—and they knew Julianna's escape was the kind of error that could cost them their jobs. So when a red-faced and squinting Connor Lipkin finally screwed up his courage and knocked on Edgar's office door, Julianna had been gone for nearly two hours.

Coincidence doesn't merely love insanity: It worships it.

Back in the little town of Prescott, Maine, Elijah heard Julianna call him Ben as he settled into the backseat of the Edsel, but he chose not to correct her because he was trying to come up with the best way to ask for her newspaper. He was also fretting about how he was going to smuggle an outlawed item such as this past his mother once he was home. Mary Hunter was diligent and resourceful, and she knew her only child all too well. In the last few weeks she had even begun to frisk him for news-related contraband the instant he walked through the door.

The front windows of the Edsel were open, but the wind on his face was hot as he mulled over various strategies. The sun was almost directly above them, and he felt tired and thirsty. He rested his head on the seat behind him and closed his eyes for a minute, grateful for the ride, because the walk home would have taken him almost half an hour. The humid air pouring into the car was thick with early summer fragrances; he could pick out the scent of roses and lilacs, but most of what he smelled he didn't have a name for.

In the front seat, Julianna tugged at her dress and made a mental note to speak to her mother about sewing her something that would fit her better. Her mother was an excellent seamstress, and Julianna seemed to have had yet another growth spurt. She supposed most fifteen-year-olds went through the same thing, but she hated knowing she wouldn't be able to wear this exquisite green dress much longer. It was such a shame. She'd gotten so little wear out of it; she almost felt as if she'd never even worn it before that very day.

She glanced in the rearview mirror at "Ben" and smiled to herself when she saw him close his eyes. She was glad he had accepted a ride; the poor boy was obviously exhausted. He didn't get enough to eat, she knew, and it was a wonder he could even stay on his feet.

She pulled up to the stop sign at a T intersection about a mile and a half out of town. To the right and not far away—though she had no idea of this—was Elijah's farm; to the left was the open highway, leading eventually to the New Hampshire border, and from there to the rest of the country.

She looked both ways, as if confused. She wasn't, though; she was just waiting for guidance. Ever since she had begun her journey that morning, she had needed no map. Something had been advising her, telling her which way to go, and she implicitly trusted whatever this something might be. She knew all she had to do was wait a moment, and it would speak to her again.

And it did, of course.

Home is this way, she thought, turning left.

Chapter 2

Almost six thousand, Elijah concluded. *That's how many people die in the world every single hour. Holy SHIT.*

His fixation on the global mortality rate had sidetracked his plan to acquire Julianna's newspaper. More importantly, it had also kept him from paying attention to his surroundings. With this latest equation solved, however, he opened his eyes at last and straightened up, gazing around. The intersection where Julianna had made her choice was now almost a mile behind them.

Dammit, he thought. *If she tells Mom I let her go the wrong way, I'll catch hell.*

His parents didn't allow him to curse aloud, but in his own head he followed a different set of rules.

"Uh, ma'am?" He leaned forward, embarrassed. His shirt was sticking to his back. "We need to turn around."

Julianna found his eyes in the rearview mirror and giggled. "Since when do you call me 'ma'am,' silly?"

Elijah didn't know how to respond to this, so decided an apology was in order. "Sorry." He cleared his throat. "My house is back that way."

Julianna shook her head and giggled again. "Honestly, Ben, you act as if I were born yesterday."

Elijah blinked. The gravel road they were on would soon merge with a blacktop highway. The woman was driving fast, stirring up a lot of dust, and she showed no signs of slowing.

He raised his voice a little to make sure she could hear him above the noise of the wind and the crunch of the tires on the gravel.

"My name is Elijah." The dust from the road made him cough. "And our farm really is the other direction."

"Elijah?" Julianna guffawed. "Where on earth did you come up with a ridiculous name like that, Ben Taylor?"

Her laugh was throaty and full, and under other circumstances Elijah would have enjoyed hearing it. There wasn't much laughter in his home; Samuel and Mary Hunter were a bit stern and rarely laughed aloud. But given that this woman apparently thought he was someone else, her mirth set him on edge.

"My name isn't Ben," he insisted. "It's Elijah. Elijah Hunter." He grabbed the front seat for balance as the car slid onto the shoulder for a moment.

Julianna made a dismissive sound with her lips that sounded like "pfff." About a half mile in front of them was where the gravel road became blacktop. She could see the coming change in the road surface and she smiled, relieved.

She called over her shoulder. "I can't wait to be off this gravel! It's so loud, isn't it?"

Elijah didn't answer. He had finally noticed the hospital wristband on her left forearm, and was staring at it with queasy fascination. He was beginning to suspect that he might not actually be in the company of a Methodist Bingo Lady from Prescott, Maine, after all.

Ninety-seven miles away from Elijah and Julianna, on a rural highway in the middle of New Hampshire, it was raining heavily, and Jon Tate stood on the side of the road with his thumb out, praying for a ride from the only car he'd seen for the last half hour. The blue Plymouth Fury didn't even slow down, though, and as its taillights vanished over a nearby hill, Jon raised his hand high above his head and exchanged his thumb for his middle finger. He stood this way for a long moment, feeling like an obscene parody of the Statue of Liberty, before at last allowing his arm to drop to his side again.

His blue T-shirt and khaki shorts were soaked through and clinging to his skin; his canvas sneakers were also waterlogged. He was carrying a plastic bag with his only remaining possessions in it: a toothbrush, a razor, three paperback books, his wallet, two pairs of clean boxer shorts, one pair of clean socks, and three hundred seventy-two dollars in stolen cash.

Jon had been on the road since five o'clock that morning, when he'd caught a ride with a southbound trucker on the outskirts of Tipton, Maine. The trucker's name was Clive Upton, from Montreal, and to Jon's immense relief, Clive had asked no questions. He'd taken Jon out of Maine and into New Hampshire, but when they'd stopped to get breakfast, a radio had been playing in the diner and Jon grew agitated as the news came on. Clive was taking far too long to suit him, so Jon thanked him for the ride and lit out on foot, forsaking the Interstate in favor of an older highway where he thought he'd feel less exposed while hitchhiking.

He was no longer happy with this choice. Two hours had passed since he'd left the diner and no one had stopped to pick him up.

Jon was five foot nine and weighed 160 pounds. He was built like a wrestler, but he had never wrestled a day in his life; his broad shoulders and wiry frame came from good genes rather than disciplined exercise. He had deep-set gray eyes that always made him look tired, and a square, stubborn jaw. The rain plastered his short black hair to his scalp and streamed down his face, mingling with tears he could no longer suppress. He was frustrated and exhausted, and he couldn't believe he was standing where he was, doing what he was doing.

"I am so stupid," he whispered. "I am just so *fucking* stupid."

Jon had lived in Tipton, Maine, all nineteen years of his life and had never intended to live anyplace else. His family was there, and all his friends, and he had a good job at Toby's Pizza Shack, working in the kitchen. He didn't make a lot of money at

Toby's, but he was able to pay the rent for his apartment above the town Laundromat, and he even had enough left over each month to keep his home well stocked with his two favorite things in the world: books and beer.

When Jon had been in high school, his teachers described him as "smart as a whip" and "good-natured." They also described him—usually in the same breath—as "lazy, apathetic, and disappointing." All of these were reasonable characterizations, and Jon took no offense at any of them. He loved to read and he loved to drink, and felt that almost everything else was a waste of time. And since his graduation the previous year, he had *done* little else, either, aside from the necessary evil of working part-time at Toby's. His parents had long since given up trying to get him to attend college, but after he moved out they began to speak about him to his two younger brothers in hushed, disapproving tones. They used him as a sort of cautionary tale, hoping that Billy and Evan, his siblings, would understand that unambitious people like Jon were little more than dead weight, dragging society down.

Jon wasn't troubled by this assessment, either, and only laughed when his brothers told him about it. Books were piling up around him, mixed with a fair share of beer bottles and cans, and he didn't bother to explain why this was all he required from his life. He knew his parents would never understand the joy that came to him when he was sitting under a lamp in the evenings with a book in his lap. They'd never know how much pleasure it gave him when the only sound in a room was the rustle of a turning page, the only light a small circle around his chair as the rest of the town lay sleeping in darkness.

Books were sacred artifacts to be studied with reverence and passion, and devoting his life to such a study seemed infinitely more worthwhile than any other occupation Jon could think of. Only when his eyes began to blur each night would he stop reading and go to the refrigerator for a beer; reading was far more enjoyable when his mind was clear. (Not yet of legal drinking age, he was forced to buy his alcohol with the aid of an older friend, who agreed to help him out in exchange for free pizza from Toby's.) He'd be exhausted by this time, but his mind would be overstimulated by what he'd read; words and ideas scampered around in his skull like mice in an attic, keeping him awake for hours. He would return to his chair, turn off the light, and drink however much beer was required to subdue his brain and let him sleep. This always happened around dawn; there were usually five or six empty cans or bottles on the floor beside him when he abandoned the chair in favor of his bed. He'd sleep until early afternoon, work until late evening, and return home afterward to do it all again.

He didn't even own a car, because he didn't want to work hard enough to pay for one. His friends assumed he was lonely, and invited him out often, but he seldom went with them. He enjoyed his friends, but not nearly as much as he enjoyed his books. He would also go out now and then for an evening with a girl, but only if he was particularly horny, and bored with masturbating. He liked sex, too, of course, but he found it far less fulfilling in the long run than a good novel or a witty essay. He knew this wasn't the normal set of priorities for a nineteen-year-old male; he also knew his life was not exciting nor productive by anybody else's standards but his own. But for him it was all the life he needed, or wanted, and he loved it dearly.

Then two months ago he'd gotten the wrong girl pregnant.

The girl's name was Becky Westman, and Jon didn't really even know her. She was pretty enough, with long red hair, a sweet smile, and a firm little gymnastic body. But from what little he could remember of their single encounter, he hadn't much cared for her. She was dumb—for one thing, she seemed to think the Revolutionary War had been fought by cowboys and Indians in Wyoming—and she was childish, and she was a liar.

She was also fourteen.

The party that led to Jon's downfall was given in honor of Paul Revere's Midnight Ride, and so took place on April 18, in the neighboring town of Welford, about ten miles from Tipton. The host of this shindig was Tommy Somerset, a fellow worker at Toby's Pizza Shack, who had a fondness for celebrating historical events that had, in his sober judgment, never received enough public acknowledgment. Recent galas at Tommy's house had commemorated (with several kegs of Budweiser and a pantry full of Cheetos) the Battle of Fredericksburg, Sir Thomas More's beheading, and the birth of Harriet Tubman.

Jon, who knew almost nobody at the party and had only attended because he'd been promised access to Tommy's large collection of books, helped himself to a great deal of beer, and then found himself with Becky in an otherwise deserted room, next to the bookcases. Their fellow party-goers had been drawn outside by then to watch a stirring reenactment of Revere's ride, involving flashlights and bicycles in lieu of lanterns and horses.

Jon had never met Becky Westman before, and she'd basically leapt into his lap the instant they were left alone together. Minutes later, as she rode and bucked on top of him on the floor behind the couch, he'd drunkenly joked that he was beginning to understand how Paul Revere's horse must have felt. This had elicited her less-than-impressive "cowboys and Indians in Wyoming" remark, and the next thing he knew she was climbing off again, finished, and they were straightening their clothes in embarrassed silence. It was the only time they ever saw each other, and aside from those few sketchy details, he'd forgotten everything about it.

Except for the fact she'd sworn she was eighteen.

And two months later—on the night before Jon found himself standing on the road in the rain—his world had come crashing down. Becky Westman's dad and mom, Phil and Carol, discovered their daughter was pregnant, and had forced her to reveal who the father was. Phil made a few phone calls to track down Jon's dad and mom, and soon after that all four parents had shown up at Jon's apartment, shouting, moments after he arrived home from work. Becky didn't come with them; it was a school night for her and she was home in bed. She had been forced to attend summer school after failing most of her spring classes—including, sadly, both American History *and* Sex Education.

Phil and Carol Westman, who bore a disturbing resemblance to the couple in Grant Wood's *American Gothic* painting, wanted to call the police and have Jon arrested for statutory rape; Jon's horrified parents attempted to bargain with them by offering to have Jon marry Becky and take responsibility for the baby. The Tates' first suggestion that an abortion might be in order had been dismissed offhand; the Westmans were Catholic to the core and could not be swayed on this issue.

Jon had remained mute with shock through the ordeal, sitting on one of the dozen or so milk crates that served as various pieces of furniture throughout his apartment. He kept his gaze squarely on the floor, except for shooting an occasional desperate glance toward his mother, who turned away each time from these silent pleas for understanding and forgiveness.

Marline Tate was a short, slim woman, with light blue eyes and a delightful, childlike laugh that Jon loved. She wasn't laughing that night, however, nor had she so much as smiled in Jon's presence for nearly two years. Marline adored her son, but her disappointment with him had grown so pronounced she couldn't even bear to look at him. His habitual laziness and burgeoning alcoholism had been hard enough to deal with, but this newly revealed inability to control his penis was the final straw for her, and she was fresh out of sympathy.

Earl Tate (who looked like an older, grizzled version of Jon) also loved his eldest son, and was more compassionate about his apparent penis problem than Marline. But he, too, was fed up with Jon's general lack of responsibility, and his unhealthy, bizarre addiction to literature. In truth, part of him was secretly pleased to see the boy finally having to face the consequences of his actions. A baby would put an end to the bohemian existence Jon had been living, and Earl couldn't help but feel this kind of requital was long overdue. After all, life was not about fun, in Earl's opinion, or doing whatever you wanted, and it was high time Jon learned this lesson.

Anyway, after almost five hours of yelling and bickering, Becky's parents at last agreed that having Jon arrested immediately would serve no purpose. It was then decided, with no input from Jon, that all of them would meet again later than day, to continue their "discussion" about his future. They filed out the door and down the stairs at half past four in the morning, the fathers silent and the mothers weeping.

And the instant they left him alone, Jon had run away.

It was getting close to sunrise on Saturday morning when he fled. He had no car, and no suitcase, and the only money he had was locked in a bank that wouldn't open until Monday. He didn't know where he was going or what he was going to do, but two things, at least, were certain:

1. He wasn't going to jail over Becky "Cowboys and Indians" Westman, and
2. There was no way in *hell* he would marry the stupid girl, either, and be saddled with her and her stupid baby for the rest of his life.

In a blind panic, he'd grabbed a few things from his bathroom and bedroom and stuffed them in a plastic bag. It didn't occur to him he'd need more than a few toiletries and some clean underwear; the only thing he could think to do was to get out as fast as he could and never look back. It broke his heart to leave his books behind, but he had no alternative. He rescued his three favorite paperbacks (*Moby Dick, Walden,* and *The Fellowship of the Ring*) from the floor by his bed, though, and stuffed them in his bag before leaving, then ran down the stairs and out onto the dark street with his breath coming in hitches and his heart clamoring in his chest.

Acting on blind instinct, he'd made his way over to Toby's Pizza Shack and used his key to get in. His hands had been shaking as he cleaned out the cash register and the little metal safe under the counter. He crammed the small pile of bills into his plastic bag and scrawled a barely legible note to Toby, apologizing and promising to pay him back as soon as possible. Jon was no thief, but without money he knew he had no chance at all, and this was the only cash available to him. He hoped Toby might someday forgive him, once the circumstances behind this betrayal of trust became public knowledge.

And then he ran.

He ran without thought or reservation, like a hunted fox. He ran down empty streets and sidewalks; he ran past the houses of people he had known his entire life; he ran past the high school and the public library and the dark, menacing windows of Rita's Coffee Shop and Hackey's Variety Store. He ran all the way out of town, all the way to the ramp leading to the Interstate. He fell to his knees at last by a yield sign, dry-heaving from the exertion.

He put his forehead in the dirt and sucked air into his overtaxed lungs, and he prayed for help as he had never prayed before. He knew he didn't deserve such help, nor did he expect it, but he prayed anyway, because he didn't know what else to do. He wasn't normally religious, but he'd been reading a lot of C. S. Lewis in the past few days, and was very impressionable. The week before he'd been on a Nietzsche kick and wouldn't have dreamed of praying, but that was last week, and so mostly forgotten.

Just as he'd risen to his feet again, salvation had appeared out of nowhere, manifesting itself in the lumbering shape of Clive Upton's miraculous Canadian truck. Clive had put on the brakes and pulled over the moment Jon stuck out his thumb, and Jon ran to catch up as if he were on his way to meet Jehovah in the flesh. Summoning a ride in such a manner had felt like pure magic, and Jon told himself this was surely an omen that he was doing the right thing.

He'd climbed into the semi's cab, introduced himself as Steve Simpson, and lied that he was on his way to visit friends in upstate New York. Clive had just nodded, accepting the story, and only then was Jon able to relax a little, slumping back against the seat. Later, he had even managed to drop off to sleep for a short while, until Clive woke him to say they were stopping for breakfast.

But that respite from ill fortune now seemed like centuries ago, before the rain began to fall on him in southern New Hampshire. He shielded his eyes with his hand, and gazed down the empty highway in misery. All he wanted to do was go home, but he knew that wasn't possible. Not for a very long time; maybe not ever. The only thing waiting for him back in Tipton, Maine, was misery.

He couldn't stop thinking about his favorite chair in his apartment, and his beloved books stacked up around it, waiting for him to come back. Picturing this familiar, cozy scene made him more unhappy than he'd ever been in his life. If he'd only stayed home two months ago with his books instead of going to a pointless, idiotic party, none of this would have happened.

"Books don't get PREGNANT, for Christ's sake!" he suddenly howled at the empty fields around him. "I am so fucking STUPID!"

He dropped his arm at last and started to trudge south, clutching his plastic bag to his chest like a life preserver. He couldn't stay out in this downpour much longer; he had to find shelter. Lightning was sundering the sky, and the ground under his feet was trembling nonstop from continuous blasts of thunder. He felt as if he were being punished for his sins, and would never be safe and dry again. He stared down at his soaking sneakers and tried not to cry as each step took him farther away from everything he loved.

Please, God, help me, he pleaded silently. *Help me find a way to go home.*

"Honest to God, lady, we're going the wrong way!"

Elijah was on the verge of panicking. He had been cautioned by his parents, time and again, to always be polite to adults—especially *white* adults with the power to harm him—but his voice was becoming strident in spite of this warning. The strange woman in the front seat wasn't listening to him at all. They were now on the blacktop road, and the Edsel's speedometer said they were rolling along at almost eighty miles per hour.

"Oh, for goodness sake, Ben." Julianna's eyes found his in the rearview mirror. "Stop fooling around."

She reached over into one of Edgar Reilly's grocery bags on the floor and pulled out a Butterfinger candy bar. "Here, have some candy. I know you'd prefer beef jerky, but I don't think

Momma packed any in the picnic basket. She didn't know you were coming with me today."

Elijah gazed with despair at the candy bar she was holding over the seat for him. He had no idea what she was talking about: For one thing, he truly *hated* beef jerky; for another, there was no picnic basket in sight. He took the Butterfinger from her at last, though, because he didn't know what else to do and she just kept holding it there for him.

It was boiling in the car and he was having trouble breathing. Even with the front windows open and wind pouring in, the Naugahyde upholstery reeked of cigarette smoke. (He didn't know it, but the closed ashtray on the dash was chock-full of Edgar Reilly's cigarette butts.) Elijah undid the top button on his shirt and struggled to remain calm. There had to be a way to get her to stop and let him out of the car, but he couldn't see how. They were going very fast, on a lonely highway, without a stop sign or a town in sight. There weren't any other vehicles about, either, but even if one showed up all he could do was wave at it in passing, and that wouldn't help him at all.

Hoping the woman wouldn't notice what he was doing, he leaned forward to look at her gas gauge. He squinted at it for a moment, then slumped back against his seat again. There was more than half a tank left, so they could probably travel a long time before needing a refill—maybe as much as a couple hundred miles. He had to get away from this looney-tunes lady long before then, though; for all he knew she could have a gun, and might decide to shoot him long before they reached a station.

Thinking about her having a gun made him want to pee. A bead of sweat ran down his back and he undid another button on his shirt and squirmed around on the hot seat. The Butterfinger in his hand was turning to mush in its wrapper. Why didn't she at least turn on the air conditioner?

He sized her up from behind. She was nearly as big as he was, but he was pretty sure he must be stronger than her. His dad told him all the time how strong he was getting when they worked together on the farm. Still, she was a fairly large woman, and he wasn't about to try anything while they were moving. They'd wreck for sure and end up dead. If she stopped someplace, though, he might be able to control her long enough to get away from her safely. He supposed scrambling out a window was a possibility, too, but he'd still have to find a way to disable her first, or she'd probably just grab him and pull him back into the car while he was trying to get clear.

Maybe I can knock her out! he thought, and began looking around the backseat for something he could use to hit her in the head.

Thus occupied, Elijah didn't notice that Julianna was watching him in the rearview mirror with concern. She could tell something was upsetting him, but she didn't have a clue what that could be.

"Did I do something wrong, Ben?" she asked. "If I did, I really didn't mean to. Honest!"

Elijah's head flew up again in fright. His search for a weapon had proven fruitless. There was nothing at all in the back of the car, except for a woman's sweater and headscarf on the seat and a flimsy-looking window scraper on the floor. The scraper had a long wooden handle, but it was so thin a child could have snapped it in two with no effort.

He shook his head after a moment, perplexed by an odd quaver in her voice but also relieved that she seemed to have finally figured out she needed to take him seriously.

"That's okay," he answered after a brief hesitation, laying the Butterfinger on the seat beside him. "But can we please stop? I'll just walk home from here, so you don't even have to turn around or anything."

The formality of his tone caused Julianna's eyes to well up. "Don't be angry with me, Ben," she implored, her bottom lip trembling. "I didn't mean to upset you, and I'm truly sorry."

This heartfelt apology baffled Elijah more than anything else Julianna could have done. For one thing, he wasn't used to seeing a woman cry; his mother, Mary, never wept. Even when Elijah's grandmother, Mary's own mother, had died a few years ago, Mary had remained dry-eyed throughout the entire funeral. Nor did she cry in the privacy of their home later. She wasn't unfeeling, he knew; she was just "tough as nails," as Elijah's father, Samuel, was fond of remarking. One of Mary's favorite catchphrases she trotted out whenever Elijah was feeling bad was, "Boo-hooing about a thing you don't like won't change it a bit, little man."

Another reason Elijah was confounded by Julianna's remorseful reaction was because she still wasn't slowing down at all, and showed no sign of intending to let him out.

"I'm not mad," he mumbled, feeling oddly guilty for having considered knocking her out as a means of escape. Now that he had seen how emotionally fragile she was, the idea of her having a gun seemed ludicrous to him. "I just . . . feel like walking, that's all."

Julianna shook her head hard enough to make a tear fly from her cheek. "I won't hear of it. It would take you forever to get home on foot, especially with no shoes."

Elijah looked down at the white sneakers on his feet and swallowed hard. The woman might mean no harm, but she was seriously nuts.

"But I've got shoes." He hitched up his right leg and rested his foot on the seat between them. "See?"

Julianna turned her head for a moment to gaze with affection at the naked foot next to her shoulder. It was covered in dirt, and had thick calluses on the heel. She snorted and felt immediately better. Ben was teasing her again, so he must have forgiven her.

"Oh, you," she said. "You are such a fool."

Thinking that she must look quite a sight from her short crying jag, she glanced in the mirror again and cried out in horror.

"Oh!"

She let go of the wheel for a moment and the car veered wildly into the other lane before she regained control and brought it back to the right side of the road. Elijah, off-balance from having his foot propped up, tumbled over in the backseat.

"What the hell?" he yelped.

Julianna tried to say something reassuring but couldn't quite manage it. Her heart was hammering with fear.

That's ridiculous, she was thinking. *You're imagining things.*

When she had looked in the rearview mirror at what should have been her own reflection, she had seen a middle-aged woman with short brown hair and alarming green eyes staring back at her.

Her knuckles were white on the steering wheel and her neck was stiff with tension. She tried to keep her eyes firmly on the road, but she could almost feel the mirror taunting her, daring her to take another look.

She squared her shoulders. *Pull yourself together, you silly girl. It was just a trick of the light.*

Biting her lip, she gazed boldly at her reflection again. The only thing in the mirror this time was herself: a thin, rather pretty young lady, with long brown hair and smooth, glowing skin. She sighed with relief and her breathing slowly returned to normal.

"Goodness gracious." She gave an odd little laugh. "I must be losing my mind." She glanced over the seat at Elijah, who was upright again, but clutching his door handle in a death grip.

"Are you all right, Ben?" she asked. "I'm sorry for the rough ride, but the strangest thing just happened."

Elijah was too rattled to ask her what she was talking about, but the "rough ride" was no longer his chief concern: He had just seen something that might allow him to put an end to the whole bizarre situation he found himself in. Half a mile in front of them was an intersection with a four-way stop sign. And approaching this intersection from the other direction was a white Ford pickup, which looked as if it might be stopping at almost the exact same time as the Edsel.

Here's my chance, Elijah thought.

Cecil Towpath's wife of thirty-seven years, Sarah, wouldn't shut up, and he was sick of it. She'd been at him for the better part of six hours now, ever since they'd left their granddaughter's home in upstate New York, and it was all he could do not to reach across the seat and slap her silly.

"For God's sake, Cecil," Sarah was saying. "Stop pretending it's fine she married that little weasel. I told you Wally would never make a good husband and provider for Tina, but did you listen?" She sniffed and stared out the open passenger window of their pickup.

Cecil knew what that snooty little sniff of hers meant. It meant she thought Wally wasn't the only one who didn't qualify as a "good husband." *Damn her,* he thought.

The Towpaths lived in Bar Harbor, Maine. Their only grand-daughter, Tina, had married Walter Abernathy three years ago and moved to New York, where Walter ("Wally") had since shown himself, in Sarah's words, to be "a worthless, free-loading skunk." He couldn't hold down a job, because he claimed to be an artist of some sort. What kind of art he did had never been clear to Cecil. It had something to do with half a dozen ugly metal-and-wood things in their backyard that Wally called "sculptures," but if you asked Cecil, they looked a lot like a bunch of monstrous dog turds, lying in the grass.

Tina worked for a lawyer and supported Wally through thick and thin, and wouldn't listen to a thing Sarah said about him. Cecil didn't much care one way or another about Wally, but Tina loved him, so he, unlike Sarah, had decided to just let them be. Tina seemed happy about her life, and that was good enough for him.

And this irritated Sarah beyond all bearing.

A stop sign was coming up and Cecil tapped on the brakes to begin slowing. There was another vehicle getting close to the in-tersection, too, but it was headed the other way. It looked like an Edsel, he thought. The front bumper was separated in the middle by a silver, shield-like ornament on the grille.

Yep, it's an Edsel, he nodded to himself. *No other car has a grille like that.*

"I swear to God, Cecil, you're not listening to a word I say," Sarah complained.

Now or never, Elijah thought as they approached the stop sign. The white pickup facing them was slowing down, too, and he could see a man with a white beard driving it, sitting next to a woman with a big head of poufy white hair. Elijah had to get out of the car almost immediately to flag them down, or it would be too late. He didn't want to hurt the crazy lady, but if he could just get hold of the wheel once they came to a full stop he was pretty sure he could aim the car into the little ditch at the side of the road if she tried to take off again.

His mouth was dry, and his heart was beating so loudly in his own ears he could barely hear anything else. He leaned forward and put his feet flat on the floor, readying himself to move as fast as he could. Julianna pulled up level with the stop sign and ground to a halt. The white pickup across the road from them stopped, too, and she waved politely at its driver, indicating that he should go first.

And Elijah, seeing his chance, popped up into the air behind her like a flushed pheasant and launched himself over the seat.

Sometimes Sarah Towpath's husband, Cecil, made her so damn mad she couldn't see straight. She'd been giving him a piece of her mind for what felt like eternity now, but it was like talking to a lump of coal.

If he had just put his foot down three years ago, their gullible granddaughter, Tina, would never have married that jackass Wally. But all Cecil had said was, "It's her life, Sarah. Let her live it, for God's sake."

But just look what had come of *that* asinine strategy: Their granddaughter was working her fingers to the bone to support a useless, moronic slug of a man, that's what. And Sarah, who had seen the whole miserable train wreck coming from the second she'd laid eyes on her future grandson-in-law, couldn't even get Cecil to admit he'd been wrong.

She took a deep breath, preparing to fire off another volley, but before her tongue could get up and running again, she happened to glance across the road and see a car facing them at an intersection. A tall woman was at the wheel; her head was almost touching the ceiling of the cab.

My, she's got a pretty car, Sarah thought, admiring the cream-colored roof and the shiny brown hood. *Why can't we have a pretty car like that, instead of this nasty old truck?*

She started to say as much to Cecil, but her words were swallowed in a scream of shock. Right before her eyes, a young black man had just lunged over the front seat of the pretty car, and was viciously attacking the tall white woman driving it!

"Cecil!" Sarah wailed. "Do something!"

Shortly after Dr. Edgar Reilly had purchased his 1959 Edsel Ranger, he went through a belated midlife crisis. He found himself wanting to own a car with some "muscle," and the Edsel's Super Express V8 engine, though by no means lacking in the get-up-and-go department, wasn't quite muscular enough to offset the decline of his youthful self-esteem. Rather than purchasing an entirely different car, however, Edgar had asked a gifted mechanic to make a few "modifications" to the engine, to satisfy his newfound lust for speed.

And the mechanic, who loved a challenge, had outdone himself. The specifics of the transformation were lost on Edgar, but he listened in a delighted trance as the mechanic uttered mysterious, manly words like "camshaft," "differential," "headers," and "intake manifold" by way of explanation. Such terms were meaningless to Edgar, but he could sense the masculine potency in them, and each syllable was a balm to his aging soul.

Julianna knew nothing of this, of course (she had been going at a good clip down the highway, but hadn't yet goosed the accelerator) and it wouldn't have meant a thing to her even if she had been aware of it. But prior to this overhaul, Edgar's Edsel could only do a standing quarter mile in 15.2 seconds. Afterward, it could do the same distance in 11.4 seconds.

In other words, when given proper inducement, it could haul ass.

Elijah made it halfway over the seat in his brash bid for freedom, but his crotch caught on the seatback just as his hands seized the steering wheel.

"Oof," he grunted.

Julianna was too surprised to say anything at all. One moment she'd been humming to herself as they paused by a stop sign; in the next, Elijah was wrenching the steering wheel from her hands. Without thinking, she fought back, fearing he was going to wreck them. At the same time, she stomped on the brake, which she had just taken her foot from an instant before.

Unfortunately, she missed, and landed squarely on the accelerator instead.

"Oh!" Julianna cried.

"*Oh, FUCK!*" Elijah gasped.

With Julianna pulling to the left on the wheel as hard as she could and Elijah cranking with all his might to the right, Edgar Reilly's midlife-crisis-enhanced Edsel shot through the intersection and missed Cecil and Sarah Towpath's pickup by less than eight inches. Julianna had only an instant to register the old couple and their panicked faces before they disappeared from view.

"Shit, shit, shit!" Elijah howled over the roar of the engine. He was no longer trying to gain control of the wheel; he was now only hanging on for dear life.

"Benjamin Taylor!" Julianna bawled back. "Have you lost your ever-loving mind?"

The intersection was out of sight by this point, and they were in the middle of the highway, swerving from one lane to the other and doing well over a hundred miles an hour.

"Let go of the wheel!" Julianna squealed.

"Not until you take your foot off the gas!" Elijah bellowed.

Julianna gaped at him. She at last realized she was responsible for their speed, and wisely abandoned the accelerator. At the same time she also decided, less wisely, to slam both feet down on the brake pedal.

The Edsel went into a chaotic skid as Elijah flew forward, banging his forehead into the dash and crumpling into a heap on top of Edgar Reilly's bags of junk food. The car turned full circle nearly twice, but Julianna, her mouth open in a soundless scream, somehow managed to keep the wheels on the highway. When she at last fought the Edsel to a standstill, it shuddered once, in protest, then its engine stalled out with what sounded like a vast sigh of relief. Its right wheels were on the shoulder, but by some miracle the hood was still pointing in the direction they had been traveling before going into their spin.

Julianna collapsed against the steering wheel and closed her eyes, her whole body trembling. The peaceful sounds of early summer in the country wafted through the windows—birdsong, and wind in the tall grass by the side of the road, and the faint rumble of a tractor, far in the distance. Julianna stirred at last and sat up again, blinking in the sunlight, and her gaze fell on Elijah.

The boy was now entirely in the front seat. His upper body was on the floor with the groceries, and his knees were touching Julianna's side. He wasn't moving, and there was blood on his face. He looked like a child's discarded doll.

"Oh, Ben," Julianna moaned. "What have you done?"

She jumped out of the driver's door—stopping to fight for a moment with the automatic lock before remembering to hit the release button—and ran around the front of the car. She flung open Elijah's door and leaned in over his body, praying aloud.

His breathing was slow and regular, and his pulse was steady, in spite of a large, acorn-sized lump on his forehead and a small trail of blood running from his hairline to his cheek. She carefully inspected his head and neck, then moved on to his arms and legs. Her hands moved of their own volition, appearing to know exactly what they were doing. She tested all his joints and lightly fingered his spine, and only when she had finished her examination did she allow herself a tiny smile.

"Oh, thank God," Julianna whispered.

She put her arms around his chest and dragged him out of the car, groaning with the strain. She was a strong woman, but the boy weighed nearly as much as she did. Once she had him free of the vehicle, she laid him out on the road's shoulder and cradled his head in her lap.

"Oh, Ben. What am I going to do with you?" she muttered, looking down at his sleeping face with mingled anxiety and affection.

Crooning to him, she tugged his white shirt out of the waist of his jeans. She unbuttoned it and tore two long strips from the front; she wiped the blood from his face with one and used the other as a bandana for his injured head. The lovely, familiar smell of sweat and Ivory soap was rising from the skin of his torso; it reminded her of the way her brothers always smelled when they had been working in the hayfields surrounding their house.

"There," she said, surveying her handiwork. "All better."

He was still out cold, but Julianna was no longer worried. She somehow knew he would be fine. She raised him to a sitting position to free her legs, and once she had regained her feet, she half dragged, half carried his body over to the Edsel. The tatters of his shirt hung from his frame like rags on a scarecrow.

"Good Lord, Ben," she grunted, struggling to stuff him into the backseat. "You're much heavier than you used to be."

Ever since Cecil and Sarah Towpath had witnessed the horrifying scene at the intersection, they had been speeding along in the opposite direction as fast as Cecil could make their pickup go, desperately hunting for a phone.

It was the first time in a long and difficult marriage that Cecil and Sarah were in agreement over anything, and this unfamiliar sense of unity was intoxicating. The silly quarrel about their granddaughter Tina's marriage to Wally the Weasel had been forgotten, swept aside by an act of violence on a quiet country road. In fact, if it hadn't been for the unforgivable crime they were on their way to report, they may have even found time to smile at one another, or to share a few kind words.

But for all they knew, the woman whom they had seen assaulted might even be dead by now, and this grim possibility was rendering them somber and silent. Their silence held even after Sarah spotted a farmhouse on a distant hill, and Cecil spun onto the gravel lane that would take them to it.

It galled them both to no end that they had been so helpless during the attack. Cecil had wanted to follow the Edsel himself, but he had been too afraid. He knew he was no match for the young Negro assailant, even if they had been able to catch up. For her part, Sarah was suffering from a bout of intense empathy; she believed that she could just as easily have been the victim of the assault. She had never felt so old and vulnerable in her life. This shared sense of helplessness had since festered into righteous indignation, and as a result the phone call they would make to the Maine State Patrol would be slightly hysterical. Words like "armed madman" and "murderer" would get tossed around with no circumspection or concern for consequences.

And the Maine State Patrol would begin a manhunt.

Julianna casually pulled the Edsel back onto the highway and resumed her journey home. In her backseat was a slumbering boy with a ruined shirt and a lump on his forehead. As she looked to the south, toward New Hampshire, she could see the sky before them was dark with thunderclouds.

"Oh, dear," she clucked softly. "I do believe we're in for a storm."

Chapter 3

The rain was slowing to a drizzle when Jon Tate finally caught a ride. He'd been standing under a concrete overpass for over an hour, but it had given him little protection from the elements. Strong crosswinds had flung water at him again and again, mocking his attempt to stay dry. He was just as drenched and forlorn as he had been before he'd found this nominal shelter, and he felt feverish as he ran to catch up to the car that had pulled over and was waiting for him on the side of the road.

It was a cream and brown Edsel, but the side windows were fogged over so he couldn't see inside. The front passenger door was locked the first time he tried it; he tried again after hearing a metallic click, and this time the door opened for him.

A tall, thin, middle-aged woman in an elegant green dress leaned across the front seat and he bent to talk to her.

"You poor thing!" she whispered up at him. "You look like a drowned cat."

Jon responded with a tired nod and wondered why she was whispering. He waited for her to ask where he was headed, but she just beckoned him to get in. Her lack of curiosity was a blessing, but there were several grocery bags on the floor where his legs were supposed to go, and he didn't know what he was supposed to do with them.

"Should I get in back?" he asked. He was lightheaded from hunger and exhaustion, and he felt stupid.

"Shh!" The woman put a finger to her lips. "Ben is taking a nap."

He glanced in the rear of the car. A skinny black kid was sprawled across the backseat, faceup and apparently fast asleep. His white shirt was in shreds and he had what appeared to be a bloodstained bandana of some sort wrapped around his head. Jon gawked at him. The blood and the torn shirt caught his eye, of course, but the real attention grabber was the kid's dark skin. Everybody in Tipton, Maine, was white, and Jon had never been this close to a black person.

The woman gestured at the groceries. "Just move this stuff to the floor in the back, then you can sit up front with me."

As much as Jon wanted a ride, he hesitated. Hitchhiking with strangers was one thing, but getting into a car with a passed out, wounded black kid was quite another. A head injury like that could have happened in a fight or something, and the last thing Jon wanted right now was to be around a violent Negro.

He looked at the boy again, both fascinated and leery. "Is he okay?"

She sighed. "He's fine. He just got a bump on his noggin when he was horsing around. He'll wake up soon."

She studied Jon's gray eyes and his square jaw. His left hand was gripping a white plastic bag, tied tightly at the top; Julianna thought she could detect the outline of two or three books through the plastic. The protective way he clutched it to his side was endearing, and there was a vulnerability in his expression that reminded her of Ben. She took an instant liking to him, but something about the anxious way his eyes kept darting up and down the road made her guess he was in some sort of trouble.

"My name is Julianna," she said. "What's yours?"

Jon looked away. "Steve."

Julianna suspected he was lying to her, but it didn't bother her. Whatever his reason for standing out here in the rain on a deserted country road, Julianna didn't believe for a minute he was dangerous. She lifted one of the grocery sacks and thrust it toward him.

"Here," she said gently. "Put this in back."

The rainwater dribbling from his legs into his shoes helped Jon make up his mind. He took the sack from her, awkwardly juggling it with his bag of belongings, and opened the rear door to tuck the groceries on the floor by the sleeping kid. On first glance, Elijah was so still he looked like a corpse, but as Jon set the sack down he could see the boy's raven-black stomach moving as he breathed. Jon transferred the other groceries from the front to the back, too, trying to be as quiet as possible, then he closed the rear door and got in front with Julianna.

As he settled into his seat she hit the lock button for the doors and pulled back on the road without another word. It was hot in the car, but Jon was grateful for the heat because his sopping clothes were cold on his skin. He wished he had taken time to at least wring out his shirt before getting into the Edsel, and was kicking himself for fleeing his apartment that morning with nothing else to change into but two pairs of underwear and a pair of socks. He couldn't even change socks now, either, because if he opened the bag to get his dry pair the woman might see the cash he'd stolen from Toby.

He wiped his forehead with a damp hand and studied the side of the woman's face as she drove; the clouds ahead were breaking up a little and a ray of sun lit her long nose and her brown hair. He was pretty sure she knew he was watching her, but she didn't seem to mind. The car smelled of cigarettes and sweat, so he cracked his window to get some fresh air. After a few minutes of this silence he could barely keep his eyes open, in spite of the discomfort from being so wet. He set his bag carefully on the floor, next to his feet.

"Where are you guys going?" he asked at last, yawning.

She glanced at him for a long moment and smiled. "Home."

Something about the way she said this moved him, but it was probably only because it reminded him that he no longer had a home of his own to return to. He waited for more, but nothing came. He yawned again, remembering this time to cover his mouth for the sake of politeness. "Where's home?"

She pointed at the road through the windshield. "That way."

*   *   *

Mary Hunter was pacing back and forth on the front porch of their yellow farmhouse, waiting for Elijah to return. Her husband, Samuel, was inside, watching her through the screen door. It was early afternoon and a rainstorm from the southwest was headed their way, but the wall of approaching clouds hadn't reached them yet and the sun was still beating down on the house, throwing shadows from the porch rails across the wooden boards at Mary's feet. The shadows looked like prison bars. Mary kept shielding her eyes with her hand to see the gravel road half a mile away, at the end of their driveway.

She's so pretty when she's worried, Samuel thought.

On the rare occasions when Mary was unsettled about something, the resemblance between her and Elijah became far more pronounced than usual. Their son had inherited his mother's striking brown eyes and small nose, and a lot of her mannerisms—like how she tilted her head to the side when she was listening to things, or the way she stuck out her chin when she was annoyed. But Elijah's fretful temperament was nothing like Mary's. Mary was a polished stone with a few rough edges. Elijah was a hummingbird.

Even as a baby, he'd been like that. He'd yell and scream for hours in his crib if something startled him, and as he got older loud noises threw him into a tizzy, as did the sudden movement of a cat or a bird glimpsed from the corner of his eye. A fireworks display was Elijah's worst nightmare, and Halloween was the end of the world. He'd shown some improvement in the last couple of years, but Samuel and Mary occasionally still found him hiding behind the couch or under his bed if he heard a sound in the house he couldn't identify.

He didn't get his disposition from Samuel, either. Samuel was a mild, quiet man, who could never figure out why his son was so nervous. Elijah had gotten Samuel's height and his sharp, almost aristocratic cheekbones, but Samuel's calmness hadn't been handed down to his only child. It seemed a shame you couldn't pick and choose what to pass on to your kids, but Samuel supposed the Lord had a reason for preserving some traits from generation to generation while dumping others off at the side of the road. He just wished he knew what that reason was.

He wished a lot of things at the moment. He wished he knew where his son was, for instance, and why he hadn't come home for lunch. He was getting ready to drive into town and find him, but he hated to be an overprotective father, and was putting the trip off as long as he could stand it. Mary hadn't told him to go yet, either, but she wasn't likely to do that, no matter how worried she got.

Samuel adored his wife, but wished that they lived in the kind of world where she'd feel comfortable letting other people see her the way she was now, when Elijah was long overdue. Mary Hunter came across as cool and detached, and her face, though beautiful, was off-putting to strangers because it had so little expression in it. Most people thought she was haughty and they weren't completely wrong; she had a chip on her shoulder about a lot of things. She could be snappish, for instance, if she thought somebody was "looking down" on her, nor did she have any qualms about letting people know when she believed they weren't doing their jobs right, or were being lazy or stupid.

Like last winter, when the county was too slow getting their road plowed after a snowstorm. The Hunters were initially told it might be as much as a week, but Mary was on the phone with every elected official in Prescott, Maine, by the morning of the second day, and on the third day—while Samuel was down in the timber behind their house breaking up ice on the creek so the cattle could have water—she put chains on the tractor's tires and drove into town to badger Mayor Bridge in person. Her protest proved effective, and shortly after she returned home, a snowplow showed up in their driveway to do her bidding.

"A lot of busier roads needed that plow first, Sam," Mayor Bridge had whined later, when Samuel stopped by town hall to thank him for his help. "But Mary would have driven your goddamn tractor right through my front door if I hadn't said yes to her."

Samuel had just nodded. Mary would have done no such thing, of course (at least not without a lot more provocation), but he figured it didn't hurt for people to be a little afraid of her now and again. Most of their neighbors were decent souls, but there were a few idiots in town who had a problem with black people, and Sam was glad Mary intimidated them.

The Hunters were no fools. When Mary had become pregnant sixteen years ago, they sold their farm in Alabama and moved to New England, to get as far away as they could from Jim Crow. Once there, though, they had raised Elijah to always be deferential and courteous, knowing full well that a black man with a smart mouth was more often than not a target for violence, even in a relatively tolerant place like rural Maine. Samuel, too, kept a low profile and was well liked because of it.

But both Mary and Sam believed the situation was different for Mary. In their experience, "nice" black women became victims just as often as outspoken black men, and so Mary purposely adopted an almost Amazonian demeanor when she was in public. Over the years she had gotten astonishingly good at projecting an aura of menace, and nobody in Prescott, Maine, ever thought twice about messing with her.

But she didn't look so frightening right now, with their son gone AWOL. She was chewing on her lower lip, and her dark eyes, usually so steady and unblinking, were full of fear.

"He's fine, Mary." Samuel spoke through the screen door. "He's probably just reading magazines at the library and trying not to upchuck from all the bad news."

A hint of a smile played across her lips. "If that's the only reason he's late, he'll get his share of bad news when he gets home, too."

Both Mary and Samuel were spare and strong from physical labor; Mary cleaned houses in town and helped Sam with the farm chores when she could, and neither of them was any good at sitting still if there was work to be done. Lunchtime was normally just a short break in the day, but Elijah's absence was so unusual it had thrown a two-hour wrench in their routine.

Samuel waited another minute, watching her pace. "Think I should go look for him?"

Mary squinted out at the road again, not answering.

Samuel opened the screen door and stepped out on the porch. She stopped pacing and leaned back against him as he put his arms around her waist. The top of her head only came up to his chin.

"He probably just lost track of the time," Samuel said, gazing out at the field of knee-high corn that bordered each side of their driveway. "Teenagers are like that, remember?"

She shook her head. "Not Elijah," she murmured. "This isn't like him at all."

Samuel sighed, knowing she was right, as usual. Both of them had been trying to encourage Elijah to be braver and have more self-reliance, but the boy remained a painfully timid homebody who would never go lollygagging around town when food was on the table and his parents were waiting for him.

"I'll take the truck and go find him," he said, squeezing her. "We'll be back in a jiffy, you'll see."

Mary's hands tightened on his forearms for a moment before she released him.

As Samuel got in his blue Dodge pickup parked next to the house, he waved at her reassuringly. She waved back but resumed her pacing on the porch as he drove down the long driveway between the rows of corn. He kept glancing in his rearview mirror at her. She was standing tall and moving slow, and from a distance she looked cold and formidable as always, like a sentry on guard duty. Anybody who didn't know her wouldn't have a clue that all kinds of terrors were going through her head.

But Samuel knew. Other than Sam himself, Elijah was Mary's only weak spot. Their son had his share of quirks, but he was a good boy, through and through. He was sweet, smart, and loving, and he was the very best part of Mary's life. Sam's, too, for that matter, but if someone ever harmed Elijah it wouldn't be Sam they'd have to worry about. Mary Hunter would go to hell and back to keep her son safe, and God help anybody who tried to take him away from her.

Elijah woke with a throbbing headache and a layer of sweat all over his body. For a moment he didn't remember where he was, and he stared blankly at the tan underside of the Edsel's roof, trying to get his bearings. There was a thin strip of cloth tied around his head and his hand drifted up to inspect it, probing the tender bump over his left eye.

"Ow," he muttered.

Memory came rushing back: He'd banged his head while trying to get away from the crazy lady. Full awareness of his surroundings returned with this recollection and his eyes darted to the front of the car.

She's still got me prisoner!

A larger shock followed as he registered a young white guy with short black hair now sitting in the front passenger seat. The guy's head was resting on top of the seat and he seemed to be asleep.

Elijah goggled at this new threat. *Who the fuck is THAT?*

The windows were steamed over and the car was uncomfortably hot. Elijah sat up gingerly, and only then noticed his shirt was in shreds. He fingered it with dismay. The collar and short sleeves were intact, but the only other fabric left in front was the pocket covering his left breast. He felt like he was wearing a cape.

He flushed with embarrassment as he figured out where the bandage around his head had come from, and who must have torn up his shirt. He crossed his arms over his chest, feeling naked and vulnerable.

Elijah never went to the town pool (even though he loved to swim) because he didn't want other people to see him without clothes, and he loathed gym class since he had no choice but to shower with the other boys. Sometimes he'd take his shirt off when he was working on the farm with his dad, but the instant he saw the mailman or somebody else coming down the driveway he'd bolt for cover. It bothered him to know that while he'd been unconscious the woman and the stranger in the front seat had both seen him partly undressed.

There were groceries on the floor beside him, and as he stared at the Pepsi bottles and candy bars in one of the bags he realized how thirsty and hungry he was.

"Oh, good!" Julianna's cheerful voice made him jump. "Welcome back, sleepyhead."

Their eyes met in the rearview mirror.

Elijah frowned. "How long have I been asleep?" Keeping one arm firmly pressed to his sternum he wiped condensation from a side window with his free hand and peered out at the world. The weeds on the side of the highway were wet from a recent rain, but the sun was peeking through the clouds again.

She shrugged. "Several hours, I should think."

The stranger woke at the sound of their voices and raised his head. He looked at Julianna for a minute before turning in his seat to study Elijah. His face was guarded, but not unfriendly.

"Hi," he said.

Elijah was not in the best of moods. His head hurt, his shirt was ruined, and he was apparently hours away from his home. Worst of all, he was still a captive of the lunatic woman, and this guy might be her accomplice, for all he knew. Frustration and fear overrode his usual good manners.

"Who the hell are you?" he demanded.

The stranger blinked. He had a black stubble of beard on his chin and cheeks, but he didn't look much older than Elijah.

"Benjamin Taylor!" Julianna chided. "What on earth has gotten into you?" She dropped her voice to talk to the newcomer. "You'll have to forgive Ben. He's been acting strangely all day."

She spoke louder to address Elijah. "This is our new friend Steve, Ben. Say hello."

In spite of himself, Elijah felt a little abashed. His arms tightened over his exposed torso. "I'm Elijah," he muttered, looking at the floor.

Julianna's voice fell to a whisper again. "His name is Ben," she said, sounding distressed.

"No, it isn't," Elijah snapped, glaring at the back of her head. "It's Elijah."

In the mirror he could see her big green eyes rolling.

Jon Tate looked from one to the other of them, confused. "Uh, I'm Steve." He held out a tentative hand. "Nice to meet you."

Elijah stared with suspicion at the offered hand for a few seconds before taking it in his own. Both boys were sweating and Elijah let go promptly. He didn't like touching other people, especially when perspiration was involved.

His stomach growled and he gazed with longing at the bags of groceries next to his feet. His throat felt raspy as he raised his head and looked at the woman again. "Can I have some of your food?"

Julianna realized she was hungry, too. "Of course you can, silly. I could use a bite myself. Find me a chicken leg, will you?" She smiled over at Jon. "Momma always packs the best picnic lunches. Would you like to try some of her delicious fried chicken?"

Jon was starving and his mouth started watering. "That would be great."

He watched the top of Elijah's head as the other boy dug around in Edgar Reilly's grocery bags. Jon was trying to figure out what the connection was between Elijah and Julianna. It seemed odd that a middle-aged white woman and a young black kid would be traveling together, but the woman acted as if the two of them were old friends. The kid was bent out of shape about something, but maybe it was just because he'd hurt his head, like the lady said.

Elijah handed up a couple of bottles of Pepsi and a bag of potato chips and Jon thanked him, then asked if Elijah had a bottle opener. When Elijah shook his head, Jon shrugged and said "No problem," and promptly pried open the bottles with the latch of his seatbelt, impressing Elijah in spite of himself. Jon grinned and explained he'd learned to do this trick on beer bottles, then he passed one of the sodas to Julianna and tried to make conversation as he waited for Elijah to find the chicken.

"So how long have you guys known each other?" he asked.

Hearing this, Elijah abruptly straightened in the backseat, realizing that the older boy wasn't with the woman after all.

Maybe he can get her to stop the car! he thought in excitement.

"Oh, forever," the woman answered, taking a sip of warm

Pepsi and smiling appreciatively at its sweetness. "We grew up together."

Elijah poked his head between Julianna and Jon. "We did *not*," he said emphatically. He thrust a bag of Chips Ahoy! cookies at the other boy as if he were presenting him with a sworn affidavit. "Honest to God, I've never seen this lady before this morning. I don't even know her name!"

Jon ignored the offered cookies. Julianna's assertion of having grown up with somebody who was clearly forty years her junior was bad enough, but her hospital wristband had now caught his attention, as well. He was eyeing it with concern.

"She doesn't have any chicken, either," Elijah added sullenly.

Julianna pursed her lips, worried. "Oh, Ben, how could you possibly forget my name? We've been best friends since we were babies!"

Jon's mouth was hanging open, revealing a partially digested potato chip on his tongue.

"She's out of her goddamn mind," Elijah muttered to the other boy.

Julianna overheard this, but before she could chastise him for his rudeness a flashing red light appeared behind them on the highway, distracting her.

Gabriel Dapper answered the phone in the office of his downtown Bangor hardware store.

"Dapper's Tool Emporium," he said.

The office was small and cramped (especially for Gabriel, who was six foot four and weighed nearly three hundred pounds), but the piles of paper on his desk were stacked in tight, neat piles, and the catalogs and ledger books on the wall shelf were plainly marked and alphabetized. The desktop itself was clear, save for a notepad, a compass, and a pencil, all of which Gabriel had been using when the phone rang.

Edgar Reilly's polite, pompous voice came through the receiver. "Gabriel? It's Dr. Reilly."

Gabriel had been drawing interlocking one-inch diameter circles on the notepad with the compass; a closer inspection of the pad would have revealed dozens of virtually identical pages, with seven circles per page. Gabriel loved circles, and was also rather fond of the number 7.

"Hey, Doc," he responded cautiously. He knew better than to hope Edgar was calling to tell him Julianna's condition had improved, but he made himself ask anyway. "Is Mom doing any better?"

For Gabriel's entire life, his mother had been more sane than anyone else he knew. Living in the same town as they did, he had seen her at least once a week for years, and prior to setting the fire in her neighbor's garage a month ago, nothing in her behavior had warned him that her mind was preparing to desert her. On the contrary, she had seemed sharper than ever, reading book after book in preparation for the literature classes she taught at Shelby Cabot Grammar School; she had recently begun tutoring several students privately, too, in every subject from algebra to Latin. Ever since the garage fire, though, she had referred to him as "Lars, the blacksmith," and whenever he looked in her eyes the woman he had known as his mother was altogether absent. It made his heart hurt just to think about it, and for the last few weeks he'd found himself on the verge of tears at the oddest moments: standing in line at the grocery store, tossing a steak on the grill, sharpening all his office pencils until they were a uniform length.

On the other end of the line, Edgar Reilly held the phone in one hand and a cigarette in the other. Before dialing Julianna's son, he'd placed an open bag of lemon drops in front of him on the desk, for courage.

"I'm afraid I have some very bad news, Gabriel." Edgar did his best to sound calm and professional but he was unable to keep a tremor from creeping into his voice. "I'm very sorry to have to tell you this, but it seems your mother has escaped."

A prolonged silence followed this announcement and Edgar's forehead began to sweat. He popped a lemon drop into his mouth and waited anxiously.

Gabriel cleared his throat at last. "I don't understand." His voice was quiet, but ominous. "Where did she go?"

Edgar explained as quickly as he could, recounting all he knew about Julianna's escape from the hospital, her theft of his Edsel, and the subsequent police hunt for her. Then, sucking hard on the lemon drop every few seconds, he shared the information Deputy Oakley had given him only moments ago:

"Late this morning, a young black man was seen assaulting a white woman in what was almost certainly my car, in southern Maine." He forced himself to go on. "The physical description of the victim was vague, but I fear it could all too easily have been your mother." His voice shook. "I'm so sorry, Gabriel, but the police think it's likely she's been kidnapped."

Gabriel stared into space, not seeing anything in his orderly office.

"Christ," he whispered. "Sweet Christ in heaven."

Everybody believed Gabriel was older than he was. His size and his seriousness made him appear almost the same age as Julianna, but he was only thirty-six years old, and in many ways he felt even younger than that. He had never been in love, for instance, and his sole romantic relationship of any consequence had been with Tammy Sue Ogilvie, when he was a junior in high school. The time he spent with Tammy Sue was sweet and fun, but to be honest she hadn't meant much to him. And no woman had since come along, either, that he felt was worth the trouble of more than a single night.

The simple truth was that none of them could hold a candle to his mother.

Gabriel's father, William Dapper, had been kicked in the head by a horse and killed when Gabriel was only three years old, in a tiny town called Veteran, Maine. Gabriel had no memory of his father, nor of Veteran. Julianna had been a very young schoolteacher when William died; they were married for less than four years, and his premature death broke her heart. She couldn't bear to continue living in Veteran, and so she and Gabriel relocated to Bangor to start a new life.

They knew no one in Bangor when they arrived, but Julianna was a gifted teacher and soon found work at the school where she still taught to this day—or *had* taught, until her recent psychotic episode. She never even dated another man; losing William had hurt her too badly, and she frequently told Gabriel—who thought she should remarry—that she had experienced more than her fair share of that sort of pain for one lifetime, and didn't care for any more of it. She felt it was much safer to pour her entire heart and soul into her teaching, instead.

And into her only child, of course.

If Gabriel were forced to come up with an anecdote from his childhood that would best illustrate why he adored his mother as much as he did, he would have chosen a memory from when he was sixteen, shortly after America had just entered the second World War. In addition to her teaching, Julianna had begun volunteering as a nurse's aid at the Bangor hospital; she worked long hours each night, taking care of wounded soldiers who had been shipped back to the States, and she often didn't get home until after midnight, exhausted. Gabriel soon became worried about her, and he asked why she was working so hard when she didn't have to.

She'd turned to him with a tired smile. "Because I made a deal with God."

"What are you talking about?" Gabriel had smiled back warily, thinking she was pulling his leg. Julianna was far less religious than Gabriel, and often teased him for being what she called "too churchy" for his own good.

Julianna had shrugged. "Well, since you've decided to enlist in the army next year, I promised God I'd help out at the hospital for the entire war. All *He* has to do to hold up His part of the bargain is to bring you back in one piece."

Gabriel had stared at her. "You're not serious."

"I surely am." Her smile had deepened. "If the war lasts a long time I'll probably end up helping a lot of soldiers to get better, so God's getting an excellent deal, if I do say so myself. All the doctors and nurses tell me I should have been a nurse instead of a teacher because I'm so good at it."

"You're talking crazy, Mom," Gabriel had protested. "God doesn't make *bargains*."

She'd raised an eyebrow. "I had a dream where we shook

hands on it, and that's good enough for me." She paused. "It was a very odd dream. God had two thumbs on His right hand and a hideous wart on the end of His nose that I couldn't help staring at. But He promised He'd look after you, and I believed Him."

Gabriel had narrowed his eyes. "You're making this up."

She'd laughed. "Only the part about the wart. The rest is true, I swear." She'd reached out and pulled him to her, then, gripping him tightly against her body. "Don't you dare make a liar out of God, Gabriel," she whispered in his ear. "I couldn't bear to lose you."

Edgar Reilly's voice on the phone abruptly pulled Gabriel's mind back to his hardware store office. "Gabriel? Are you still there?"

Gabriel blinked. "Yeah," he rasped. "I'm here."

"Oh, I thought for a minute there we'd been disconnected," Edgar said, sounding relieved. "Well, as I was saying, I know this is a terrible blow for you, but the police are doing everything in their power, and I'm sure we'll hear something very soon. You mustn't . . . well, you really mustn't give up hope."

Gabriel's big fingers turned white as they clutched the receiver. He suddenly couldn't bear to listen to any more of Edgar's platitudes, so he thanked him brusquely and asked him to call if he heard anything else, then hung up. He stared at the walls of his hardware store office for a minute or two, and he began to tremble.

Images of a rabid black man flooded his mind. He could see his mother screaming for help; he could see her body lying on the side of the road somewhere, flung from the car like a bag of trash; he could see the light leave her lovely green eyes and her face turn still as stone as she gazed up at the sky.

"Mom," he murmured aloud, his voice cracking.

He dropped his forehead on his desk and began to cry.

Lloyd Eagleton of the New Hampshire State Patrol was more excited than he'd been in his whole life. He'd become a state trooper in '59, but in the three years since he'd never made what he considered an "important" arrest. Oh, sure, he'd busted at least half a dozen drunks for causing bad accidents or raising hell on the roads, but the bulk of his days were spent handing out endless speeding tickets to pissed-off tourists and truck drivers. He couldn't believe his luck in finally being given a chance to bag a major scumbag.

It was really happening this time, though. The 1959 Edsel he was following was definitely the car everybody was looking for. It was a cream and brown Ranger, sure enough, and as he got close enough to verify its Maine plates, he flipped on the cherry light "gumball machine" on top of his squad car and snatched up his radio microphone to notify the dispatcher he was making the stop.

Like a lot of young troopers, Lloyd enjoyed the feeling of power that came with a badge and a .357 Magnum. He loved everything about his uniform, too, from his flat-rimmed Smokey Bear hat to his glossy, black leather gunbelt and shoulder strap.

"Car twenty-seven to station!" he bawled into the mic. "I've got the bastard!"

This wasn't supposed to be the sort of thing he said on the radio, but he was far too worked up to deal with the usual formalities.

A skinny Negro in the backseat of the Edsel was visible through the rear window. He had a strip of white cloth wrapped around his head, and he was leaning over the front seat, by the driver, who appeared to be a white woman.

Lloyd gaped. "I'll be damned," he muttered. "She's still alive!"

When he'd heard the bulletin that afternoon to watch for the Ranger, he'd assumed (along with every other cop who received the broadcast) that the lady victim from Maine they'd been told about was already dead, killed by the black son of a whore who'd assaulted her while she was driving.

Lloyd was not necessarily the dumbest cop on the road, but neither was he—as his supervisor once remarked—the "shiniest penny in the fountain." He had made more than his share of errors in his three years of service with the state police, the worst of them involving an altercation with a teenaged drunken driver whom Lloyd bullied into a fistfight. This sort of behavior wasn't uncommon for Lloyd, who enjoyed a good tussle, but the situation became nearly lethal to his career when the boy was afterward revealed to be: (a) sober, and (b) the youngest son of the lieutenant governor of New Hampshire.

Once Lloyd was in possession of these facts, he let the kid off scot-free, of course (save for a black eye and a fat lip), but the lieutenant governor had not been forgiving. Lloyd was suspended for three months without pay, and then stuck on probation for an entire year following his return to duty.

His year of purgatory for that lapse in judgment was now over, thank God, but Lloyd knew he was still deeply in the doghouse with his superiors. The only way to redeem himself in their eyes at all, he believed, was to make a high-profile arrest, so he had been praying for months for something just like this to come his way.

And now his prayers had been answered.

"Holy shit!" he yelled with glee at the dispatcher through the radio. "We've got a hostage situation here!"

He hit the siren and stepped on the gas.

Jon Tate was in a full-blown panic. The instant he saw the flashing red light behind them he assumed it had to do with the money he'd stolen back in Maine, or even worse, Becky Westman's pregnancy. The improbability of a New Hampshire state trooper already having information about either of these offenses never crossed his mind; his conscience was running roughshod over his common sense. He slumped down in the front seat as much as he could, to get out of the line of sight.

"Oh God, oh Jesus, oh Jesus God," he whispered hysterically as the squad car's siren began to wail. He could picture himself being led away from the Edsel in handcuffs. "I am so fucked!"

Julianna, of course, was viewing things a bit differently than Jon, though with an almost equal sense of dread. "Oh, for pity's sake!" Her voice betrayed her dismay. "Daddy will never let me drive again if he finds out I did something illegal!"

Jon gawked at her, uncomprehending, and attempted to stuff his bag of stolen cash under the seat.

In the backseat, Elijah was flushed with triumph and waving happily through the rear window at the trooper he believed to be his savior. He didn't know how this miracle had happened, but he was betting his mother, Mary, had something to do with it.

Oh, thank God! he thought. *This freak show is finally over!*

"I ain't believing this," Lloyd Eagleton grunted into the radio, shaking his head as he glared at Elijah through the windshield. "The fucking asshole is *waving* at me, like this is all some kinda big joke."

The radio squawked back at him.

"Car twenty-seven? What's your location?" Brenda Freeman was the dispatcher. "Maybe you should wait for some backup?"

Lloyd was aware Brenda thought he was an idiot. She'd been on duty the night he'd beaten up the lieutenant governor's son, and she wasn't about to let him forget it.

He'd show her, though. He'd show them all.

"There's no time," he barked back. "He might kill this lady if I wait any longer."

He flipped the siren off as the Edsel lurched over to the side of the road and came to a gradual stop in front of him. He pulled in behind it and reached down to unsnap the holster on his Smith & Wesson.

"The suspect has pulled over," he advised Brenda. His hands were sweating, but he chalked that up to excitement more than fear. "I'm going to go get him now."

He drew his gun and opened his door.

"Dammit, Lloyd, don't be a dipshit!" Brenda screeched through the radio loud enough to make him wince. "Where are you?"

He almost didn't answer, but at the last second he decided it couldn't hurt anything to reveal his location.

"Highway ten, right by the Ashuelot River Bridge," he said. A grin spread across his face. "But if the other guys want in on this they better hurry!"

There was no way anyone else could get there in time to hone in on his glory. He dropped the microphone into the seat before Brenda could answer and stepped from his car, crouching behind the door for cover.

The gravel on the side of the road was wet and the ground was riddled with potholes as Julianna put on the brakes and steered them onto the shoulder of the highway, followed immediately by the police car. The Edsel bumped along and came to a rest a few feet away from a small bridge over a river. To the south was a cranberry bog; to the north was a thickly forested area. A wild tangle of birch, maple, and pine trees was little more than a yard from Jon's door, and even with all the windows closed the sweet, pungent smell of the pine trees filled the car.

Elijah tried the door handle but it was still locked.

"You better let me out, lady." He was feeling more assertive now that his release was at hand, but he supposed there was no point in being rude. "I promise to tell him it was all a big mistake if you'll just let me go, okay?"

Before Julianna could answer they heard a man's voice shouting behind them.

"What did he say?" Jon whispered from the floor of the front seat. His cheeks and forehead were coated with sweat.

Julianna looked in her rearview mirror. "I don't know." Her mouth fell open. "Why would Sheriff Burns hide behind his door like that?"

Elijah turned around and got on his knees in the backseat so he could get a better look out the rear window. All he could see was the trooper's black shoes under the open driver's door of the patrol car.

The trooper yelled something else they couldn't make out.

"Oh, for heaven's sake," Julianna said in confusion. "Why doesn't he just come talk to me?" She hit the lock release and opened her door a crack.

"Hello, Sheriff Burns!" she shouted politely through the opening. "Can I help you?" She turned her head to Jon and dropped her voice. "Maybe he has me confused with somebody else, do you think?"

Elijah lunged for the rear door handle while it was still unlocked, but before he could grab it the trooper's strained voice
rang out once again.

"Put your hands up where I can see them right now, goddammit, or I will open fire!"

Elijah froze, facing the front again, realizing the situation
could get out of control very quickly. He didn't want to be shot
accidentally, nor did he want Julianna to be hurt if there was
any way to prevent it. The woman may have kidnapped him,
but it wasn't really her fault. She wasn't in her right mind, and
he hoped she wasn't going to do anything stupid.

The trooper resumed yelling. "I mean it, *nigger!* You've got
until the count of three! One . . ."

Elijah's face went blank with shock.

"No, oh no, oh no no no," he spluttered.

Julianna's head flew up in rage. "That is the lowest, rudest
thing I've ever heard in my entire *life!*" She was beside herself
with indignation. "People in polite society say 'Negro!' Everybody knows that!"

"Two . . ." bellowed the trooper.

Jon Tate slowly raised his head in the front seat. "What's
happening?" he demanded.

His relief to discover that the cop wasn't there for him was
tempered by his inability to make sense of what was going on.
From where he was crouching he could only see Elijah from the
nose up, but the kid was crying, and he looked petrified. Their
eyes locked over the seat, and Jon's confusion deepened.

"But why are the cops after *you?*" he asked, bewildered.
"You haven't done anything wrong, have you?"

Whatever else could be said about Lloyd Eagleton, he was an
excellent shot with his revolver. In target practice he could routinely hit the bull's-eye ten out of ten times at a distance of
twenty-five yards, and he even had a gold marksmanship pin on
the breast of his uniform to prove it.

At the moment he was less than fifteen feet away from the
Edsel, and he could see the young black man's head through its

rear window. It was an easy shot, and Lloyd was more than prepared to kill the SOB if he didn't surrender. He'd yelled out a
couple of warnings already but so far there had been no response.

The driver's door on the Edsel popped open a crack and a
woman's voice sang out.

"Hello, Sheriff Burns! Can I help you?"

"What the hell?" Lloyd muttered. "Who the fuck is Sheriff
Burns?"

His face began to flush as he puzzled over this and came up
with an answer: The black bastard must be *forcing* the woman
to call him the wrong name, just to piss him off. He hated it
when punk-ass little delinquents pulled shit like that, and he
wasn't about to put up with any crap from such a lowlife
douche bag.

"Put your hands up where I can see them right now, goddammit," he yelled back, "or I will open fire!"

Silence was the only answer.

Lloyd filled his lungs with pine-scented air. "I mean it, *nigger!*
You've got until the count of three! One . . ."

Lloyd supposed he shouldn't have said "nigger," but it
sounded tough to his own ears and he thought it might help
scare the prick into giving up. He didn't like to think of himself
as a racist, but in his opinion there were times when "nigger"
was the only word that fit the bill, and this was definitely one of
those times.

"Two!" He aimed his .357 through the gap between his open
door and the body of the car. He was surprised to notice the
barrel of the gun was shaking quite badly. He'd never shot anybody before, and to tell the truth he was terrified.

Why the fuck didn't I wait for backup? he thought.

For some reason he was beginning to feel like a little boy
who'd gotten into something way over his head. This sudden
drop in confidence made him mad, and his jaw stiffened with resolve.

"Don't be a weenie, Lloyd," he whispered to himself. "Just
do your job."

His arm steadied against the door frame and he took another breath to yell one last time.

Jon Tate was young enough that he still didn't know a lot about himself. For instance, he had no idea he was the kind of person who might risk his own life for a stranger. Yet as he stared across the seat at the stricken Elijah, it occurred to him that the kid's head was visible through the rear window, and the cop, for whatever reason, had threatened to shoot him on the count of three.

And several long seconds had now passed since the trooper had yelled out, "Two!"

"Jesus Christ, Elijah, get down!" Jon howled.

He flung himself over the front seat, banging his head on the ceiling light en route, and grabbed Elijah around the neck, pulling him out of the line of fire just as the trooper's first gunshot punched a quarter-sized hole through the rear window, turning the safety glass white with a thousand tiny cracks.

Lloyd Eagleton very nearly soiled his neatly pressed pants when he saw Jon Tate pop up out of nowhere and fly over the front seat of the Edsel. This unwelcome manifestation stunned him so much that his arm jerked as he squeezed the trigger on his gun, and his shot went high. The Edsel's rear window seemed to frost over all at once as the bullet pierced it, and Lloyd, panicking as he realized he'd not only missed his target but now had to contend with two kidnappers instead of one, snatched up the microphone in the seat next to him.

"SON OF A BITCH!" he wailed to the dispatcher. "There's TWO of them! I need help right now, goddammit!"

He fired another wild shot at the Edsel and the woman in the driver's seat began to scream.

"Sheriff Burns has gone insane!" Julianna cried as Lloyd's second shot took out the side mirror on her door. The first bullet had embedded itself in the car's ceiling less than a foot from her head. "He's trying to kill us!

Most of the safety glass in the rear window was still clinging to its frame, but a small piece had flown through the air and cut her forearm, close to the elbow. She had blood on the sleeve of her green dress. She stared at the sticky red mess for a moment, then without hesitation she turned the key in the ignition.

"Hold on, boys!" she cried.

Crazy or not, Julianna Dapper was a warrior.

As Edgar Reilly's magnificent, souped-up engine roared to life, she popped the car in reverse and stomped on the accelerator.

Lloyd had expected the kidnappers to flee in the opposite direction, and he watched in stupefaction as the Edsel came straight at him, charging backward in a spray of gravel. He couldn't decide whether to run or shoot, and his irresolution proved to be his undoing.

In the final moment—as he squatted, frozen, behind his open door—a dispassionate voice spoke in his head. What it told him was clearly untrue, yet still comforting.

There's no way in hell they can be moving that fast, the voice said. *It's just a fucking Edsel.*

The last thing he heard was an apocalyptic crash.

Chapter 4

Otto "Red" Kiley of Prescott, Maine, liked to think of himself as a great sheriff. True enough, he was not fond of working and did everything he could to avoid it. But he'd kept the peace in Prescott day in and day out for thirty-plus years, and he'd never once shirked his responsibilities. If he had to investigate a crime he was thorough and honest, even if it meant putting in extra hours and dealing with stupid assholes who didn't deserve his help. He'd broken up hundreds of bar fights and domestic brawls, yet he'd only had to draw his gun once, when an eggnog-crazed Irma Flederman threatened a group of Baptist carolers with a shotgun on Christmas Eve in '49.

Red had sympathized with Irma (who had passed out before things got out of hand). He disliked Christmas carols, too, and even though eggnog wasn't for him, he had a weakness for Budweiser beer, and a history of doing questionable things while drinking it.

For example, he was fond of chugging a Bud or two in his squad car on the way home from work each day. If the beer was too warm he'd reach out the window as he drove along and set a can in the gap between the hood and the windshield, so the wind could chill it for him. What aided this ingenious cooling process even more, he'd found, was to go very fast and make the can slide back and forth across the hood by swerving left or right every few seconds or so. It was just a bit of harmless fun, and he'd never even come close to having a wreck while doing it. But he knew some people might nonetheless object to this unique method of refrigeration.

As far as he was concerned, though, they could all go fuck themselves.

Red—who got his nickname from his ruddy complexion and a thick red beard—had a similar attitude about a lot of things. He had little patience for the nervous Nellie types in town who fussed about every little thing and wasted his time by coming into his office to badger him with their silly-ass problems day after day. It made him irritable, and it was a wonder he'd been reelected so many times when he'd told much of the voting public to "stop being a burr in my butt crack."

But Samuel Hunter wasn't a whiner. Not by a long shot.

Fifteen years ago, shortly after the Hunters moved to Prescott, some anonymous little dickhead had tried to make life unpleasant for the young black couple from Alabama by painting the words "Whites Only" on the *Welcome to Prescott!* sign, posted on the main highway into town. The sign was less than a mile from the Hunters' farm, and Red had figured Sam and Mary would be pretty bent out of shape by something ugly like that. But when he talked to them about it, Mary hadn't even blinked, and Sam had just shrugged and said, "Could be a lot worse."

In other words, the Hunters weren't whiners, and Red had approved of them ever since. More than that, he'd even grown to *like* them over the years, and for Red that was really saying something, because Red didn't like most people. But Samuel Hunter never kissed ass, nor asked anyone else to kiss his, though he was always friendly and respectful. And if someone in town took exception now and then to Mary Hunter—who scared people shitless—and her "stuck-up" ways, it tickled Red to tell Samuel all about it, because Samuel's only reaction was to hide a proud grin behind his hand. Sam Hunter didn't give a crap what anybody else thought of his bitch-on-wheels wife, and Red loved that about him.

So when Samuel showed up in Red's office late Saturday afternoon, Red didn't mind sticking around to talk to him, though it was getting close to the end of his shift and he was looking forward to the warm six-pack waiting for him out in his squad car.

"Something's happened to Elijah," Samuel said, shaking Red's hand and taking a seat in front of his desk.

Apparently Samuel had been searching for his son for the last three hours, and the kid had been missing for two hours before that. Samuel had stopped in at the public library, the drugstore, and everywhere else he could think to look, but the only person he'd spoken to who'd even laid eyes on the boy that day was Bill Keenan, the pharmacist. Bill told Samuel that Elijah left the drugstore sometime before noon, but he hadn't seen him go. "He was rooting through the magazines, frowning and talking to himself," Bill had related, smiling. "But he always does that, so I didn't pay him any mind."

Samuel told Red he'd called Mary once every half an hour from the pay phone outside the drugstore, in hopes Elijah had returned home. But Mary had answered the phone so fast each time it told him everything he needed to know without asking. She was going out of her head with worry.

Red didn't say so to Samuel, but he thought Mary had cause to be alarmed.

Prescott was not much bigger than a pimple. It had a handful of stores, a school, a city hall, a park, a bank, and a couple of churches, but that was about it. It was unusual for a kid to go missing in such a small place, and Red could normally find just about anybody he was looking for in a matter of minutes. Still, if it were any other boy in town, a five-hour absence wouldn't have alarmed him, and he likely would have told the father to go home and stop pestering him.

But Elijah Hunter wasn't any other boy. Considering that every single soul who lived and worked in the area was white except for Samuel and his family, a kid with dark skin stuck out like a black olive in a bag of marshmallows.

No sooner had this thought flitted through his brain than Sally Shepherd, his dispatcher, began caterwauling in the next room.

"Dammit, Otto!" Sally was the only person that called Red by his given name. "Who let all the paper run out on the tele-type machine again?"

He hated it when Sally got worked up about something. Her voice went high and tight and reminded him of a model airplane engine.

Red rolled his eyes for Samuel's benefit and yelled back through the open door. "It's not my job to keep your machines up and running, Sally."

"Well, it's been out of paper all afternoon," she huffed. "The whole world could have blown up and we wouldn't have known about it."

A few seconds later the clackety-clack of the teletype started up.

Red apologized to Samuel for the interruption. "Did you try the pool, Sam? Maybe he went for a swim."

Samuel shook his head. "He only swims in our pond. He hates public pools."

Sally shrieked again and both men jumped. An instant later she appeared in the doorway, clutching a teletype report to her bosom.

Red waved her away. "Go away, Sally. I'm busy." The sun coming through the blinds was making him hot and irritable, and the ceiling fan wasn't doing a damn thing to cool him down.

She ignored him and galloped over to his desk. "You need to look at this right now," she said, thrusting the paper at him.

Red glowered up at her but took the report. After two sentences he started craving the Budweiser in the trunk of his squad car.

"What is it?" Samuel demanded, noticing the consternation in Red's beefy face.

The teletype report was from the Maine State Police, warning to be on the lookout for an Edsel, a white woman, and "a tall, thin, Negro male, approximately eighteen years of age" who was being sought for kidnapping, assault, and theft. The crime had occurred less than twenty miles south of Prescott, Maine, but the suspect was now being hunted all over New England.

Red scanned the teletype message again, wordlessly, then held it out to Samuel.

Samuel's dark eyes studied Red's face before he reached for the paper. As he read it his long black fingers began to tremble.

"No, Red," Samuel said, furiously shaking his head. "There's no way in *hell* that's my boy." He read the paper again, desperate for reassurance. "For one thing, Elijah's only *fifteen*. This is just a dumb coincidence."

Red nodded to make the man feel better, but he felt sick with dread. Coincidence or not, Elijah was missing, and three felonies had been committed that very day in the vicinity of Prescott by a teenaged Negro matching the boy's description. The age discrepancy didn't really matter; Elijah had grown a lot recently and from a distance he could easily pass for eighteen. Everything Red knew about the Hunters told him this was some sort of mistake, but his gut was telling him otherwise. It didn't bode well for the Hunter family, and Red almost couldn't bear to look at Samuel. Elijah had somehow gotten mixed up in something bad, and that was all there was to it, like it or not.

Red looked up at Sally, who was staring at him with poorly concealed excitement. She was chomping on a piece of gum as if it were a wad of caffeinated cud.

"Get me the state police on the phone," he ordered, feeling tired. He held up a hand to head off Samuel's protest until she left the office to make the call.

"You've got to be joking," Samuel snapped as soon as they were alone again.

"Sorry, Sam. I don't like this any better than you, but if Elijah's in trouble—"

"It's not Elijah," Samuel insisted.

Red talked over him. "If Elijah's in trouble, then we need to make sure everybody knows he's just a kid, okay?"

He didn't say the rest of what he was thinking: *Because if they know how young he is, the cowboys in the state patrol might be less likely to get trigger-happy.*

The idea that somebody might actually shoot Elijah Hunter before the day was done made him want to puke. There were a

ton of people Red wouldn't mind seeing shot, but Samuel
Hunter's boy wasn't one of them.

He had no way of knowing he would soon feel much worse.
Within an hour, another teletype message would arrive, report-
ing the attempted murder of a New Hampshire state trooper
named Lloyd Eagleton.

Edgar Reilly's stolen Edsel plowed into the squad car and
drove it backward nearly three feet on the shoulder of the road.
The open door Lloyd Eagleton was cowering behind was prevented from slamming shut, however, because Lloyd's stocky
body—or more specifically, his ribcage—got in the way. Lloyd's
gun and Smokey Bear hat went flying as five of his ribs snapped
and the back of his skull bounced off the side of the car; he
passed out an instant later, facedown on the gravel.

Julianna didn't even glance in the rearview mirror before
throwing the Ranger into drive once more and flooring the accelerator. The Edsel spun out again and lunged forward, detach-
ing itself with a squeal from the demolished front bumper of
Lloyd's cruiser. Within seconds the scene of the collision was
well behind them on the highway, but Julianna didn't ease up on
the gas pedal.

"Are you boys hurt?" she cried over the noise of the engine.
"Ben? Steve?"

There was no response at first and she risked taking her eyes
from the road to assess the situation in the rear of the car.

"Oh, thank heaven," she breathed a moment later. "I thought
Sheriff Burns had killed you."

Jon and Elijah peered up at her with twin looks of shock.
They were on the floor of the backseat, where they had landed
in a jumble of limbs and junk food. Both had minor cuts here
and there, but otherwise appeared unhurt. Julianna, relieved, returned her attention to her driving.

"Wait till I tell Daddy about this," she said. She was trembling from the violence of the last few minutes and had to struggle to keep her voice cheerful. "Sheriff Burns is completely
demented."

"Jesus Christ," Jon groaned, stirring.

He slowly lifted his chin off Elijah's ear and looked around. He was on top of the younger boy; Elijah was on his side, wedged between the seat and the floor, and Jon was sprawled across him. Jon's face was full of horror as he stared down into Elijah's stunned eyes.

"Please, please tell me she didn't just kill a cop," Jon begged.

Both boys were sweating profusely from fright, and neither smelled very good. Jon's clothes were also still wet from the rainstorm, and he was dizzy from the heat in the car.

Elijah's lower lip quivered as he tried not to cry. "Can you get off me, please?" The makeshift bandage around his head had fallen off and the bump on his head was throbbing. "I can't breathe."

Elijah felt he was on the verge of a nervous breakdown. *THAT COP ALMOST KILLED ME!* he kept thinking. *My BRAINS were almost SPLATTERED all over this car!*

Jon rolled onto the seat with care, trying to avoid more glass. It was only then he noticed a more serious gash above his left knee. It was three inches long and looked deep.

"Shit!" He probed at the wound and grimaced. "I'm bleeding bad!"

The Edsel swerved as Julianna shot another glance over the seat. "You'll be fine," she said, recovering control of the wheel. "Apply pressure to it. Ben, get a tourniquet ready for Steve, just in case the bleeding doesn't slow down."

Elijah clambered off the crushed grocery bags on the floor and gaped at the wound on Jon's leg.

"A tourniquet?" He looked around, dazed. "How do I do that?"

She sighed. "Tear off another piece of that silly cape you're wearing, and twist it into a rope."

Elijah and Jon shared a despairing look.

"I think she means your shirt," Jon whispered.

"I *know* what she means," Elijah snapped. He didn't want to sacrifice any more of his shirt; he was positive he was going to be killed soon and he didn't want to die half-naked. He spotted the checkered headscarf on the floor next to a bag of potato chips and held it up. "Can't I just use this instead?"

Julianna inspected it in the mirror and shook her head. "Absolutely not! That scarf belongs to my mother, and she'll be furious if I ruin it."

"I want out of this car," Elijah moaned. "I want out right now."

Julianna was calming down. She lightened her foot on the accelerator and the needle on the speedometer gradually fell into a more reasonable range. "Don't be ridiculous, Ben," she said. "We're almost home."

This was the last straw for Elijah.

"MY NAME IS *ELIJAH!*" he howled. "STOP CALLING ME *BEN,* BECAUSE IT'S NOT MY NAME, OKAY? AND I DON'T KNOW WHERE THE *FUCK* WE ARE, BUT IT'S NOWHERE NEAR *MY* HOME! I LIVE IN PRESCOTT *FUCKING* MAINE, LADY, AND YOU'RE OUT OF YOUR *FUCKING* MIND!"

The scream was earsplitting, and Julianna and Jon both recoiled from the force of it. Elijah, too, seemed shocked by the immensity of what had just issued from his mouth, and they all sat still, dumbstruck, in the ringing stillness that followed his outburst.

"Shame on you, Benjamin Taylor," Julianna said primly, recovering at last. "Your mother would blister your little bottom for speaking like that."

Elijah put his face in his hands and screamed wordlessly through his fingers before at last falling silent.

Jon looked through the rear window and cleared his throat. "What happened to the trooper?" he asked Julianna. "Is he . . . is he still alive?"

Julianna frowned. "What trooper, Steve?"

Jon made a face, realizing he had to step into Julianna's fantasy world for her to understand what he was talking about. "Sheriff whatever-you-called-him. Burns, I guess. Sheriff Burns."

Julianna's eyes met his in the mirror as he faced front again;

she seemed perplexed by his question. "Sheriff Burns lives in Hatfield, so he doesn't get over our way very often. I really haven't seen him in *ages.*"

Jon opened his mouth, then promptly shut it again, giving up.

Elijah dropped his head in despair, but as he did so he noticed that the cut on Jon's leg was now dripping blood onto a crushed grocery bag on the floor. All of a sudden it occurred to Elijah he'd be dead if it weren't for the older boy, and he began to feel ashamed for not doing anything to try to help him with his injury. He shrugged out of the remains of his shirt and ripped another long piece from the back to use as a tourniquet. When he had it ready to tie around Jon's thigh, he looked up at the other boy for guidance.

Jon grimaced. "Sorry. I don't know how to do it, either."

"How heavy is the bleeding, son?" Julianna asked.

Until that moment, her speaking voice had been high and breathy, like a schoolgirl's. But as she asked this question her voice deepened perceptibly, becoming lucid and more adult in an instant. Both boys heard the change and gaped at the back of her head.

"Steve?" she prodded. She was unaware of their scrutiny. "Is it slowing down at all?"

Jon tore his gaze away from her and lifted his hands to inspect the cut again. "Yeah. I think so."

"You might not need a tourniquet, then. Just keep pressure on it for a little while." There was a brief pause, and when she resumed speaking her voice had reverted to its girlish timbre. "You can use the rest of Ben's cape as a bandage."

The boys looked at each other again.

"Jesus," Jon whispered. "We are so screwed."

Elijah nodded but said nothing. He tried to cover himself again with the pathetic remnants of his shirt, but so little was left of it that he soon gave up. Fresh tears welled in his eyes as he let the soft white cloth fall from his fingers to the floor, and he turned his head so Jon wouldn't see him cry.

"It's not a cape," he grated at Julianna, fighting to keep from having another panic attack. "It's my *shirt.*"

Jon had been watching him. He was almost as upset as Elijah, but at the moment he was less worried for himself than he was for the younger boy. For whatever reason, Elijah was the one being hunted by the police, and he looked so sad and vulnerable sitting there in his bare skin that Jon's heart ached for him.

"You want my shirt, man?" he asked. "It's wet, but you can have it if you want it."

Elijah stared at him. The kindness behind Jon's offer astonished and moved him, and he eyed the other boy's blue T-shirt for a moment before shaking his head.

"Nah. That's okay." He hesitated. "Thanks, though."

As much as he hated being unclothed, he hated the idea of wearing somebody else's dirty shirt even more.

Jon shrugged. "Sure."

There was a long, shy silence as they searched for more to say to each other. Julianna was humming what sounded like a hymn, and the trees on both sides of the road were blurs of green and brown through the windows.

Jon finally cleared his throat and leaned closer to Elijah so Julianna wouldn't hear him. The corners of his mouth turned up as he spoke in Elijah's ear. "Just be glad she didn't think your underwear was some kind of surgical gauze," he whispered.

Elijah flushed, but when he realized he was being teased he almost grinned, too, in spite of everything. He was still trying to think of an appropriate reply when the Edsel's engine sputtered and died.

"Oh, dear!" Julianna cried, wrestling with the wheel to bring them to the side of the road before they stopped moving altogether. "Now what?"

Samuel and Mary Hunter weren't the only parents on tenterhooks about a missing child in trouble with the law. One hundred and three miles north of Prescott, Maine, in the quiet little town of Tipton (home of Toby's Pizza Shack), Earl and Marline Tate were praying as hard for Jon as the Hunters were for Elijah.

The Tates felt they'd failed as parents. Their eldest child had not only run out on his responsibility to the underage, pregnant

Becky Westman, but on his way out of Tipton he had also robbed Toby, his friend and employer, of nearly four hundred dollars. Because of this, he was now wanted by the police, and there was nothing Earl and Marline could do about it except wait for him to be caught, and fret about the consequences.

Marline, especially, was so torn between agitation and rage she couldn't sit still.

"What will happen when the Westmans find out he's skipped town?" She was pacing the floor in Jon's apartment, pausing now and then to aim a vicious kick at various stacks of paperback books that kept getting in her way. "What if they decide to tell the police about Becky's baby?"

When the Westmans and the Tates had left Jon alone in the wee hours of the morning, the plan had been to meet again for lunch with both Jon and Becky to discuss their future. But before this meeting could occur, the Tates had gotten a call from the Tipton sheriff, informing them Jon had stolen cash from the Pizza Shack and was now a wanted criminal. The last thing Jon needed was for the sheriff to discover he was fleeing from more than a simple misdemeanor theft, so Earl and Marline had decided to go to lunch with the three Westmans anyway, to stall for time until Jon could be apprehended. Once there, they'd made up a story about his not being able to join them due to a sudden onset of flu-like symptoms. The Westmans were suspicious about his absence, but Marline was at last able to convince them she'd spent the morning nursing Jon herself, and that he was at home in his bed with a high fever and chills, and was clearly in no condition to be around a pregnant young girl like Becky.

When Marline was desperate, she could be a particularly effective liar.

"Calm down, Marline," Earl grunted from Jon's comfy reading chair. Earl was attempting to be stoical, but his hands were trembling on the chair's arms. "Don't borrow trouble."

"Don't borrow trouble?" Her lips quivered. "Statutory rape, Earl," she whispered. "They'll charge him with statutory rape. He could go to jail for years."

She resumed pacing. Her small, thin legs were moving so fast it reminded Earl of those little tiny birds he'd seen the last time time he and Marline had taken their sons to the beach.

What were those funny little birds called? he wondered, rubbing his temples.

It bothered him that he couldn't remember. They'd watched the birds for hours, though; the nervous little guys with their tiny stick legs fleeing the tide, then sprinting back onto the wet sand to hunt for food every time the ocean withdrew. Jon and his younger brothers, Billy and Evan, had made a game of imitating them, and Marline had laughed herself silly. The boys were all tan and handsome that day, and Earl had been so proud to be their dad.

"What were those birds called?" he asked. "You know, the funny little ones at the beach a couple of summers ago."

"What?" Marline stopped pacing and stared at him. "What on earth are you talking about?"

He shook his head, knowing it wasn't worth explaining. "It doesn't matter." He swallowed. "I was just trying to remember something."

She kept staring at him. She'd already forgotten what he'd asked her; her mind was wandering as much as his was.

They look so much alike, she thought. *How can they be so different?*

The resemblance between Earl and Jon was remarkable. Earl's face was puffier than Jon's, of course, and his hair had gray in it, but the two of them were peas in a pod, from their wide shoulders and thin waists to their gray eyes and flat chins. If you saw their baby pictures, too, you'd swear you were looking at the same infant. Even Marline had trouble telling the photos apart if you put them side by side.

But the similarity between her husband and her oldest son was limited to the surface. Earl was a model of sobriety and maturity, and Jon was nothing but a spoiled child. Marline mostly blamed herself for this; she'd let Jon have his way far too much of the time when he was growing up. He was her oldest and brightest son, but he'd squandered all his gifts, one by one, and now he'd turned into the kind of kid who ran away when the going got tough.

He's become a coward, she told herself, grieving.

Earl didn't notice that Marline was still staring at him. *Jon was really something that day,* he was thinking. *He was good as gold to Billy and Evan.*

Jon had helped his younger brothers build a sand castle, and he'd played Frisbee with them, and when some other kids who were Jon's age came over and asked if he wanted to join them for volleyball, he said no, because he knew how hurt Billy and Evan would be if he ditched them to play with the older kids.

Marline started pacing once again, but then halted almost immediately to bend down and look at a book with no cover, resting on a milk carton. It was *Anna Karenina.* She'd adored that book when she was in college, and she thought this battered copy may have even been hers: Jon had been stealing books from her shelves for years. There was a small pyramid of empty beer cans by the milk carton, too, and something about the sight of those filthy cans next to her beloved book felt like desecration. It made her want to scream.

"Where in God's name is he?" she cried at the ceiling. "He's ruining his whole life!"

She picked up *Anna Karenina* and swung it like a ping-pong paddle at the aluminum pyramid. The beer cans went flying in every direction, making a horrendous racket as they bounced along the floor and against the walls. It took a long time for the last one to come to a standstill in the corner by the lamp.

In the silence that followed, she slowly straightened. Her lungs felt as if they weren't working; her breathing sounded odd to her own ears. But when she gazed over at her husband her throat closed, and she stopped breathing entirely.

"Oh, my dear," she whispered.

Earl's face was composed, but his eyes were brimming with tears.

Plovers, he was thinking, knowing it didn't matter. *Those little birds were plovers.*

* * *

Julianna put the stalled Edsel in park and turned the key in the ignition to "off." To the left of the car was a heavily wooded area; to the right was a stone fence, surrounding what appeared to be a dairy farm. Julianna sighed, then shifted in her seat to face the boys in the back.

"I believe we're out of gasoline," she said, flustered. She very much wanted to get home, and she was uncertain how to deal with this unforeseen delay. "Daddy must have forgotten to refill the tank earlier this week."

"Wonderful." Jon's voice was tinged with hysteria. "We just killed a cop, and now we're stranded in the middle of nowhere." His eyes darted from window to window, as if he were expecting dozens of police cars to surround them at any moment. "That's . . . yeah, that's just great!"

Fewer than twenty minutes ago, Elijah would have been thrilled at the notion of the Edsel failing them, but now all he felt was dread. He was thinking more clearly than he had been when Julianna first ran over the state trooper, and it seemed to him his sole remaining hope of living through this day was to get as far away as he could from the scene of the crime.

And to do that, he needed the Edsel.

He needed the Edsel right *now.*

"How did this happen?" he demanded. "How could you have let us run out of gas?"

Julianna seemed oblivious to their distress. She was making small sounds of dismay over the blood on her outfit.

"Oh, no," she said. "My dress is *ruined!* I'll never get this stain out."

The cut on her forearm was superficial, but it had bled quite a bit. Both Jon and Elijah gasped in horror when they saw the large red splotch on her sleeve.

"You're hurt," Elijah said, surprised. He temporarily forgot the direness of their situation as he leaned over the seat for a closer look. "Why didn't you say something?"

Jon's head appeared next to Elijah's. "Do you need a doctor?" he asked. "How bad is it?"

Julianna was touched by their almost parental concern for

her. But before she could thank them for their solicitousness, her forgotten years as an English teacher resurfaced, and her big green eyes flickered with amusement.

" 'I bleed, sir,' " she quoted. " 'But not killed.' "

Elijah frowned, not understanding, but Jon stared at her, taken aback.

"*Macbeth*?" he asked.

Her smile widened as she shook her head. "Nope. *Othello.* Iago says it at the end of the play. Good guess, though."

He studied her with curiosity, wondering more than ever who she was, and what she was doing here. "You know Shakespeare?"

She giggled. "Not personally, silly."

Her little girl voice was back, and the adult woman had vanished.

Jon stared at her for another long minute, then began to bump his forehead against the front seat over and over. "Great," he muttered, between bumps. "Oh, yeah. This is just *terrific.*"

The heat in the car was stifling; all three of them were dripping with sweat.

Elijah clasped his arms around his naked stomach to keep from vomiting. "What are we gonna do?"

Julianna peered out the windows, then gestured over the stone fence at the dairy. "Do you suppose the Millers are at home? I bet they might give us some lemonade, if we ask nicely."

Interlude

Pawnee, Missouri, (population 137) was little more than a village wedged between steep, brooding hills, nine miles south of the Iowa border. Named after the Pawnee Indians—who'd been sent packing to a reservation in Oklahoma in the 1870s—the town was home to mostly Irish and Scottish immigrant farmers and their offspring. There was only one street to speak of, but it was a busy one. There was a smithy, a general goods store, a school, a doctor's office, and a post office; there was even a telephone/telegraph office and a bakery (*Nellie and Eunice's Sweet Home Kitchen*). Northern Missouri in the summer was as hot as a boiler room in hell, and in the winter it was bone-numbingly cold. Yet it wasn't a bad place to grow up, especially if it was all a child had ever known.

As was the case with Julianna Larson.

Julianna was fifteen years old that summer, and had never been farther than twenty miles from Pawnee. Her father, Eben Larson, was the county tax collector, and her mother, Emma, was Pawnee's postmistress and sole telephone operator. Julianna's two older brothers, Michael and Seth, still lived at home and took care of the family farm; Eben had ceded the place to his sons after a hay conditioner shredded his left foot and permanently crippled him. The Larson farm was a mile and a half north of Pawnee, and their nearest neighbor was Clyde

Rayburn, whose beat-to-hell old farmhouse was several hundred yards closer to town, hidden from sight by a high hill and a row of maple trees.

If somebody had told Julianna she'd be fleeing Pawnee in three days and wouldn't attempt to return for the next thirty-nine years, she would have thought the idea preposterous. She loved her family and friends, and even though her world was gradually getting larger—Pawnee's school was for kids in the eighth grade or younger, so the past year she'd ridden her horse to Hatfield, five miles distant, to attend high school—she was still content with her life, and had no idea what kind of hell awaited her in the coming week.

It all started with a large, angry farmer named Rufus Tarwater.

In spite of Prohibition, Rufus was a drunk, and everybody knew it. Worse than that, he was a mean drunk, who was said to enjoy waling on his wife, Josephine, whenever he felt she was getting "uppity." His farm was on good land and should have provided everything he needed, but Rufus was rumored to spend all his earnings on moonshine, so he and Jo were always strapped. The only reason they survived at all was because the minister of the Lone Rock church was a soft touch, who could always be counted on to tide the Tarwaters over with food from his very own pantry whenever Rufus came begging.

Julianna's dad, Eben, was new to the tax-collection business; the accident with the hay conditioner had just occurred the previous autumn. After his injury, the only job in the area he was still up to was tax collector, because it allowed him to stay off his bad foot most of the day. This meant, of course, that every taxpayer in the county came to call on Eben Larson in his home office at least once a year, and usually more often than that.

Which is why Rufus Tarwater, taxpayer, came calling on a Saturday morning in June.

Rufus was in his mid-forties, and therefore old enough to remember a time when no taxes had been imposed on his farm at all. It rankled him beyond reason to be forced to visit the tax collector every three months and make a payment of twenty-seven dollars; in his mind, that money belonged to Rufus Tarwater, and no one else. Twenty-seven dollars was worth a lot of moonshine, and he hated handing cash over to the government on demand—especially to a snooty little pencil pusher like Eben Larson.

Rufus didn't know Eben well at all, but he didn't have to be overly acquainted to take his measure. Eben was said to be a brilliant man, who'd taught himself to read Greek and could do complicated math in his head, and Rufus believed that anybody who engaged in that kind of uppity horseshit was nothing but a cocky son of a bitch who thought he was better than people like Rufus.

In truth, Eben *did* look down his nose at Rufus, but not for the reasons Rufus thought. Eben didn't mind that Rufus wasn't educated, but he minded a great deal that he got drunk and beat his wife. Eben adored his own wife, Emma, and thought that any man who could hit a woman—especially a woman he'd vowed to love, honor, and cherish—was nothing but a scoundrel and a coward.

Eben's early life had not been easy. His father passed away before he was born and his mother died giving him birth, so he was taken in by an elderly couple named Charles and Lily Lamb. Charles Lamb perished shortly after Eben moved in with them, and Lily remarried a man named Zachariah Pittman, who only made it to Eben's fifth birthday before having a fatal heart attack of his very own. Lily died of grief a year later, and Eben was forced to spend the rest of his childhood in an orphanage.

But his life as a grown man had been altogether different, and blessed. He had a loving wife and three beautiful children; he and his sons had escaped the Great War by virtue of being both too old and too young, respectively; he had a fine intellect (that his daughter, Julianna, had inherited); and even though his foot had been mauled, he counted himself lucky to be alive, and never complained once about the chronic pain that came with the injury.

Rufus Tarwater, of course, knew none of this about Eben Larson, but even if he had, it wouldn't have changed what he thought of him. To be honest, Rufus didn't much care for anybody else but Rufus Tarwater.

He learned this attitude at the knee of his father, Tilson. Tilson Tarwater fought in the Civil War on the side of the Confederacy, and was one of those unhappy men who survived the carnage of the war but came home still spoiling for a fight. Tilson had four boys—Rufus was the youngest—and he raised them to hate everyone and everything, including each other. Rufus's mom, Eleanor—a quiet, grim-faced woman from Kentucky—disappeared one day when Rufus was still in diapers, and never came back. Hence Rufus grew up thinking the only way to survive in the world was to be a better fighter than anybody else, and this philosophy was supported by the daunting physical size and strength he attained as an adult, which allowed him to dominate and intimidate almost everybody he encountered.

Rufus was a mountain of a man. He wasn't exceptionally tall—only six foot two—but he weighed 350 pounds, and most of that was muscle. When he was a little boy, though, he had a rough go of it with his older siblings, and endured years of cruelty and abuse at their hands. This all ended, however, when he outgrew his tormentors; the first thing he did once he came into his own was to break his brother Frank's jaw and collarbone with a crowbar, and chase the other two boys from the house. Tilson didn't escape his youngest son's wrath, either; Rufus believed his dad was owed payback, as well, and came damn near to killing him one day when Tilson made the mistake of backhanding Rufus for mouthing off at the supper table.

Regardless, the Tarwater farm eventually came into Rufus's sole possession. Tilson left no will when he died (strangely enough, he went peacefully, in his sleep, with a sweet smile on his battle-scarred face), and since Rufus had driven his brothers clean out of the state by then and the law had no way of tracking them down, the family farm passed to him by default. Rufus felt no guilt about this; in his view, he'd fought for the place and he'd won, fair and square, and if his brothers were stupid enough to come back home and try to get their share, he'd have been more than happy to give each of them a six-foot plot of land in the cow pasture, and a pinewood box for a house.

Anyway, prior to that Saturday in June, Eben and Rufus had only met twice to do tax business, as Eben had been the county collector for such a short time. Neither meeting had been a pleasant affair; it would be difficult to imagine two souls less alike, and each man loathed the other on general principle.

The second meeting had been particularly confrontational. Rufus had been unable to make his payment, and so had consented—with no intention of doing any such thing—to pay double the next time. Yet when Eben forced him to sign an agreement to this effect, Rufus's temper ignited. He flung the signed contract at Eben, knocked over a card table, and stormed from the premises, muttering threats.

And the following morning Eben's beloved dachshund, Cerberus, was found dead on the road, his neck snapped.

Eben couldn't prove this vile act was Rufus's doing, but he was sure of it. He shared his suspicion with Emma and the boys, but he forbade them to speak about it with Julianna, instructing them to say instead that Cerberus, whom Julianna had adored, had been accidentally run over by a car. By doing this, Eben was not trying to coddle his daughter with a prettified version of events; far from it. Indeed, his only concern was keeping her alive, were she to discover the truth.

Julianna was a sensitive, loving girl, but when she was provoked she also had what Eben called "an Old Testament temper," and nothing in the world set her off more than cruelty to an animal or a small child.

When she was eight, for instance, she had come across Sully Nixson, a teenaged boy, tormenting a tomcat behind the school, and she had picked up a stick and flown at Sully with a Sodom-annihilating fury that was worthy of Jehovah Himself. Sully Nixson was amused by this attack at first, but his laughter abruptly ended when he fell to the ground with a grape-sized knot over his right ear. Lars the blacksmith saw the finale of the skirmish, and had called Julianna by the nickname of "Amazon" ever since.

But Rufus Tarwater was a far, far cry from Sully Nixson, and Eben was terrified of Julianna finding out what had really happened to poor old Cerberus. If she were to go after Rufus like she'd gone after Sully, it could well be the last thing she'd ever do. Rufus would have no compunction about killing someone who dared attack him, even if that person were a young girl.

And especially if he thought she was guilty of being "uppity."

Julianna had been in school both times before when Rufus visited, but she was home on this occasion, washing dishes in the kitchen. Emma was working at the post office and the boys were in the fields, so Eben and Julianna were alone when Rufus banged on the front door.

Eben's office was right next to the entryway, and before Julianna could respond to the knock she heard her father's uneven footsteps as he clumped his way to the door: *taTUNK, taTUNK, taTUNK.* He had been crippled for months, but it still saddened her to know he would never again walk without limping.

"Hello, Rufus."

The living room and a swinging door separated Julianna from the men, but she could hear Eben's words with no difficulty. His voice was courteous, but much colder than usual.

Julianna frowned while drying the dishes. She knew Rufus, of course, and she didn't care for him. She'd heard all the gossip about how mean-spirited he was, and she'd often seen his wife, Josephine, walking around town with multiple bruises and cuts on her face. What was most damning, though, was that her father clearly disliked the man. Julianna needed no other reason than this to dislike him, too.

Rufus ignored Eben's greeting. "I got no money for taxes, Larson."

There wasn't a trace of civility in his manner, and Julianna felt her spine stiffen.

Eben cleared his throat. "You said that the last time, too, Rufus."

The vexation in his tone was plain; Julianna could tell her father thought Rufus was lying. But he sounded nervous, as well, and it shocked her to realize her father feared the other man. There was a long pause, and she could picture the two of them standing in the doorway, glaring at each other.

Eben Larson was as tall as Rufus, but nowhere near as muscular. He was a beanpole (as were all his children), and though he was strong from years of farm work, he was frail in comparison to Rufus. Rufus, in spite of his drinking, was easily the most powerful man in the county. Julianna herself had once seen him lift a quarter-ton calf in his arms as if it weighed no more than a parakeet.

Eben finally broke the silence. "Well, don't just stand there. Come in and we'll discuss your options."

Rufus didn't seem to care for this suggestion.

"There ain't nothin' to talk about," he snapped. "If I ain't got any money, the government can't take any, right?" A porch board creaked under his weight. "It's my money, anyway, goddammit."

"Nobody likes paying taxes, Rufus," Eben shot back. "But if you don't pay them, you'll be arrested. I'll have no choice but to report you to the sheriff."

Rufus's voice dropped, and Julianna strained to hear what he said next.

"You ain't gonna say nothin' to nobody," he rumbled. There was a tense pause. "Not 'less you wanna lose another dog, that is."

Julianna clutched at the sink as the blood left her face.

He killed Cerberus!

As shocking as this ugly revelation was, she nonetheless understood intuitively, now, why her father had sounded fearful a few moments ago. He wasn't afraid for himself; he was worried for her. He had no doubt assumed she was listening, and was apprehensive about the possibility of Rufus making just such a terrible comment in her hearing. She was also wise enough to grasp why her whole family had chosen to deceive her about the dog's death three months ago.

They knew her too well.

She had loved the little dachshund with her whole heart. Ever since he was a puppy and she was a little girl, Cerberus had slept with her each night in her room at the top of the stairs. Had she been told right away what Rufus had done to him, there was no question what her reaction would have been: She would have gone after Rufus Tarwater with a meat cleaver. She would have torn his foul, evil eyes right out of his stinking sockets with her bare fingers. Her family knew this, and had tried to protect her.

Oh, Cerberus.

Her throat closed with grief as she imagined Cerberus—trusting and gentle—coming to say hello to Rufus on the road. She could picture his little body being lifted into the air, all the while wagging his thin, whiplike tail as fast as he could. He would have tried to lick Rufus's fingers; she was sure of it.

Oh, my sweet little dog.

Her paralysis lifted, and her grief was subsumed by rage. A red haze filled her brain and she began to pant.

So help her God, she would make the man pay for what he had done.

She snatched a brass candlestick from the kitchen table and charged straight at the living room door, murder in her heart.

In the entryway, meanwhile, Eben's face, too, had gone white with fury at Rufus's words. But the response he'd intended to utter ("Get out of my house, you son of a bitch!") died on his lips as he heard Julianna coming.

"Oh, sweet Jesus," he muttered, paling.

He spun away from Rufus and hobbled into the living room as quickly as he could. He was sure his bum foot wouldn't allow him to intercept Julianna before she appeared, yet he had to try.

Rufus stood in the doorway, perplexed, and watched Eben lurch away from him across the living room floor. He didn't know what reaction he'd expected after telling the uppity cripple what had happened to his dog, but this wasn't it. He took a hesitant step into the house, trying to decide if he should chase Eben down or just leave.

He had no time to do either.

Julianna burst through the living room door, brandishing the candlestick. Her face was deranged and her eyes were wet, and she didn't even glance at Eben as he made a desperate attempt to grab and restrain her. She darted around his outstretched arms and flew directly at Rufus, screaming like a Pawnee warrior.

Juliannna was tall for her age, and quite strong, and she had speed and courage to spare. She also had the element of surprise on her side, and was insane with anger and shock, and was wielding a heavy brass candlestick as if it were a mace. In addition to all this, her nickname was, appropriately, Amazon, and she was intent on meting out justice for what had been done to an innocent creature she had loved unreservedly.

And had it been anybody else she was after besides Rufus Tarwater, these things might have mattered.

Rufus was indeed caught off guard by Julianna's wild assault, and it was a measure of her wrath that he took a step backward in concern as she flung herself at him. Rufus was not an easy man to frighten, and retreat was not in his vocabulary. But Rufus had been raised in a family that regularly employed unpredictable tactics of warfare, and his survival instinct kicked in just as she swung the candlestick at his head. He caught her wrist with his left hand, and with his right fist he struck her, full in the face.

Eben Larson watched his daughter crumple to the floor, and he rushed to her defense, crying out her name. He knew he stood no chance against Rufus, but he hated the man and he loved the girl, so there was little else for him to do. Julianna's nose and mouth were bleeding and she wasn't moving, and Eben flung himself at Rufus with the same abandon his youngest child had just displayed.

Had he been more agile, things would likely have gone much the same for him. At the last second, though, his limp caused him to stumble, and before he could engage Rufus in his own useless assault, the cavalry arrived: Julianna's older brothers, Michael and Seth, materialized on the porch behind Rufus.

Michael Larson was seventeen, his hero was Copernicus, and he wanted to be an astronomer. He didn't really have the makings of an astronomer, however, because he couldn't stay awake more than an hour or two after the sun went down. His "observatory"—a telescope on a tripod, beside an old crate he used for a seat—was in the hayloft of the barn, but each evening after supper when he went out to study the stars, he began yawning immediately, and soon would feel the need to stretch out in the hay until someone came to fetch him. Michael's older brother, Seth, was nineteen, and though easily the most serious of the Larson children, he had a smile that could thaw an iceberg, and an appealing sense of whimsy to go with it. (Thanks to Seth, the scarecrow in the cornfield was dressed as Kaiser Wilhelm, with a spiked, Pickelhaube helmet constructed of a chamber pot and a chess-piece bishop.)

Michael was six foot one and blond, Seth was slightly taller and dark haired, and both were sunburned and sweating as they came up behind Rufus Tarwater that Saturday morning in June. They had been working in the hayfield to the west of the house when Rufus rode by on his horse, and they had decided to come home, just in case Rufus took it into his head to cause their father trouble, as he had the last time. As they drew closer they'd heard Julianna screaming, and so had sprinted the rest of the way. They were not so fierce as Julianna, but they were tough, lean, and brave, and more than willing to defend their father and sister with their lives. Nor were they stupid. They knew it was Rufus Tarwater they had to deal with, so they had taken an extra moment to stop at the barn for weapons: Michael was carrying a pitchfork, and Seth had a metal fence post in his sturdy hands.

Rufus's fist was raised to strike Eben, but Michael's voice stopped him cold.

"Hey, Rufus!"

Rufus hadn't heard them coming, and he spun around, startled. His red face, which was full of glee at the prospect of beating up Eben Larson, became markedly less cheerful as he gawped at his new opponents. Unarmed, the Larson boys would have been no match for him, either, but with no weapon of his own, he was now at a serious disadvantage.

He spat on the floor by Julianna's feet and tried to bluster. "I'm gonna shove that pitchfork up your ass, boy."

He'd be damned if he was going to back down from a fight with a couple of scrawny kids and a cripple.

The pitchfork shook a little in Michael's hands. But after he shot a quick glance at his unconscious, bleeding sister on the floor, and another at his father, standing guard over her body, his hands steadied.

"Come on and get it, then," he answered. His green eyes, large and bright like Julianna's, were unblinking. "I'll be real happy to give it to you."

Seth raised the sharp end of the fence post so it pointed at Rufus's forehead. "How'd you like to spend the rest of your life looking like a unicorn, Rufus?"

Rufus wasn't sure what this meant, but it sounded uppity, so it enraged him. He wanted nothing more than to grab the post and beat Seth to death with it, but there was no way he could do this without first being impaled by Michael's pitchfork. He clenched and unclenched his fists and tried to think of what he might do to even the odds, but nothing sprang to mind.

He swore in frustration, and the boys could smell the moonshine on his breath.

"Why don't you chickenshits put down them toys?" he growled. "Fight me fair and square."

Eben spoke from behind him. "Like how you just fought my fifteen-year-old daughter, Rufus?"

His voice was quiet, but there was something in it Rufus didn't care for at all. He flushed, but kept his eyes on the weapons pointed at his head and stomach.

"I only hit her 'cause I had to, Larson," he muttered. "The little bitch attacked me."

The pitchfork and the fence post darted nearer to his body.

"Don't call her that!" Michael ordered.

Eben Larson was no hothead, yet he was perilously close to telling Michael and Seth to go ahead and stab Tarwater. Julianna was breathing, but her eyes were still closed and her nose appeared to be broken, and Eben badly wanted to punish the man who had done this to her. Besides that, Rufus had also admitted to killing Cerberus, and Eben feared what else the crazy son of a bitch might do if he were allowed to walk away from this confrontation unscathed. There was a strong possibility he'd feel that Michael or Seth needed a comeuppance of some sort for having had the temerity to threaten him today.

We could say that Rufus went berserk, and the boys had no choice but to run him through, Eben thought. *There's not a soul in town who'd question that story.*

It was an appealing notion, and he went so far as to fantasize about it for a few seconds. But then Julianna began to stir on the floor, and his native decency resurfaced. He sighed, knowing he couldn't go through with it. As much as Rufus deserved retribution for his actions, the problem was in this instance he *had* acted in self-defense. Julianna had been doing her level best to kill him when he struck her, and that was a fact. And though Rufus had been far too rough with her, she appeared to be mostly unhurt. Seeing this cooled Eben's temper, and allowed him to think straight again. The last thing any of them needed was for Julianna to wake up with Rufus still in the house: She'd just go after him again, and to save her the boys would end up with blood on their hands, losing their innocence forever.

Eben took a deep breath, and then another.

"Get the hell off my porch, Rufus," he said, tiredly. "Just go on home."

Rufus blinked. In his experience, situations such as this were never resolved without a lot of bloodshed, and he had fully expected Eben to tell the boys to skewer him. It's what he himself would have done, had their positions been reversed. To be sure, he was enormously pleased by Eben's decision, but he smirked at Michael and Seth to conceal his relief.

They saw his expression and their faces turned mutinous.

"We can't just let him go, Daddy," Seth protested. "Let's at least tie him up, okay? Mikey and I will guard him, and you can take Julianna to the doctor and call the sheriff."

Eben shook his head. The only phone within miles was the one at the telephone/telegraph office in town, and Sheriff Burns was in Hatfield. It would take forever for Burns to arrive, and once here, he could do nothing. Rufus couldn't be arrested for defending himself against Julianna, nor given aught but a slap on the wrist for killing Cerberus. Aside from this, Eben wasn't about to leave his boys alone with Rufus Tarwater, even if the man were hog-tied. He might find a way to get loose, and there was no telling what he'd do.

"Just let him go, son," he said, resigned. "It's for the best."

Rufus barely even registered Eben's words. Seth's last suggestion was still churning through his brain, and he could focus on nothing else.

Coincidence is fickle, and thrives on chaos.

When Rufus was seven, his brother Frank had tied him to a post behind their barn and gagged him, then left him there for nearly five hours. Rufus had messed his pants and screamed himself hoarse through the gag, but no one had come to release him until his father at last stumbled across him while feeding the chickens. Tilson had set him free, but had laughed at him, and done nothing to Frank by way of punishment. Rufus had never felt more helpless, before or since, and he'd sworn to kill the next person who tried to tie him up like that.

As the eldest Larson child had just proposed to do.

"Put that little pigsticker down, boy," Rufus hissed. "See what happens."

He almost didn't care if he got stabbed or not now, but he wanted to make sure he lived long enough to get his fingers around Seth's throat.

"Shut up, Rufus, and go home," Eben demanded. He knew nothing of the line Seth had just crossed in Rufus's mind, of course, but he heard the intensified anger in the big man's tone and it scared him. "Michael, Seth, back away from him right now, but keep your weapons ready."

His sons did what he asked this time. They had sensed the sudden shift in Rufus's mood, too, and Eben's alarm was evident. Yet Rufus didn't budge for a long moment, even after they cleared a path for him to leave. He swung his head from side to side like an infuriated bull, hoping if he waited a few more seconds the boys would give him an opening he could exploit.

We'll see about this, he thought, livid with rage. *We'll see who ties who up.*

Michael and Seth showed no sign of relaxing their guard, however, so he finally snarled a string of obscenities at them and stalked off the porch. He kept up this outpouring of impotent curses until he reached his horse on the other side of the yard, but once back in the saddle, an odd, disquieting change came over him. His font of foul words ceased in midsentence, and he sat still on the beast for nearly a full minute.

His face was flat and unreadable as he studied the two-story Larson home. His gaze took in the living room window, the swing on the front porch, and the storm cellar door on the south side of the house with equal attention; he seemed to be no less interested in the paint job (white with blue trim) than he was in the rain gutters and the windows. He gave no indication of looking for anything specific.

When he had finally completed this slow inspection, he nodded in an almost friendly manner at Michael, Seth, and Eben, who were all watching him.

None of them moved a muscle in response. The sun glinted off the tines of Michael's pitchfork as Rufus at last dug his heels into the horse's flanks and galloped away.

No one spoke until he disappeared over a hill by Clyde Rayburn's place.

"Christ," Seth muttered at last, unnerved. "What was that about?"

His dark hair was wet with sweat as he set the post down on the porch. He glanced over at his younger brother first, and then back at Eben and Julianna.

Eben had knelt beside Julianna. Her big, green eyes were open again, and Seth wondered how long she had been awake.

The blood on her upper lip and chin made her look ghastly, but she managed a trembling smile as their father took her hand.

"You shouldn't have let him go, Daddy," she murmured. Her smile fell apart. "That man is a monster."

She had been conscious long enough to see Rufus on his horse, looking at the house, and something in his brutish face had frightened her out of her wits.

Eben nodded. "I know, sweetheart," he whispered. "I know he is."

He gazed up at his sons for a moment, who were now standing side by side in the doorway. Seth's arm was around Michael's shoulders, and both boys were staring down at him, troubled. Eben bit his lip and looked again at his daughter, who was holding tightly to his hand. He wanted to reassure them all, but he had seen the same cold, calculating look on Rufus's face that they had, and it had frightened him, too. He squeezed Julianna's fingers and sighed.

Just fifteen minutes ago, Eben Larson had believed his little farm in Pawnee, Missouri, was about the safest place on earth for him and his family. Now he was no longer sure of that at all, and he was stunned by how swiftly things seemed to have changed. He needed to go find Emma at the post office and warn her about Rufus; he wished she were with him right now, to help him figure out what to say to their children.

What just happened? he wondered. *Why was Rufus looking at the house like that?*

He took a hanky from his breast pocket and began to clean Julianna's chin. He couldn't bear it if Rufus hurt any of his children again; he had to find a way to keep them all safe.

I should have let the boys kill that son of a bitch when we had the chance.

"Better get the car ready to go to town, son," he said to Seth. "Julianna needs to see Doc Colby, and your mom needs to be told about all this."

And then Eben needed to buy a gun.

Chapter 5

"Yoo-hoo! Anybody home?" Julianna rapped on the screen door of the dairy farmhouse a second time. "It's Julianna Larson, and Ben Taylor." She lowered her voice and whispered to Jon. "They don't know you, Steve, so I'll wait until they answer to introduce you."

The main door behind the screen was wide open, allowing Julianna to see a long hallway with a wooden floor leading back to the kitchen, but no response came from within the house. Jon stood beside her on the narrow porch, gripping his bag of belongings and sipping nervously at a warm bottle of Pepsi, but Elijah waited at the bottom of the steps with his hands jammed in his jeans pockets. He felt exposed and childish with no shirt, and he kept his gaze firmly on his white sneakers as he kicked at a stone by the bottom step. He'd noted Julianna's name without much interest; he guessed it didn't really matter if he knew what to call her or not.

The air was thick with sharp smells: cow manure and hay, roses and freshly turned dirt, honeysuckle and cut grass. The sun was beating down on the earth, but mud puddles from the recent rain were everywhere, and the siding on the house was wet. An herb garden next to the porch had attracted dozens of fat, slow-moving bees, and the buzzing they made as they circled the mint plants was peaceful and hypnotic, punctuated now and then by the wild drumming of a woodpecker in a grove of trees behind the barn.

Jon Tate had an almost overpowering urge to run. His eyes darted down the hill to the Edsel on the shoulder of the highway, where they had left it five minutes ago. He was certain the police would soon find the car, and every instinct was telling him to get as far from this place as possible before that could happen. He knew he wouldn't stand much of a chance on foot, though, so he was praying for another miracle. In his opinion, the only hope any of them had was to buy (or steal) some gas from the dairy, and get the Edsel back on the road before another New Hampshire state trooper came along.

"We can't just keep standing here," he said impatiently.

Julianna frowned at the silence coming from the house. "It's odd that Polly's not home. I wonder where she could be?"

She stepped over to the edge of the porch and peered across the yard. There was a silo, a barn, and a long, sturdy milk house that appeared to hold about fifty Jersey cows, but no human beings were in sight. The mailbox by the gravel driveway clearly declared this to be the home of "The Stocktons," but Julianna paid no heed to it. In her mind, Günter and Polly Miller lived here, and that was that.

On the way up the driveway, she had informed them that Günter Miller was a first-generation immigrant from Germany who had married Polly Brightman from Hatfield, Missouri, shortly before the couple purchased this dairy farm on the outskirts of Pawnee. She assumed Elijah (Ben, to her) already knew this about the Millers, of course, but considering how strangely he'd been acting she felt he might need to have his memory jogged.

"Günter's such a sweet man," she now said as she leaned on the porch railing. "But he has the funniest German accent, doesn't he, Ben?"

Elijah barely even registered that Julianna had once again called him Ben. He, like Jon, was wrestling with a compulsion to run for his life, and was too frazzled to care anymore if she knew his real name or not. He saw she was waiting for an answer, though, and he rolled his eyes at Jon and grimaced.

"Yeah," he muttered. "When good old Günter talks he sounds just like Hitler."

A swig of Pepsi spurted from Jon's nose onto his shirt.

"Gross," he coughed, wiping his face on his sleeve. He grinned down at Elijah, in spite of himself. "Wise ass," he said.

Elijah gave him a strained smile, but both boys sobered quickly. Their predicament was no laughing matter, and they knew it.

Julianna missed this exchange; she had returned to the front door and was looking in the house again. She opened the screen door and put a foot over the sill as if intending to enter. "Polly? Günter? Are you here?"

"I don't think you should do that," Elijah blurted. "We should just find some gas and get out of here."

Jon nodded vehemently. "Yeah. We've got to get going."

"Don't be silly. The Millers won't mind a bit." She stepped through the door. "Besides, your leg will get infected if we don't clean that cut."

She disappeared into the house, humming a tune neither Jon nor Elijah recognized.

Jon glanced down at his leg in frustration. He had used the strip of Elijah's shirt as a bandage, tying it around his left thigh, and though the wound was no longer bleeding, the white cloth was mostly red and looked none too hygienic. Regardless, they really couldn't afford to stay here long enough to do anything about it.

He looked at Elijah, who was fidgeting as if he needed to urinate.

"What are we going to do?" Elijah asked.

"I don't know." Jon chewed on his lip for a minute, glaring at the Edsel on the empty highway, then he tossed the Pepsi bottle into a nearby rosebush and spun around to hiss through the screen. "We don't have time for this, Julianna!"

There was no answer, and precious seconds ticked by, one after another.

"Okay, that's it." Jon hopped off the porch, landing lightly beside Elijah. "I'm going to look around for some gas. See if you can get her out of there, okay?"

He took off running for the barn, not waiting for an answer.

Elijah blinked and yelled after him. "What if she won't come out?"

Jon ground to a halt and looked back at him. "We'll just have to leave her." He frowned at the look on the other boy's face. "I don't like it, either, but we really don't have a choice, do we?"

This time he waited long enough to see Elijah's hesitant nod before resuming his run for the barn.

Bebe Stockton had epilepsy. It never bothered her, though; she just had to remember to take a spoonful of phenobarbital twice every day, and this simple regimen worked like a charm to ward off seizures. Unfortunately, Bebe was easily distracted, and could never remember if she'd taken her medicine or not.

Her husband, Chuck, however, bless his heart, had the memory of an anal-retentive elephant. Every day he reminded her at lunch, and then again before bed, that it was time for her tablespoon of "ucky juice" (as Bebe insisted on calling it). Quite often he also had to tell her she'd already taken a dose; she simply couldn't keep track of such things.

Chuck and Bebe Stockton had owned this dairy farm in southwestern New Hampshire for thirty-six years. They raised two lovely daughters (both grown and moved away, now) and one fine, handsome son, who had been killed in World War II. Bebe was small and squat, with short gray hair and a dimpled double chin. She laughed easily but she also cried a lot; her feelings were easily hurt by a harsh tone or an impolite word, and she didn't like raised voices, or conflict of any kind. Aside from this hypersensitivity, though—and a poor memory—there was nothing out of the ordinary about Bebe at all.

Except, perhaps, her fetish for glass swans.

Her house was chock-full of swan figurines, in every color and size imaginable. (The cobs tended to be red, blue, and green, but the pens were almost always yellow, orange, or purple. The cygnets, though, for some reason, were often sculpted from clear glass.) When her husband, Chuck, was in a bad mood he referred to the place as "a goddamn crystal aviary." Bebe didn't care, though; her glass swans were the epitome of beauty and grace, and they made her feel beautiful and graceful by association. The funny thing was she didn't like actual swans half as well as she liked her figurines. What drew her to glass swans was their stillness; she could hold and caress them whenever she wanted. The living, breathing birds moved too much to suit her, and were fearful of her touch.

When Edgar Reilly's stolen Edsel ran out of gas in front of the Stockton farm, Chuck was out making deliveries in the milk truck, and Bebe was home alone, napping with one of her swans in the upstairs bedroom. Saturdays were Chuck's longest days; he had been gone since early morning and wouldn't return until almost nightfall.

Bebe was in a deep sleep. She had remembered to take her dose of phenobarbital at noon, but as she was also baking corn muffins and trying to find batteries for her kitchen radio, she forgot all about the first tablespoon of medicine she had swallowed, and promptly took another.

This often happened on Saturdays when Chuck was absent. Happily, her dosage was low enough that she could have an extra tablespoon now and then with little risk, and the only side effect she had experienced in the past from this sort of unintentional drug abuse had been drowsiness.

But today, when she at last located the batteries for the radio and removed the muffins from the oven, she hadn't been able to remember for the life of her if she'd taken any ucky juice at all. She was almost sure she had, yet when she'd looked in the sink to see if there was a dirty tablespoon as evidence of this, she'd found nothing. (She had forgotten washing the first spoon along with the bowl she had used to mix the muffins, and the second spoon was still in the refrigerator, where she had absent-mindedly left it while getting a splash of milk for her coffee.)

I guess I forgot again, she'd thought, shaking her head with rue. *Lordy, Lordy! Chuck would be furious!*

She'd then slurped down a third tablespoon, and ten minutes

later she couldn't keep her eyes open. Stumbling upstairs to her bedroom, she'd seized a lovely blue swan—a cob, and one of her favorites—from the dresser top, and collapsed on the mattress as if she'd been shot in the head. It was fortunate she'd stopped at three tablespoons; a fourth would likely have put her in a coma. As it was, she was destined to not wake up for several hours.

Uh oh. Her last thoughts before she lost consciousness were astonishing for their clarity. She'd read about phenobarbital overdoses, of course, and recognized something unusual was occurring. *I better call the doctor! I must have had too much ucky juice!*

Thinking this, though, she fell into an untroubled sleep like an enchanted princess, still clasping the blue cob to her bosom. She did not stir from this position one little bit until Julianna's knock on the door in the late afternoon at last began to filter through the haze in her mind, but even so it would take her several minutes to open her eyes again.

And at least another five minutes after that to realize she was no longer alone in the house.

The tune Julianna had been humming on the porch earlier was one her father sang all the time when she was a child. It was no wonder neither Jon nor Elijah had recognized it; Julianna herself hadn't heard it for almost forty years. She couldn't remember many of the words, but the chorus was stuck in her head and she was now singing and whistling it as she washed the cut on her right arm in Bebe Stockton's kitchen sink.

"Oh, joy! Oh, boy! Where do we go from here?"

The kitchen was charming, with clean gold linoleum and sparkling countertops. Bebe's corn muffins were on top of the stove where she had set them to cool earlier that afternoon, and a window over the sink looked out over a lush green pasture, just beyond the barn.

Julianna winced as she found a small sliver of glass from the Edsel's rear window still embedded in her forearm. She tugged

up the sleeve of her dress and used her fingernails to carefully remove the shard from the wound.

"*Dahdadada, dahdadada . . .*"

"What are you doing?"

She spun to find Elijah hovering in the kitchen doorway. He
looked unhappy and anxious, and his narrow chest was sweating in the heat. He was also shifting his weight from one foot to
the other, like a small child with a full bladder.

Julianna smiled at him. "Benjamin! You gave me a fright."
She turned back to the sink. "I'm just cleaning myself up a bit.
Where's Steve?"

"He's looking for gasoline." Elijah cleared his throat. "He
told me to come get you."

She glanced over her shoulder and frowned. "What about his
leg? That cut won't clean itself."

"He said there wasn't time."

She made a face and turned off the water. "Boys," she muttered. She dried her hands on a dish towel and sighed. "I guess
we can clean his wound in the car, but we'll need some alcohol
and bandages to take with us."

She began opening cabinets and hunting through them, and
Elijah decided the fastest way to get her out of there was to steer
her in the right direction.

"They probably keep stuff like that in the bathroom," he suggested.

"The bathroom?" Julianna giggled. "You're so silly. You
know full well no one in Pawnee has an indoor bathroom except Judge Mason, and he's rich as Midas. Mother keeps asking
Daddy if we can get one, too, but he says it's a luxury we can't
afford."

Elijah didn't bother to respond, because the moment he'd said
the word "bathroom," he realized he had a ferocious need to
pee, which he'd ignored for about as long as it was safe to do so.

"I'll be right back," he said, turning away quickly.

He hurried down the hallway. On his way into the house he'd
passed several closed doors, and he was praying one of them led

to a bathroom. He figured after he used the toilet he could find some hydrogen peroxide and some Band-Aids, then he'd grab Julianna and drag her back to the Edsel. With any luck, Steve would already be there with some gas.

Elijah had nodded in the front yard when the other boy said it might be necessary to leave Julianna here, but in spite of wanting to get away from her he didn't feel very good about the idea of running out on someone in her condition without first making sure she was safe. Nonetheless, he didn't know how long Steve would be willing to wait for them, and he was terrified of finding the Edsel already gone by the time he managed to get Julianna back outside.

She left her keys in the ignition, he remembered. *What if he decides to just take off without me, too?*

Julianna's voice lilted down the hall after him, as if she didn't have a care in the world.

"Where do we go from here, boys?" she sang. *"Where do we go from here?"*

Bebe Stockton opened her eyes and stared blankly at the ceiling of her bedroom. Her head felt as if somebody had filled it with wet clay, and for a moment she couldn't even recall where she was. The glass swan in her hands was slick with her perspiration, and her heart seemed to be beating at only half its normal speed.

Oh, my, she thought, remembering at last. *The ucky juice.*

Her arms and legs were numb, her mouth was dry, and she felt stupid and slow. She turned her head to view the clock on the bedside table. She was astonished to find she'd been asleep for nearly five hours; it was now 5:07 p.m. She needed to use the restroom, but she didn't want to get up. She would have to make the long journey down to the bathroom on the main floor; the upstairs toilet wasn't flushing properly. She stayed still as long as possible, fondling the smooth blue head of her swan until the pressure in her bladder became impossible to disregard.

At 5:13 she rolled onto her side with a groan, and only then did she notice there was a woman singing downstairs.

At first this didn't alarm Bebe. She was so foggy, and the woman's voice was pleasant and soothing. She recognized the song immediately, of course; her uncle—a World War I soldier who had lost a leg during the second battle of the Marne—had taught it to her in 1918, right after being discharged from the army. Bebe felt as if she were hearing it in a dream, except the dream-woman on the first floor didn't seem to know many of the words.

"Dahdahdah to Kaiser Bill and make him dahdahdah . . ."

"Slip a pill to Kaiser Bill and make him shed a tear," Bebe corrected, sotto voce, as she tried to sit up.

She couldn't imagine who might be in her house. She and Chuck no longer had relatives who lived in town, and most of her female neighbors were younger women who wouldn't know that song. But surely it was somebody who belonged there; nobody would be so brazen as to just come into a strange house and start singing a cheerful ditty if she were up to no good.

"And when we see the enemy, we'll shoot him in the rear . . ."

The voice wafted up the stairs and floated into Bebe's bedroom like pipe smoke. She rubbed the sleep from her eyes, smiling, and decided the singer must be her cousin Ruth, here on a surprise visit from Minnesota. It would be just like dear old Ruth to show up out of the blue! It sounded as if she was in the kitchen, where she was no doubt making herself a pot of coffee and helping herself to the corn muffins Bebe had made earlier that day. Bebe didn't mind a bit, of course; Ruth hadn't visited in years, and Bebe couldn't wait to see her again.

She rose unsteadily to her feet—impaired coordination, she knew, was a side effect of too much ucky juice—and as she set her swan back on the dresser a twinge in her groin reminded her she'd have to make a detour to the downstairs restroom prior to greeting Ruth. Ruth was a champion hugger, and Bebe was afraid her bladder might pop like a balloon if Ruth were to get hold of her before she had the chance to urinate. Giggling at this indelicate image, Bebe lurched toward the bedroom doorway, humming along with the woman in the kitchen.

"Oh, joy! Oh, boy! Where do we go from here?"

Jon Tate kicked the huge, unyielding door on the right side of the barn and cursed at the padlock that was preventing him from seeing into that part of the building. The left side of the divided barn was wide open, but even though it was crowded with farm equipment and junk—a green and yellow John Deere tractor, a riding lawn mower, the remnants of an old chicken coop, empty plastic containers, cans of nails and screws—there was no gasoline in sight. He kicked the door again, and bit back a scream of impotent rage.

Jon had already given up on Julianna, and was questioning his own sanity for even considering waiting around for Elijah. He didn't want to ditch the kid, but the truth was that it seemed to be Elijah the cops were after, and if Julianna truly *had* killed that trooper, it was likely no one else knew Jon had been in the Edsel at the time. Things had happened so fast, after all, and Jon was sure the cop hadn't had time to get a good look at him, let alone call in a description on the radio.

All of which meant, of course, the dumbest thing in the world for Jon to do would be to keep associating with the younger boy. If the cops found them together, Jon would be in just as much trouble as Elijah.

The plastic bag with his belongings was dangling from his wrist, swinging in the breeze like a pendulum. It bumped against his leg and he stared down at it blindly. A corner of one of the books he'd brought along was digging into his calf muscle, and a wave of self-pity threatened to overwhelm him. The book reminded him of his home, and tears sprang to his eyes. Right at that moment he would have given anything, anything at all, just to sit in his armchair again, reading to his heart's content. He thought of his parents and brothers, and his apartment, and his refrigerator full of beer, and his job at Toby's, and his friends, and his bed. His life in Tipton had been so simple, and he had loved it.

"Well, you can just forget about it now, jackass," he said aloud, furious at his own stupidity. "It's all gone."

Breathing hard, he bent to inspect the lock. It looked brand new, as did the metal plates it was attached to, and the door itself was solid oak. Nonetheless, he was sure he could get it open in about two seconds with a hammer or a pry bar, but when he'd searched the premises a minute ago nothing remotely like that had turned up. All the tools were probably behind the locked door, he assumed—no doubt right next to a stupid *fucking* gas can.

The sun on his back was hot, but his clothes were still sopping from rain and sweat. It suddenly occurred to him that besides the books and money, the plastic bag also held dry underwear and socks. There was no time to change, of course, but after another fruitless struggle with the lock, he decided he might as well get more comfortable while he was figuring out what to do.

He darted into the shadows by the tractor, out of sight of the farmhouse, and stripped naked, tossing aside his wet underclothes and wringing out his T-shirt and shorts as quickly as he could. The water he squeezed through his fingers was enough to create a small river in the dirt at his feet. As he dressed again, he wished once more he'd thought to bring a complete set of clothes with him that morning when he'd fled his apartment. The fresh underwear and socks were a distinct improvement from the old set, however, and as he returned to the sunlight and pulled his damp shirt back over his head, his mood had lifted slightly.

It lifted even more an instant later. A few feet to the side of the barn entrance was a well, and next to the pump was a rock the size of a coconut.

"That should do the trick," he said aloud. "Let's see what's hiding behind that big goddamn door."

Julianna opened a catchall drawer by the stove and spotted a box of wooden matches. Without seeming to notice what her hands were doing, she opened it and fished out a single match-stick.

"*He saw a dead man next to him,*" she sang, "*and whispered dahdahda . . .*"

She paused abruptly and cocked her head, listening. She could have sworn she heard another woman's voice, singing along with her from another part of the house, but now there was only silence.

A movement out the window caught her eye, and she looked across the yard, just in time to see Steve step from the barn into the sunshine. He'd taken off his shirt, but was now tugging it back on as he walked, and Julianna blushed to see him like that. He was a lovely young man, with a slender waist and broad shoulders, and Julianna wondered yet again what he was running from. She caught herself gawking at him until he was fully clothed again, and shook her head in embarrassment, grateful he hadn't been looking toward the farmhouse at that moment.

"Oh, I'd have just DIED if he'd seen me watching him!" she muttered, blushing deep red. "He'd have thought I was nothing but a silly little girl!"

The bloody rag around his left thigh reminded her what she was supposed to be doing. She tucked the wooden match behind an ear for safekeeping, then resumed her search for alcohol and bandages. She wondered what was taking her friend Ben so long and almost called out his name before deciding to give him another minute to get back from the outhouse.

"I don't know where that boy's head is these days," she complained, sighing.

Elijah panted with relief as he urinated in Bebe Stockton's downstairs toilet. The bathroom had been the fourth door he'd tried in the hallway; the first two were closets and the third opened on a staircase that led down to the cellar.

"Oh, thankGodthankGodthankGod," he murmured to himself, feeling lucky that he hadn't actually exploded like he thought he might.

The bathroom was spotless and welcoming, with Winnie-the-

Pooh wallpaper and a claw-foot tub. A window next to the tub was open, and a hot breeze blew through the curtains, drying the sweat on his back as he studied an elegant, matching pair of red glass swans perched on top of the toilet tank. The door behind him was shut, but unlocked; humidity had swollen the wooden jamb and made the door impossible to latch.

A soap dish on the sink caught his eye. It was in the shape of a scallop shell, and his throat closed the instant he recognized it. His mother, Mary, had one just like it in the bathroom of their house, and all at once he was so homesick he couldn't stand it. Tears blurred his vision as he realized what his absence must be doing to his parents; they were no doubt worried sick. He desperately wanted to call and tell them what was going on, yet he knew he didn't dare. He was sure the instant they heard his voice they'd order him to go to the police and give himself up, and he knew there was no way he could do that.

Elijah knew what happened to black kids who got mixed up in stuff like this. Almost every night on the news he saw boys and girls his age and younger getting clubbed down on the street just for taking part in peaceful demonstrations; what were the cops likely to do to a black teenager they thought had killed one of their own?

He brushed angrily at his eyes with the back of a wrist. *I'll call them when I'm far away from here, and out of danger,* he told himself. *I'll call when I can talk to them without bawling like a goddamn baby.*

He forced his mind back to the present. Julianna was still singing in the kitchen, but Elijah could barely hear her over the noise of his pee hitting the toilet water. For a moment it sounded as if two women were singing in the house, but a second later he decided he'd only imagined this.

There was a medicine cabinet over the sink and a small closet by a clothes hamper in the corner. He eyed both of these with anticipation. Either location was a likely spot for antiseptic and bandages, and once he found the medical supplies all he had to do was get Julianna out of the house before Steve decided to leave them both behind. He was sure the older boy had already located gasoline, and was at that very moment back at the Edsel, attempting to get it restarted. If he'd just wait a little longer, though, all three of them could still get away from the dairy farm and back on the highway together, safe and sound.

Elijah finished his business at last with a satisfied grunt, but just as he flushed the toilet and began zipping up his pants, the door behind him flew open and crashed into the wall.

Bebe had nearly fallen three times on the staircase before she reached the bottom. She was most definitely feeling the aftereffects of her ucky juice binge, but during her descent she had kept a death grip on the handrail and somehow managed to stay on her feet.

Now safely off the steps, she did her best to tiptoe down the hall toward the bathroom, wanting to use the facilities before sneaking up on her cousin in the kitchen.

Poor old Ruth will jump through the ceiling when I walk in on her! Bebe thought, grinning. *I just have to make sure she doesn't hear me!*

She made it to the bathroom door without being detected, and put her hand on the knob. She gave a push, but the door wouldn't budge.

Oh, gosh darn this doggone humidity! She bit her lip and pushed harder, but the bottom of the door held tightly to the jamb, as if nailed to it. Bebe put a toe on the corner that was causing the problem, intending to just give it a quiet shove with her foot. Unfortunately, this proved to be too much of a challenge for her drug-weakened equilibrium. She slipped in the hallway and fell forward, and the entire weight of her stocky little body slammed into the door, popping it open and wrenching the knob from her hands.

Jon raised the stone over his head and brought it down on the padlock with all the force he could muster.

BANG!

The blow gouged into the red paint of the barn door, but the lock held firm.

"Oh, come *on*, you son of a bitch," Jon breathed in exasperation. He raised the rock again and aimed with more care.

BANG!

This time the lock broke apart with gratifying ease, but any elation Jon might have felt was obliterated two seconds later by the screams of a woman inside the farmhouse. Even from across the yard her shrieks hurt his ears; they were shrill and incredibly loud, like the feedback of a microphone pumped through an amplifier.

"Jesus Christ!" he gasped, nearly dropping the rock on his foot.

Jon knew instinctively that such a sound was not coming from Julianna, which meant that the owner of the house was home after all. Julianna may have been crazy, but after witnessing the unflinching way she had dealt with the trigger-happy trooper, he believed her incapable of the outright hysteria he could hear in the screamer's voice. He snatched up the plastic bag from the ground and clutched it to his chest, wondering if the woman had seen him break the padlock, and if that was the reason she sounded so upset. It didn't seem likely, but she hadn't started screaming until he broke the lock so he supposed it was a strong possibility. Elijah and Julianna might have done something to set her off, too, he supposed, but either way she was seriously out of control.

Which meant bad news for all of them, no matter who was at fault.

He glanced over at the barn door with the ruined padlock still hanging from the latch, but his quest for gas now seemed pointless. He stared at the house and then over at the woods, and he began to swear in a steady stream as the woman's unnerving screams blotted out every other noise on the hilltop.

"Fuck it," he said, making up his mind at last. He bolted for the woods, jackrabbit quick, with panic nipping at his heels like a ravenous basset hound.

WAP!

The bathroom door collided with the wall and Bebe Stockton

tumbled into the room and sprawled on her knees on the floor, catching a startled Elijah with his hands still on the open zipper of his jeans as he spun to face her. The woman and the boy gaped at each other with equal horror, struggling to digest the unpleasant fact of each other's presence in this cozy farmhouse bathroom.

BANG!

The sound of Jon's first attempt to break the lock on the barn door across the yard made both of them jump, as if someone had just detonated an M-80 right outside the window.

Bebe thought she had fallen into the clutches of Lucifer Himself, and that her time on the earth was limited to the next few seconds if she couldn't get away from him. She couldn't see the fright and bewilderment on Elijah's handsome young face; what she saw instead was a tall, half-naked black man, standing over her and fingering his zipper. She was convinced he was a homicidal rapist, intent on having his way with her and then slitting her throat.

BANG!

The second outdoor explosion caused both of them to jump again. Bebe was at her wit's end, though, so this time she misread the boy's innocent spasm as a prelude to an attack on her person. She could take no more, and her mouth opened to its widest dimensions, like a small, toothy portal into hell.

"OHSWEETJESUSOHLORDOHJESUSJESUS," she screamed. "PLEASE DON'T HURT ME OHDEARGODOHJESUSOH MYSWEETLORDJESUS, NONOOHNO, PLEASEPLEASE-PLEASEPLEASE I WON'T TELL ANYONE, JUST DON'T HURT ME, OHGODOHGODOHGOD . . ."

Buffeted backward by this volcanic aural assault, Elijah lost his footing and fell on top of the toilet, crying out in pain as he bruised a rib on the corner of the tank. The grandmotherly looking woman on the floor in front of him was plump but not large; he simply could not fathom how someone so short was able to make such a cataclysmic sound.

"Please, lady," he whispered. He was too shocked and scared

to speak any louder, so he put up his hands in a placating manner. "Please, *please* calm down!"

Bebe couldn't hear him over her own screeching, and his soothing gestures—which she interpreted as an attempt to deceive her—only made her more desperate to escape than ever. Still wailing at the top of her lungs, she struggled to her feet and tripped into the hall, sure at any second she would feel the grip of the black man's strange, white-palmed hands on her neck. She had forgotten all about the other woman in the kitchen; her only thought was to get away from the madman in her house.

Julianna heard the bathroom door crash into the wall, but she thought it was just poor old Ben Taylor being clumsy and knocking something over in the hallway as he returned from his visit to the outhouse. She wished he'd be more careful; Polly Miller would be upset if he made a mess in her nice clean home.

A loud bang out the window drew her attention to Jon and the barn once again, and she almost cried out as she realized what he was attempting to do.

"What on earth is he *thinking?*" she hissed. "That's vandalism! He'll break Günter's lock and get us all in terrible trouble!"

She gathered her breath to yell out the window at him, but she was too late; he had already raised the rock for a second strike, and he now heaved it at the door again, destroying the lock. Her angry protest died on her lips, however, overmastered by Bebe Stockton's screams from the bathroom.

Bebe once again did not take into account the effects of the phenobarbital on her limbs. In her panicked rush to flee from Elijah, her feet got tangled as she plunged down the hall toward the front door, causing her to take a spill right beside the staircase that led back to her bedroom. She was still howling an ear-piercing prayer to God when the side of her head bounced off the edge of the bottom step, and just like that, her screaming stopped.

*   *   *

Jon Tate was a hundred yards from the farmhouse when he realized the hysterical woman had at last shut up. He knew he should just keep on running, but his legs quit moving of their own accord and he bent double, gasping for air and trying not to pass out after his wild sprint across the pasture. The edge of the woods was only fifty feet in front of him, yet all of a sudden the wall of trees looked less appealing. Now that the screaming had ceased he found he was able to think again, and he was no longer sure that an escape on foot through the dark, wet woods was such a great idea. Julianna and Elijah had apparently managed to calm the woman down, because otherwise Elijah would surely have come outside by now, either seeking help or trying to flee, too. The yard remained empty, however, and everything looked as peaceful and reassuring as it had when they first arrived. Jon shielded his eyes to check out the Edsel on the highway; it was still the only car on the road.

"Shit," he muttered, ashamed for panicking. Julianna and Elijah could have been having a friendly chat with the owner all along, until Jon set her off by breaking into the barn. All the ruckus had probably been his own fault.

He looked at the woods again, and then back at the farm. Any second now Julianna and Elijah would emerge, and if Jon wasn't there, they'd figure he'd run out on them. They'd get gas from the owner and leave, and he'd be on his own. Almost without realizing what he was doing, he started walking back to the barn. Within a few steps he picked up his pace, and began to jog.

If the dairy lady is pissed about her padlock, he thought, *I can always say I was going to leave some money for it.*

"This isn't Polly Miller," Julianna whispered.

She was on her knees beside the dead woman in the hallway, and her eyes were full of tears as she gave up trying to find a pulse in Bebe Stockton's wrist. Elijah stood next to her, holding a hand to his injured ribcage and breathing in hitches; he was so upset it was all he could do to keep from collapsing on the floor and sobbing.

Julianna smoothed the dress on the stranger's body. "Do you think she might have been Günter's sister?"

Her voice sounded thin and haunted, even to her own ears, and her hands shook as she touched Bebe's round face. A small pool of blood was encircling the dead woman's head like a grotesque halo.

This will not go unpunished.

Sanity flickered behind Julianna's eyes, and the person she had been before her break with reality looked down at the corpse of Bebe Stockton and grimly assessed the situation.

We will be made to pay for this.

Elijah watched in horror as a stream of urine began to spread around Bebe's body. His gorge rose instantly, and without warning he leaned over and vomited on his sneakers, barely missing the hem of Julianna's dress.

When the dairy lady had fled from the bathroom he had scrambled to his feet, intending to run also. Then there had been a sickening thump in the hallway, and the woman's screams ended abruptly, as if somebody had flicked off the siren on a fire engine. This odd *thump* had scared him more than anything else in his life, and for almost a minute he hadn't been able to move a muscle. He had stood in the bathroom, gazing through the open door into the hall, and there had been no other sound in the house for what seemed an eternity.

Finally, he had heard quiet footsteps in the hallway, and Julianna glided past the bathroom. She had glanced in at him as she passed, but she didn't speak; her attention was focused on something ahead of her Elijah couldn't see. When she disappeared from view he followed her as if in a dream, one slow step at a time. She had been waiting for him right outside the bathroom, however, and only when he had joined her in the hallway did she move to examine the sprawled body at the base of the staircase.

The body of the woman who was dead because of him.

Elijah promptly threw up again. Fortunately he hadn't eaten in a long while so most of what came up was water, but the smell was still foul, and he reflexively muttered an apology to Julianna. She didn't even seem to notice, though; she just got to her feet, knees popping, and took a slow, shaky breath.

"I don't think Günter's sister is feeling well," she whispered, still staring at the woman on the floor.

Elijah blinked several times before raising his head to gape at Julianna. "What?"

"Maybe we should just let ourselves out, don't you think?" she asked. "She probably just needs a nap." She turned her head to gaze at Elijah. "Were you able to find the alcohol and bandages for Steve's leg?"

She was standing less than a foot from the corpse, on a dry spot of floor between twin puddles of piss and puke, yet she looked for all the world as if she were simply inquiring about a homework assignment.

Elijah shook his head in disbelief as he realized that the hallucinatory narrative Julianna had been telling herself all along was still intact, regardless of the dead woman beside them. "No, but don't you think we . . . I mean, we can't just . . . this is . . . this . . ."

He trailed off in despair.

Fifteen minutes ago, Elijah had thought things couldn't possibly get any worse. The assault on the state trooper had seemed like Armageddon as it was happening, but it didn't even come close to *this*. Unlike the state trooper, the woman at their feet had not been shooting at them when she died, nor had she threatened any of them in any way. She had done nothing, in point of fact, but to enter her own bathroom and have the misfortune of running smack into Elijah Hunter.

Elijah Hunter, who had no excuse whatsoever to be in her home. Elijah Hunter, whose uninvited, illegal presence had literally frightened the poor woman to death.

"Oh, Jesus," he whispered. "I can't believe this is happening."

Julianna was aware that her friend Ben was distraught about something but her compassion for him was tempered by a growing sense of urgency. Something was telling her they were wasting precious seconds, and if they didn't leave soon their trip home might actually be jeopardized. She reached out and put her hand on his shoulder.

"We really must hurry, Benjamin."

She gave him a gentle squeeze. It was a reassuring, loving touch, and Elijah looked down at her hand on his skin and fought to keep from crying. He wanted very much to be held and comforted right then, but he hadn't yet learned how to ask for this sort of thing, and Julianna was too intent on what had to be done to perceive just how badly he was hurting.

He swallowed hard a few times, still struggling for control. He knew she was right, but he couldn't seem to make himself care.

I deserve to be put in prison, he thought. *I deserve the electric chair.*

He lifted his head to tell her to go on without him, but as he looked into her face he found he couldn't speak. Something in her unwavering green eyes—and in the strength of her grip—told him she would never agree to leave her friend "Ben" behind, and for the first time he began to wonder about the boy she had mistaken him for all along. If he were still alive, he'd be in his fifties, like Julianna, but some instinct told Elijah that the real Ben Taylor was long since dead.

He couldn't have said why, but understanding the reasons behind Julianna's delusions now seemed critical to him, as if they might help explain why this nightmare was happening. She was clearly on a mission of some kind, and Elijah was part of her insane journey, like it or not. His fate was now bound to hers by at least one death, and probably two, and whatever happened to him would surely happen to her, as well.

Who was Ben, Julianna? He almost asked aloud, but he knew she'd tell him he was being silly. *What happened to him?*

He forced himself to take a deep breath, and then another. If he stayed here and turned himself in, Julianna would be taken into custody, as well, and no doubt she would soon be returned to the mental ward she had apparently escaped from. And while that might be the best place for her, there was something about the trust on her face that made him feel bad, in spite of himself, at the idea of being responsible for her recapture. There was also Steve to think about; if the other boy got caught with them, he would likely share in their punishment even though he had done nothing wrong. Turning himself and Julianna in was one thing, but getting Steve arrested, too, surely wasn't the right thing to do, was it? Elijah could tell the police the older boy was innocent, of course, but he doubted the cops would believe anything that came out of his mouth—especially not since they already thought he and Steve had run over one of their own on the highway.

"Jesus," he murmured again. "This is so insane."

Julianna was still watching him, still waiting for him. It occurred to Elijah that he'd never had anybody besides his parents look at him the way she was looking at him; whoever she thought he was, the softness of her gaze held real love in it, genuine and unmistakable.

What am I supposed to do, God? he demanded. *Tell me what to do!*

No answer from on high was forthcoming, however, and Julianna was beginning to fidget.

Elijah swallowed hard, pulling himself together as best he could. "I know where the medicine cabinet is," he rasped. "I'll try to find the stuff for Steve's leg."

Julianna rewarded him with a dazzling smile.

"Very good." She released his shoulder with a final squeeze and gazed back at the kitchen doorway, thinking fast. "Okay. After you've done that, run and tell Steve to hurry with the gasoline. I'll join the two of you by the car in a moment, but I have a couple of things to take care of in here first."

The sudden command in her voice was startling, but in spite of himself Elijah felt a surge of relief. The Julianna who had run over the state trooper was apparently back, and Elijah couldn't help but be grateful. Insane or not, this version of Julianna had proven herself able to deal with emergencies, and they very much needed her right now.

"Hurry, Ben," she urged. "We don't have much time."

She strode past him on her way to the kitchen, but before she stepped out of sight she turned to face him. Her expression was stern.

"Once you're outside, stay there," she ordered. "Don't come back in the house. Understand?"

Elijah opened his mouth to ask why, but she vanished around the corner before he could say anything. He stared down one final time at the dead woman on the floor, and his heart twisted. There was an ugly, fist-sized bruise on her left temple, and her pale lips were frozen in a frown. He closed his eyes and prayed for her soul—and his own, too, in pity and sorrow.

Julianna's voice floated down the hall from the kitchen, jarring him back into motion.

"And don't forget to zip up your pants, dear," she called.

Chapter 6

Gabriel Dapper sat behind the wheel of his bright red Cadillac and watched Edgar Reilly trundle down the steps of the state mental hospital in Bangor, Maine. Edgar had drooping jowls and a bulging torso; his eyes were sad and brown, and much too small for his bald, wrinkled head.

"He looks like a walrus," Gabriel muttered to himself.

It was half past seven on Saturday evening, but the temperature was still unpleasantly warm, so Gabriel had the windows rolled up and the air conditioner at its highest setting. Even with the arctic blast coming from the vents, however, he was sweating profusely; he felt as if he had a fever.

Edgar opened the passenger door of the Cadillac. "Hello, Gabriel."

Gabriel nodded, unconsciously tapping his steering wheel seven times with his left forefinger before answering. "Hi, Doc. Hop on in."

As Edgar settled into the passenger seat of the Cadillac and pulled the door shut, he sighed with relief at the cooler temperature in the car. He simply couldn't abide being hot, and he'd feared that Gabriel might be a "fresh air" type of man.

He gave Julianna's son a strained smile. "Thanks again for letting me tag along with you tonight."

Gabriel shrugged, wrinkling his nose at the smell of cigarettes on Edgar's breath and clothes. "Sure."

I hope he's not a yakker, Gabriel thought, putting the Cadillac in gear and turning west out of the parking lot. Gabriel was consumed with worry about his mother and had no patience for small talk.

I certainly hope he doesn't expect me to make conversation all the way there, Edgar Reilly thought. Edgar had a lot to mull over before they reached their destination, and he didn't feel up to explaining his complicated mental processes to a layman. He reached into his pocket and dug out a bag of M&M's, staring resolutely out the window to forestall a dialogue.

Earlier that evening Edgar had received a phone call from the Bangor Police Department informing him Julianna had been spotted by a state trooper in New Hampshire. This same trooper was now in the intensive care unit of a county hospital and had not regained consciousness since being run over by Edgar's stolen Edsel. To make matters worse, the trooper's last words to the dispatcher had been a shouted warning about a second kidnapper in the vehicle with Julianna.

Nor had this been the last of the grim tidings:

Edgar's Edsel had been found abandoned on the highway in front of a dairy two miles from the border between New Hampshire and Vermont. There had been no sign of Julianna and her two captors, but there was a bullet hole in the rear window, blood on the steering wheel and on the backseat, and the dairy farmhouse itself had been burned to the ground—with the wife of the dairy farmer presumed to be still inside. The only other news Edgar had been given was that the first kidnapper was believed to be a teenaged Negro named Elijah Hunter, who had gone missing that morning from Prescott, Maine. Nothing was known about the Hunter boy's companion.

Edgar had promptly dialed Gabriel Dapper to tell him what he'd learned, and Gabriel—who had spent the day at Julianna's silent, book-stuffed house in Bangor, working himself into a frenzy of restlessness and rage over his mother's abduction—had decided on the spot that he'd be damned if he'd sit around waiting for more such news. He'd stated his intention to leave Bangor that night to find Julianna on his own, and Edgar—who for his part had spent the day berating both himself and his staff for allowing Julianna's escape—offered his assistance. Gabriel had accepted, and they had agreed to begin their search that night at the dairy farm in New Hampshire.

"Mind if I smoke?" Edgar now asked, reaching for the pack of cigarettes in his pocket.

Gabriel loathed the smell of cigarettes. "Sorry, I'm allergic," he lied.

Edgar looked crestfallen. "That's fine," he muttered, doing his best to be a good sport. "I smoke too much, anyway."

They lapsed into silence once more. Gabriel kept his eye on the mile markers along the highway, and every seven miles he tapped the steering wheel seven times. Edgar watched this ritual occur again and again and finally caught the pattern. He stirred in his seat and cleared his throat.

"You've got *Zwangsneurose*," he said to Gabriel.

Gabriel turned to stare at him. "I've got what?"

"*Zwangsneurose*," Edgar repeated. "It means 'compulsion neurosis.' It's a nervous disorder that often manifests itself in a behavioral tic such as yours."

Edgar tapped the dash of the Cadillac seven times to demonstrate what he meant.

Gabriel flushed. "I don't know what you're talking about."

"You've been tapping your steering wheel seven times, every seven miles," Edgar explained kindly. "Many people who suffer from a compulsion neurosis fixate on a specific number, just like you're doing. For example, I once had a patient who washed and dried his hands exactly five times whenever he went to the bathroom."

Gabriel narrowed his eyes. "I'm just keeping track of the miles, Doc. I'm not crazy."

"Of course not," Edgar agreed. "A compulsion neurosis is nothing to be overly worried about. But you might want to consider undergoing psychoanalysis sometime to deal with the underlying motive for why you feel compelled to keep track of the miles in such a tactile, systematic manner. It's a highly interesting quirk, to say the least."

"It's not a quirk," Gabriel protested. "It's just something I do to keep awake when I drive."

"I see," Edgar murmured. "Well, then, I'm glad it serves a good purpose."

Gabriel scowled and returned his attention to the road, deciding to let the matter drop. He rebelliously tapped the wheel seven times again at the appropriate mile marker, however, refusing to interrupt his routine just because Edgar thought there was something wrong with it.

Edgar smiled indulgently and began sorting through a colorful handful of M&M's, popping them in his mouth one by one (starting with brown, as always, then proceeding in alphabetic order through the other colors). As the chocolate melted on his tongue he stared out the window and let his mind wander.

Unbeknownst to Gabriel, Edgar had spoken on the phone less than an hour before to a profane man named Otto Kiley, who was the sheriff of Elijah Hunter's hometown of Prescott, Maine. Sheriff Kiley had told Edgar that the report about Julianna's kidnapping sounded like "a steaming pile of horseshit" to him; he insisted Elijah Hunter was a "fine young Negro" who would never dream of committing such a crime, let alone the other barbarities he was accused of, and that something "pretty fucking peculiar" had to be going on. Edgar had listened to Kiley's protestations about what he viewed as a rush to judgment of Elijah Hunter, but Edgar's immediate reaction had been to assume that the man probably had close ties to the Hunter family, and was therefore an unreliable source of information. This being the case he had decided not to share Kiley's doubts with Julianna's son, feeling that the last thing Gabriel needed to hear at the moment was idle speculation about the innocence of his mother's kidnapper.

But what if it turned out Kiley was right after all?

The more Edgar thought about it, the more unsettled he became. All anybody had been thinking about was Julianna's welfare, but what if things were not exactly what they seemed? Edgar and his staff were already vulnerable to a lawsuit for allowing Julianna to escape, but what if they were *also* responsible for far worse than that? What if, for instance, Julianna had picked up the Hunter boy when he was hitchhiking or something, and he was actually *her* prisoner, instead of the other way around?

Edgar squirmed in his seat, considering the legal implications.

He didn't see how Julianna could have overpowered the teenager without a gun, and surely she hadn't managed to procure a weapon before she came across Hunter. Even if she had, though, it still wouldn't explain the second kidnapper in the car. She surely couldn't have kidnapped this person, as well, could she?

But she COULD have set the fire at the dairy farm, he reminded himself.

Julianna had a predisposition for arson; it was why she had been committed to Edgar's care in the first place. And if the police were right about the woman who lived on the dairy farm being killed in the fire earlier that night, then Julianna could now be implicated, at least by extension, in a murder.

Edgar swallowed a yellow chocolate without chewing it and almost choked.

"Are those M&M's?" Gabriel asked. "Can I have some?"

Edgar wiped sweat from his upper lip and wordlessly poured a generous helping of candy into the big man's palm, wishing it were as easy to pour out this terrifying new suspicion. He almost said something to Gabriel, but then abruptly changed his mind, deciding it would be wiser to wait until he had more information.

"Thanks," Gabriel muttered.

"My pleasure," Edgar said, fretfully fingering the teardrop mole on his left cheek. He emptied the last of the M&M's into his own hand, automatically reaching for a brown one first.

Gabriel was unaware of Edgar's disquiet. An image of Julianna from when he was a small boy had just popped into his mind for no reason whatsoever; he was remembering the feel of her arm around his shoulders as the two of them stared through the screen door of their house, watching a spring rainstorm. Neither of them had spoken as the rain fell, and both of them breathed deeply, relishing the smell of the fresh air as the dust in the street settled. Gabriel had leaned into his mother, resting his head against her side; she had been wearing a red-and-yellow flowered dress that was soft on his cheek and ear. The rain had fallen fast and hard and caused a small river to form by the curb; twigs and leaves caught in the stream bobbed madly along the street and finally vanished in the storm drain at the corner. Julianna had lifted Gabriel in her arms and taken him outside; she'd swung him around in the rain and tried to teach him how to waltz, putting his feet on top of hers and waving gaily at every car that passed them by.

"Umbrellas are for sissies!" she'd cried, soaked to the skin and giggling like a child.

Gabriel hadn't thought of that rainy day in years.

"These damn things are absolutely *addictive*," Edgar Reilly said, fishing another bag of M&M's out of his pocket and pulling Gabriel from his reverie. "I simply can't get enough of them."

Gabriel blinked away tears. His hair and face were damp with perspiration, as if that long-ago downpour had somehow left a residue.

At 8:57 p.m. Mary Hunter was pacing the floor of her kitchen as she listened to Sam speak to Red Kiley on the phone. She was having difficulty following Sam's side of the conversation, though, because he wasn't saying much. He was mostly just listening and frowning, and as his frown deepened, Mary felt fear touch her heart with a clammy finger.

Mary was not accustomed to this feeling at all, and she did not much care for it. In fact, it made her furious.

Where is my son, Lord? she demanded silently, glaring up at the ceiling. *What were you THINKING when you let him get in the car with that crazy white woman?*

Mary Hunter had no reservations about upbraiding the Almighty if she felt He wasn't doing His job properly.

A few hours earlier, Sheriff Kiley had walked Sam through the details of why Elijah was being sought for the kidnapping of an escapee from a mental institution, and also the attempted murder of a New Hampshire State Trooper. Sam had then returned home and shared it all with Mary, and the two of them had gone over it time and again as they waited by the phone for more news, praying fervently for Elijah to walk in the door, safe and sound, and tell them it had all been some kind of silly mix-up.

Nothing they had heard thus far made any sense to them. They both knew Elijah simply wasn't capable of the things he was accused of doing. Yet two witnesses to the kidnapping—an elderly couple named Cecil and Sarah Towpath—claimed otherwise, and there was also an inexplicable radio report to a police dispatcher from Lloyd Eagleton, the Edsel-mauled trooper. Eagleton had pulled over the car Elijah was purported to have hijacked from Julianna Dapper, only to be run down, moments later, like a hapless possum on the highway.

But not before he had called in a frantic plea for assistance, alarmed by the appearance of a second kidnapper.

Please, God. Mary moderated her mental tone to something half plea, half command. *Don't let my son be hurt. I'll do anything you ask, anything at all. But don't you DARE let them hurt my son.*

To Sheriff Kiley's credit, he hadn't believed Elijah was guilty of anything, either. He had spent a good hour on the phone earlier that evening, trying to hammer this point home to everybody he could think of while Sam sat across the desk from him in the sheriff's office. Red had spoken to five or six muckety-mucks in the New Hampshire and Maine State Patrols, and even to Julianna Dapper's headshrinker in Bangor, imploring them all to not allow any harm to befall Elijah.

But apparently nobody had bothered to listen to Red Kiley.

Samuel's eyes went wide with shock as he clung to the phone receiver. "I don't understand," he said. "Why would they think such a thing?"

"Why would *who* think *what?*" Mary asked. Something in Sam's voice made her throat constrict.

Sam waved her to silence as the blood drained from his face.

"I see," he whispered. "So she's dead, then?"

Mary stopped pacing and leaned on the table for support. *Oh, Jesus.* "The crazy woman's dead?"

Sam shook his head and covered the receiver to speak to her. "No. But some other lady got burned to death at a dairy in New Hampshire."

Mary's heart began to pound in her ears. "And they think Elijah did *that?*"

Sam didn't answer, but he didn't have to. His expression said it all.

The muscles in Mary's legs gave out. She sank into a chair and stared at the clean yellow walls and the polished wooden cabinets of her kitchen, and she began to tremble.

"Oh, my darling boy," she whispered. She bit her tongue hard enough to draw blood. "Why is this happening to you, of all people?"

Elijah was too fragile for his own good. Mary had always known this, and had feared, in secret, that someday something bad might befall him simply because he was much too vulnerable to protect himself. There were terrible people in the world, and you had to be strong to deal with them. She had tried to teach him this, but it was like trying to teach a tulip to be a machete. From the moment her son had been born it had been obvious to Mary she had been put on this earth for the sole purpose of protecting him; he had no defenses against those who might do him harm, and she had sworn to herself she would always keep him safe.

And she had failed.

Mary Hunter had no illusions whatsoever about what might happen to Elijah were he to be caught by the police. She had been born and raised in a town just eleven miles north of Birmingham, Alabama, and many young black men she had known during her childhood had ended up dead—or worse—after being accused of similar crimes. Most of these boys never even saw the inside of a courtroom; they were just hunted down and "dealt with," someplace out of sight. Granted, New England was a long way from Birmingham, but her life experience had taught her to have precious little faith in white men with guns and badges.

It took her a moment to realize Sam had hung up the phone and was now sitting across the table, speaking to her. She had to ask him to repeat himself, and then she listened as best she could as he told her of Bebe Stockton's death. Sam went on to describe the bloodstained, bullet-pocked Edsel, abandoned on the highway by the smoldering remains of a dairy farmhouse, and after that, in hushed tones, he told her of the fragment of a white shirt the police had found in the backseat of the stolen car.

Mary put her hands over her mouth to keep from crying out. She knew full well what Elijah had been wearing that morning when he left home to mail a letter to his grandpa; she had straightened his collar before he walked out the door. He'd looked so handsome and grown-up, and she'd given him a rare smile of approval.

Disregarded tears fell from her chin to the table, one after another. She couldn't comprehend how the same child who had stood in the doorway that very morning as she inspected his appearance could now be so far away from her, and in such peril. She remembered picking lint from his breast pocket, too, having to reach up a little to do it. She couldn't get used to his being so tall lately.

"My baby," she whispered.

Sam's face was the color of ashes as he looked at her. He reached out to her and tried to say something, but his voice no longer worked.

As bad as the tidings were about their son, it was far worse for Samuel to see the toll his words had taken on Mary. It was almost inconceivable to him that she could be so helpless. As a teenager Sam had once seen Mary stare down a pair of suspected Klansmen who attempted to harass her on the sidewalk in Birmingham, making them hang their heads and walk away in shame; as an adult he had watched her smack a bad-tempered bull between the horns with a milk bottle and frighten the beast into running for cover. She was easily the bravest person Samuel knew, and to see her like this was agonizing.

He should have known, though, he realized.

It was for Elijah that she and Sam had left their home in Alabama and moved to a place they thought would be safer and better; it was for Elijah she worked herself to exhaustion each and every day, to make sure he'd never want for anything, or be ashamed of who he was. Her love for her son eclipsed everything, even the love she had for Samuel himself, which was no small thing.

"Oh, Mary," he whispered, grieving for her. "Just say the word, and I'll do whatever you ask."

Mary clasped his outstretched hands and sobbed aloud. She wept as she had never wept in her life; she wept as if she would never stop weeping again. She had thought she could bear anything, but she couldn't take the idea of a world without Elijah. She was certain he would not survive this ordeal, and she would never again be able to speak to him, or hold him, or hear him singing in his room at night, when he didn't know she and Sam were listening to his clear, sweet tenor voice from across the hall. This last thought, especially, was unendurable, and she wanted to die herself before such a thing came to pass.

But as she clasped her husband's fingers in her own, the trembling in her body gradually subsided, and her breathing quieted.

Sam and Mary had known each other most of their lives. They had gone to the same church and school in the dirt-poor, ramshackle town of Bluff Ridge, Alabama; they were only a year apart in age, and had been constant companions since they could talk. There had never really been a question about the two of them eventually ending up together. They'd always fit together like butter and cornbread, and everybody, including Sam and Mary, just assumed they'd get hitched soon after high school, which they did. (Not even World War II was able to interfere with these expectations: Sam's feet were flat as a board and exempted him from the draft.) Since their wedding day more than twenty-two years had passed, and their almost preternatural bond had gotten only stronger through the years.

But Mary had never needed Sam as she needed him now. Until this moment, she had never experienced despair. She had known sadness, of course, and suffering, but she had never felt anything akin to this utter wretchedness. In her life she had lost her parents (both to cancer), and two brothers (one to a car accident, the other to alcohol abuse), but she had absorbed these losses stoically, and to be truthful, a bit arrogantly. She had felt pride in her ability to "keep on going" no matter what, and she had cultivated, with hidden pleasure, a reputation for being hard-nosed and unemotional. And though she had been grateful for Sam's support on these occasions, she hadn't really needed it, nor ever dreamed there might be a time when she would reach the limits of her endurance.

"I am such a fool," she murmured.

Sam tightened his grip on her hands, and Mary squeezed back with all the strength she had, trying very hard to remember who she was. She was humbled by the compassion and love she saw in Sam's eyes, and felt ashamed of her weakness. Sam was hurting just as badly, she knew, and yet there he was, patient and solid as an old tree, doing what he could to help instead of sitting around feeling sorry for himself.

Her shoulders straightened almost imperceptibly. "I don't know what's the matter with me," she blurted. "I guess you married a great big baby who falls apart the second things go wrong."

Sam considered this for a moment, then cleared his throat before answering.

"I don't believe you've met my wife, ma'am," he said solemnly.

There was a pause, then Mary snorted in spite of herself.

Klansmen and bulls weren't the only ones Mary Hunter had outfaced in her tenure on this earth. When she was properly roused, as Sam knew all too well, it was a sight to behold. Her slight, five-foot-four frame seemed to swell to gigantic proportions and her eyes began to smoke and burn, and when she got going full force it was enough to make a stone gargoyle lose control of its bowels. In her time she had tangled with violent drunks, burglars, politicians, salesmen, Baptist preachers, mud wasps, and Dobermans, and not one of them had been a match for her. She had been born with a God-given genius for intimidation, and if Sam could just get the wind back in her sails, Elijah's odds for survival would increase dramatically.

Mary drew a long, slow breath, and then another as Sam watched her intently, like a nurse caring for a wounded soldier. After another minute she was able to sit up straight again, and her brown eyes glittered in the bright fluorescent light.

"So," she rasped. "I guess everybody's out hunting for him."

Her voice was still shaky, but Sam had a sudden, perverse desire to grin.

"Yes," he answered. "Red said he'd do everything he could to bring him home, though, and that we should just wait for him to call."

"No."

Her tone sent shivers up Sam's spine. Mary released his hands and rose to her feet in one smooth, graceful motion, like a ballerina.

Or a lioness.

That's my girl, Sam thought.

"Go start the truck, Sam," Mary said. "We're done waiting for somebody to shoot our boy."

On this same Saturday evening in June, a lime-green Volkswagen Beetle was chugging along a lonely highway in upstate New York. The sun was nearly down, and the western sky was an immense, spectacular canvas of red, orange, and gold. The fields and hills surrounding the road were blanketed with thick green grass and wildflowers, and in the growing shadows Julianna Dapper could see the flickering of fireflies. It was an idyllic, stirring scene, yet she was the only one in the car who appeared to be enjoying it.

"Oh, my goodness!" she cried from the cramped confines of the backseat. "Would you look at that?"

Elijah Hunter, sitting up front in the passenger seat, chose to ignore her burst of enthusiasm. He took another bite of a cold meatloaf sandwich and gave the driver a forlorn look.

"Can't you make this stupid thing go any faster?" he muttered around the food in his mouth.

Jon Tate shook his head and sighed. "Every time I try to go faster the engine starts to overheat."

The Beetle belonged to Chuck and Bebe Stockton. Which meant, of course, it was stolen, but Jon wasn't particularly worried about this. Considering he was now an accessory to murder and arson, the theft of a 1957 Volkswagen seemed rather inconsequential.

We're all gonna die, he thought. This blunt phrase had been running through his head in a monotonous loop for the last few hours, ever since they had driven away from the burning farmhouse. *We're all gonna die.*

Three-and-a-half hours earlier, Julianna had waited until Elijah was outside the house before doing what she believed was necessary. She first found a paper grocery bag and ransacked Bebe Stockton's refrigerator, cramming as much food into the bag as it would hold. Bebe had apparently loved to eat; the refrigerator was jam-packed with leftover ham and meatloaf, pickles, deviled eggs, shepherd's pie, cheeses, muffins, casseroles, bread, fruit, coffee cake, and green olives.

The boys will be starving, Julianna thought, her mind racing. *And we mustn't stop for a while.*

Hands flying, she filled the bag in less than a minute, then closed the refrigerator door and stepped over to the window above the sink, wanting to make sure Ben and Steve were out of harm's way. She located them by the barn, standing in front of the big sliding door that had until recently been padlocked.

"Günter is going to be *furious* with us," she clucked. "Somebody should take a switch to Steve for breaking that lock."

She was able to hear their voices through the open window, but she couldn't make out what they were saying. She smiled, though, to see Ben actually engaged in a conversation with the older boy; Ben had few friends other than herself and her older brothers, and she always worried about him being lonely.

Get on with it, girl. She shook her head, realizing she was stalling. *The sooner you're done, the better.*

She took a final look around the bright, cheerful kitchen. The stove and refrigerator were so clean and white they were almost blinding in the sunlight coming through the window, and the muted-gold linoleum beneath her feet didn't have a speck of dirt on it. A pair of delicate, blue glass swans were on the kitchen table, and a warm, fragrant breeze was blowing through the curtains. The entire house had the feel of a place that had been meticulously cared for, and loved, for years.

Julianna blinked back tears, then reached up and removed the wooden match from behind her ear.

Elijah had no idea what Julianna was preparing to do when she ordered him outside. He was far too rattled to even think of disobeying, though, so right after he snatched a bottle of hydrogen peroxide and a box of bandages from the medicine cabinet in the farmhouse bathroom, he ran for the front door, doing his best to ignore the corpse of the woman in the hallway. (This took some doing, as Bebe's body was splayed across the hall and he had no choice but to leap over it to get to the front porch.) His shoes, wet from his own vomit, made squishing sounds on the hardwood floor as he came down on the other side of Bebe's chubby legs, and it was a tremendous relief to burst through the screen door and out into the early evening sunlight.

The sweet, sharp smells of honeysuckle and mint instantly filled his nostrils, and the sun on his skin was warm and reassuring. Bumblebees still hovered around the herb garden, cows lowed in the milk house, and a cheerful circle of yellow and orange marigolds ringed the base of the mailbox like a lei. It was all so serene and nonthreatening, and made the macabre scene he had just left behind him seem even more grotesque by comparison.

Jon was over by the barn, struggling with a massive sliding door. Elijah sprinted across the lawn to help, but as he neared the barn he slowed, dreading Jon's reaction to the tale of the dead woman in the house. He came to a halt and set the hydrogen peroxide and the bandages at the base of the water pump, next to the plastic bag containing Jon's belongings. He squirmed a little when the older boy glanced over his shoulder and met his eyes.

For his part, Jon had only just resumed his search for gasoline. His wild flight across the pasture and the jog back had winded him, and he'd needed to rest for a minute before finishing what he'd started when he'd broken the padlock. The barn door had proven obstinate, though, even when unlocked, and by the time Elijah arrived he'd only managed to budge it an inch or two.

He started to speak but fell silent as he studied the other boy. Elijah was plainly upset; his face was tight with strain and he looked as if he were trying not to cry.

Jon's stomach sank as he let go of the door and turned around. "What's wrong?" he asked.

Elijah blinked, distressed. It bothered him that he couldn't keep a secret when he wanted to, but he supposed it was to be expected. His folks had always told him his face was as easy to read as a billboard.

He began to sputter. "Uh, well, there's a . . . we were in . . . I mean *I* was in the bathroom and this old lady . . . I guess she's not that old, but she kind of . . . well, walked in on me while I was peeing, and she screamed really, really loud and ran out again but then she . . . well . . . it was . . . she must have tripped and . . . and . . . she sort of . . . I mean I think she did, 'cause I didn't see it . . . but she must have hit her head on the stairs or something, and . . . and then . . . well, she just . . . I . . . she, then she . . . ."

He looked away, chin trembling.

The skin on Jon's scalp began to crawl. "Then she *what*, Elijah?"

Elijah's voice broke. "She died," he whispered. "She just died."

Jon fell backward. His butt banged into the barn door and he slid to the ground.

"Christ. Oh, Jesus Christ," he whispered, burying his head in his hands. "Oh, Jesus."

"It was an accident," Elijah pleaded. "I swear to God it was an accident. We didn't even know she was in the house."

Jon's shoulders were shaking. "Jesus God, who *are* you people?" he moaned into his palms. "Why did I ever get in that *fucking* car with you two *psychos?*"

Elijah stepped back, stung.

"I was just peeing!" he protested. "I tried to calm her down but she wouldn't listen!" He stared down with resentment at the top of Jon's head. "You were the one who told me to go inside," he mumbled.

Jon's head sank between his knees. "Holy shit." His voice came out muffled. "We are *so* fucked."

Elijah hugged his bare ribs, wishing he'd kept his mouth shut. He racked his brain for something else to say, desperate to change the subject.

"Did you find any gas, Steve?" he blurted. "Julianna said we should meet her by the car with the gas."

Jon raised his head. "My name isn't Steve." His gray eyes were stunned and weary. "It's Jon."

Elijah gaped back at him. "What?"

Jon shrugged. "Long story." He felt disconnected from his own body; he couldn't seem to feel anything from the neck down. *You're in shock*, a matter-of-fact voice in his head informed him. *This is what shock feels like.*

He rubbed his temples and squinted up at Elijah. "I didn't want you to know my real name," he said drily, "but since we're both going to be dead soon I figured I should go ahead and introduce myself."

Elijah stared at him, bewildered. His fingers fidgeted with the hem of his jeans as he tried to come up with an appropriate response. "Why'd you lie?"

Jon sighed. "It doesn't matter." He continued to watch the

other boy for a minute, then held out a hand. "Help me up, would you?"

Elijah's inborn reluctance to touch other people usually prevented him from doing such things, but after a brief hesitation he grasped Jon's outstretched hand in his own and pulled him to his feet. Jon grunted thanks and released him before glancing down the hill once again at the lifeless Edsel on the shoulder of the empty highway. His shock was passing, and panic began to fill the vacuum it left behind.

"Elijah," he said urgently. "We have to get out of here."

He could sense Elijah's eyes studying the side of his face, and he turned to confront him.

"We should just forget about finding gas for Julianna's car, too, because every cop in the country is going to be on the look-out for it. The two of us should just take off on foot, and not stop running until we're a hundred miles from this place."

Elijah bit his lip and gazed across the pasture at the forest for what seemed like an hour.

"What about Julianna?" he asked at last.

Jon scowled. "She'll be fine." He waved away a horsefly trying to land on Elijah's shoulder. "They'll just take her back to the looney bin, or the circus, or wherever the hell it was she escaped from. But if you and me get caught, we're screwed."

Elijah was rigid with fear, but he slowly shook his head as he met Jon's eyes again.

"I can't," he whispered. "She trusts me."

Jon gawked at him. "Are you nuts, man?" Frustration and terror welled up in him, and he was suddenly furious. He began to yell. "That cop almost KILLED you, remember? And that was before you went and MURDERED an old woman in her own goddamn house! What the fuck do you think they'll do to you NOW?"

Elijah stumbled, almost falling, and his dark brown eyes spilled tears down his cheeks.

"I didn't murder anybody!" he cried. He looked away, sobbing. "She fell!" he choked out. "It was an accident!"

Jon knew that screaming at Elijah wasn't helping anything,

but he couldn't seem to make himself stop. The younger boy was being unbelievably thick-witted, and he had a wild impulse to grab him by the shoulders and shake him until his moronic little head popped off.

"Are all black people as dumb as you are?" he pressed, glaring. "Do you really think anybody will believe you when you say it was an accident? Jesus, Elijah, Julianna killed a COP, and they're gonna blame it on us! You might as well strap yourself to a goddamn electric chair and flip the fucking switch yourself if you think we can afford to wait around here and babysit Julianna!"

Elijah closed his eyes and put his hands over his ears. "I KNOW!" he howled. "I KNOW, all right?" He opened his eyes again and dropped his arms, trying to calm down. "But I still don't think it's right to leave her, okay? It's just . . . not right, that's all."

Something inside Jon snapped.

"Fine!" he bellowed into Elijah's face. "Just stay here and get caught, then, you retarded little douche bag, but I'm leaving!"

Elijah had never heard the expression "douche bag" before, and normally he would have been quite taken with it. He loved learning new curse words, especially when he wasn't sure what they meant. But he didn't like being called retarded one little bit, and his own temper flared in response.

"GO AHEAD!" he yelled back. "Just run away like a big fat CHICKENSHIT, then! See if I care!"

The accusation of cowardice hit too close to the bone for Jon. He was already feeling lousy about running away from his family and his hometown that very morning, and he thought it was unfair to be labeled a "big fat chickenshit" by someone whose life he had saved less than half an hour ago. Without thinking, he threw a full-body tackle at Elijah and brought him down in a screeching heap in the dirt by the water pump.

"What are you DOING?" Elijah wailed in horror, struggling to free himself from Jon's grip.

"I'm not a chickenshit!" Jon huffed, trying without success to pin the other boy's flailing arms. "Take it back right now!"

"No!" Elijah cried.

As a shy, nonconfrontational child with no siblings and few friends, Elijah had never wrestled with anybody before, let alone been in a fight, and he didn't have a clue what he was supposed to do. He had taken more than his share of verbal abuse at school, of course, but had somehow always managed to avoid violence, largely by keeping his mouth shut and his eyes downcast. He had seen many westerns with barroom brawls, of course—*Shane* was an all-time favorite—but this frenzied, spastic clash of elbows and knees was not anything he had been prepared for.

"Get off!" he squalled, writhing. "Get the hell off me!"

"Not until you take it back!" Jon gasped, narrowly avoiding a sharp knee to the groin. "Say it! Say I'm not a chickenshit!"

"No! Not until you say I'm not a murderer!"

Whatever counteroffer Jon might have made was never given utterance; Elijah's right hand lashed out and connected with Jon's left ear in a wide-fingered slap. Jon tumbled off Elijah with a yowl and sprawled in the dirt beside the other boy, cradling the side of his head and swearing.

"Ow, goddammit! What'd you do that for?" he yelped. "That really HURT!"

Elijah rolled away from him, both astonished and appalled by this development. "I didn't mean to!" he said. "You were trying to kill me!"

"I wasn't either!" Jon worked his jaw from side to side in an attempt to silence the high-pitched ringing in his ear. "I was just trying to . . . I don't know . . . trying to get you to stop being such a dick!"

Elijah stared at him, nonplussed. He still had tears in his eyes, but his heartbeat was slowing down again.

Was I being a dick? he wondered. Another disadvantage of being a loner was that he always felt as if an arbitrary set of rules governed every social interaction, and everybody else in the world except for him knew and understood these rules. Was it possible that "chickenshit" was a worse insult than "douche bag"?

"But you called me a bad name before I called you one," he said uncertainly.

Jon made a face. "That's because you were being a dick, man," he insisted, sitting up. There was an angry red palm print on the skin next to his ear. He looked at the ground as Elijah brushed dirt off his jeans and sniffled.

"I wasn't being a dick," Elijah said under his breath. "*You* were."

"I was not."

"Were so."

Both boys fell silent. Elijah sniffled again and then, unable to help himself, began once more to cry in earnest.

"I'm not . . . not a murd . . . murderer," he hiccuped. "It was an acci . . . accident."

The suffering in his voice was palpable, and Jon bit his lip, suddenly ashamed of himself.

"I know," he mumbled, his own eyes starting to burn. "I'm sorry I said that. I really am. I know you didn't murder her." He swallowed hard. "You didn't do anything wrong, okay? Please stop crying."

Elijah's shoulders hitched as he fought for control. "I want my mom and dad," he sobbed, turning away. He was aware this was a childish thing to say, but he didn't care. "I want to go home."

Jon waited beside him in remorseful silence. The need for haste was gnawing at him, but he forced himself to remain motionless as an act of penance. He stared over at the younger boy's quivering, naked back, and tried to think of what else he could say to convince Elijah to come away with him, but he soon gave up, believing any argument he might make would be useless. He looked down the hill at the Edsel one last time, and then over at the woods with hopeless longing. He had no idea why he wasn't already running for his life; he had already done everything he could do for Elijah, and there was nothing left but to say good-bye.

I must be out of my fucking mind, Jon thought angrily. He

plucked a tuft of grass from the ground and flung it away, then rose to his feet, shaking his head in wonder at his own stupidity. *Whatever's wrong with Julianna must be as contagious as a goddamn cold.*

He spun toward the barn again and put his hands on the side of the door, tugging as hard as he could. The crack he'd already made widened another couple of inches.

"Oh, come on, you piece of crap," he muttered at the door.

Elijah raised his head in surprise, having been sure the older boy was preparing to flee. He wiped his face and swallowed as he watched Jon labor with the door, then he forced himself to stand up, too. He took a deep breath and stepped forward to help, and Jon quietly made room for him at his side. Working in tandem, the two of them pried the door open bit by bit, causing the rusted wheels in the long metal track above their heads to screech in protest.

"Whew," Jon breathed when they had created an opening wide enough to allow them to finally see inside the right side of the barn. The acrid scent of cat urine made him wrinkle his nose as he took the first step inside. "We better pray there's some gas in here, man," he said bleakly.

The sun pierced the darkness at the front of the barn, lighting up a dirt floor and a wall of neatly hung tools. A large glass-doored cabinet full of veterinary supplies and medicine bottles stood alongside an impressive tool bench with two expensive-looking electric saws bolted to it; a flimsy-looking ladder was nailed to the wall and led up to a mostly empty hayloft.

"I don't see any gas," Elijah said, coming up behind him.

Jon didn't, either, but he was too distracted to answer. He was staring at the back of the barn, in the shadows, where a canvas tarp spattered with bat and swallow droppings was draped over what appeared to be a small, humpbacked automobile.

"Bingo," he said.

"Goodness," Julianna had whispered as she wandered from room to room in Chuck and Bebe Stockton's house. She was clasping the bag of stolen food to her breast as if it were a sleeping toddler. "Look at all these swans!"

The dairy farmhouse reminded her somewhat of her own house in Pawnee. Julianna's mother, Emma, collected glass knickknacks, too—though she preferred unicorns and angels to waterfowl—and, like Bebe, Emma Larson ran a tight ship when it came to housecleaning. More than this, however, was the warm, welcoming feeling Julianna sensed no matter where she turned. The wood floors had been worn smooth by the bare feet of children and the boots of men; bright, handcrafted afghans adorned overstuffed chairs; the walls were filled with black-and-white photographs of graduation celebrations, anniversaries, birthdays, and family reunions.

Julianna had a lump in her throat as she spotted a stack of newspapers next to the sofa in the living room and a kerosene lamp on a table in the corner.

It's such a shame, she thought, fingering the match she had taken from the kitchen drawer. She heard raised voices coming from outside and paused to listen.

"What on earth?" she murmured. She tried to make out what was being said, but could only distinguish a few angry words. She shook her head, wondering what her companions were arguing about. It wasn't like Ben to yell, and this further example of aberrant behavior disturbed her. He was acting so erratically, and she simply couldn't understand what had gotten into him. He was usually so good-natured and forgiving.

"It could be puberty, I suppose," she muttered.

A picture on the wall caught her eye. It was of three well-dressed and groomed young children, two girls and a boy, standing in front of the house. Bebe Stockton's "brood" had posed for Bebe on an Easter Sunday, long ago, as the Stockton family prepared to leave for church. The girls looked to be about nine and seven, but the little boy—Bebe Stockton's son, Virgil—could only have been four years old or so. Julianna took a closer look at the boy in the photograph and almost dropped the grocery sack.

"Gabriel?" she whispered.

Coincidence loves to play with a disturbed mind.

The name had popped into her head for no reason she could comprehend. Nor did she have any idea why the sight of a child she had never seen before had given her such a shock. But the boy—towheaded and smiling, in an adorable plaid vest and dark pants—looked quite familiar to her, and she felt certain she had once known somebody very much like him, with an unruly cowlick and a gap-toothed grin. She clutched the bag to her chest with one arm and reached out her free hand to touch the picture, trying to remember who the darling little stranger reminded her of, but nothing else came to her.

Another bout of bellowing from the boys outside startled Julianna from her musing. The words were strident enough this time that she could hear most of them. "Retarded little douche bag" and "Big fat chickenshit" came through loud and clear, and she winced. She hated it when the boys were vulgar; it reminded her of Rufus Tarwater.

Her mouth went dry with fear, and she wished she hadn't thought of Rufus.

The volume of the altercation ratcheted up even higher. It sounded to Julianna as if Ben and Steve might have actually come to blows, and she had to restrain herself from running outdoors to make sure they did no harm to each other. "Boys will be boys," she reminded herself. Her brothers, Michael and Seth, often engaged in heated horseplay, and never seemed to be any the worse for it, no matter how much it seemed to Julianna that their intention was to kill each other.

Maybe it will be good for Ben and Steve to have a little tussle, she thought. *They'll get whatever's bothering them out of their systems, and Ben might start to act more like himself again.*

She suddenly wondered if Ben could be a little sweet on her. She had never considered such a thing before, but if it were true, he might be regarding Steve's presence as a threat. She blushed at the notion of Ben feeling that way about her; they had always been the best of friends, but surely Ben realized the two of them would never be allowed to date. Still, though, it might explain why he had been so prickly and excitable for the last few hours.

Without really seeming to notice what she was doing, she stepped over to the table and removed the glass chimney from the kerosene lamp. She carefully set the chimney on the table beside an orange swan, then upended the lamp base, sloshing kerosene on the tablecloth and the rug. She walked backward, toward the newspapers, splashing the floor here and there as she went, but saving most of the fuel for the paper mound itself. After the lamp was empty she placed it on a bookshelf, directly in front of a copy of the King James Bible; her father had a bible just like it in his study.

With no warning, an horrific image flitted through her mind. For a long, terrible moment, she believed she could see the silhouette of a very large man standing on the lawn next to her own home in Pawnee, late at night. The man was holding a burning torch above his head, preparing to fling it through the open window of her father's study; in his other hand was a rifle.

"Rufus," she gasped, her face blanching.

She lost all track of time. She continued to stare sightlessly at the kerosene-soaked papers for what could have been days, and only regained her senses when a nasal car horn began beeping again and again in the driveway.

"Julianna!" Elijah's voice echoed through the house. He was yelling through the screen door from the safety of the front porch. "Let's go!"

She shuddered, shaking her head several times to clear it. "Don't come inside, Ben! I'll be right there!"

Like a seasoned smoker, she lit the match in her hand with a thumbnail and took one last look around the orderly, attractive living room. She peered into the flame as it crept toward her fingers, then she dropped the burning match on the newspapers. There was an instant *whoosh* as the kerosene ignited, and Julianna marched toward the door without so much as a backward glance, the grocery sack clutched in her arms like a sleeping child.

The sun was now entirely down in western New York, and the last of the vivid colors that had filled the sky at sunset and caused Julianna to gasp with pleasure had vanished, swallowed without a trace into the darkening sky. Jon Tate found the headlight switch on the Volkswagen's dashboard and flipped it on, praying that both lights were working.

"If we get pulled over for a busted headlight, we can just say sayo-fucking-nara," he murmured.

He needn't have worried. Chuck Stockton had maintained the Volkswagen with an almost religious fanaticism ever since buying it five years before, although he really had little need of it. Chuck's usual mode of transportation was the dairy truck, and as Bebe was unable to drive—the written part of the driver's test had never made any sense to her at all, and after failing nine times to pass the exam she had given it up as a lost cause—the only time the lime-green Beetle came out of the barn was on Sunday mornings, for church. But Chuck treated the little car as if it were a Rolls-Royce, polishing it after every outing and tinkering with the engine before tucking it back under its protective tarp. His reason for doing this was a mystery to everyone who knew him, including Bebe, but the truth was he found the Volkswagen oddly erotic. From the first moment he had seen the car for sale on a lot in Portsmouth, there was something about its rounded roof that always made him think of a woman's breast, or the sensual curve of a single, shapely buttock.

Bebe had her swans; Chuck had his Beetle.

This being the case, the Volkswagen was in fine condition. Jon and Elijah hadn't been able to believe their good fortune when they discovered that the car in the barn was not only unlocked, but also had its key in the ignition. (Chuck always locked the door of the barn, but not the car itself. He liked knowing it was out there, "ready and raring to go" any time he should feel the need to pay it a friendly visit.) Without a moment's hesitation, the boys had scampered back to the barn door and finished opening it, then Jon had settled behind the wheel and driven the vehicle out into the early evening sunlight. It was Elijah, however, who had insisted on taking the time to close the barn door again before leaving, and had also carefully rehung the broken padlock back on its latch, attempting to cover their tracks.

"Okay," he'd said, getting into the car. "Maybe nobody will notice anything for at least a couple of hours."

Except for the dead body in the house, Jon thought darkly, holding his peace to keep from further upsetting the younger boy.

They retrieved Jon's plastic bag and the medical supplies from beside the well before driving over to the porch to collect Julianna. Elijah worried when he got out of the car to summon the woman from the house that Jon would abandon him, but Jon had left the Volkswagen in neutral, idling, as Elijah leapt on the porch and yelled through the screen door. Julianna had appeared seconds later, toting a bag full of groceries, and crawled into the tight confines of the backseat.

"Is this your car, Steve?" she'd asked.

"Yeah," Jon lied, knowing the truth would make no sense to her. "We couldn't find any gas for yours, so I thought we should take mine instead."

Julianna's resolution to reprimand Jon for his act of vandalism to Günter's padlock had not faded, but she was grateful to him for providing a vehicle, and didn't want to start a row. Still, though, he mustn't be allowed to believe she was the sort of girl who didn't care about the wanton destruction of someone else's property.

"I really wish you hadn't broken Günter's lock," she'd chided, though with no real heat.

"Jesus Christ!" Elijah yelped as he'd leapt into the Beetle's front seat and slammed the door. "The fucking house is on fire!"

Interlude

None of Emma Larson's children looked a thing like her. They all took after their father, Eben, and Emma was thankful for that. Eben was tall and thin, with big green eyes and a lively, clever face. It always made Emma laugh when she caught him napping, because even when he was asleep his mouth and eyebrows never stopped moving. With his eyes closed and his breathing slow and steady, he still looked for all the world like a little boy who'd been caught making mischief and couldn't decide whether to smirk or pout about it.

Emma was plain and stout, with round, unremarkable features and no neck or waist to speak of. Her lips moved so little when she spoke her children often teased her by calling her "The Ventriloquist." Her brown hair was short and neat, and she cut it herself every week to keep it that way. She wore wire-rim glasses and was nearly blind without them, and she dressed mainly in black and white, except for church on Sundays, when she wore a bright green skirt and a dark green blouse—an unfortunate color combination for her, as it made her resemble a well-fed frog, floating on a lily pad. She was soft-spoken and wary with strangers, and people meeting her for the first time often forgot all about her within seconds of shaking her hand.

But Emma's husband and children worshipped her, and with good reason.

In the Lone Rock church, two miles from Pawnee, Missouri, the worn wooden floors looked newly burnished in the sunlight pouring through the open windows, as did the high-backed, diabolically uncomfortable pews the congregation was required to sit on. A stuffed owl perched on a ceiling beam above the pulpit—put there by the minister in the vain hope its presence would deter bats and swallows from taking over the building—and Emma had spent the better part of the sermon this particular Sunday morning service staring up at it and trying not to fidget. The relentless sunshine was gradually turning the small, square church into a roasting oven; beads of perspiration stood out on every face.

Eben was on Emma's left, Julianna and the boys on her right. As ever, Emma was proud to be seen with her family when they were all dressed in their finest. Eben looked unaffectedly elegant in his navy-blue suit, Seth and Michael were neat and handsome in matching black trousers and starched white shirts, and Julianna was radiant in a pink and white summer dress Emma had made for her earlier that spring. She looked to Emma like an exotic flower growing in the pew beside her.

An exotic flower with two black eyes, a broken nose, and a bruised upper lip, all thanks to Rufus Tarwater.

When Eben and the children had come to town the day before to tell Emma about Rufus's assault on Julianna and their uneasiness about what else the man might do, Emma had been working in the post office. When her family all came in together she calmly put down the mail she had been sorting and hung the *Back in a Minute* sign on the door. She inspected Julianna's face in grim silence and listened to their story; she asked a few questions and told them all to wait as she went next door to the telephone office to ring up Sheriff Burns in Hatfield. When she had finished this conversation and returned to her family, she raised a thin eyebrow at Eben.

"You're thinking about buying a gun," she said flatly.

Eben had stared at her for a moment, wondering how she'd guessed that, but in truth he wasn't that surprised. Emma always seemed to know what people were thinking, and this was especially true when it came to the members of her own family.

He nodded. "I think I better, don't you?"

They already owned a .22 rifle for shooting rabbits and other pests, but it was old and tended to jam, and wouldn't be much good for anything else.

She'd studied his face for a long minute, and then the anxious faces of her children. Seth and Michael stood on each side of their sister, like a pair of sober, sunburned bodyguards. Julianna was watching both of her parents with a knowing half smile on her injured lips; Emma wasn't the only one in the Larson family with the ability to read minds.

Emma had turned to Eben again and nodded back. "Yes." She paused. "And you better teach me how to shoot it, too."

That was yesterday, and she now had a revolver in her handbag as she ignored the minister in his pulpit and stared up at the stuffed owl in the rafters. The only things on her mind were Rufus Tarwater and what she would like to do to him for hurting her daughter and threatening her sons. She believed Eben had been right to not allow the boys to lose their innocence by skewering Rufus on the porch, but she herself wouldn't scruple to murder the man if he were stupid enough to show his brutish face at her house again. She'd never shot a gun in her life until last night, but after two solid hours of target practice in the backyard, she felt certain she could at least point the thing in the right direction and have a fifty-fifty chance of hitting whatever she aimed at.

Eben had fallen asleep in the pew beside her, and he now snorted loudly in his sleep and woke himself up. Julianna and the boys giggled as every head in the congregation turned to look at their father, and in spite of herself, Emma stifled a laugh. She nudged Eben in the ribs and he flushed, and for a moment she almost managed to convince herself everything was fine, and nothing untoward had occurred in the last twenty-four hours.

She knew better, though. The trouble with Rufus Tarwater wasn't over, and her family was in danger until she figured out a way to deal with him.

*   *   *

Unlike his mother, Michael Larson wasn't thinking much about Rufus Tarwater that Sunday morning. Michael had been very worried the day before, but the shock of the confrontation with the big man on the porch was gradually wearing off, and he was feeling more like himself. Knowing that Emma had a loaded gun in her handbag was particularly reassuring, all the more so because she had proven herself to be a crack shot as they were practicing the previous night. Eben had purchased a matched set of revolvers at the general store, and after supper they had all gone out behind the barn to learn how to use them. Michael had taken his turn with the weapons, as had Eben, Seth, and Julianna, but none of them save Emma had shown any aptitude as marksmen. Julianna and Seth both missed the big Folger's coffee can on the fence post ten times in a row, and Michael and Eben fared only slightly better, no matter how close they were to the fence or how many bullets they wasted. Emma, however—to Eben and Julianna's delight, and the envy of Michael and Seth—became more accurate each time she tried, and by the end she was pinging the can again and again, even from as far away as twenty-five feet.

The main reason, however, that Michael wasn't dwelling on Rufus that Sunday morning was because Sarah Ann Bowen kept turning her head to smile at him from across the aisle in the church.

The dating pool in Pawnee, Missouri, was severely limited, so Michael had little experience with girls. Be that as it may, he still knew enough to know he very much liked Sarah Ann Bowen, and he also knew how very much he wanted to see her naked. He'd imagined many times what she would look like without her dress; just catching a glimpse of her long black hair and dimpled chin was enough to make him cross his legs, flush the color of rust, and stop breathing. She was only a year younger than him, and she was the prettiest girl in town by far.

Does she want to see me naked, too? he wondered.

The flush on his face deepened as he considered this, and he squirmed a little in the pew between his brother and sister. The church felt intolerably hot all of a sudden, and he couldn't wait for the service to end.

Maybe I could ask her to come swimming with me in the pond when no one else is around.

He knew this would never happen, of course; the fishpond behind their house was in plain view from the back porch, and he'd never find a way to meet her without somebody seeing them. But the mere thought of sliding into the cool water with her, wearing nothing but their skin, was so delicious he almost couldn't bear to let it go.

Julianna leaned close to whisper in his ear. "Sarah Ann uses pig manure for toothpaste, Michael," she murmured. "I swear to God, her breath smells worse than an outhouse."

Michael was jarred from his pleasant reverie and glared over at her. "Shut up," he whispered back.

Michael's infatuation with Sarah Ann Bowen had not gone unnoticed; both Julianna and Seth—overjoyed at being given the rare opportunity to provoke their normally easygoing middle brother—had been teasing him unmercifully for the past few weeks whenever they caught him mooning over her.

Seth bent his head to address Michael's other ear. "Sarah Ann keeps looking at me," he breathed. "Think she'd let me play with her titties if I asked nicely?"

Seth already had a girlfriend in Hatfield named Hessie Trotman—aka "Hussy Trollop" to Michael and Julianna—and Michael knew full well that Seth wasn't the least bit interested in Sarah Ann. He also knew that both Julianna and Seth would only torment him further if he reacted badly, but he couldn't help getting mad anyway.

"Sure," he hissed back. "Hussy let me touch hers just last night, so I guess it's only fair."

Emma Larson, alerted to her children's misbehavior by the frowns of fellow worshippers in the surrounding pews, put a warning hand on Julianna's knee and wagged a finger at her sons and daughter. All three straightened immediately and resumed staring at the minister with attentive expressions. Emma kept her hand on Julianna's leg as a precaution, knowing her brood would likely resume their whispered conversation the instant she dropped her guard.

Temporarily saved from the taunts of his siblings, Michael gratefully returned to daydreaming about Sarah Ann, and all the wonderful things they might do together if he could only get her alone.

Seth Larson was a natural-born worrier, but he, like Michael, was feeling much better that morning than he had the day before. Seth's improved outlook, however, owed less to the revolvers Eben had purchased than it did to Emma's phone conversation with Sheriff Burns. According to Emma, the sheriff had promised to speak to Rufus Tarwater, and had also sworn to "keep a close eye" on the man for the next few days until Rufus's volatile temper had cooled. Seth wasn't foolish enough to believe there was no longer any danger, but he trusted Burns to do what he said, and was relieved somebody in authority had been apprised of the situation. He felt that not even a dumb son of a bitch like Rufus would be so stupid as to try anything when he knew the county sheriff was watching him. Besides this, everybody who had seen Julianna that morning as she entered the church had noticed her bruises right away and were openly indignant after hearing what had happened; the news would spread quickly, and if Rufus decided to try something else, somebody was sure to see him coming and would either show up themselves or send help to deal with him.

A fly landed on a cowlick in Michael's short blond hair and Seth automatically brushed it away. Michael didn't notice; he had resumed gawping at Sarah Ann Bowen and couldn't spare attention for anything else. Seth caught Julianna's eye and grinned, and she shook her head with a disconcertingly adult-like amusement.

Seth and Julianna had never had any problem getting along, but until lately Seth hadn't felt as close to his sister as he did to Michael. Over the last few months, though, Julianna had begun to mature at an almost alarming rate, and every time he saw her now she seemed to be a finer, more interesting person. There was a new look in her eyes, a curiosity and a directness, that reminded him of their mother, and when she spoke she sounded smart and thoughtful, just like their dad. Seth supposed she'd always had these qualities, but the four-year difference in their ages had kept him from really noticing it before. It was as if she'd been a little girl for fifteen years, and then bloomed overnight into an attractive, intelligent young woman.

His good humor slowly faded as he studied her face. Her bruises looked puffy and painful, and he found himself getting furious all over again as he remembered how she'd cried out when Doc Colby reset her broken nose. He understood why Eben had made them let Rufus go, but he couldn't help thinking it was a huge mistake to do so. Eben was the wisest man he knew, but in this case he'd been too fair-minded and forgiving by far, in Seth's opinion. Seth almost wished that they'd gone ahead and killed Rufus when they had the chance; he and Michael could've pinned the miserable bastard to the side of the house like a big, ugly moth, and put an end to him once and for all.

He became aware that Julianna was watching him. Her face had softened as his mood darkened, and she now gave him a reassuring smile, as if she knew exactly what he was thinking. Seth blinked in surprise, then noticed that his little brother was looking at him, too. The goofy, love-struck expression on Michael's face had completely vanished, replaced by a concern that made him, too, seem more like an adult than a teenager. Michael had always been attuned to Seth like this; whenever Seth was troubled he would show up and sit beside him in silence, just like this, for however long it took for Seth to work through whatever was bugging him.

Michael and Julianna both had Eben's unsettling green eyes (as did Seth), and they looked very much alike, with long freckled noses and sharp, high cheekbones. Seth's throat closed as he gazed at them, sitting side by side. He wasn't normally sentimental, but every once in a while the unquestioning, routine love he felt for his brother and sister flared up inside of him, intense and startling, like a torch in the dark. His eyes began to sting, and he looked away quickly to hide what he was feeling.

Rufus better stay the hell away from them, he thought.

The drone of the minister's voice had lulled Eben Larson to sleep again. It was a troubled nap, though, and not just because he was sitting upright on a hard wooden pew in a stifling church. Eben had not slept any easier the night before; Rufus Tarwater had disturbed his dreams, and was disturbing them again that morning. In this particular one, Rufus was sitting on his horse in front of their house, just as he had done after striking Julianna. Where Rufus's eyes should have been were two black, cavernous holes, and when he opened his mouth to say something, his words were lost in the sound of a savage, corrosive wind.

Eben awoke with a start, once again, to renewed giggling from his children and another jab in the ribs from Emma. He shook his head sheepishly and sat up straighter to avoid falling asleep a third time, and he pondered the fading fragments of his nightmare with a pounding heart. It was all he could do to stay seated; every nerve in his body was telling him to take Emma and the children and get as far away from northern Missouri as fast as possible. His eyes flitted around the room, and he half expected to see Rufus lurking in the corner, watching them at that very moment. Rationally, he knew Tarwater never came within a mile of the church except to beg food or money from the minister, but the sick feeling in his stomach was overmastering his customary reasonableness.

He looked down to find that Emma had taken his hand in her own. She was watching the stuffed owl in the rafters, not him, but her fingers were tight and warm in his, and very strong. Her free hand was resting on Julianna's knee, and even as disquieted as Eben was, the wry symbolism of this image didn't escape him—Emma as the link between himself and his children, Emma as the link between himself and everything he cared about. He squeezed her hand back just as tightly, and his heart-beat gradually returned to normal.

She'll know what to do if Rufus comes back, he thought.

Eben held to his wife's hand in gratitude, as if it were a life-line. Part of him was embarrassed that she was so much braver than he was, but he was an honest man, and thought it silly to pretend otherwise. Emma always knew what to do; it was one of the reasons he loved her as much as he did.

Everything will be fine, he told himself, trying to believe it. *Everything will be just fine.*

Julianna Larson was more at peace that morning than any-one else in her family, even Michael. Her face still hurt from being punched, of course, and she was still seething over what Rufus had done to their dog. But the fear she'd felt yesterday on the porch was gone. She was surrounded by family and friends, and it was a bright, hot summer morning, and she refused to have her good mood spoiled by a sorry excuse for a man like Rufus Tarwater. Her father had told her she could drive the Model T home after church, and Seth had promised to help her fix a broken drawer on her desk that afternoon, and Ben Taylor was coming to supper that night. After dark, too, was going to be fun; Ben would no doubt join her and her brothers in the hayloft to look at the stars through Michael's telescope.

It was going to be a perfect, wonderful day.

She remembered watching her mother shoot one of the new revolvers last night, standing by the barn with her squat, slightly bowed legs rooted to the earth and her arms as steady as tree limbs as she aimed with two-handed, deadly accuracy at the cof-fee can. Rufus was a big man, but he wasn't bulletproof, and if he tried anything stupid, Emma Larson would deal with him faster than he could say "Amen."

"Amen," echoed the minister, finishing his sermon.

Chapter 7

"I'm going to stop for gas," Jon said, pulling into a Phillips 66 service station on the outskirts of the torpid town of Sedling Falls, New York, less than twenty miles from the Pennsylvania border.

Elijah had been dozing in the passenger seat and he sat up, blinking at the bright light above the fuel pumps. "Already?"

He wanted to get much farther from the dairy farm before stopping, even though they had been driving for nearly four hours straight, excluding a quick piss break on the side of the road some miles back.

Jon nodded, too exhausted for more of a response. There was no gas gauge on the Beetle's dashboard, but he figured they had to be almost empty by this point, even if they'd started with a full tank. His buddy, Tommy—from Toby's Pizza Shack in Tipton—had owned a Volkswagen similar to this one, and Jon knew from experience the only way to tell when it was out of gas was to wait for it to lose power and die on the road. Flipping a switch on the dash would activate a reserve tank and maybe give them enough juice to get to a station, but it seemed smarter to refuel now while they had the chance.

"Thirty-one cents a gallon?" Julianna exclaimed in the backseat as Jon turned off the engine. "That's extortion! No wonder Daddy always has gasoline delivered to the house instead of going to the filling station in Bethany!"

An attendant who was about Jon's age stepped from the station and began walking toward them. As he got closer Jon could make out greasy blond hair and a pasty complexion.

"Shit," Elijah whispered, digging in his jeans pockets. "What are we going to do for money? All I've got is a couple bucks."

Jon glanced over his shoulder. His plastic bag with the stolen cash in it was on the seat beside Julianna, next to the groceries she'd looted from Bebe Stockton's refrigerator.

"I've got it covered," he muttered.

As the attendant approached Jon's open window, Julianna leaned up between the seats to get a better look at him.

"Who's that?" she hissed. "He's not the usual boy who works here."

The kid bent down to speak to Jon. "Fill 'er up?" He glanced over at Elijah and visibly recoiled.

"Yeah," Jon said, frowning. "Check the oil, too, would you?"

The attendant nodded, then his eyes flicked over to Elijah once more before he slouched to the front of the Beetle to fill the tank. Jon turned to Elijah.

"What was that about?" he whispered. "You don't think he's heard about you on the news, do you?"

"Nah," Elijah answered quietly. He and the blond kid were keeping a wary eye on each other through the windshield. "He just doesn't like black people."

Julianna pursed her lips. "If that's the case, we should take our business elsewhere." She tapped Jon on the shoulder. "Let me out, Jon, will you? I want to stretch my legs."

Jon had told her his true name soon after leaving the dairy farm, but this was the first time she'd spoken it aloud. Elijah turned to her with irritation.

"How come you can remember *his* name but not *mine?*" he demanded.

She rolled her eyes as Jon, grinning in spite of himself, stepped out of the car and pushed the driver's seat forward to make way for her.

"Don't be difficult, Benjamin," she pleaded. "It's not funny anymore."

She squeezed out of the Beetle's backseat and stepped toward the station. The attendant called out that he was closing up for the night in just a few minutes, but if she needed the restroom it was on the left side of the building. She thanked him with a wave and disappeared around the corner.

Jon climbed back in the car. "Aren't you going to use the can, too?"

Elijah shook his head, staring after Julianna with a bemused expression. "I'm okay."

Jon reached back for his possessions with reluctance. He had been hoping the other boy would exit the car for a few minutes, because he didn't want to be forced to explain why he had so much money with him. He sighed as he worked at the knot in the plastic handles.

"I ripped off my boss this morning," he blurted. "I needed the money to run away, and I didn't have any other choice."

Elijah shifted in his seat to study him. He wasn't surprised by this information, but he didn't know what to say, either. A bead of sweat ran from his armpit down his side and he wiped it off his ribs, grimacing. The night was hot and sticky, and his skin felt as if it had a layer of oil on it.

"Is that why you lied about your name?" he asked at last.

Jon nodded. "Yeah." He paused. "Well, mostly. I also got a fourteen-year-old girl pregnant. Accidentally."

"Oh," Elijah said. He looked away, blushing. Sex was still a deeply unsettling topic for him, even though wet dreams and masturbation had been a regular part of his life for the past two or three years. His father, Samuel, had not yet chosen to have a father-son conversation with him (to the dismay of Elijah's mother, who did all the laundry, and had secretly been at Samuel for months to "talk to that horny little man"), and since he had nobody else he could discuss such things with, he had been forced to glean what information he could from what other boys at school said to each other in the showers following gym class. Needless to say, the things he'd heard had done little to demystify the subject.

Jon finally got the bag open and removed a ten-dollar bill from the loose pile of cash resting against his copy of *Walden,* then he quickly retied the handles of the plastic.

"Can you pay the guy when he's finished?" he asked, handing the ten to Elijah and returning his belongings to the backseat. "I need to take a whiz."

He paused and wrinkled his nose before getting out of the car. Now that they had stopped moving and fresh air was no longer pouring through the windows, there was a sour, unpleasant smell he hadn't noticed before that seemed to be coming from inside the Beetle.

"What stinks?" he wondered, turning his head and trying to track the scent. "It smells like spoiled milk in here or something."

Elijah blushed harder. "I think it's my shoes," he muttered. "I threw up on them."

"You did what?" Jon squinted at Elijah's formerly white sneakers, trying to see them in the shadows under the dash. "When did you do that?"

Elijah stared at his lap. "At the dairy farm."

His stomach rebelled at the memory of the dead woman on the floor of the house, and it was all he could do to keep from vomiting yet again.

Jon winced. "You should wash them off, man. They'll just get worse if you don't."

Elijah knew he was right, but he also knew he couldn't bear to remove his shoes in a gas station restroom.

God only knows what kind of germs are on the floor in there, he thought.

"Is there a hose or something I can use outside?" he asked desperately, scanning the brick walls of the station. The majority of the little building was a dark blur, well out of the range of the circle of light surrounding the pumps.

Jon shrugged and opened the door to get out again. "I dunno. Ask the guy."

Elijah made a face and mumbled something. Jon didn't hear what he said and asked him to repeat it.

Elijah bit his lip and spoke louder. "He won't let me use it, even if there is one."

Jon raised his eyebrows. "Why the hell not?"

Elijah didn't bother to reply. The attendant was still shooting hostile glances at him every few moments, and the reason for this seemed to Elijah like the most obvious thing in the world.

Jon waited a minute, at a loss, then finally appeared to grasp the problem. He cleared his throat, feeling uncomfortable and naïve. "You could still clean them off in the bathroom sink. That would work just as well."

Elijah looked horrified. "I can't," he whispered. "What if there's pee on the floor, and I accidentally stand in it while I'm not wearing shoes?"

Jon gaped at him. "Are you shitting me?"

Elijah dropped his gaze to the ten-dollar bill in his hands and began twisting it. "No, I just mean what if I have a cut on my foot or something, and there's some kind of disease in the pee? Couldn't the germs get into my blood?"

Jon closed his eyes and rubbed his temples. *Oh, for Christ's sake,* he thought. *He's as much of a nutcase as Julianna.*

"Give me your goddamn shoes," he ordered, scowling. "I'll do it."

Dealing with someone else's puke was not appealing, but Jon had a strong stomach; he had two younger brothers, after all, and when they were little and got sick he had helped his mom clean them up more times than he could count.

Elijah's face fell. "I didn't mean that," he protested. "I just meant . . ."

"It's okay," Jon interrupted. "The guy's going to close the station in a minute, and I'm not going to sit in this stupid car for the next four hours with your goddamn shoes smelling like *that*." He gestured impatiently. "We're in a hurry, so just give them here."

Elijah was speechless. This was the sort of thing his parents would do for him, but for anyone else to make such an offer was unthinkable. He knew he should refuse, but there was no way he could perform this foul chore himself, and he couldn't come up with an alternative plan. He felt terrible, yet he was deeply moved by the older boy's generosity. He gawked at Jon's waiting hands and swallowed, then reached down to tug off his sneakers.

"Socks, too," Jon said tersely. "They must stink just as bad."

Elijah nodded, not trusting his voice to speak. He peeled off his socks and tucked them in the shoes, then passed the whole evil-smelling pile to Jon, who accepted it without comment.

"Thank you," Elijah rasped.

Jon got out of the Beetle and closed the door, but a second later he stuck his head back through the window. "Keep an eye on my stuff while I'm gone, okay?"

It was almost full dark outside when the policemen's flashlight beams crisscrossed the blackened, limbless lump of Bebe Stockton's body in the smoldering ashes at the Stockton Dairy Farm. Chuck Stockton—who had been out making deliveries in the boonies, and returned to a yard swarming with emergency personnel and a hellish inferno where his house should have been—had managed to maintain his composure while watching the fire consume the last of his home, but the moment Bebe's corpse was spotted, he crumpled to the ground and became incoherent.

Bebe's body was unrecognizable, of course, and it would be the following morning before the police could sift through the wreckage to recover her soot-coated wedding ring. Chuck knew it was Bebe, though, the instant he saw her lying there; there was something horribly familiar about the mound of burned flesh, and he needed no further proof to accept that the worst had occurred. He had to be led away from the site by his neighbors, leaving the police to speculate in vain as to the whereabouts of the Edsel's driver and passengers.

The fire trucks had arrived in time to save the barn and the milk house, but they'd been too late to do anything at all for Chuck and Bebe's residence. The blaze Julianna had set was fast and fierce; in less than an hour the entire house was reduced to a charred ruin, and there was nothing to do but wait for the coals to be fully extinguished. The fire marshal, a man by the name of Orville Horvath, deemed it unsafe to remove the body until first light, and so it would be the following afternoon before Bebe's autopsy revealed she had died of a blow to the head, rather than burning to death as first thought. Because of the abandoned Edsel on the highway, however, foul play was suspected from the outset of the investigation.

This being the case, officers had combed all the other buildings on the property, even as the house fire was still raging. The broken padlock hanging from the barn door piqued their curiosity, of course, but since Chuck was not yet home when they entered the barn—and none of them knew the dairy owner well enough to be aware of his most prized possession—the absence of the lime-green Volkswagen Beetle escaped their notice. Orville Horvath had fully intended to ask if anything was missing when Chuck came screeching up the driveway in his milk truck, but Chuck refused to move away from the fire until he knew the fate of his wife, and after Bebe's body was revealed he was too distraught to answer questions for well over an hour. Horvath tried several times to get him to talk, but Chuck simply stared at him, as if Horvath were speaking in tongues.

Hence the reason no one began to hunt for a missing 1957 Beetle until almost eleven o'clock that night, when Chuck at last recovered enough to inspect the barn with Horvath. Unfortunately, the theft of his beloved, erotically charged automobile hit the grieving widower almost as hard as the loss of Bebe. It was a devastating double blow, and nearly the death of him, too.

Many people had believed Chuck and Bebe to be a laughable mismatch. Chuck was tall and whip-thin, with a sparse, white mustache and stooped shoulders; his disposition was gruff and dour, and he seldom socialized with anybody. This aversion to company extended even to his own daughters. Chuck was fond of his girls, as he had been of his son, too, before the boy's death in the war, but to be honest he had never given his kids much thought. He had a limited supply of love, it seemed, and was unwilling to share his small stockpile with anyone but Bebe. Bebe's flightiness and forgetfulness were a constant source of aggravation to him, yet he'd find himself smiling at her sometimes, for no reason, and his heart always lifted a little bit when he'd come home in the evenings and see the light shining from the kitchen window.

He had fallen in love with her the moment he'd met her at an auction, decades before. She had been hovering around a table of glass figurines, and Chuck, surrendering to an odd, carnal impulse, had purposely bumped into her as he was strolling by. She had blushed and giggled, then scurried off with her friends, and he had watched her go in stunned silence, still able to feel the softness of her body where it had connected with his. He'd shown up on her porch the next day, carrying the small glass swan he'd seen her ogling at the auction. She'd flushed with joy and then burst into tears seconds later, overwhelmed to be courted by this earnest and attractive stranger, with such an obvious flair for gift giving. He didn't care that she was silly and sentimental, nor that she was his polar opposite in almost every way imaginable.

All he cared was how she made him feel when she touched him.

It was the kind of touch, he believed, that could make the blind see or the lame walk, and for the first time in his life he felt whole, and healed. Before that moment he had not even known he was sick. Yet this supernatural, restorative touch of hers was all too fleeting; he found he needed it every day to reclaim his sense of well-being, and if he were away from Bebe for too long he began to wilt, like a thirsty rhododendron.

The only other time he experienced a similar sensation of peace and completion was when he sat in the driver's seat of the Beetle.

That he derived nearly as much sensual satisfaction from a Volkswagen as from his wife sometimes disturbed him, but not often. The truth was the Beetle reminded him of Bebe; their comely curves and undemanding, durable demeanors made them seem somehow related, like sisters, in his mind. Cheerful, solid, and unpretentious, neither required anything from him but patience and affection. He had never been attracted to glamorous women and sleek cars; elegance and grace were wasted on him. The only thing that fired Chuck's soul was reliability, and a certain coy vulnerability that Bebe and the Beetle each possessed in spades.

Chuck Stockton harbored no thoughts of vengeance for the barbaric, thieving criminals who had destroyed, in a matter of minutes, his entire reason for existence. If he'd returned home as they were committing their atrocities it would have been a different story, of course; but after the fact, vengeance was only a poor excuse to go on living, and as such he wanted nothing to do with it. In the suicide note he penned in the wee hours of Sunday morning, he asked to be buried with as many as possible of Bebe's ash-covered swans that had survived the fire. He wrote he had never liked the "silly damn things" in life, but in death he wanted something of Bebe's with him, and he supposed her beloved swans might be better company than most.

In the final conversation he had with Fire Marshal Horvath that evening, Chuck was told of the crime spree that had started in Prescott, Maine, and had proceeded to rip through his own home like a tornado eight hours later. He learned of the separate plights of Julianna Dapper and Trooper Lloyd Eagleton; he was informed that a young black man named Elijah Hunter was likely to blame for everything that had happened, and he was promised that everything possible was being done to bring the savage, depraved animal to justice.

He was also one of the very first people to hear the name of Elijah Hunter's equally bestial accomplice.

The underwear Jon Tate had so carelessly tossed aside by the tractor in the barn when changing his shorts and socks earlier that evening was an old set of boxers from his high school days. In his haste to return to the sunlight, Jon had forgotten that his mother, Marline—who believed high school locker rooms were full of towel-snapping, garment-stealing perverts—had sewn labels into most of his clothing, including his underpants, in an attempt to discourage theft.

Thus it was that Orville Horvath successfully identified the second most-wanted man in the northeastern United States. The names of Elijah Hunter and Jon Tate would soon be broadcast on every police radio and teletype machine from Maine to Pennsylvania, and pictures of the two boys—as well as their victims, living and dead—would begin appearing in newspapers and on national television newscasts by the end of the weekend.

Chuck Stockton was past caring about such things, however, and well before he'd finished speaking to Horvath that night, he'd decided to end his life as soon as he could arrange to be alone. At 4:00 a.m. on Sunday he left a note for his daughters in the guest room of his neighbor's house, and made his way on foot back to the dairy farm. Everybody had gone home by then, and he lingered undisturbed for a moment by the ruins of the house before moving over to the barn. He slipped through the open door, lifted a rope from the wall, and climbed the ladder to his hayloft. Straddling a beam for balance, he scooted out until he was directly above where the Volkswagen should have been, shortened the rope to an appropriate length, and began tying his knots. Securing the rope around the rafter was easy and quick, but his hands shook a bit, surprising him, as he tightened the noose around his throat.

Things didn't go quite the way he had planned, however.

In the moonlight streaming through the doorway, a stray black cat with long, matted hair and an erect, bushy tail cautiously padded into the barn. It looked up and froze when it saw Chuck sitting on the rafter above it, and Chuck froze, as well, not having anticipated a witness to his last moment on earth.

"Get out of here," Chuck rasped after a moment, breaking the silence. "Go on, scat!"

The cat flicked its tail once or twice, then casually sprawled on the dirt floor and began to clean itself, wetting a front paw with its tongue and using it like a washcloth to scrub its forehead and ears.

Chuck tugged at the rope around his throat, unable to get enough air to yell loudly.

"Get the hell out of my barn!" he rasped again with mounting frustration. "Leave me the fuck alone!"

The cat ignored this second croaked entreaty entirely, raising a back leg and arching forward gracefully to lick its anus.

"Goddammit!" Chuck choked out.

Chuck couldn't have said why he didn't want to commit sui-cide in front of a stray cat; all he knew was that he wanted the flea-infested, mangy thing *out* of his barn, right that very damn minute. He kicked his legs wildly, trying to frighten the stray, but it was too engrossed in what it was doing to pay the thrash-ing dairy man above it any attention.

Chuck finally managed to loosen the noose around his neck. Ripping the rope from his head in rage and filling his lungs for a properly intimidating scream proved to be his undoing, how-ever; he lost his balance and fell from the rafter, plunging to-ward the barn floor like a meteor. He landed badly, breaking both an ankle and a wrist, and the subsequent pain he felt was enough to make him howl so loudly that the black cat had no choice but to take him seriously at last, bolting through the open door and disappearing into the night. The patrolman as-signed to keep a close eye on the dairy farm was passing by at that very moment, and since the patrol car's windows were open, the accursed cat wasn't the only one who heard Chuck's yell of agony. The officer came to investigate and caught Chuck in the act of trying to re-climb the ladder in the barn, in spite of his in-juries, with a rope coiled around his shoulders. An ambulance was summoned, and Chuck was taken to the hospital, sedated, and put under close observation.

It had been a busy twelve hours at the Stockton Dairy Farm.

A few minutes past 2:00 a.m. (and a couple of hours before Chuck Stockton's attempted suicide), Samuel and Mary Hunter pulled into the driveway of the Stockton Dairy Farm and asked to speak to Fire Marshal Orville Horvath of the New Hamp-shire State Police. Chuck Stockton had vacated the premises long before the Hunters' arrival, on his way to spend the re-mainder of the night—or so Horvath believed—at a neighbor's house. Most of the emergency personnel had left, as well, but a few of Orville's underlings, grumbling and irritated at being kept so long at a site where they could do little real work until the sun rose, were still milling about with flashlights, halfheartedly inspecting the Edsel, the barn, and the still-smoldering wreckage of the house. The sky was crowded with stars, making flashlights almost unnecessary.

Orville Horvath was not an imposing man. He was five foot three and weighed slightly less than his pet rottweiler, Lucy (Lucy was 114 pounds, Orville only 112). His fireman's jacket and bright yellow helmet were too big for him; his knee-high boots made him look like a small child playing beside the ruins as larger, more adult-looking men in similar apparel performed grown-up tasks around him. His voice, too, was less than commanding; it was thin and high-pitched, and he tended to mumble.

He was also a man who loved his job a bit more than he probably should have, which was why he'd insisted on staying so late, even though there was really no point in keeping his men there so long.

Fire, and its aftermath, excited Orville. From the red, glowing cinder of a cigarette tip to the deafening hell of a forest conflagration, he could never get enough of it; fire was the one true love of his life. He had been married and divorced three times and scarcely remembered the names of his ex-wives, yet he could recall the details of every fire he had investigated for the past twenty-eight years. He was in the habit of putting himself to sleep at night by reciting the chemical compounds in soot, and the smoky aroma of an outdoor barbecue was enough to make him reach for his binoculars, hoping to catch a glimpse of his next-door neighbor's open grill through the hedge separating their lawns.

But fires resulting from arson were his favorites. Especially when there was an apparent homicide involved. It was torture to postpone his investigation until first light, when it would be safe to comb through the ashes and debris, and he knew that no matter how many aromatic hydrocarbons he recited that night in bed he'd get no sleep. It had been all he could do to conceal his impatience while consoling Chuck Stockton about the loss of his wife—even though he felt genuine compassion for the bereaved man—simply because he wanted nothing more than to sit by the ashes and think about the fire he had witnessed that evening. The dying tongues of flame, running low on combustible material, had licked lazily at the cement foundations of the house before at last surrendering to the water hoses of the fire trucks, and Orville had watched their flickering, sensual death throes with his mouth slightly open and his eyes narrowed into lustful slits.

Mary Hunter's first impression of Orville Horvath was not favorable.

"My son did not set fire to this house and kill that poor woman," she said, after the introductions were out of the way. "And if you think he did, you better put your dog here in charge of this show, because it has more brains than you do."

Lucy the Rottweiler went everywhere with Orville. Orville found her presence to be very comforting, and he enjoyed watching the fear she inspired in even the biggest of men. No one had ever dared to become aggressive with him when Lucy was at his side. In addition to her muscular frame and belligerent brown eyes, she also had a mouthful of jagged, yellowish teeth that could mangle an arm or a leg with a single snap of her jaws, like a bear trap.

Lucy began to growl, deep in her throat.

"Try it," Mary murmured, glancing down at Lucy with indifference. "You just come right on and try it."

Lucy abruptly ceased growling and sat on her haunches.

Orville blinked several times and resisted a peculiar urge to crouch beside his dog. "We have an eyewitness account of your son attacking a woman in that car," he said, pointing down the hill at the hulking shape of the stranded Edsel.

Sadly, this sentence did not come out as clearly as it might have. Orville's mumbling always worsened when he was nervous, so it sounded to the Hunters as if he'd said: "Weaven I wiz cunt you son-snacking woman thacker."

"I beg your pardon?" Mary responded coldly. She wasn't sure what Horvath's cryptic insult meant, but she didn't care for it one little bit.

Elijah is in even worse trouble than I imagined, she thought. She shot a grim look at Samuel, who was equally perturbed. He frowned back at her and raised his eyebrows, but he stayed silent, knowing it was best to let Mary handle the fire marshal as she saw fit.

Lucy the Rottweiler watched this exchange with confusion, swinging her massive head back and forth from Orville to the Hunters. She whined a little in support of her master, but appeared reluctant to offer any further challenge to the tiny woman confronting him.

Orville made another attempt to assert control. "There's also a report he assaulted a police officer this afternoon."

It was best to say these hard truths forthrightly, he found, rather than beat around the bush with the parents of criminals, who were always unwilling to believe their offspring could be capable of such things.

Mary's eyes narrowed. She could have sworn Horvath just said, "Salsa rubbery asshole tit up Lucifer the zephyroon."

"What?" she demanded. It wasn't just Orville's filthy mouth that enraged her; she also believed he was toying with her.

Orville cringed at the hostility in her tone, and Lucy all but prostrated herself on the ground.

At that moment a passing car on the highway screeched to a halt next to the Edsel, then lurched into the driveway where the four of them were clustered. Its glaring high beams made them wince as it approached; gravel crackled underneath its tires as it parked next to the Hunters' blue pickup. It was a Cadillac, Orville noted, shielding his eyes, and there appeared to be two large men sitting in the front seat.

Now what? he wondered, praying these new arrivals weren't related to the Hunter woman.

The Cadillac's engine stopped and its lights snapped off, leaving them all momentarily blinded. The doors opened and Lucy leapt to her feet with a relieved-sounding snarl, as if anxious to once again challenge somebody who behaved the way one was supposed to behave when facing a displeased rottweiler.

The two newcomers stepped from the car and closed their doors as sight returned to the tense little group watching them.

"I need to speak to the guy in charge," the driver of the Cadillac called out.

That would be my wife, Samuel Hunter thought, biting his lower lip to keep from saying the words aloud.

Orville raised a hesitant hand. "I'm Fire Marshal Horvath." Proclaiming his title in this manner made Orville feel more confident, and his speech became somewhat less garbled. "May I help you?"

"Shouldn't that dog be on a leash?" The Cadillac's passenger, an older man, was lagging behind his companion and eyeing the growling beast with obvious apprehension as they drew closer.

Mary Hunter sized up the two strangers, trying to determine if they might pose yet another threat to her son. The older man seemed harmless enough; his voice had been deferential, and his steps were fearful and wobbling as he approached the bristling rottweiler. He had a round, jowly face and a substantial paunch, and his bald head glistened in the starlight.

He looks like a walrus, Mary noted to herself.

The other man was even larger than his companion, but much of his bulk appeared to be muscle. He had wide, round shoulders and thick, sturdy legs, and he moved easily over the rough earth. He planted himself squarely in front of them, and there was something about him that disturbed Mary. He was close enough by then that she could make out his face. He was an attractive man, with sharp, regular features and probing, alert eyes, but he looked both angry and worried, and under a great deal of strain. She intuitively grasped he was there for a reason similar to her own, and this scared her more than she wanted to admit.

This man could be dangerous, she thought. *Someone he loves has been hurt.*

"Sit, Lucy," Orville ordered, responding to Edgar's query. The dog obeyed with gratifying haste. Orville glanced at Mary to see if she'd witnessed this demonstration of his authority, and was disappointed to find her glowering at the younger of the two strangers instead.

"I'm Mary Hunter, and this is my husband, Samuel," she said. Her tone was polite, but for some reason Orville got goose bumps on his arms listening to her. "Who are you?"

The driver answered, but he addressed Orville, clearly not understanding who the small woman was or why the fire marshal was deferring to her.

"I'm Gabriel Dapper, and this is Dr. Reilly," he said curtly. "My mother was attacked and kidnapped by the same two sons of bitches who did this." He jabbed a thumb at the ruins of the Stockton house.

Until he and Edgar arrived at the dairy farm, a part of Gabriel Dapper had still believed he might find his mother in time to save her, but he now realized, with a wrenching grief, that this wasn't going to happen. The savage thugs who had murdered Bebe Stockton and burned her house to the ground would also murder Julianna the instant they no longer needed her as a hostage. The ashes and rubble might just as well have been the cremated remains of Julianna's body, spread in mockery on the earth before him. He stared blindly at an overturned, blackened milk pail and fought to control his breathing as tears rolled down his cheeks.

"Hello, Gabriel. I'm pleased to make your acquaintance," the small black woman said quietly, "and I'm very sorry to hear about your troubles." She paused, sighing. "But regardless of what this *gentleman* here may tell you"—she indicated Orville Horvath with a disdainful flick of her wrist—"our boy wouldn't dream of hurting your mother."

She now had Gabriel's full attention.

"Your son was the one who took my mom?" he asked, stunned. The middle-aged black couple standing before him looked like ordinary, decent people; they didn't look to him like the type to raise a homicidal maniac for a child.

Mary shook her head firmly. "Our boy would *never* do such a thing," she said. "I don't know what's going on here, but I promise you Elijah is not to blame."

The flashlights of Horvath's coworkers were sweeping across

the front yard a few feet from the ruins of the front porch, nos-
ing for evidence in the badly scorched grass. A cow lowed
mournfully in the milk house, then fell silent again as Gabriel
studied Mary in the semidarkness, his throat working.

"Then what's he doing with my mother?" he asked at last, making no attempt to hide either his anguish or his skepticism. "Why
did those people this morning say they saw him attacking her?"

Mary held up her hands in a helpless gesture. "I don't know,"
she said. "All I can tell you is what I've already said: Our son
would not do any such thing. He's the sweetest, gentlest boy in
the world, and that's the God's honest truth."

Next to Gabriel, Edgar Reilly fumbled a cigarette from his
shirt pocket and stared with anxiety at the sad remains of the
dairy farm. Now that he'd seen the devastation firsthand, his
fears about Julianna's role in all that had occurred—and his
guilt for his part in her escape from the hospital—were beginning to overwhelm him. What if there really had been some kind
of colossal misunderstanding? What if the Hunter woman was
right, and her boy was somehow being made into a scapegoat
for crimes that Julianna Dapper had committed?

He tasted bile in his throat and came close to vomiting up all
the M&M's he'd eaten in the past few hours.

"Do we know any more about the other man who was seen
in my car with Gabriel's mother earlier tonight?" he asked,
lighting his cigarette with trembling fingers.

Surely Julianna couldn't be responsible for *everything*.

Fire Marshal Horvath's lips parted and he seemed to stop
breathing as he watched the sensuous yellow flame blossom on
Edgar's cigarette lighter. "The Edsel belongs to you?" he asked.

"Yes." Edgar released an unsteady stream of smoke from the
corner of his mouth and wished he'd brought some lemon drops
with him. "Julianna Dapper is my patient at the state mental
hospital in Bangor. She stole my car this morning before she was
assaulted."

"I see." Horvath glanced at the Hunters as if debating how
much to reveal in their presence. "We believe the second kidnapper's name is Jon Tate," he replied hesitantly, "but I'm

afraid that's all we've been able to learn. The state trooper who was run over by your car this afternoon is still unconscious, and he's the only one who's actually seen him."

"How do you know this Tate person's name, then?" Mary Hunter interrupted.

Horvath answered even more reluctantly this time. "We found his underwear beside the tractor in the barn," he muttered.

Mary raised her eyebrows. "You found his underwear." The sarcasm in her voice was lacerating. "Is there some sort of national underpants registry I'm not aware of?"

Horvath flinched and his speech became indecipherable. "The wise Manhattan ate egg!" he blurted, confusing Edgar mightily.

Mary's face froze. "You had best shape up, mister," she grated. "And I do mean right now."

The menace in her words conspicuously frightened Horvath, and Edgar sympathized with the man, even though he had not understood whatever it was the little fire marshal had mumbled, nor why it had angered Mary so. His own throat had gone a little dry from simply observing Mary's demeanor, however, and he was very grateful she wasn't upset with him.

"The waistband had a name tag!" Horvath now squealed with exaggerated clarity, stepping backward a full two paces.

Gabriel Dapper shook his head in frustration. "Can we stop chitchatting about *underwear*, for Chrissake?" He rounded on Mary, giving up on Horvath. "If it wasn't your son who attacked my mom, then who was it?" he demanded. "Where was your kid when that cop got run over, and where was he when this place got burned to the ground? Where is he now? If he's as innocent as you say he is, why doesn't he just turn himself in?"

Gabriel knew he was badgering Mary but he couldn't help it. Samuel Hunter—obviously not liking the way Gabriel was behaving toward his wife—opened his mouth to intervene but Mary shook her head slightly, stopping him.

"As I said before, we're just as much in the dark as you are," Mary answered Gabriel calmly. "Elijah has never gotten in any trouble in his life, and if you knew him you'd understand just how ridiculous it is to suspect him of being behind any of this. He could no more set fire to a house or run over a police officer than he could jump over the moon."

Edgar Reilly was only half listening to the conversation. He'd just remembered the bags of junk food he'd purchased that morning on his way to the hospital, and he was wondering if Julianna had left them in his car. When he and Gabriel had arrived at the dairy farm and seen the Edsel sitting on the highway, he'd been too upset by the damage to his beautiful, powerful automobile to think of anything else. The Edsel's shattered rear window and crushed bumper had made him gasp aloud in sorrow, as if its injuries had been inflicted on his own body. But now that he'd absorbed the initial shock of that tragedy—and been subjected to the far graver spectacle of the ruined farmhouse— he badly wanted to see if he could at least salvage a 3 Musketeers bar from his battered vehicle to help soothe his nerves.

"Orville?" One of Horvath's subordinates, Dick Gopp, called to the fire marshal from the darkness of the front lawn. "We've got something over here."

"What is it?" Orville responded, looking delighted to have an excuse to turn away from the tension between Mary and Gabriel.

"Just an empty soda bottle," Gopp said. "Should I bag it for prints? It looks like it was far enough from the fire to not get tons of shit all over it."

"Bag it," Orville answered shortly. "But then let's knock off for tonight, shall we?"

Gabriel broke in on Orville's conversation. "So are they on foot, Horvath, or did they steal another car?"

Orville turned back to them with an anxious expression on his face. "Where's Dr. Reilly?" he asked, in a transparent attempt to evade Gabriel's question.

Neither Gabriel nor the Hunters showed any interest in Edgar's whereabouts; all three of them remained silent and unmoving, like models in a tableau. Lucy the Rottweiler, however, had been tracking Edgar's progress down the hill toward the

Edsel all along, and seemed to believe Orville had just commanded her to follow him. She darted down the driveway to obey, her heavy paws skittering on the gravel.

Orville attempted to call her back, but Gabriel stopped him by asking his question again, oblivious to the dog's swift departure. "Do they have a car or not, Horvath?"

Mary stepped closer to Orville. "Answer him," she hissed.

"We think they took Chuck Stockton's Volkswagen," the little marshal stammered immediately. "It's a green 1957 Beetle, but we have no idea where they've gone."

"JESUS CHRIST ALMIGHTY, GET IT OFF ME, GET IT OFF ME!"

Edgar Reilly's petrified screams came from the vicinity of the Edsel, at the base of the hill. In the soft glow of the starlight, two large forms could clearly be seen running in frenzied circles around Edgar's car. One was Lucy, growling and snapping in fury; the other was the pudgy psychiatrist, sprinting for his life with what looked to be only inches between his meaty thighs and the dog's jaws.

"OH FUCKING HELL SAVE ME SOMEBODY PLEASE GET IT THE HELL OFF ME!" Edgar yelped.

Gabriel Dapper barely even noticed Edgar's plight. Now that he knew what vehicle the kidnappers were driving, the only thing he was interested in was where they might be headed.

"Do you know where your son is taking my mother?" he asked Mary as Orville began to whistle frantically for Lucy.

"JESUS FUCKING CHRIST WOULD YOU PLEASE GET THIS FUCKING DOG OFF ME!" Edgar wailed from the highway.

"You're not listening to me, Gabriel," Mary replied impatiently. "My son isn't taking your mother anywhere. I believe *she's* taking *him.*"

Orville Horvath at last managed to get the rottweiler's attention. Tantalizingly close to catching her prey, Lucy broke off her pursuit with visible reluctance; Orville had to call her name four more times before she finally bounded back up the hill, looking disappointed. Edgar dropped to the ground by the Edsel, clutching his chest and retching.

"You can't really be serious!" Gabriel snapped at Mary the instant Orville stopped yelling. "You're actually accusing my mother of kidnapping your son?"

"It makes far more sense to me than *him* kidnapping *her*," Mary said.

"And just how is she supposed to have accomplished that?" It was all Gabriel could do to keep from screaming. "In case you haven't heard, my mom doesn't even have a clue where she is, or what she's doing! How in God's name do you think she managed to kidnap an eighteen-year-old kid—"

"Fifteen," Mary corrected.

"—who's probably a lot bigger and stronger than she is? Those two eyewitnesses this morning SAW your goddamn kid attacking her, for shit's sake, not the other way around!"

Mary's eyes narrowed into slits. "Swearing at me won't help your mother, or my son," she said icily, supremely uncowed by Gabriel's burst of temper. "So you may as well stop your huffing and puffing this instant."

"I'll swear at whoever I want to, goddammit!" Gabriel fired back. "You need to wake up and smell the coffee, lady!"

She raised her eyebrows. "Oh? And just what exactly do you think it is I'm missing?"

"That your son has gone off the fucking reservation, that's what! Isn't it obvious?"

In Sam Hunter's memory, he had never seen a man less afraid of his wife than Gabriel Dapper. Mary's face was as cold and forbidding as a dead moon; anyone else Sam knew would have frozen solid by now under her gaze. But if Mary herself noticed that Gabriel wasn't responding in the normal way to her considerable powers of intimidation, she gave no indication.

"No, it is *not* obvious," she said. "And I will not allow you or anyone else"—her eyes briefly bored into Orville Horvath before returning to Gabriel—"to pin these crimes on Elijah based on the say-so of two strangers and a whole bucketful of guesses.

So how about you just cool your jets, mister, before you make things worse than they already are?"

Gabriel bit back a scathing retort, but only barely. He badly wanted to keep raging at the small black woman, but something about her that he couldn't quite put his finger on made him think twice about it. As upset as he was, he was also forced to acknowledge, at least to himself, that at least part of what she was saying was true: He was indeed rushing to judgment. He took several deep breaths and forced himself to speak with less hostility.

"I'm sorry," he muttered awkwardly. He met Mary's eyes and grimaced. "I didn't mean to swear at you, but my mother is missing, and I don't know how to help her. It's making me a little crazy."

Mary watched his face for a long moment before answering. "There's no need to apologize, Gabriel. To tell the truth, I feel exactly the same way."

Gabriel blinked at the sudden compassion in her voice, then looked over at his Cadillac, his chin trembling. "I think I need to be by myself for a minute," he rasped abruptly. "Will someone please come get me in my car if you hear anything?"

"Of course," Mary answered. "Of course we will."

Gabriel thanked her and turned away quickly, and Mary, Sam, and Orville watched him return to his Cadillac. Orville was called over to the barn to speak to one of his men just as Edgar Reilly rejoined the Hunters in the driveway by the ruins of the house.

"That stupid damn dog should be euthanized," Edgar whispered in indignation, watching Lucy the Rottweiler trot along beside Orville.

The lime-green Volkswagen with New Hampshire plates passed just north of Mansfield, Ohio, at 2:12 a.m. that same Sunday morning. Julianna was at the wheel by then and singing quietly to herself as Jon and Elijah slept; the hills and deep valleys around them were filled with phantoms and shadows, lit only by the stars and an occasional lonely porch or bathroom light from otherwise dark farmhouses beside the highway. Elijah's socks and sneakers were in the small space behind the rear seat of the Beetle, drying, and the car smelled like unwashed bodies and leftover meatloaf. Elijah, shirtless and shoeless, was in the front passenger seat, his head resting against the window. Jon was curled up in the backseat and snoring lightly, though he kept waking every few minutes to shift position, unable to get comfortable.

"There's a place in my mem'ry, my life, that you fill," sang Julianna. The song was called "Mother Machree," and it was another of her father's favorites. *"No other can take it, no one ever will . . ."*

Chapter 8

Chuck Stockton's beloved Volkswagen Beetle made several surprised, plaintive choking noises and then died on the road a little after 4:00 a.m. on Sunday, shortly after crossing into Indiana from Ohio. Julianna was driving, and her dismayed cry of "Oh!" awakened both Elijah and Jon.

"What's going on?" Elijah asked, scrambling upright in the passenger seat and blinking rapidly. The Beetle coughed once more before lapsing into silence, like a mortally wounded man gasping out a farewell to a grieving spouse.

"The main tank's empty," Jon said, sticking his head between the two front seats as Julianna wrestled with the wheel to bring them safely to the side of the road. Jon's neck was stiff from being curled up in the confines of the backseat and he felt stupid with sleep. "We've still got the reserve tank, but that's only good for thirty miles or so."

He stared out the windows into the darkness and swore under his breath when Julianna flipped off the headlights. They were on a deserted highway with nothing but the stars to see by. He twisted in his seat to peer through the small oval rear window, searching in vain for a hint of human habitation. He could detect a faint brightening in the eastern horizon, but it was only the first suggestion of the coming dawn, still an hour or two away.

"Why didn't we stop to fill up someplace?" He couldn't hide

the irritation in his voice, even though he knew Julianna wasn't really to blame for this.

She probably thinks she's in a fucking covered wagon, he thought. *It's my own damn fault for not staying awake.*

Julianna turned her head to look at him mildly. "I think there may be something wrong with your car, Jon."

She didn't say what else she was thinking, of course, but she believed her father's automobile was far superior to this slow, uncomfortable vehicle of Jon's, and she regretted the necessity of leaving the Model T behind at the Millers' Dairy Farm.

Jon rubbed his eyes and sighed. His mouth was dry and his breath tasted sour. He knew it was futile to press Julianna for answers, but he couldn't think what else to do. "Have we passed a gas station recently?"

She frowned. "Since Mullwein, you mean?"

"Mullwein?" Jon asked, perplexed. "Where's that?"

"In *Iowa,* silly." Lines appeared on her large forehead. Both boys were staring at her as if she were speaking a foreign language, and it was unsettling her. "Right where it's always been. We filled up there ages ago."

Julianna pondered the last few hours on the highway with a sudden feeling of vertigo. She remembered stopping to urinate next to the railroad tracks somewhere between the last gas station and wherever they were now, but that, too, seemed as if it had occurred quite some time in the past. The creases on her forehead grew more prominent and she turned to Elijah. "Shouldn't we be home by now, Ben? Mullwein is only thirteen miles from Pawnee."

Elijah's heart had slowed again after the initial panic he'd experienced when Julianna had cried out and awakened him. He studied her long, elegant face and could see her confusion as she tried to puzzle out the inconsistencies in whatever story she was telling herself about their journey.

"We're a long way from Iowa, Julianna," he said quietly. "You're not where you think you are."

"But how can that be?" Her eyes probed his. "Did I take a

wrong turn somewhere?" Her frown deepened. "I *know* we filled up in Mullwein, but I'm afraid I may have gotten us badly lost since then."

No shit, Jon Tate thought. He forced himself to speak patiently as he made another attempt to reach her rational mind. "You didn't happen to notice if we went through any towns in the last half hour or so, did you?"

She shook her head. "I haven't seen anything resembling a town in forever." She bit her lip and faced front again, visibly troubled. "Just where do you suppose we are?"

Jon grimaced at the back of her head. "East Bumfuck," he mumbled in frustration, too softly for her to hear. He reached for a Pepsi in the paper bag by his feet and spoke to Elijah. "So where do you think the closest gas station is? Should we keep going straight, or turn around?"

"Home is that way," Julianna asserted, pointing west through the windshield. "I know that much for certain."

This was the first time Elijah had seen Julianna questioning her own skewed perceptions; her version of reality seemed to be in a serious state of flux, and he couldn't help but wonder what was going through her head. He continued watching her in fascination as he answered Jon's question.

"I don't know," he said. "I was asleep, too, but I don't think we've gone through a town for a while. I probably would've woken up."

"Yeah," Jon agreed, prying off the bottle cap with a seatbelt latch. "Me too."

He supposed he should be grateful Julianna hadn't known about the reserve tank on the Volkswagen. If she had, she might have flipped the tank switch and burned through their emergency fuel, too, while he and Elijah were sleeping, and they might never have known they needed gas until it was too late to do anything about it.

His bladder felt uncomfortably full, but he didn't really like the idea of getting out of the car to pee. If a cop happened by while they were pulled over it could lead to disaster; the last thing they needed was to arouse the suspicions of some over-vigilant state trooper working the late shift by allowing him to set eyes on Elijah—or worse, have a conversation with Julianna. Still, it was hard to take such a scenario seriously. It didn't seem likely the police in this part of the country would have information about them quite yet, and even if they did, the rural highway they were on was as devoid of traffic as the surface of the moon.

He took a swig of Pepsi and nudged the back of Elijah's seat. "Let me out, okay? I need to take a leak before we go on."

Elijah opened the door and all three of them squinted and winced as the dome light came on. Julianna opened her own door a second later and got out quickly, stretching her back before moving away from the car, murmuring that she, too, needed to "use the ladies' room." The night was hot and sticky, but the outside air was much fresher than the air in the car, and Jon took several grateful breaths as Elijah gingerly stepped out on the gravel shoulder in his bare feet and tugged the seat forward to allow Jon to get out, too. Jon wiggled free of the car and walked a few feet away for privacy; in the predawn stillness of the Indiana countryside he could hear his companions already urinating as he unzipped his fly.

"Maybe you should drive for a while, Jon," Julianna called out from the opposite side of the narrow highway. "I must be more tired than I thought."

"I think that's a really good idea," Elijah murmured from somewhere by the rear of the Beetle.

Jon, yawning, heard the worry in Elijah's voice about Julianna and simply nodded, forgetting that the other boy couldn't see him in the darkness. They'd closed the doors on the Beetle after getting out, extinguishing the dome light, but the stars provided enough illumination for him to make out a telephone pole surrounded by tall grass on his left, and what appeared to be a snow fence not far from the shoulder of the highway. With his free hand he took another gulp of warm Pepsi and looked up at the night sky, listening to himself pee. A slight breeze blew through his hair and rustled the corn in a nearby field; he thought he could hear an owl hooting somewhere for an instant before it quieted again. In such a bucolic setting it was hard to come to terms with the idea that his world had fallen apart in the past twenty-four hours; the fear and dread that had consumed him ever since his parents and Becky Westman's folks had come crashing into his apartment almost seemed as if it belonged to somebody else.

He allowed himself to pretend for a moment he was just on a camping trip with friends, and there was a roaring fire and a full cooler of beer waiting for him once he finished emptying his bladder.

We'll roast some hot dogs and get drunk, he thought, *and when we wake up in the morning we can all go back home.*

He pictured himself working a double shift at Toby's Pizza Shack, then returning at last to the silence and peace of his own living room. His favorite chair would be there waiting for him, and a book, and when he flicked on his reading lamp it would create a small, cozy cocoon of light, just for him, like a spotlight on a stage. The shadows would be herded into the corners of the room and held at bay until he finished reading, and after that he'd have a beer or two and go to bed, where he'd sleep for twelve blissful, dreamless hours, safe from fire, bullets, pregnant girls, and lunatics.

"Oh, for heaven's sake!" Julianna exclaimed in disgust, disrupting his fantasy. "I must have taken a left instead of a right at the Iowa state line! That explains *everything!*"

Jon zipped up his pants wearily. Thinking about beer had made him crave some; he wished he'd asked Julianna to buy him a case somewhere earlier that night. She probably would have said no, he supposed, but he should have asked her to do it anyway.

I could've just told her it was ketchup, if she'd asked, he thought. He felt a surge of despair rise in his throat about the absurdity of their predicament. *She wouldn't have known the difference anyway.*

He shook his head and hawked up a loogie on the highway.

"Jesus," he whispered, turning around to go back to the car. "What am I doing here?"

He'd only gone a few steps when Elijah's subdued voice came from less than a foot away from him, close to the front bumper of the Beetle.

"Jon?"

Jon jumped, startled. The younger boy's skin was so black Jon could barely make out his silhouette in the darkness.

"Jesus, Elijah!" Jon gasped. "Don't scare me like that!"

"Sorry." Elijah hesitated. He'd heard Jon's despairing whisper a moment before and didn't know what to say. He'd intended to share his apprehension about Julianna's apparent instability, but now it seemed like the wrong time. He scratched at a mosquito bite by his belly button and tried to get a better look at the older boy's face.

"Are you okay?" he finally asked.

Behind them, Julianna opened the driver's door and crawled into the backseat. The door was still open, and the Beetle's lime-green paint looked pale and sickly in the faint glow of the dome light shining on its hood through the windshield. She began singing softly to herself as she waited for them; the words *"If you're happy and you know it, clap your hands"* floated out out of the Beetle as the two boys stood together in the night.

Jon made a face and tossed the Pepsi bottle in the ditch. "Yeah, everything's just hunky-dory, man." He stared with ill-humor at Julianna through the glass. "I've never been better in my whole fucking life."

He was ashamed of the childish self-pity in his voice, but he couldn't seem to do anything about it. He tried to apologize, but Elijah cut him off.

"It's okay," he said. "I'm not feeling so hot, either."

Jon raised his head. In the scant light, Elijah's face was drawn tight with worry; his skinny, naked torso looked gangling and defenseless, and he was balanced precariously on the sides of his feet, cautious of the gravel under his unprotected soles. Something about him, though, seemed to have changed from the last time Jon had looked closely at him. For one thing, he was carrying himself differently; his hands were no longer jammed in his pockets but hung loosely at his sides, and he was meeting Jon's gaze instead of staring at the ground.

"Hey," Jon said, surprised. "You're taller than me."

Elijah smiled shyly, but still didn't drop his eyes. "I grew close to half a foot this last year. I'm almost as tall as my dad now."

Jon tried to return the smile. "My dad and me are exactly the same height. Mom keeps calling us twins because I look just like him." His smile crumbled as he recalled his last encounter with Earl and Marline Tate, and bitterness crept back into his tone. "I guess I won't hear her say that again anytime soon."

He stared at the car bumper, hoping Elijah hadn't noticed the tears running down his face.

Stop being such a goddamn crybaby, he chided himself angrily. *It doesn't help ANYTHING.*

Elijah had seen Jon's tears, and he felt an answering sorrow rise in his throat. He, too, was thinking about his parents, and the hell they must be enduring right at that moment because of him. He had to find a way to call them, soon; they were probably going out of their heads with worry. He cleared his throat and struggled to control an unwanted quiver in his chin.

Headlights suddenly appeared in the distance, coming from the west. Both boys started in fear, gaping down the highway at the approaching car. It was still a good mile off, but they scrambled to get back inside the Beetle before the driver of the other vehicle could get a good look at them. Jon dove behind the wheel seconds before Elijah fell into the passenger seat, yelping in pain from the rocks he'd stepped on in his rush to get there. They slammed their doors simultaneously and Jon fumbled for the switch that would transfer gas from the reserve tank into the Beetle's engine.

"Don't be a cop, don't be a cop, don't be a cop," Jon breathed. He knew the panic he was feeling was irrational, but he couldn't shake the feeling that, cop or not, anybody who was out on the road at that hour and saw them would know who they were and what they'd done. He flicked on the headlights as the other car drew close, to keep whoever it was from seeing into the Volkswagen.

"If you're happy and you know it," Julianna sang, oblivious to the tension her friends were feeling, *"then your face will surely show it . . ."*

"Duck your head, man," Jon ordered Elijah, talking over Julianna and reaching for the ignition key. The Beetle came back to life with a gratifying growl. "If somebody knows to look for us, you're the one they'll want the most."

Elijah obeyed Jon without hesitation. The other car drew even with them before Jon could put the Beetle in gear; it looked to be a Rambler, not a police car, and although the driver turned his head to look at them, he passed without slowing, his face a pale blur.

Julianna abruptly stopped singing and sat up.

"What's Fred Marcy doing out so late at night?" she asked, her eyes following the taillights of the Rambler. "If he doesn't get home soon, his wife will skin him alive." She faced front again, feeling much more like herself now that she'd solved the mystery of why they weren't back in Pawnee yet, where they belonged. "You don't know Esther Marcy like Ben and I do, Jon," she continued. "But she's got a frightful temper. She once caught poor old Fred making eyes at Alice Boswell at the Fourth of July picnic, and she dumped a whole pitcher of iced coffee in his lap, right in front of everybody! Remember that, Ben?"

Elijah was badly shaken. The random encounter with the other car, though harmless in itself, had reminded him just how much danger they were in. His concerns about Julianna and Jon had distracted him, and until the Rambler's approaching headlights had intruded on his conversation with Jon, he had actually forgotten that even the routine act of stopping to pee on a remote highway now posed a significant threat. It would have been an ugly, unfair coincidence for a cop to show up right then and there, of course, but considering their recent history anything was possible: They simply couldn't afford to be so careless.

I need to get my head out of my ass and quit acting like a douche bag! he told himself angrily. He still didn't know what a douche bag was, but he knew he'd been behaving like one.

Julianna leaned forward. "Ben?" she prodded, sounding anxious. "Didn't you hear what I said?"

Elijah sighed, pulling himself together. "Yeah." He was still bent over in his seat with his forehead on the dashboard. He sat up again with an effort. "Sure I remember that picnic, Julianna. I laughed so hard I crapped my pants."

He glanced over at Jon and they stared at each other for a moment in silence. Jon raised his eyebrows at him and a second later both of them began to grin in spite of themselves.

"Language, Ben," Julianna reminded, lightly flicking Elijah's ear with an admonitory forefinger. "We'll be home again soon, and if your mother hears you talking like that she won't let you out of your house for a year."

It took every ounce of Jon Tate's remaining self-control to keep from cackling like a madman. *Maybe I'm nuts, too,* he thought. *Maybe I've been in the asylum with Julianna this whole time, and I'm just hallucinating. Maybe some doctor snuck some drugs into our pureed potatoes during supper, and I'm really strapped in a wheelchair someplace watching an episode of Gunsmoke.*

"She's right, Elijah," he murmured in a strained voice. "You could get into a lot of trouble for that sort of thing."

Elijah actually laughed aloud. It came out as more of a sob than a chuckle, though, and it died quickly. "Yeah," he agreed, wincing as he rubbed his ear. "If I'm not careful I might even get my mouth washed out with soap."

Both boys attempted to hold on to their grins a little longer, but it was no use. They each took a deep breath at the same time, and let the air slowly out of their lungs in a synchronized sigh that only Julianna found amusing. Elijah looked out the passenger window as Jon put the Beetle in gear and pulled back on the highway.

Dr. Edgar Reilly looked out the passenger window of Sam and Mary Hunter's blue Dodge pickup, whistling softly between his teeth. His whistle was almost inaudible, but the tune he had chosen was familiar enough to both Sam and Mary that neither had any trouble identifying it from the few snippets of melody they could pick out above the hum of the tires on the pavement.

Edgar Reilly often whistled "I'm a Little Teapot" without being aware he was doing it. All of his staff at the mental hospital in Bangor were familiar with this quirk, though none of them could have said for sure what provoked it. Connor Lipkin (the nearsighted Jungian) had postulated to the others more than once that it was likely only an unconscious attempt to alleviate stress, but Nurse Gable (who had known the good doctor longer) contended it went deeper than this, and was almost certainly a nervous reaction to repressed feelings of inadequacy. Jeptha Morgan (the freckled young orderly who was new to the hospital and unaccustomed to the nuances of psychoanalytical thinking) had only heard Edgar's rendition of the teapot song once, yet argued forcefully it indicated nothing beyond a "shitty taste in music."

In this case, all three diagnoses would have been accurate.

The current round of sub-tonal whistling had begun shortly after Edgar realized he was taking up nearly half the pickup's ample seat. The Hunters were conspicuously trim and neat, and as such required little space for themselves. The two of them together, in fact, were more compact than Edgar by himself, and no matter how tightly he wedged himself against the passenger door to allow Sam and Mary more room, he still felt flabby and intrusive. Mary's request that he not smoke heightened his discomfort, as did the lack of air conditioning in the truck, yet it wasn't until Edgar made his fourth attempt to share his M&M's with Mary—and was rebuffed, yet again—that his lips parted to emit their first soulful, sibilant lament.

Sam Hunter had also declined to accept any candy (with a polite but firm "No, thank you"), but it was Mary's nonverbal rejections that Edgar found particularly unsettling. He sensed no judgment of him per se in these refusals, yet there was still something hurtful to him about the curt, disinterested shake of her head, something distancing and remorseless, that made him feel the need to conceal just how many M&M's he was consuming. To his own chagrin, therefore, he had begun to sneak them from his pocket, one by one, and pop them into his mouth whenever Mary's head was turned. It was a distressing stratagem on many levels, but the most vexing aspect was that Edgar could no longer alphabetize the chocolates by color before eating them. And as this lessened his enjoyment of the entire snacking experience to a remarkable degree, Edgar couldn't help but resent Mary for putting him in such a position. To be forced to engage in such a childish subterfuge was humiliating, and far beneath his dignity as both a doctor and a man.

I'm projecting, he scolded himself, palming an M&M in his left hand (much as Julianna Dapper had concealed her caplets of Thorazine in the dementia unit). *She's not forcing me to do anything.*

He knew this was the case, yet the more he tried to reason away his resentment, the more influence it gained over his psyche. Mary's inflexible behavior had begun to feel like an ascetic, sugar-free gauntlet, flung down on the seat between them, and he found himself taking it personally.

Maybe she just doesn't like chocolate, he speculated. Air hissed through his two front teeth. *Or maybe she's too worried about her son to eat anything at all.*

It was a little past four in the morning in upstate New York. Fire Marshal Orville Horvath and the Stockton Dairy Farm—where Chuck Stockton would soon make an unsuccessful attempt to hang himself—were ninety miles behind them, Gabriel Dapper was following them in his Cadillac at a hundred yards' distance, and Julianna and her two "captors" had just finished urinating under a starlit sky somewhere in eastern Indiana. Edgar knew nothing of Chuck Stockton's suicidal intentions, of course, or the whereabouts of Julianna and her companions, yet he still had more than enough to occupy his attention without also obsessing over Mary Hunter's unwillingness to respond to his overtures of friendship.

I'm behaving like a lovesick boy who's just been spurned by the most popular girl in school! He flushed at this heartless self-assessment. *What in God's name is the matter with me?*

He squared his shoulders and peered manfully through the

windshield, reminding himself there was no time for such foolishness. Lives might well depend on him in the coming hours, and the only thing that truly mattered was to find Julianna before she hurt herself or anybody else, and return her safely to the hospital.

His hospital, where people wouldn't dream of brushing aside whatever kindnesses he wished to bestow.

The key to Julianna Dapper's psychosis, he believed (attempting to ignore Mary as much as she appeared to be ignoring him), was already in his grasp. It clearly had something to do with all the people Julianna had spoken of time and again in the past month. Her parents and two older brothers figured prominently in many of the remarks she'd made, but many other names seemed almost as important—the young boy "Ben," for instance, whom she never failed to mention. The selective nature of her memories regarding these individuals who had once been dear to her made for a fascinating case study in itself, but the problem was that Edgar had no idea how much of what he had gleaned from her was rooted in fact, and how much was sheer fantasy.

Thus far, he had not been able to confirm the existence of the town of Pawnee itself, nor a single soul she had referred to. This by itself wasn't necessarily a reason to discount her tales, however. The events she described had occurred (ostensibly) nearly four decades ago, and a tiny town such as the one Julianna said she came from might have changed names or been assimilated into a neighboring community in the intervening years, and its citizens, too, would have been swallowed by time, a world war, and God knew what else. Nevertheless, since Edgar had been able to learn nothing useful about Julianna's early life from any of her coworkers and friends in Bangor, he was forced to question almost everything she'd said.

Oddly enough, Gabriel Dapper, too, possessed little knowledge of his mother's childhood—or so Gabriel had explained to Edgar early on in Julianna's treatment. She had always been closemouthed about her past, even with her son, and the most she had been willing to share was that she had grown up on a farm in Missouri, and that her parents and brothers had died long before he was born. Whenever Gabriel pushed for more information, however, she changed the subject, or became cross with him and abruptly ended the conversation. She was apparently just as taciturn about Gabriel's father, and Gabriel had long since given up asking the kinds of questions he knew would only cause her pain.

Edgar's mind drifted again.

The M&M's are a metaphor of some sort, he thought irrelevantly, pursing his lips as his inner demons renewed their assault on his peace of mind. *Perhaps I'm seeing them as a symbol of a shared spiritual journey, which would explain why Mary's rejection feels so emasculating.*

Edgar's "shared spiritual journey" with the Hunters had begun an hour and a half earlier, when he had worked up the nerve to speak to the black couple in the driveway of the dairy farm while Fire Marshal Horvath was over by the barn and Gabriel was sitting alone in the Cadillac. Edgar was still out of breath from Lucy the Rottweiler's vicious attack, and from the hike back up the hill in the pale moonlight. His growing suspicions about Julianna's role in her own kidnapping—and the subsequent house fire—were also contributing to his breathlessness; he was trying to work up the nerve to share these concerns but didn't quite know how to broach the subject.

"That stupid damn dog should be euthanized," he'd rasped, hoping the Hunters would be willing to respond to this conversational gambit.

Sam and Mary had turned to him. Mary's tone wasn't harsh when she spoke, but neither was it welcoming. "What can we do for you, Dr. Reilly?"

Edgar had clasped his hands in front of his waist and looked furtively around the yard before answering. Orville and his underlings were all out of hearing range, yet Edgar instinctively lowered his voice.

"I believe I may know where to look for your son," he'd blurted.

The Hunters' dark eyes had fastened on him with an intensity that made his mouth go dry. The naked, desperate hope he could read on their faces tugged at both his heart and his conscience.

"How is that possible?" Mary, too, had spoken in a whisper. Her voice and gaze were unwavering but her narrow shoulders trembled ever so slightly. "What do you know that we don't?"

"It's only a guess." Edgar fidgeted, choosing his words with extreme care. "But I think ... well, it's certainly possible, that is, though not necessarily the case at all ... but I think Elijah may actually be ... well, he just *might* be taking Julianna home."

This hadn't been exactly true, of course, but Edgar allowed himself the little white lie, not yet willing to overly implicate Julianna in all that had occurred.

"You think Elijah is doing *what?*" Mary's voice rose enough to alarm Edgar, but she'd regained control of her emotions quickly. She glanced at Sam for several long moments, then at last turned back to Edgar. "You don't think our son kidnapped Julianna," she said bluntly. "You think *she's* the one calling the shots."

The quickness of her perception alarmed Edgar; he'd thought it safer not to answer.

"What do you mean, Elijah is 'taking Julianna home'?" Sam had demanded, struggling to keep up. "Why would he do that?"

Edgar looked away, feigning an interest in the ashes of the farmhouse. "I'm not sure," he said. He had felt their eyes probing the side of his face and he began to squirm. "Perhaps he's just being a good Samaritan," he muttered.

Mary had snorted. "I don't believe that for a moment," she said, "and I don't think you do, either, Dr. Reilly." She glanced down at the forlorn shadow of the Edsel on the highway, with its nose pointed due west. "But if you're right about where they might be headed, then they're going the wrong way, aren't they? We were told Julianna lived in Bangor before she got sent to the funny farm."

Edgar didn't care for the phrase "funny farm," but he'd decided it was wiser not to scold Mary for using it. He faced the Hunters once more and shook his head, relieved to have a question he could answer without prevaricating.

"Julianna has no memory of her life in Bangor." He wanted something to soothe his nerves but his fingers hovered indecisively between the cigarettes in his shirt pocket and the candy in his suit coat. "That's why I think it's far more likely they're on their way back to where she grew up. She thinks her home is still there."

Orville Horvath's high, reedy voice called out in the night, telling his subordinates to pack up for the night, but the Hunters and Edgar had barely heard him.

"And where exactly is that?" Mary's lips barely moved.

"A little town in northern Missouri called Pawnee," Edgar had answered.

The wind stirred restlessly, as if something were troubling its sleep. The few remaining coals in the ruins of the dairy farmhouse had flared up, and the firemen and officers on the lawn behind them began moving across the trampled and scorched grass. Inexplicably, the hair on the back of Edgar's neck stood up as he watched the men drift toward the Hunters and himself like ghosts in a graveyard. The officers' flashlights began snapping off in the darkness as they passed by without speaking on the way to their cars; two or three went out at the same time, but the others flickered off within seconds, too, leaving only the moonlight and the stars to see by.

Sam, too, appeared to be unnerved by the spectral scene, but if Mary felt a similar unease, she didn't show it.

"Why didn't Gabriel say something to us about this?" She'd paused, her dark eyes studying Edgar with disturbing shrewdness. "And why aren't the two of you already on your way to Pawnee, if that's where you think you can find Julianna?"

Edgar was growing more ashamed of himself by the second; his fear of inviting a lawsuit by admitting what he suspected about Julianna now seemed both self-serving and cowardly.

"I haven't told him yet," Edgar mumbled, sweating through

the back of his suit coat as he'd glanced over at the Cadillac. He could see Gabriel's dark form sitting behind the steering wheel, huge and motionless. "I didn't want to say anything until I was more certain."

Mary Hunter had reached an opinion by then about the type of person Edgar Reilly was. She was far from impressed, yet she was nonetheless thankful he had chosen to speak up at last—and that he'd approached her and Sam before telling Gabriel Dapper. If Gabriel had found out earlier, he'd likely already be halfway to Missouri by now, and she and Sam would've had no chance to run interference for Elijah.

She'd searched the darkness again to make sure no one could hear them. She could see the outlines of tiny Orville Horvath and the massive rottweiler still standing by the doorway of the barn, but all the other men had already left or were in their vehicles and pulling away down the driveway.

"Very well," she'd said at last, turning back to Edgar. "I'm assuming you didn't say anything to the fire marshal for . . . similar reasons?"

Edgar nodded, looking sheepish. "Should I tell him now, do you think?"

Mary pursed her lips. "My son got shot at by the last policeman he saw, Dr. Reilly," she said. "There's blood in your car, and for all we know Elijah may have been badly hurt. As far I'm concerned, the police don't need to know a God-blessed thing."

Her voice was soft, but there was something in it that had made Edgar's tongue cleave to the roof of his mouth. Unable to reply, he'd nodded ardently, just to make certain she knew where he stood.

The three of them had walked over to the Cadillac and broken the news to Gabriel. Gabriel rolled down his window as they approached, and Mary told him everything Edgar had just related to Sam and herself. Gabriel listened in silence until she was finished—his large, unblinking eyes intent on her face but also occasionally flicking over to an increasingly uncomfortable Edgar.

"Jesus Christ, Doc," Gabriel had murmured when Mary was done. "Don't you think this was probably something you should have mentioned?"

Edgar's hand drifted into his pants pocket and fingered a butterscotch toffee he'd been saving for an emergency. "I'm sorry, Gabriel. I didn't want to say anything because it was only speculation—and still is, by the way—but I was very wrong not to share what I was thinking with you."

Gabriel stared hard at the older man. "But you honest-to-God think my mother *knows* what she's doing?"

"No, no, I wouldn't go quite that far," Edgar said quickly. "I'm just saying that Julianna's psyche is very complicated, and she's under a great deal of strain." He glanced over at the smoking ruins and swallowed before continuing. "But we do know she already committed arson once, before she was committed to the hospital."

"That was completely different," Gabriel protested. "That was a garage, and no one got hurt. And Mom didn't have any idea what she'd done." He paused for a minute, stewing, then returned his attention to Mary as something else occurred to him. "Even if Dr. Reilly is right"—his face made it clear how much he doubted this—"it still doesn't explain what your son is doing with her. Why would he be *helping* Mom, after attacking her? What's in it for him? Why take her someplace he doesn't know anything about, halfway across the damn country? What about the other guy that's with them, for Chrissake?"

Mary had sighed wearily. "I don't have any answers, Gabriel," she said, "but what I *do* know is that we're not doing any good just standing around here, twiddling our thumbs." She put her hands on Gabriel's door and leaned down to look directly in his face. "So here's the deal. We're going to Missouri, and I think you should come with us." Gabriel began to interrupt but she talked over him. "I know you don't believe your mother has had any say in what's happened to her, but what if Dr. Reilly is right, and you're wrong? What if she's headed *exactly* where she wants to go?"

"It's just a guess," Edgar had demurred anxiously.

Gabriel made a sour face. "What if I'm *not* wrong, and we end up a thousand miles away from where we need to be?" His thick fingers had drummed restlessly on the steering wheel as anger resurfaced in him, making him want to lash out at the self-possessed woman leaning on his car. "What if your kid and his buddy have dumped my mother's body in a river someplace, and are now headed to Key West, or the Grand Canyon, or wherever the hell else they feel like slaughtering people?"

Mary had remained unruffled. "Then we can drive to Key West or the Grand Canyon *after* we check out Missouri." She paused. "Or do you have a better idea? If you do, I'll listen."

Gabriel's scowl had deepened. "It's a wild-goose chase, Mary." He saw the lines of fatigue etched around her eyes and spoke less harshly. "I'm sorry, but that's all it is. If you think that's what you should do, though, then who's stopping you? Go find Pawnee, Missouri, or whatever the hell it's called, and good luck to you. But if it's all the same to you, I'm going to stick around here until I hear something that makes more sense."

Mary had leaned in closer to the Cadillac. "I'd be happy to part company with you, Gabriel," she said bluntly. "You think my son is a killer, and that makes you dangerous. But if your mother—and I'm saying *if*, Gabriel, so please don't throw another hissy fit—*if* your mother is somehow forcing Elijah to stay with her, then we may need you to deal with her. She doesn't know Sam and me from Adam, and if we can't get through to her, there's no telling what we might have to do to save Elijah. The last thing on earth I want is to see your mother harmed, but what choice will we have if she won't let our son go? What will she make us do? Don't you think you should be there to help her through this?"

Mary's eyes were unblinking, and her quiet voice was hypnotic. Suddenly unsure of himself, Gabriel looked past Mary's shoulder at the blackened ruins of the house, his fingers still drumming (in seven-beat patterns) on the steering wheel. Mary had impulsively reached through the window and put her hand on his wrist. Her fingers were as small as a child's, but they were warm and strong as they gripped him.

"Please come with us, Gabriel," she'd murmured. "Your mother needs you, and so do we."

Edgar's original intention had been to drive his own car, but Mary and Sam had known without asking that the police would not release the Edsel to its rightful owner during an ongoing investigation. Since Gabriel was still visibly annoyed with him, Edgar thus found himself in the Hunters' pickup an hour and a half later, missing the comfort and power of the Edsel and obsessing over Mary's apparent disdain for him and his M&M's.

Edgar now looked over his shoulder, squinting through the rear window of the cab at the headlights of the Cadillac tailing them.

"Gabriel is still there," he murmured unnecessarily.

Sam nodded to acknowledge Edgar's observation, his eyes flicking to the rearview mirror and then back to the road. Mary just kept staring straight ahead, though, as if she hadn't heard.

Edgar sulked, feeling snubbed.

Would it kill her to eat just ONE fucking M&M?!! he fumed, resting his arms on his belly as he stared out the window.

Chapter 9

Sal Cavetti gazed through the windshield of the Volkswagen Beetle parked alongside the gas pump at his father's service station and composed, on the spot, a free verse poem:

"A naked-breasted, narcoleptic Negro and a weary, willowy white boy a-snooze in bucket seats." Sal paused, putting both hands on the Beetle's hood and leaning as close to the windshield as he could get. "In back, a fey-faced female slumbers like a dehydrated daffodil," he continued, "waiting for the sunlight's wet kiss to re-blossom her maternal milky momhood into wakefulness."

Sal was the sole employee at the only gas station in Wainwright, Indiana. He was twenty-nine years old, had a ponytail and a luxurious red beard, and often referred to himself, without a trace of irony, as "the Allen Ginsberg of eastern Indiana."

It was 8:47 a.m. on Sunday, and Sal had breakfasted that morning on three walnut brownies, each laced with a substantial amount of marijuana. Marijuana was a reliable muse for Sal, but he could already tell this Sunday morning in June was going to be particularly productive.

"White-black-white, like a Wonder Bread Chocolate sandwich," he intoned. "A sweet snack for the eyes, boy-girl-boy in a stubby lime-green car. The glue-bond of spirit-love lies between their somnolent, sun-dappled souls like invisible mayonnaise."

Jon Tate opened his eyes and saw a hairy, beer-bellied giant of a man in jeans and a dirty white T-shirt looming over the Beetle, staring in at them and apparently talking to himself. The man's face was close enough for Jon to get a good look at a small forest of hair sprouting from his large nostrils.

Jon recoiled. "Jesus Christ!" he yelped, flailing his arms and legs.

His seat was reclined back a few inches and he scrambled to find the knob to bring it to its normal position again. Elijah stirred in the passenger seat and Julianna raised her head and blinked in the hot sunlight.

They had pulled into Wainwright at a little after 5:00 a.m. that morning, running on the fumes of their reserve tank. After noting the business hours sign on the service station door, they'd decided to wait until it opened at nine, assuming they would find no other filling station open before then within range of their remaining fuel. The entire downtown area of Wainwright was less than two blocks long, with no city hall, sheriff's office, or streetlights in evidence, so it seemed unlikely they'd draw attention to themselves. After Jon turned off the engine, all three of them had promptly passed out and slept through the sunrise, with the windows on both doors cracked wide for air.

"Wake up, you guys!" Jon demanded, finally getting his seat upright. "We've got trouble!"

He had his hand on the ignition key, ready to make a run for it, but even though the red-bearded stranger in front of the car was still leaning on the hood and gazing in at them with an unsettling intensity, Jon hesitated.

Why is he grinning like that? he wondered, unnerved.

Elijah came fully awake in an instant and also jumped in fright. Sal's head was less than a foot away from the windshield by this point, and his smile reminded Elijah of the wolf character in the picture book of *The Three Little Pigs* his mother used to read to him when he was a child.

"What the hell?" he hissed, frantically seeking his own seat knob. "What's wrong with him?"

Julianna sat forward. "I think it's Larry Badder," she said, frowning uncertainly at their scruffy observer. "But Larry's beard is black, isn't it?"

Sal continued beaming in at them all, admiring the contrasting colors and contours of their alarmed faces, framed perfectly by the windshield. "A trinity of touring tellurians watches me," he extemporized, "as if I, and not they, were a portrait hung in the museum of man." This image so delighted him he began to chuckle with pride at his powers of invention. "Who is the painter? Who is the painting?"

Sal Cavetti had grown up in Wainwright, but had left home to attend college in Indianapolis as a philosophy major. Midway through his freshman year, though, he'd happily stumbled upon his true calling as a poet (at the very same party where he was introduced to his herbal muse) and dropped out of school to work for his father at the family gas station. He found the work much to his liking; pumping gas and performing oil changes left his mind free to wrestle with the universal nature of man, and he thought himself the luckiest person in the world—if still sadly undervalued as a poet. His father, especially, seemed incapable of acknowledging Sal's gifts, but Sal took no offense when Benito Cavetti referred to his son's poetry as "the most God-awful crap I've ever heard." Sal knew the hallmark of poetic genius was to be unappreciated, and he also knew that his father and the rest of the world would one day sing his praises.

"Good morning," he said, raising his voice so the three strangers in the Beetle could hear him. A crow sitting on the fender of his dad's tow truck across the parking lot caught his eye, and he took a few seconds to delight in its sleek black feathers before remembering what else he'd intended to say. "You folks need gas?"

Jon and Elijah glanced at each other as the man straightened again and removed a key chain from his pants pocket. As he shuffled over to unlock the padlock on the fuel pump, both boys slowly relaxed.

"I guess he works here," Jon breathed to Elijah. "For a minute there I thought we were in deep shit." He unrolled his window all the way and stuck his head out. "Can you fill it up, please?"

Sal nodded, looking forward to inhaling the gas fumes. "I'll check your oil, too."

Julianna brightened. "Yes, that's Larry," she said. "I'd recognize that voice anywhere."

Jon opened his door and stepped out onto the asphalt parking lot. He groaned as he stretched, turning from one side to the other to crack his spine.

"Do you have a bathroom?" he asked.

Sal glanced over at him affably. "Yep. I'll have to open up the station first, though. It's inside." He stared at the padlock in his hand, then at the gas pump, and lastly at the front door of the station. "An earth-child ambles through an orchard of possibility," he rhapsodized, "plucking choices like immaculate apples from serpent-bejeweled trees."

"What?" Jon asked, his face going blank.

Elijah opened his door, as well, and turned to face Julianna. "Could you hand me my shoes, please?" He indicated the space behind the backseat, hoping his sneakers and socks had dried enough by now that he could wear them.

Julianna began to do as he asked but then halted and made a face. "Oh, you! You know full well you didn't bring any shoes with you today, Ben Taylor. Stop teasing me."

"Oh, for God's sake," Elijah muttered.

"I'm a poet," Sal explained patiently to Jon by the gas pump. "I'm the Allen Ginsberg of eastern Indiana."

Jon blinked. "Oh." He chewed on his tongue to keep from laughing.

Julianna's expression soured in the Volkswagen. "Ginsberg is entirely overrated," she whispered to Elijah. "Anybody who says differently should have his head examined."

Elijah froze. He'd been preparing to step from the car and let Julianna out so he could crawl into the back and retrieve his shoes, but he'd forgotten what he was doing the moment she spoke. He stared at her over his shoulder.

Julianna's young girl persona had withdrawn again, ousted

by the older and far more mature woman Elijah now assumed was the "real" Julianna. Not only was her voice lower and more decisive, but her face had grown sterner, and her back had straightened, too, adding a striking elegance to her posture. For the first time since Elijah had known her, she looked at ease in the formal green dress, as if she wore such things all the time.

It's like she's got a short circuit, he thought, torn between apprehension and pity. *A wire gets jiggled or something and she's normal again, but only for a second.*

He couldn't imagine what she must be thinking during these flashes of sanity. Maybe some small part of her knew all along what was happening, and now and then it broke free, only to be trapped again by a waiting hand, and stuffed back into the cage of her madness. If there were only a way to keep her out of that cage for even a few minutes . . .

His pulse quickened.

If Julianna would just stay like she was now long enough to make a phone call, she could tell the cops what had been going on! They wouldn't believe Elijah or Jon, but they'd believe her!

"Why don't you like Ginsberg, Julianna?" he asked urgently, his fingers clenching the door frame. He couldn't have cared less about the poetry of Allen Ginsberg, but the newly awakened hope in his breast warned him not to change the subject until he was sure Julianna could focus on something more useful.

She toyed with a seatbelt latch and peered through the open door at the red and white gas pump. "It's not that I don't like him. I do." She closed her eyes and pinched the bridge of her nose, as if her head hurt. "But so many other poets out there are just as good as he is, and I feel he gets an unfair amount of publicity."

"Who do you like, then?" Elijah prodded, suddenly desperate to not allow her mind to slip away again.

She opened her eyes and met his gaze. There was an enormous, active intelligence in her expression; she seemed to be reading his mind and his heart at the same time. Elijah was certain she knew who he was, at last, and was going to tell him something that would make it possible for him to go home again, putting an end to all the sorrow and terror of the past twenty-four hours; he was barely able to contain his excitement.

She started to answer, but a wide yawn erased whatever she'd intended to say. She covered her mouth and shook her head, waiting for the yawn to run its course.

"I don't know about you, Ben," she said at last, smiling warmly, "but I could eat a horse."

Elijah almost bit through his lower lip to keep from screaming.

Meanwhile, Sal was still juggling his options at the gas pump. "Should I fill your car first, or let you into the restroom?" he asked Jon, feeling as if a little spur in the flanks from a nonliterary layman might be helpful. "Either way works for me."

Jon told him to fill the tank first and Sal nodded agreeably, removing the hose from the pump and making his way around to the front of the Beetle. He was moving in what seemed to be slow motion and Jon started to feel exposed again as a station wagon with two adults and three children, all staring at him, passed by on the highway.

"Don't worry about checking the oil," he said. "We're kind of in a hurry."

"Haste makes waste, daddy-o," Sal answered.

Elijah got out of the car and turned around to let Julianna out, too. The pavement was already hot under his feet as he moved away from the door to allow her to rise beside him.

"I wish we still had Daddy's car instead of Jon's," she murmured, wincing as she stretched stiff muscles.

Elijah slid into the backseat to get his sneakers. They hadn't dried yet but he put them on anyway, figuring he could take them off again after he'd used the restroom. He was tying the laces when Jon opened the driver's door and leaned in.

"Hand me my stuff, will you?" Jon indicated the plastic bag with his books and the stolen money on the floor behind the passenger seat. He lowered his voice and grinned. "Did you hear the gas guy say he thinks he's Allen Ginsberg?"

Elijah grinned back and passed the older boy his things. "Maybe we should get his autograph," he whispered.

Jon snorted. "Yeah, I'll be sure to do that." He shook his head, untying the bag handles. "Jesus, people are weird."

"What books are those?" Elijah had noticed the paperbacks when Jon had paid for gas at the last station, but he'd been too intent on the wad of cash at the time to get a good look at any of Jon's other possessions.

Jon removed his three treasures from the bag and lovingly fingered their spines. "*Walden, The Fellowship of the Ring,* and *Moby Dick.* I had to leave almost everything else in my apartment, but I couldn't stand to be without these guys." He put them back in the plastic, feeling oddly vulnerable. "Do you like to read?"

Elijah blushed a little, thinking about what he'd been reading lately and how much trouble his preoccupation with unpleasant news had gotten him into at home.

"Yeah," he said. "Mostly magazines and newspapers, though." He glanced involuntarily over at the window of the station, trying to see inside. "Do you think maybe they sell *U.S. News and World Report* here?"

His blush deepened as Jon raised his eyebrows. Before either of them could say anything else they became aware that the attendant and Julianna were talking by the pump as the bearded man returned the gas nozzle to its slot.

"My name is Sal, not Larry," he was saying. "Sal, as in Salvatore. But my pen name is Salvation. Salvation Onassis Cavetti."

Julianna made an exasperated noise. "Don't you start pulling my leg, too, Larry Badder. Did Ben put you up to this?"

Jon sighed. "We better get out there before she says something she shouldn't," he muttered. He dug around in the plastic bag and took out his toothbrush and razor. "Can you keep an eye on her when it's my turn in the john?"

Elijah nodded. "Sure." He looked over at the station again. He felt stupid for asking about a magazine; what he really wanted was a toothbrush of his own and some deodorant.

And a shirt, too, he thought belatedly. He was surprised at himself for almost forgetting to add this item to his wish list. Before the tragic events of the previous evening his partial nudity would have been foremost on his mind, but it hadn't even occurred to him to worry about it for quite a while. He tilted his head to sniff at an armpit and winced at the sour odor.

Jon smiled sympathetically. "Yeah, I'm getting pretty ripe, too," he said. "I doubt they sell much of anything here, but if they've got any BO juice I'll get us some." He paused. "We can see if they have magazines, too, I guess, while we're at it."

Elijah mumbled thanks.

The door to the station bathroom was flimsy and didn't latch properly, so as Jon brushed his teeth by the sink he could hear everything Elijah, Julianna, and Sal said out by the cash register. Sal had turned on a radio, as well; Jon hummed along with a Winston cigarette jingle ("Winston tastes good like a cigarette should") but winced as the advertisement ended and Shelley Fabares began crooning "Johnny Angel."

"Oh, for Christ's sake," he muttered.

For the past three months, one of the girls he'd worked with at Toby's Pizza Shack had serenaded him with "Johnny Angel" every time she saw him. He didn't care for the girl at all—she told stupid jokes and smelled like sauerkraut—and as a result he'd grown to detest the tune. He tried to blot out the sugary melody by focusing on Julianna's voice instead.

"Seth told me your cousin Annie just got engaged, Larry," she was saying. "Who's the lucky fellow?"

Jon wondered who Seth was. He spat out a mouthful of water, wishing he had some toothpaste.

"I don't have a cousin named Annie," the gas guy answered. His deep voice reminded Jon of a record player set at the wrong speed. "And like I told you before, ma'am, my name is Sal."

"And I'm the Queen of Sheba," Julianna replied with asperity. "I don't know why every boy I know has to be so difficult."

Jon grinned. He rubbed at the dark stubble on his chin but decided not to bother shaving since he didn't have any shaving cream. He'd been right about the station having little for sale; there wasn't even any coffee available. He tugged off his shirt and hung it on the doorknob over his plastic bag of belongings, then did his best to wash the stench and grime from his torso. It had only been about a day and a half since his last shower, but he felt as if he hadn't bathed in months. He ran water over his head, too, getting the floor and the toilet seat as wet as his hair, and for a minute he lost the thread of the conversation in the next room. When he turned off the faucet again, Julianna was in the middle of telling a story to Elijah.

". . . and then Larry's sister and I ate the whole jar of rock candy! We were sick for days."

"I don't have a sister," Sal protested. "Hey, do you guys want to hear one of the poems I wrote yesterday?"

"No, thank you," Elijah blurted.

"It's really good," Sal coaxed.

"I'd rather you didn't," Julianna said. "You know how I dislike those pornographic limericks of yours, Larry."

Jon laughed aloud. He was feeling better than he had in a while; the cold water had revived his spirits somewhat. He dried himself with a handful of coarse paper towels, then mopped up the water on the floor and the toilet seat. The bathroom was tiny but surprisingly clean for a gas station; the only graffiti on the wall was a neatly written sentence beside the mirror that read: *For a good time, call your mom.* The nine o'clock news broadcast mercifully replaced Shelley Fabares on the radio, and Jon tossed the towels in the trash and retrieved his soiled shirt from the doorknob. He started to put it back on, but on a whim decided to wash it instead and let it dry in the car. Snatches of the news broadcast caught his ear as he ran the shirt under the faucet: President Kennedy was vacationing on Cape Cod; the Tigers and the Yankees were playing a game that night at Tiger Stadium.

Elijah knocked on the door. "Jon? I have to pee pretty bad."

Jon reached over to unhook the latch. "Come on in," he said, opening the door. "I'll be done in a sec."

Elijah blinked, embarrassed to find Jon partly undressed. "Sorry," he mumbled. "I didn't mean to rush you."

Jon turned off the faucet. "It's cool." He wrung out his shirt in the sink, then shook out the wrinkles in the fabric and stepped around the other boy. "It's all yours, man."

"You forgot your toothbrush and razor," Elijah said.

"I left them for you." Jon reclaimed his bag from the doorknob. "I know it's kind of gross to share a toothbrush, but it's better than nothing, right?"

Elijah's stomach churned at the very idea of using someone else's toothbrush, but he was nonetheless touched by Jon's generosity. "Thanks," he muttered, trying to hide a grimace as he handed the toiletries over. "I'll just use my finger."

Jon shrugged, unoffended. "Sure. We'll buy some stuff for all of us the next place we stop."

Julianna watched Jon emerge from the bathroom, closing the door behind him, and she flushed a little, admiring the loose fit of his khaki shorts around his slender waist. Thinking about the other time she'd seen him without a shirt, however, made her recall watching him break Günter's lock at the Millers' Dairy farm, and she pursed her lips.

He's a common vandal, for goodness sake, she thought, annoyed at herself. *I can surely find a better boyfriend than that!*

"Unblemished and incorruptible as a clarion call," Sal improvised, noting Jon's wet hair and scrubbed skin. "Washed sinless and sparkling by holy water from a virginal, vaginal font, like a baptized baby Jesus." He paused to let the profundity of his words resonate, then solemnly opened a notebook on the counter. "I'll write that down for you."

Julianna rolled her eyes and Jon bit back a laugh.

"That's okay," Jon said. "I'm pretty sure I'll remember it."

Julianna turned away with an abrupt motion, and Jon realized she was struggling not to laugh, too. He watched her with a surprising tug of affection, suddenly wishing he'd known her before her mind cast loose from its moorings.

The news roundup was still on the radio but he was only half listening to it as he paid for the gas—holding the plastic bag beneath the counter, where Sal couldn't see how much cash was in it. Preoccupied by thoughts about what items they were going to need to purchase soon, he began to ask Sal for a map of Indiana, wanting to find a good-sized town where stores would be open on Sunday. The radio broadcast interrupted him, however, before he could finish his sentence:

"The FBI is conducting a nationwide manhunt for two men accused of the attempted murder of a New Hampshire State Trooper and the brutal slaying of a New Hampshire woman in her home."

Jon flinched and dropped his bag of belongings. The copy of *Moby Dick* slipped out of the bag onto the concrete floor with a five-dollar bill sticking from its pages; Jon stared down in shock at the cover of the book—a bleak picture of a ship on the ocean during a storm—not comprehending what he was seeing.

"According to a spokesmen for the FBI," continued the broadcaster, *"one suspect has been identified as fifteen-year-old Elijah Hunter of Prescott, Maine."* (A squeal came from behind the bathroom door, but Jon barely registered it.) *"Hunter is a five-foot-eleven Negro male, approximately 145 pounds, last seen wearing a white shirt and blue jeans. Little is known about Hunter's accomplice, but his name is believed to be Jon Tate. In addition to the murder charges, Hunter and Tate are being sought for arson and grand larceny, as well as the kidnapping and assault of a mentally ill woman from Bangor, Maine. The men are believed to be driving a green Volkswagen Beetle, and headed west. No other details are available at this time, but the FBI is asking for assistance from all state and local law enforcement agencies, and has requested that anyone with information about the fugitives immediately contact their local police. The men are considered armed and extremely dangerous, and a reward of five thousand dollars is being offered for information leading to their capture.*

Jon Tate raised his head to stare across the counter at the open-mouthed gas station attendant.

"Oh, man," Sal Cavetti moaned piteously, eyes darting from Jon to the blood-stained sleeve of Julianna's dress. "Fuck me running."

* * *

Elijah flew out of the bathroom half a minute later, still attempting to button his pants. Julianna was looking curiously at Sal—who was crouched behind the counter, uttering a remarkably nonpoetic string of obscenities—but Jon was nowhere in sight.

"Where's Jon?" Elijah demanded.

"Oh, Jesus!" wailed Sal. "Please don't kill me, man!"

Julianna frowned. "Hush, Larry. You're behaving like a five-year-old." She turned her attention to Elijah. "Did you boys have another spat? Jon seemed very upset."

Elijah darted out the door without answering and stared wildly around the parking lot in the hot morning sunshine. The Beetle was still by the pump, he noted with relief, but Jon wasn't in it; it took another few seconds to catch sight of the other boy in the alley across the highway, already a block away and running fast in the opposite direction. Jon's back was pale in the sunlight, and he was carrying his bag and his shirt in his right hand. Without thinking, Elijah sprinted after him, his arms and legs windmilling furiously. He was a fast runner, but so was Jon; after another block the distance between them hadn't narrowed by more than ten feet. Elijah willed himself to go faster, panting and gasping, yet no matter what he did he couldn't close the gap.

"Jon!" he cried out.

The gravel under his sneakers seemed to blur as he threw himself forward, but his lungs already felt as if they were on fire, and he was having difficulty getting enough air. Jon had just crossed another street, still more than thirty yards ahead of him. Realizing it was pointless to keep going, Elijah suddenly broke off his pursuit and skidded to a halt.

"Goddammit, Jon!" he cried, his voice cracking from frustration and sudden anger. "Come back here, you PUSSY!" He bent over and retched, his stomach heaving from exertion.

Elijah didn't care that Jon had their only money. The truth was he couldn't bear the idea of going on alone with Julianna on her mad, disastrous journey. Jon's departure meant the end of all hope, because at least when the three of them were together it felt as if there were still a slim chance they might eventually figure out a way to somehow survive this nightmare. At least when Jon was there, there was somebody to talk to who actually knew his *real* name—somebody who tried to take care of him, somebody who shared the responsibility of keeping them one step ahead of the police, somebody who made him feel as if the whole world had not gone absolutely, stark raving mad.

Somebody he trusted.

With a twist of pain in his heart, he realized he had begun to think of Jon as a friend. He knew it was stupid to believe this; they'd only met a day ago, and knew next to nothing about each other. Besides that, what Elijah *did* know about the other boy was hardly reassuring: He'd gotten an underaged girl pregnant, for God's sake, and robbed a few hundred bucks from an employer.

Yet he'd also washed Elijah's shoes and socks for him the night before, and less than five minutes ago had offered Elijah the use of his own toothbrush.

Elijah lifted his head, startled by a noise in the alley. Jon was standing a few feet away from him, his shoulders and chest wet with perspiration and his face flushed.

"I'm not a pussy," he said in a subdued voice. "I was just stretching my legs."

Elijah cleared his throat. "I know," he answered, averting his face. He wiped his eyes as he stood up straight again. "I was just kidding."

He looked back at the gas station, two blocks behind them. Julianna was beside the Beetle, looking toward them; the gas station attendant was apparently still cowering inside the station. Elijah thought it was likely the big man had already called the police, but for the moment he couldn't seem to make himself care. There was a lump in his throat, and he was having trouble seeing Julianna clearly.

Jon Tate sighed as he stared at the back of Elijah's head. "Sorry, man," he mumbled. "I don't really know what the fuck I'm doing."

Elijah nodded, not willing to risk speaking again quite yet. He didn't look at Jon as they fell in step together, separated only by a strip of green grass growing in the middle of the alley. They picked up the pace together immediately, though, and began to jog toward the Volkswagen. By the time they recrossed the highway, they were running full tilt.

Interlude

Michael led the ascent to the hayloft, right before sunset, followed closely on the ladder by Ben Taylor and Julianna. Julianna insisted on going last because she was afraid that Ben, who was barefoot, might get a splinter and take a tumble, and she wanted to be sure there was someone under him to cushion his fall. Her worry was for nothing, though; he scooted up the crude ladder and disappeared into the loft in a matter of seconds.

At fifteen, Benjamin Taylor was shorter than most kids his age, and thin as a postage stamp. He hated having his hair cut, and as a result he had a wild mass of black curls surrounding his head like a dark, fuzzy corona. His face was normally lit by a sunny smile, and even though he was sometimes bullied into crying by classmates who did not care for Negroes, his tears never lasted more than a minute or two. He'd spot a fox or a rabbit darting across the road into the woods by his house, or he'd catch a whiff of bread from the bakery window when he was downtown, and he'd wipe his eyes on his forearm and brighten up again.

Julianna and Ben were only a month apart in age, and had been friends since they were infants. Emma Larson, eight months pregnant with Julianna and bloated to twice her normal size, had actually helped Doc Colby deliver Ben when Mary

Taylor had given birth. Mary's health had not been good for weeks before Ben was born, and Colby had asked Emma—who had served as a midwife for more than a dozen births in Pawnee—to come with him to the Taylors and lend a hand, just in case things "went poorly" during the delivery. Fortunately, Ben's birth was free of complications, and Emma and Mary formed an easy friendship that day that eventually extended to their children.

On the Sunday night before everything changed forever in Pawnee, Julianna scaled the ladder in the barn almost as gracefully as Ben had managed a few moments before. She had almost reached the hayloft when Seth stepped into the barn and started up after her.

"Hey, baby girl," he called out, taunting. He and Michael only called her "baby girl" when they wanted to get her goat. "Your panties are showing!"

Julianna, who was wearing a light blue, knee-length skirt, paused in her climb and looked down at him, unfazed.

"Thank you, Seth." She smiled fondly at him. "I'd forgotten how childish you can be."

Seth found himself a little taken aback, yet again, by the recent change in her. Until the past few months or so, she would have squealed with indignation over the kind of comment he'd just made.

"You used to be a lot more fun," he complained. "Why'd you have to go and get older?"

Her smile grew. "I'm so sorry." She stepped off the ladder into the loft. "But if you're looking for someone to annoy, you can always pick on Michael. He's even more immature than you are."

"Hurry up, you guys," Michael urged from the other end of the barn. He and Ben had helped themselves to Michael's hidden stash of chewing tobacco and were standing side by side, leaning out the open half door the Larsons used—when it wasn't in service as a stargazing portal—for loading and unloading hay. Michael was nearly a foot taller than Ben, but Ben's Medusa-like helmet of hair narrowed the gap by several inches. "You're missing the sunset."

Seth made it to the loft in time to see Julianna rush over to join the others at the window. He was reassured to notice she still shared Michael's enthusiasm for things like sunsets and stars; it made her seem more like her old self. Michael and Ben shifted to make room for her between them, and Seth wandered over a few seconds later to poke his head out, too.

The sun looked like a massive, overripe apricot, resting on a hilltop several miles away. The sweltering heat of the day had lessened a little but the sky was still hazy; the red and white clover of the surrounding hayfields covered the earth to the horizon, broken here and there by a dark green carpet of trees, grass, and corn.

"Oh!" Julianna exclaimed in delight. She took a deep breath and filled her lungs with the humid evening air. Clover, hay, and lilac were the dominant fragrances, but there seemed to be a thousand others, too, floating around and mixing with the pleasant, familiar sounds of a squirrel chittering in a nearby tree, and the mournful, meditative ringing of her mother's wind chime on the back porch of the house, and the distinctive chirping of a horned lark, high-pitched and sharp like the squeak of rubber shoes on a wooden floor. Julianna absorbed it all and sighed with contentment, but immediately lost her good humor as Michael leaned out farther to spit a mouthful of tobacco juice at the ground.

"Ugh," she snapped. "It looks like you've been eating cow pies."

"Yeah, it's a disgusting habit, Mikey," Seth agreed. "Can I have some?"

Michael laughed and handed over the tin. Ben lowered his head to release a brown stream, too, but then gagged and was forced to spit out the small wad of tobacco from his cheek. He wasn't as experienced a chewer as Michael and Seth, and still felt like throwing up every time he put a pinch in his mouth. But everything Michael and Seth did, he wanted to do, even if it made him sick to his stomach.

Julianna frowned and stepped away from the hay door. "If

Momma finds out the three of you are doing that, she'll kill all of you."

Michael nodded, unconcerned. "She'll have to kill Daddy, too. He knows we've been doing it and he hasn't said anything about it."

She grimaced. "He would if he knew you were giving it to Ben. He thinks you and Seth are old enough now to make your own choices, even when they're really *stupid* choices. But if he knew Ben was rotting out his stomach with you, he'd put a stop to it."

Seth laughed, amused by the sour expression on her face. "You should try a pinch, Julianna. You might like it."

Julianna ignored this and settled herself in a loose pile of hay. "And if Ben's parents find out—"

"They won't," Ben interrupted quietly. "Don't make a fuss, okay?"

Ben was always quiet. When he was with other people, even Julianna and her brothers, he mostly listened to the conversation without contributing, unless he thought something needed to be said. Consequently, whenever he did speak up, everybody else stopped talking and stared at him, as if a chair in the room had suddenly come to life and begun singing a hymn.

"Yeah," Michael said. He leapt to grab a beam a couple of feet above his head, then started swinging his legs back and forth over the floor of the loft. His boots and blue jeans were filthy from working in the fields for most of the day, but he had scrubbed the worst of the dirt from his skin before dinner. He wasn't wearing a shirt, and his long, thin torso was reddish brown from the sun. "Quit being such an old lady."

Julianna watched him swing for a moment before answering. "Just because I'm trying to keep Ben from being beaten to a pulp by his folks doesn't make me an old lady." She turned her attention back to Ben. "And the only reason I said something is because you're being ridiculous, Ben Taylor."

Ben smiled at her, unoffended. He was used to this sort of comment from Julianna, and knew she didn't mean anything by it. (He also knew she was probably right, but he wasn't about to admit that in her presence.)

"Speaking of old ladies," Michael said, dropping to the floor, "you and Seth didn't get to hear the story about Nell Cobb that Dad was telling me and Ben tonight." He glanced over his shoulder at Ben and the two of them grinned at each other.

"You want to tell them, or should I?" Michael asked. Both boys giggled.

Ben shook his head. "You go ahead."

"What story?" Seth asked. Julianna and Seth had helped Emma clear the table while Michael and Ben went out on the front porch with Eben after supper; they'd heard the three of them laughing uproariously at one point but hadn't known why.

"Dad said Luther dropped by to pay his taxes this afternoon." Michael's giggling was getting considerably worse, and Ben's shoulders had begun to shake. "Luther told him . . ."

Ben's knees suddenly gave out; he fell to the floor and lay on his back. "Bonk," he chortled, covering his face with his hands. "Bonk."

Julianna and Seth stared at each other, nonplussed, as Ben writhed on the floor. Michael struggled to maintain his composure for a moment longer, even though his face had become mottled and he couldn't catch his breath.

"Dad said . . . Dad said he asked Luther how married life was going and Luther told him . . . oh shit, you guys."

He collapsed beside Ben, holding his own stomach as tears streamed down his cheeks.

"Bonk," he gasped. "Oh, God. Bonk."

Michael finally managed to blurt out the full story to Julianna and Seth:

Until the past spring, Nell Jones had been Pawnee's oldest spinster. But when Luther Cobb's first wife passed away in March, he found he didn't care for living alone one bit, and promptly asked the fifty-three-year-old Nell—the only available woman in town who wasn't guaranteed to turn him down outright—to marry him. She wasn't exactly bowled over by the offer; Luther had a potbelly and several missing teeth, and was not a handsome man by any stretch of the imagination. But Nell was lonely, and not much of a looker herself, and she was weary of having no income save for a small monthly allowance she received from a trust fund her parents had left in her name. Luther was honest and kind, and he also owned a profitable apple orchard east of town, and so Nell eventually made up her mind that she could do far worse than to become Mrs. Luther Cobb. The two had tied the knot in mid-May, and taken up residence together in Luther's house.

To the best knowledge of anybody in town, however, when Luther kissed Nell at their wedding was the first time Nell had ever been kissed by a man. Nell was a notorious prude, and would suffer no hanky-panky whatsoever during their short engagement. This being the case, when the newlyweds attempted to come together as man and wife in Luther's bed, it was not exactly what either might have hoped for. Nell was apparently so frightened by the sight of Luther's naked body she was unable to become aroused; fifty-three years of celibacy and a distaste for all things sexual—not to mention Luther's potbelly and bad teeth—had ill-equipped her for making love. For his part, Luther was no Lothario; his only previous sexual partner had been his first wife, and while things had gone smoothly enough with her through the years, their copulation had always been quick and businesslike, and taught him nothing he could use to surmount a challenge like Nell.

As a result, Luther was unable to enter his new bride's inner sanctum. No matter how gently, or insistently, he requested admission at the barred gate he encountered, it remained closed to him. Nell tried to help; she even forced herself to kiss his nose once or twice and whisper words of encouragement in his ear, unconsciously gritting her teeth and clenching every muscle in her body as she did so. Her good-hearted willingness to share herself with Luther, however, was in the end no match for the aversion she felt about the entire ordeal. Luther was eventually forced to withdraw after the tip of his penis became so swollen and bruised he couldn't bear to risk another sortie.

When Luther had confided these painful details of his wedding night to Eben, he was still traumatized. He became inarticulate toward the conclusion of his tale of woe (or so Eben later related to Michael and Ben) and could only demonstrate what had occurred by thrusting his right fist into his left palm again and again, and saying "bonk" each time his hands made contact with each other.

The effect on Seth of Luther's story was much the same as it had been for Michael and Ben. Midway through Michael's narrative, he had found it necessary to lean against the wall for support, and he was now wiping his eyes and wheezing as Michael and Ben convulsed on the floor. Julianna sat silently in the hay, shaking her head and scowling.

She cleared her throat. "Daddy should be ashamed of himself for telling you such a thing, and you should all be ashamed, too, for laughing at those poor people like this," she said primly. "Just imagine how you'd feel if you were Luther or Nell."

Michael fought for air. "Sore as hell?"

"That's not funny, Michael," Julianna scolded. Her voice quivered and her chin began to tremble as Seth and Ben hooted. "And by the way, I can't believe you chose to tell a filthy story like that in my hearing."

She looked genuinely upset, and all three boys began to sober as they looked at her. She almost never cried, and none of them were prepared for this sort of emotional reaction from her.

"Julianna?" Seth straightened. There was a hitch in his voice he couldn't control, but his smile had all but melted away. "What's wrong?"

She met his eyes wordlessly for an instant, then without warning a very unladylike peal of laughter erupted from her lips. She clapped her hands over her mouth in horror and rolled over on her stomach to bury her face in the hay, and the others came undone once again as they watched her kick at the floorboards.

"Oh, Lord!" Her words came out muffled. "Oh Lord oh Lord oh Lord!"

Michael had always loved his sister's laugh. It was full-throated and completely unselfconscious, and it poured out of her like water from a pump.

"I'd like to hear Nell's side of the story," he hiccuped. "Do you think she'd say 'bonk,' too?"

Julianna kicked the floorboards again and plugged her ears. "Stop it, Michael!" she demanded. "Stop it right now!"

Ben adored Julianna's laugh, too. Of course, he adored everything about Julianna Larson, but her laughter was probably the thing he adored the most. He spent a lot of his time trying to get her going like this, but her brothers were the only ones who could really set her off. She smiled and chuckled frequently with everybody else, but Michael and Seth knew how to tickle her just right.

I wish she thought I was as funny as them, Ben thought.

Julianna didn't know it, but Ben had been in love with her for years. He knew she didn't feel the same way about him, though, nor did she have an inkling about his feelings for her. And she never would, if Ben could help it. There was no point to her knowing, after all, because even if she did feel the same way, they didn't live in a world where they'd ever be allowed to act on those feelings. Still, he couldn't escape the fierce ache in his chest he experienced whenever he was with her, nor keep from desperately wishing he could make her laugh just like this, all by himself.

He stared at her quaking back and made himself guffaw along with Michael and Seth. It really wasn't all that hard to do; she looked funny as hell sprawled out in the hay and flailing her arms and legs around as if she were being eaten alive by mosquitos.

She gets prettier every day, he thought. He turned his head and blinked away unwanted tears before realizing it didn't matter if anybody saw. They were all crying, and nobody would think twice about it.

Seth Larson had a flash of insight as he watched Julianna's antics in the hay. He realized he'd been worried about Julianna growing up because he was afraid she'd want to leave home once she was no longer a child. It was Seth's biggest nightmare: the people he loved the most, leaving him forever. Many of his friends had abandoned Pawnee, moving to the city and never coming back, even for a visit. He could handle infidelity like this from his friends, but not from his family. Michael talked about leaving now and then, but Seth didn't truly believe his brother would go. Michael loved their farm, and Pawnee, as much as Seth did. He might move away for a year or two on a whim, but Seth had slowly come to trust that Michael would always want to come home eventually. It was Julianna, though, that he'd been anxious about. With her mind and insatiable curiosity, the more grown-up she got the more it seemed there was nothing for her in a town like Pawnee.

But she really didn't want to go anywhere else. He couldn't understand why he hadn't seen it before, yet in that moment it was as plain to him as the weathered walls of the barn, or the strand of hay in Michael's short blond hair. Julianna was happier than any of them, right where she was.

"I hope you're pleased with yourself, Michael," Julianna moaned, finally managing to sit up again. Her dress was wrinkled and twisted and her bruised face was wet with perspiration and tears. "I think I ruptured something in my stomach."

The four of them eventually quieted. The sun sank from sight as they talked about this and that, and a quarter moon rose overhead, dim and lonely. As the western horizon faded to black the stars came out, one after another. Michael—with one eye glued to the telescope and the other closed—traced the major constellations with his finger for the others to follow: Scorpius and Libra, Virgo and Hercules, the Corona Borealis and Boötes. He quizzed Julianna on the brightest stars visible from the south side of the barn; she was able to identify Spica and Antares, but she forgot about Arcturus. Michael, predictably, started yawning long before anybody else began to get sleepy. He retired to the hay pile, and was soon snoring lightly. It was only ten thirty or so, but he'd been up since before dawn and couldn't keep his eyes open another second.

Seth lasted another hour or so before he began nodding off, too. The only light in the barn was from the moon and the stars as he leaned down and shook Michael's shoulder.

"Hey," he said. "Time for bed."

Seth was wearing a sleeveless white undershirt and it was the only thing about him Julianna and Ben could make out clearly; his bare arms, much darker in contrast, were almost invisible. He pulled Michael to his feet and brushed him off. Michael grumbled sleepily at him as he did this, but all Seth said was, "You're a mess, Mikey. You're gonna be crawling with bug bites."

They called good night to Julianna and Ben and made their way down the ladder, Seth leading the way. Julianna listened for their voices after they reached the ground but if they spoke she couldn't hear them; Michael was basically asleep on his feet, anyway, and Seth wasn't much of a talker when he was tired.

"I guess I should be gettin' home, too," Ben said. "Momma told me not to be too late tonight."

Julianna nodded in the darkness. She wasn't sleepy yet and would have enjoyed talking to Ben a while longer, but she didn't argue with him because she knew it was likely he was already in trouble with his folks for being out so late. He used to stay overnight all the time, sharing a bed with Michael, but ever since he'd gotten big enough to help his father run the farm, Silas and Mary Taylor had kept a much tighter leash on their only child.

"Be careful walking home," she said. "I'd give you a ride, but Daddy doesn't want me driving at night by myself yet."

"He's lettin' you drive in the day?" Ben asked. He sounded jealous. "Since when?"

"I drove home from church just this morning," Julianna said proudly.

Ben was usually in church but one of his father's calves had gone missing that morning and it had taken Ben most of the morning to find it.

Ben's teeth glinted a little in the starlight as he grinned. "You run over anything?"

Julianna smiled back. "Of course not. Seth and Michael screamed like fools all the way home, though, pretending I was going to get us all killed."

Ben chuckled and tried to think of something else to say. He wanted to stay and talk forever, now that it was just the two of them, but he knew if he didn't get home right away he'd catch living hell from his folks.

I wish I could kiss her good night, he thought.

"Guess I'll see you tomorrow," he said. "I'll be workin' with my dad most of the day, but I'll come find you after supper?"

She nodded again and reached out to touch his shoulder. "That'll be wonderful. Momma said she wanted to make ice cream tomorrow afternoon. I'll save you a bowl."

He lingered for another moment after she dropped her hand. The warmth of her fingers on his naked skin seemed to have immobilized him. He knew she didn't think a thing of it, of course; she was affectionate by nature and often touched him in passing, taking his arm when they'd go for walks and even hugging him now and again when he did something she liked.

"Did you fall asleep, Ben Taylor?" Her voice, soft and amused, brought him back to himself.

He was grateful she couldn't see him blushing. "Just about," he answered, faking a yawn. "G'night, Julianna."

Julianna told him good night and watched him make his way across the loft to the ladder. His skin was so black he was almost impossible to see; she called out for him to be careful going down the ladder, and wondered to herself why he'd been acting so strange lately. She turned to face the stars once more, resolving to ask him the next day if something was bothering him.

The night sky was so vast and beautiful it made her shiver in spite of the heat. She was glad Michael had shown her how to recognize certain constellations and individual stars, but it also seemed pointless to her, in a way. The stars were simply the stars, ageless and voiceless, and forever out of reach. What was the use in naming things so far beyond anybody's understanding?

"Julianna!"

She jumped and banged her knee against the telescope's

stand, nearly knocking it over. The whisper had come from the other side of the barn, down by the main door. It was obviously Ben, and she opened her mouth to reprimand him for giving her such a fright.

"Julianna!" Ben hissed again. "Get down here fast, and be quiet!"

She didn't know why, but goose pimples rose on her arms and neck. She ran across the loft as quickly as she dared and stared down at Ben, who was crouched at the base of the ladder.

"What is it?" she whispered back.

He waved his arms frantically for her to come down. "Rufus Tarwater's right outside your house!"

Chapter 10

When Julianna Dapper saw the *Welcome to Mullwein, Iowa* sign on Highway 69, she knew the long journey was nearly over.

"Look, Ben!" she cried. She turned to face Elijah, who was sitting in the backseat of the Beetle, daydreaming, and on impulse she reached between the seats and clasped one of his sweating hands in her own. "We'll be home in time for dinner!"

For want of a better plan, Elijah and Jon had allowed Julianna to guide them that day. She'd led them across Indiana and Illinois with no apparent interest in the back roads they traveled, but as soon as they crossed the Mississippi River into southern Iowa she'd begun to perk up, telling Jon, who was driving, to head straight west on Highway 2 "for a hundred and fifty miles." Both of the boys had been startled by her specificity, and when they came to Highway 69, almost exactly one hundred and fifty miles later, she turned them southwest toward Missouri, and informed them they were almost home.

Elijah sat up and looked around. There was a cattle lot and sale barn to the right of the asphalt highway, and a number of modest, unremarkable houses with well-tended green lawns on the left, but he saw nothing to explain Julianna's elation. To him, it looked exactly the same as every other small Midwest town they'd driven through that day. Jon caught his eyes in the rearview mirror and shrugged, unimpressed, as well. Elijah stared down in bafflement at Julianna's fingers in his own.

A mere twenty-four hours earlier he would never have allowed someone to hold his hand as she was doing, but for some reason he didn't really seem to mind such gestures from Julianna. To tell the truth he kind of liked the steadiness of her touch; there was something oddly comforting in it, in spite of the fact she was certifiably insane. Besides, he could see how happy she was, and he saw no reason to dampen her mood by pulling away from her.

"So is this where you grew up?" he asked, hiding his skepticism about her claims of being almost "home."

Julianna squeezed his hand. "For goodness sake, Ben," she chided, laughing. "You've been in Mullwein as often as I have. You know full well it's still another thirteen miles to Pawnee." She released him with another squeeze and turned to face Jon. "You're welcome to join us for dinner, Jon. Ben almost always eats with us on Sundays, and Momma will have made enough food to feed an army."

She felt somewhat uneasy making such an offer, considering the lingering doubts she had about Jon's character. Her parents certainly wouldn't approve of her bringing a strange boy home without asking them first, and once they heard about his breaking the padlock at the Millers' Dairy Farm, they'd likely forbid her from having anything further to do with him. Then again, she reminded herself, if Jon hadn't given them a ride in his car she and Ben never would have made it home that day. Surely her parents wouldn't be too upset with her for at least offering to thank him with a nice meal.

It was a little past five o'clock on Sunday afternoon, and the temperature was in the nineties. The windows on the Beetle were open but the breeze blowing through them was hot and muggy, and the sunlight reflecting off the hood of the cramped little automobile was blinding. They had been driving ever since fleeing Sal Cavetti's gas station, with only three short breaks from the heat-softened, blacktop highways of the rural Midwest. They had stopped twice to refill the car and use the bathroom, and once again for a quick lunch at a drive-in restaurant in Illinois, where Jon had bought an obscene amount of food for them. Jon and Elijah wolfed down four cheeseburgers each and several bags of French fries, and Julianna had eaten nearly as much as the boys. They had all been ravenous because Julianna had insisted on tossing out the leftovers from Bebe Stockton's refrigerator, leery of spoilage.

Their route for the day had miraculously skirted all large cities, and with the exception of a heart-stopping few minutes near the Iowa border—where a state trooper had followed them for two or three miles before veering off again—they had managed to stay clear of the law, as well. It was almost as if Julianna were intentionally taking precautions to avoid the police, but Elijah couldn't make himself believe their good fortune had anything to do with a conscious strategy on Julianna's part. She seemed to be relying on instinct, like a Capistrano swallow or a homing pigeon. The only downside to her choice of roads was that they hadn't been able to find a clothing store open for business, so they were all dressed as they had been since early that morning: Julianna in her green dinner dress (looking none too fresh), Jon in his khaki shorts, and Elijah in jeans and Jon's blue T-shirt.

Elijah didn't really know who he was anymore. Being at ease with holding Julianna's hand was out of character enough for him, but wearing someone else's shirt made him feel like an entirely different person. He was tempted to take it off again for the thousandth time that day—it had never really dried from the hand-washing Jon had given it earlier and was now soaked through with his own sweat, as well—yet he couldn't seem to make himself do it. He knew it was silly, but he didn't want Jon to think he was ungrateful.

Jon had offered the T-shirt to him that morning when they'd returned to Sal Cavetti's gas station from their frantic run down the alley, and Elijah had put it on immediately, without hesitation, even though he'd never before worn anyone's clothes but his own, not once in his entire life. He wasn't sure why he'd suddenly been okay with wearing something of Jon's, but he knew it had to do with the resigned, hopeless look on the older boy's face when he had come back in answer to Elijah's cry in the alley. That look had haunted Elijah, and still did, because it was obvious Jon would have had a much better chance of survival on his own. His friend's sacrifice moved Elijah deeply, and on impulse he had set aside all his habitual reticence and pulled the newly washed, wet shirt over his head, hoping Jon would somehow understand that to do so was not something he did lightly.

Elijah had never been very good at expressing himself when things came too near his heart. He accepted hugs and kisses from his parents, but he could rarely respond in kind because emotional displays of all sorts made him squirm. Saying "I love you" was even harder for him, and he was utterly incapable of putting himself through that kind of fumble-tongued, red-faced ordeal more than once or twice a year, even though Mary or Samuel said it to him almost every day. Affection was a hole in the earth, waiting to swallow him up if he didn't watch his step, and as far as he was concerned it was the better part of wisdom to stay as far away as possible from the edges of such an awful chasm. He was willing to venture near it now and then to make his parents or grandparents feel good, but he'd formed no real attachments to anybody outside his family, mostly because in his view it wasn't worth the agony of one day being called upon to share his feelings.

Whether he liked it or not, however, it seemed that both Jon and Julianna had somehow maneuvered him perilously close to the abyss. He didn't know how this was possible, but as he stared at the back of their heads he found his heart hurting in the same way it sometimes did when his mother sang to herself while she was cooking, or when his dad sat beside him on the porch at dusk and talked to him about his day. He had never thought it possible to care so much for people he barely knew, yet he found himself wishing he were the type of person who could lean forward and touch the shoulders of these near strangers, for no other reason than because it seemed like the right thing to do.

I'm going crazy, he told himself. *Julianna got her crazy germs on me or something and turned my brain into mashed potatoes.*

"Turn south at the bottom of this hill," Julianna instructed

Jon, breaking into Elijah's thoughts as they passed a small high school gymnasium and crossed over a rough set of railroad tracks. She glanced at Elijah. "Can you believe how much roadwork they've done since we were here last, Ben? I barely recognize this town anymore."

Elijah sighed and helped himself to a bottle of Pepsi from a six-pack they'd gotten at the last gas station, using Jon's trick with the seatbelt latch to remove the bottle cap. He took a long drink and stared moodily out the window at a Reorganized Latter Day Saints church on the top of a hill to the west as Jon obeyed Julianna's orders, following the highway as it curved left past a boarded-up Dairy Queen. Jon half turned to ask Elijah for a sip of his Pepsi, but he only got as far as "Can I have . . ." before his tongue failed him.

A sheriff's car had just whipped onto the road behind them, lights flashing.

Jon gasped in horror and accidentally let go of the wheel as the siren on the sheriff's car began to wail. The Volkswagen swerved wildly for a second until Julianna grabbed it with a startled cry and fought to regain control of the vehicle.

"Jon, look out!" Elijah screamed, losing his balance and tumbling over in the backseat just as he glimpsed something through the windshield that made him believe the world was coming to an end.

Jon spun around with what felt like nightmarish slowness. He barely had time to register what Elijah was screaming about before he had to stomp on the brakes and bring the little Beetle screeching to a halt. He'd forgotten to step on the clutch, too, so the engine died. He seized the ignition key to restart it, but his hand fell away again at once, dropping lifelessly at his side.

A second police car had rocketed out of an alley onto the road in front of them and was completely blocking the highway.

When Jon, Elijah, and Julianna had fled Sal Cavetti's gas station in Indiana that morning, the unstrung poet had not even seen them leave because he was still squatting on the floor behind the counter with his eyes closed, moaning to the empty room. After he heard the Beetle pull away from the gas pump, it took him ten full minutes to work up the nerve to rise and peer out the door, and then another soul-searching hour and a half before he was ready to notify the Indiana State Patrol about his harrowing brush with death. He had been afraid Elijah and Jon would return to murder him if they found he had been the one to finger them, but his hardy sense of civic duty—not to mention the five-thousand-dollar reward mentioned on the radio—at last compelled him to make the call, fortified by several reassuring bites of the pot brownie in his pocket, left over from breakfast.

By that time, of course, the whereabouts of the fugitives was anybody's guess, but Sal was still able to give the police a de-tailed description of Jon Tate (including several poetic phrases Sal was rather proud of, such as "shirtless, soulless, and san-guinary," and "angel-faced acolyte of the apocalypse"). The In-diana State Patrol passed on a more condensed version of Sal's account to the FBI, who in turn relayed the information to vari-ous law enforcement agencies and media outlets. Sal's poetry, sadly, was entirely absent from all these communications, but his call was not in vain: The good news that Julianna Dapper was still alive would be shared with all interested parties.

Unfortunately, however, the inspired marijuana madrigal run-ning through Sal's head took an ill-advised turn on the way to his tongue during the phone call to the hopelessly prosaic Indiana State Patrol. He recalled Julianna's big green eyes staring at him over the counter and belatedly read into those "verdant, Orphic orbs" the anguish of a defiled woman. Sal didn't go so far as to say he'd actually seen Julianna being violated, but he mentioned that the half-naked boys with her had reminded him of "rutting, lustful centaurs," and, as such, were clearly chock-full of "carnal-ity, brutality, and the sodomizing semen of sadists." The result of this embellishment was that yet another damning charge—al-ready suspected by Gabriel Dapper and others, but now con-firmed—was added to the long list of felonies attributed to Elijah Hunter and Jon Tate:

Rape.

*　　*　　*

Samuel Hunter hung up the receiver of the pay phone in the parking lot of a mid-Illinois truck stop and hurried back to Mary and Edgar, who were standing beside the pickup, waiting for him. Edgar was smoking a cigarette and shooting worried glances at Gabriel Dapper, who was watching them all from behind the wheel of the red Cadillac, parked ten feet away. Mary, though, had eyes only for Samuel.

"What is it?" she whispered as he drew close. Her face was grim as she read the expression he was trying to keep off his face. "What did you find out?"

Samuel took her arm and led her quickly to the driver's door of the truck. "Not a thing," he lied, speaking loud enough for Gabriel to hear him through the open window of the Cadillac. "Let's be on our way."

He waved at Gabriel, who started the Cadillac's engine and rolled up his window.

Mary got in the pickup quickly, sliding into the middle of the seat. Edgar took a last puff of his cigarette and dropped it on the ground to stub it out with his shoe, then scrambled into the passenger side with another unhappy glance at Gabriel.

Edgar had spoken to Gabriel several times over the past fifteen hours since they had all left the Stockton Dairy Farm, whenever they'd stopped for gas and food. Gabriel had made it clear each time, however, that he preferred to be left to himself in the Cadillac, insisting that he did not need to be relieved by another driver. Edgar had argued with him at the last stop before this one, telling him that it was unwise to go so long without rest, but Gabriel had merely shrugged and told him to stop worrying before shooing him back to the Hunters' pickup. Edgar was having difficulty dealing with this rejection—especially on top of Mary's ongoing lack of interest in him—and he was beginning to wish he'd never asked to come along on this journey.

"What's wrong, Sam?" Mary's dark gaze was fixed on the side of her husband's face as he peeled out of the parking lot and headed for the westbound Interstate ramp as fast as he could make the pickup go. She spoke above the sound of the wind coming through the windows. "What did Sheriff Kiley tell you?"

Sam had been making calls all day to Red Kiley back in Prescott, Maine, trying to find out what the police knew about Elijah and the others. The foul-tongued Sheriff Kiley had proven to be a good friend, and though Samuel hadn't told him exactly what they were up to, Kiley had freely shared whatever he'd heard, saying only, "I figure you and Mary are on some kind of damn-fool rescue mission, Sam, but if Elijah was my goddamn kid I'd be doing the same fucking thing."

Sam glanced in the rearview mirror at the red Cadillac following them down the ramp and drew a deep breath.

"Elijah's been arrested," he said, his voice shaking a little in spite of his best attempts to control it. "He got caught about forty-five minutes ago in a little town in southern Iowa."

Mary's small hand clamped on Sam's thigh, but she kept still, waiting for the rest.

"He's alive," Sam continued. "So's Julianna Dapper, and the other kid with them. But Elijah and the other boy have been charged with first-degree murder, attempted murder, arson, grand theft, and"—Sam's voice broke—"and rape." He fought to control his anguish, swallowing several times and blinking rapidly. "The FBI is saying Elijah raped Gabriel's mother, and maybe also the poor woman who got burned to death on that dairy farm."

Mary closed her eyes, and Edgar stared in horror at Samuel.

All the other terrible crimes Elijah had been accused of were nothing next to rape. Mary Hunter knew this charge for a ludicrous lie, of course—knew it as well as she knew her own name—but her spirit was nonetheless broken in a way it had not been before. A young black man accused of raping a white woman would not last two seconds in a white man's jail cell, and now that Elijah was in custody . . .

"Oh, my darling little man," Mary whispered, holding herself together only through a massive force of will.

Samuel forced himself to finish with the rest of his tidings. "Red said they've all been taken to a county jail, a few miles north of where they were arrested." His lips barely moved as he spoke; his tongue felt like a lump of clay in his mouth. "Some place called Maddox, near the Missouri border. Julianna Dapper's apparently going to spend the night with the sheriff and his wife, and then they'll figure out how to get her back home to Bangor tomorrow."

Edgar cleared his throat. "Shouldn't we stop and tell Gabriel?" He flushed as Mary turned her head to look at him incredulously. "I mean, shouldn't we at least tell him that his mother's alive?"

Sam's brain wasn't working properly; he couldn't seem to make heads or tails of this question. "I don't know," he mumbled.

Mary shook her head as she reached under the seat for a road atlas. "We're not going to tell Gabriel a God-blessed thing."

The firmness in her tone was enough to keep Edgar from arguing, but Samuel glanced down at her, and she answered his unspoken question.

"Gabriel can go a lot faster in that fancy car of his than we can in this truck," she said, tugging the atlas out from behind Edgar's shins and straightening again. The shock of Sam's news was wearing off, and she found herself becoming almost uncontrollably angry with the steadily worsening situation. "If Gabriel knows his mother's alive, and where she is, he'll get there before us, and find out what the police are saying has been done to her." She looked over her shoulder at the Cadillac. "And if that happens, God only knows what he might take it in his head to do to Elijah."

Edgar Reilly was starting to feel manipulated by fate, as if nothing was going to go right for them no matter what. *We're all just pawns in some kind of sick chess game,* he thought, tugging an unopened box of Milk Duds from his pants. (He'd been lucky enough to find a vending machine that afternoon and had restocked all his pockets with sweets.) *No, it's even worse than that. We're puppets. Puppets in some kind of twisted puppet hell.*

He swallowed. "Surely Gabriel wouldn't become violent,

would he?" he asked, accidentally biting his tongue as he crammed one of the chocolates in his mouth. "At least not with Elijah already in jail, and being watched by the police?"

Mary didn't answer.

"Hurry, Sam," she urged, opening the atlas to the Iowa page and beginning to hunt for the town of Maddox. "Go as fast as you can."

Gabriel Dapper knew he was tired, so he was trying to convince himself he was imagining things.

Things, say, like the sweat stains under the arms of Samuel Hunter's white shirt as he'd emerged from the pay phone at the last gas station and returned to his pickup, worry written all over his handsome features. Things like the tension in Mary Hunter's thin shoulders as she'd almost leapt into the cab of the pickup in her light blue summer dress, and the odd way both Mary Hunter and Edgar Reilly were now glancing through the rear window of the pickup—as if he, Gabriel, were some kind of predator, harrowing them down the highway.

"If they'd learned something about Mom, they'd have told me," Gabriel murmured to the empty Cadillac. "Wouldn't they?"

The long trip was starting to take a toll on Gabriel. He realized it was sheer stubbornness on his part to keep refusing Edgar Reilly's offer to spell him at the wheel of the Cadillac, but he didn't want company—especially Edgar Reilly's company—and he believed he could last several more hours before he'd need a rest. When he was a soldier in World War II, he'd routinely gone for long periods of time without sleep, and even though he was no longer a soldier, he was still a strong, healthy man in his mid-thirties, and he had more than enough stamina to stay awake and alert until they reached northern Missouri.

Or so he'd convinced himself.

He'd spent the lonely hours on the road sorting through memories of Julianna. One in particular was haunting him; he kept playing it over and over in his head, knowing he was fixating on it to an unhealthy degree but unable to stop.

When Gabriel was in fifth grade, a waspish Little League baseball coach named Doyle Matson had lost his temper at Gabriel
for dropping a fly ball during a game, humiliating him to the
point of tears in front of a good-sized crowd. Julianna had not
been able to be at the game, but after hearing about what had
happened to her son, she'd paid a late-night visit to Doyle's house.
Julianna never told Gabriel what transpired during that conversation, but she didn't have to; Doyle had arrived at practice the next
day with several long scratches on the top of his bald head, a hag-
gard expression on his face, and a much-improved disposition toward Gabriel and all the rest of the boys on the team.

"You scared the crap out of him, Mom," Gabriel now whispered in his Cadillac, reliving the memory yet again. "I wish I
could've seen it."

Up in front of him, Edgar Reilly turned around once more in
the pickup and stared back at him, pulling him out of his
thoughts. Gabriel frowned, beset by a fresh wave of suspicion; it
occurred to him that it might be a good idea to make a few
phone calls himself at the next gas station, just to make sure he
wasn't missing something important. He more or less trusted
Mary and Sam Hunter to tell him the truth about what was
going on, but the bottom line was that they were Elijah's parents, and if they'd learned something they didn't want Gabriel
to know it could only mean more bad news about their son.

And what he might or might not have done to Julianna.

Gabriel took a slow, deep breath and let it out again. He
wanted to believe Mary Hunter when she said Elijah wouldn't
hurt Julianna, but if he found out that the boy wasn't as
squeaky clean as Mary claimed when it came to how he was
treating Julianna, things between himself and the Hunters were
likely going to get very ugly, very fast.

The old memory began to play itself for him again, like a
home movie set in a perpetual loop on a projector. He thought
about how Julianna had always kept him safe, and how much
he loved her, and how much he would do to get her back.

Or, failing that, how he would make anybody who hurt
her pay.

*   *   *

The dearest dream of Ronnie Buckley's life was nearly within his grasp. After thirty-seven years as the sheriff of sleepy, rural, law-abiding Creighton County, Iowa, he had just arrested two of the most wanted felons in the entire United States of America, all by himself.

Well, almost by himself.

His deputy, Bonnor Tucker, had helped some, but Sheriff Buckley—who had spent the bulk of his long career writing speeding tickets and confiscating Pabst Blue Ribbon beer from high school kids—was the one who had first spotted the fugitives as they drove down Mullwein's Main Street, and it was Buckley who had instantly come up with the plan to trap them on the highway less than five minutes later. The arrest had gone like clockwork, too, and nobody was hurt.

Well, not too badly hurt, at least.

Elijah Hunter and Jon Tate both got knocked around a bit by the overenthusiastic Deputy Tucker when they were being cuffed, but Sheriff Buckley figured they had it coming—and then some—and didn't really mind Tucker bloodying them up a little.

Deputy Tucker, in Sheriff Buckley's opinion, was as ornery as an enema bag, but he had his uses. He was scrappy and tough (not to mention huge: six foot four, 245 pounds), and could be depended upon to throw himself in harm's way during the occasional barroom brawl or violent marital dispute, thereby keeping Buckley himself from having to do the dirty work. And today the sheriff had been more than happy to have his large, aggressive deputy be the one to search the felons and put them facedown on the ground for cuffing, while he himself, revolver drawn, watched the action from a few feet away.

When Buckley had seen the Volkswagen driving past the Sale Barn in Mullwein, he'd actually hesitated before calling Tucker on the radio. He'd recognized the lime-green Beetle with New Hampshire plates at once, of course; every sheriff, deputy, policeman, and state trooper in the Midwest had been on the lookout for that particular vehicle since early in the afternoon. But the truth was he'd been scared out of his wits to go after it. He felt he was too old and slow to be tussling with hardened criminals like Elijah Hunter and Jon Tate, and it occurred to him that sitting unnoticed in his squad car beneath the shade of a maple tree on a quiet street as he'd been doing when they passed by was a lot more appealing than being shot in the head during a confrontation. But in the end he'd somehow found the courage to tail the Beetle from a distance, and when he contacted Tucker and found out his deputy was already on the west side of town, where the fugitives were heading, he'd breathed a sigh of relief and made a quick decision where the best place would be for a showdown.

Deputy Tucker was *supposed* to have been patrolling the town of Maddox, twelve miles away, but had ignored this dull assignment and come to Mullwein that Sunday afternoon instead, hoping for more action. Sheriff Buckley would ordinarily have chewed him out for leaving Maddox unprotected like this—they were the only two lawmen in the county, and had to spread themselves thin—but for once Tucker's irresponsibility and limited attention span had put him exactly where Buckley needed him.

Sheriff Buckley still couldn't believe how absurdly easy the arrest had been, given the nature of the crimes the two young thugs had committed. But they hadn't even been armed, or tried to put up any sort of a fight, and Buckley had been truly shocked that such bloodthirsty killers could look so innocent and *normal*. If he hadn't known the grisly details about what Hunter and Tate had done, he never would have guessed they were capable of such atrocities. The Hunter boy looked like the shyest, sweetest kid you could ever hope to meet, and Jon Tate had a face right out of a goddamn Norman Rockwell picture. Buckley found it frightening that his instincts about people could be so completely wrong—he liked to think of himself as a keen judge of character—and he didn't care for the implications of such a discovery.

Strangely enough, the only difficulty in the arrest had come from the woman who had been the boys' prisoner. Julianna

Dapper was large, strong, and uncooperative, and clearly deranged from her ordeal. She was so addled, in fact, that she'd actually tried to come to the rescue of her kidnappers when Tucker had been roughing them up. Luckily, the skirt of her dress had snagged on the front bumper of the Beetle as she ran toward the altercation, causing her to trip and fall, and this had given Buckley time to grab her and pull her to safety.

It's a good thing I stopped her, too, Buckley thought, remembering the empty Coke bottle the woman had picked up from the side of the road and started swinging over her head like a mace as she charged straight at Tucker. *She might have killed Bonnor's dumb ass if I hadn't been there to save it.*

Now that they were all back in the jailhouse in Maddox, however, all Buckley had to do was get Julianna through the steel door separating the jail cells from his own residence in the same building. The Maddox "jailhouse" was a two-story brick structure that was more house than jail; there were four cells and a claustrophobic, closet-sized office that took up half of the first story, but the rest of the place was a comfortable, three-bedroom home for Buckley and his wife. Unfortunately, dealing with the mentally ill woman was once again proving to be more of a challenge than it should've been. She kept insisting the kidnappers were her *friends,* and was dead set against being separated from them.

"But why are you putting Ben in jail?" she asked, struggling with Buckley, as he tried to lead her away from her captors. "He had nothing do with breaking Günter's lock!"

The sheriff held tightly to her arm, not allowing her to approach either Elijah or Jon, who had just been shoved, none too gently, into separate jail cells by Deputy Tucker. The windowless, eight-by-eight-foot concrete cells smelled like stale sweat and mildew, with a hint of sewage from the toilets, which had a tendency to back up. Next to the toilets were rust-stained porcelain sinks, with single, cold-water spigots.

"Everything's going to be fine, sweetheart," Buckley grunted, red-faced and out of breath from the excitement of the past half hour. (Being sixty-two years old and a hundred pounds overweight didn't help his shortness of breath, either, of course, as his wife, Dottie, was sure to remind him the instant she laid eyes on him.) "You're safe now, and my little woman is going to take care of you tonight. She's right through this here door, and she'll get you cleaned up and fed, good and proper."

Sheriff Buckley wasn't really paying much attention to what he was saying. He was too busy fantasizing about watching himself on the television the following night during dinner.

This is going to make the national news for sure! he thought. *It's exactly the break I've been waiting for!*

Ronnie Buckley's dearest dream, finally coming to fruition, had nothing to do with being interviewed on television, nor with making a huge bust. These were paltry accomplishments, in his humble view, and even though he was pleased to have caught Elijah Hunter and Jon Tate—and was hoping he might even get to chat in-person with the courteous new CBS anchorman, Walter Cronkite—his dream was far more spectacular than any fleeting moment of recognition he could ever gain from his work as sheriff. He was a practical man, however, and had long understood that the only way to attain this transcendent goal was to somehow be thrust into the national spotlight, and for the first time in his life he was being given that opportunity. He had been waiting for thirty-three years for such a chance, and he intended to take it now, with no questions asked.

Thirty-three years ago, four years after he'd begun his tenure as sheriff, was 1929.

And 1929 was the year of the first Academy Awards.

Before Sheriff Buckley had spotted the Beetle that afternoon, he'd been daydreaming, as always, about winning an Academy Award—preferably Best Actor, but Best Supporting Actor was also acceptable. Ever since he'd heard the radio broadcast of the first Academy Awards, he'd envied each and every person who got to give a speech on that rarefied stage in Hollywood, but when the annual ceremony began to be televised in 1953, his desire to be up on that same stage himself became almost insupportable. He'd never acted in anything, let alone a movie, but he just *knew* he'd be a natural if he ever got the chance, and all he really needed, as he'd often told Dottie, was to be discovered by some casting director who could "think outside the box." With his dark, wide eyes and craggy, wrinkled forehead, he bore a striking resemblance to Ernest Borgnine—everybody said so— yet even though he'd secretly sent dozens of photos of himself to every talent agent in the business, for some reason no one had ever offered him a role, or even responded to his inquiries.

But that was all going to change now. The whole country was going to see him on television tomorrow night, and somebody important would finally give him his chance. Ronnie didn't know why he was so certain of this being the case, but he was. Once the right people saw him, he had no doubt whatsoever that it was only a question of time before he'd be up on that glittering platform in front of God and everybody, holding one of those golden, immortalizing statuettes above his head, just like Ernie Borgnine had done in 1955!

"But Ben hasn't done anything wrong!" Julianna insisted, interrupting the sheriff's splendid vision. "It was Jon who broke Günter's lock!" She glanced over at Jon Tate and blinked away tears. "I'm really sorry for tattling, Jon. But you have to tell them Ben's not to blame."

Jon was standing by his locked cell door with his wrists handcuffed behind him. His left eye was swollen shut and his nose was bleeding, and he was still naked from the waist up. The cut above his left knee from the previous day's run-in with the New Hampshire state trooper was bleeding again, too, as were several smaller scrapes on his shoulders and ribs. He was attempting to be stoical, but there were tears in his eyes, too, and he looked much younger than usual.

"We're not in here because of the lock, Julianna," he said quietly through the bars, his voice trembling.

"You got that right, son," Deputy Tucker taunted him gleefully through the bars. "You sure as hell got that right."

Some dreams, like Sheriff Buckley's, are larger than life; some are more modest, but no less heartfelt. Deputy Bonnor Tucker, who was only twenty-seven, had a longstanding dream of his own, and he was fairly sure he had just achieved it.

Bonnor Tucker was no glory chaser—unlike certain other public officials he could mention—and he couldn't have cared less about attention from the media, or winning an award. He also didn't give two shits about whether or not he resembled this or that celebrity (although his mother often told him he looked just like a young Babe Ruth—if the young Babe had sported a goatee and a lazy eye). All Bonnor had really wanted, for years, was to be treated with proper deference by everyone in Creighton County, Iowa, where he had grown up, and he knew an arrest of this magnitude was just the sort of thing that would do the trick.

No one will even dare to THINK that goddamn name again, he thought. *Not after they hear about what I did to these badass sons of bitches!*

Bonnor had become a deputy right after he graduated high school. Yet the gun and the authority this position had bestowed upon him notwithstanding, Bonnor Tucker had thus far been unable to eradicate a hated, life-destroying nickname he'd been stuck with ever since he was a small child. To this day, he was sure each person he passed on the street was still whispering it behind his back; when he fell asleep at night the spiteful syllables seemed to hiss in the air over his bed; when he was introduced at public functions, he imagined snickers and guffaws running through the audience like wind through a cornfield.

But it's all over now, he thought, nearly choking with joy. *After tonight, nobody's ever gonna call me "Boner Toucher" again!*

Deputy Tucker's only disappointment was that the FBI had laid claim to the interrogation of the two scumbags, and Sheriff Buckley—who had become a real candy-ass in his old age, in Bonnor's opinion—had agreed to this. Still, though, the feds wouldn't arrive until the next morning, and there were plenty of other ways he could amuse himself that evening with the suspects. Buckley and his wife always went to bed by eleven o'clock at the latest, and since there was no way the sheriff would send him home tonight and leave Hunter and Tate unguarded in their cells, Bonnor would have the murdering pricks all to himself for a good eight hours.

We'll see who's a badass, then! he thought.

"Of *course* we're in here because of the lock, Jon," Julianna protested. "Why else would we be here? Just tell them you're sorry, and that Ben didn't have anything to do with it. I'm sure they'll let us all go home."

"There's no one here named Ben, darlin'," Sheriff Buckley said to Julianna, attempting to unlock the steel door to his home without losing his hold on her. "You've had a rough couple of days, and you're just a little confused."

Bonnor Tucker decided it was time to begin the festivities.

"I don't blame you a bit for bawling your eyes out," he barked at Elijah. "The feds are gonna fry you like an egg for what you've done, sure as shit."

Elijah was handcuffed, too, and sitting on a cot in his jail cell. Tears were running off his chin, one after another, mingling with blood from a painful cut in his lower lip. As the deputy yelled at him he dropped his head and cried even harder.

"Leave him alone," Jon said from the other side of the hallway, trying not to sound scared.

"Shut up," Tucker ordered over his shoulder, not even bothering to look away from Elijah. He rapped his fist on the bars of Elijah's cell. "Hey, nigger, I'm talking to you!"

"There's no call to be using that word, Bonnor," Sheriff Buckley muttered. "You know I don't like it."

When Ronnie Buckley was younger, he'd often used the word "nigger" himself, but he had quit saying it decades ago, right after Hattie McDaniel won a 1939 Academy Award as Best Supporting Actress for her role as the Negro maid in *Gone With the Wind*. Buckley had decided on the spot that if Oscar was colorblind, then he should be, too.

"Whatever, Ronnie," Deputy Tucker muttered back.

Julianna was glaring down the hall at the gorilla-sized, homely deputy as he stood there grinning in at the boy in the jail cell. The rage she'd experienced when Tucker had brutally thrown Ben and Jon on the ground to handcuff them half an hour earlier had cooled somewhat on the trip from Mullwein to Maddox, but hearing him speak to her friends in such a vile manner was quickly bringing her temper back to a boil. She didn't really understand what was happening, but she could see that Ben and Jon were in trouble, and the heavy, obscene man with the sparse goatee and slightly crossed eyes standing ten feet in front of her was clearly an enemy.

And Julianna Larson knew how to deal with enemies.

With no warning, she seized Sheriff Buckley's nightstick from his belt and flung it straight at Bonnor Tucker. It sailed down the hall and clipped Tucker in the left kidney with considerable force, causing him to yelp in pain and dance away from Elijah's cell. The nightstick clanged against the bars of Jon's cell and then fell to the concrete floor and rolled four or five feet before coming to a stop.

"Son of a bitch!" Tucker bellowed in disbelief at Julianna. "What the hell are you doing, lady?"

"Stay away from my friends!" she yelled back. She was disappointed with her aim; she'd meant to hit Bonnor in the side of the head, but the sheriff was gripping her right arm, forcing her to use her left arm instead, and she was right-handed. "You just stay away from them!"

That's my girl, Jon Tate thought, almost grinning in spite of himself. *I wish to hell she'd been driving when we got caught. She would have run right over that asshole.*

Jon felt guilty for not having done more to try to avoid the road trap, even though he knew anything else he'd attempted probably would have gotten them all killed. Still, he couldn't help but wonder what might have happened if Julianna had been behind the wheel of the Beetle instead of him; she seemed to have a gift for survival, and may have somehow found a way to disable the sheriff and the deputy long enough to make another escape. There was no question she belonged in a mental institution, yet the woman had more balls than anybody he'd ever met.

I wish I was as brave as she is, he reflected. *She's nuts, but she's brave as hell.*

With a sudden pang of sadness, he realized it was likely he would never see Julianna again. His impulse to grin vanished, and he stared at the floor.

"For God's sake, Bonnor," Sheriff Buckley panted, struggling to hold on to Julianna. "Let me get her out of here before you say anything else stupid to these boys, okay?" He banged on the steel door. "Dottie? Let me in, would you? I can't use my key at the moment."

"What are you going to do with Julianna?" Elijah asked through his tears, his voice quivering. He'd raised his head as he heard the door into the sheriff's residence begin to open, creaking on its hinges. "You're not going to send her back to the hospital, are you?"

Elijah, too, had guessed that this was probably the last time he'd see the bizarre, damaged woman who'd kidnapped him from his hometown a day and a half ago and brought him halfway across the country. She'd effectively ruined his life since then, and Jon's, as well, but the grief and pity he felt for her was nearly as strong as the fear he felt for himself. She had begun to matter to him, despite everything; whatever was wrong with her mind had nothing at all to do with her kindness, or her loyalty, or her courage.

"What the fuck do you care, dickwad?" Deputy Tucker snapped, rubbing his lower back as he retrieved the sheriff's nightstick. "You sick fucking animals *raped* her, and now you're pretending to be worried about what happens to her? How dumb do you think we are?"

Elijah gaped at him, uncomprehending. "We did *what?*"

"Oh Jesus," murmured Jon Tate. "Oh sweet Jesus Christ."

Chapter 11

Dottie Buckley thought that Julianna Dapper was extraordinarily attractive. In fact, with her big, bright smile and watchful, intelligent eyes, Julianna reminded Dottie a little of Jayne Meadows.

"Did anyone ever tell you that you look like Jayne Meadows?" Dottie asked Julianna in a whisper, trying not to wake her husband, Ronnie, who had just dozed off in the armchair beside the sofa while watching *The Dupont Show of the Week* on NBC. Dottie couldn't understand how Ronnie could fall asleep during the season finale of *The Dupont Show*. Tonight's episode was "Seven Keys to Baldpate," starring Fred Gwynne and Jayne Meadows, and Dottie thought it was simply too clever for words.

Julianna—who did not look the slightest bit like Jayne Meadows—was sitting on the worn, overstuffed sofa with Dottie. For the past three hours she and the Buckleys had been watching television together: *Lassie, Dennis the Menace, The Ed Sullivan Show,* and *Bonanza* had all passed in a confusing blur in front of Julianna's eyes as Dottie chattered nonstop and Ronnie ate bowl after bowl of heavily buttered popcorn, licking his fingers and occasionally nodding his head at something Dottie said. Earlier in the evening, Julianna had taken a quick, cold shower (after being fed a dinner of macaroni and cheese, green beans, and Jell-O with marshmallows), but she no longer remembered cleaning up, and was thinking how good a bath would feel once she got back to Pawnee.

It was unpleasantly hot in the Buckleys' home. The windows were all open, and two small fans were pushing humid air around the second-floor living room, but Julianna was still perspiring freely, and the blue cotton bathrobe she had borrowed from Dottie was sticking to the skin of her legs and arms. Under the robe she was wearing a night slip, also Dottie's; the sheriff's wife had washed and dried Julianna's green dress and underthings, but had not given them back yet, insisting Julianna would "be much more comfortable" in the borrowed robe and slip. Dottie was as thin as Julianna, but six inches shorter, so the hemline of the robe, knee-length on Dottie, only came to mid-thigh on Julianna.

Sundays were Dottie Buckley's favorite night of the week to watch television, but to tell the truth she had been having trouble concentrating on her shows that evening. She wasn't used to having such exotic company. She and Ronnie seldom had company at all, let alone a woman as sophisticated and alluring as Julianna Dapper. Dottie's eyes, nervous and birdlike, kept darting back and forth from Julianna's high, elegant cheekbones to her long, smooth white legs.

Poor thing, Dottie thought once again. She felt an odd compulsion to pet the other woman's clean brown hair. *She's really been put through the wringer!*

Still, for a mentally impaired person who had been assaulted, kidnapped, and raped by the two vermin currently in the downstairs jail cells—safely separated from the main house by a bolted steel door—she looked remarkably fresh and cheerful, if a trifle preoccupied. Dottie didn't blame her for being distracted, of course, not after what she'd been through; it was a wonder she had survived at all.

Dottie shuddered just thinking about the cold-blooded prisoners in custody below. As she'd prepared supper for Elijah Hunter and Jon Tate that night—cooking for any lawbreakers Ronnie arrested was part of her duty as sheriff's wife in Creighton County—she'd told Ronnie she felt like spitting in their beanieweanies. She'd cooked something for Deputy Tucker, too, without complaint; she didn't much care for Bonnor Tucker and ordinarily would have balked at feeding him, but on this occasion she was grateful he was downstairs in the jail, keeping an eye on the killer rapists until the federal agents arrived in the morning. She hadn't seen the prisoners herself, of course; Ronnie had delivered their food for her, wanting to make sure she came to no harm. The Creighton County jailhouse had never hosted any felons from the FBI's Most Wanted List, and Ronnie wasn't about to take any chances with his wife's safety.

Above the television was a crude wooden plaque Dottie had made herself, featuring a shellacked painting of an Iowa sunset. Printed across the sun in dark gold letters was: *WARM FRIENDSHIP, LIKE THE SETTING SUN, SHEDS KINDLY LIGHT ON EVERYONE.* The walls of the living room were bright yellow, and similar plaques featuring rhymes Dottie adored hung on each wall: *SHARE YOUR JOY, SHARE YOUR PRIDE, SHARE YOUR FEELINGS DEEP INSIDE,* read one, and *THE LORD WALKS BETWEEN YOU AND ME, HOLDING OUR HANDS INVISIBLY,* read another, and directly behind Julianna's head was *SNOW AND RAIN AND DARKEST WEATHER, LOVING HEARTS WILL FACE TO-GETHER!* Several vases overflowing with artificial flowers were set on end tables by the couch and chairs, and the wall-to-wall carpet was a thick brown shag.

Dottie Buckley was a lonely woman. She had few friends, and little opportunity for making others. Her three sons had all left home years ago, and though two of them still lived in Creighton County, she rarely saw them, except on the holidays. She spent her days watching television and reading magazines, waiting for her husband to come home from work. She wasn't a shut-in, exactly; she left the house now and then to run errands or meet various acquaintances for coffee or lunch, and she was a member of Maddox's "As You Like It" club, which met once a month at the Methodist Church. But these infrequent outings did little to alleviate her sense of isolation. Her evenings with Ronnie were comfortable and undemanding, but whatever romance had once existed between them was long gone, and lately she had begun to feel as if her life was empty of meaning. She would never have admitted this to anybody, of course, yet she found herself crying a great deal while watching shows about tight-knit families, like the Cartwrights on *Bonanza*. Dottie adored the Cartwrights; they were all so handsome, especially Little Joe. More importantly, though, the Cartwrights lived and worked together, and almost nobody was ever alone. She hadn't cried during that night's episode, however; playing hostess to such a stimulating guest had made her far more cheerful than she'd been for ages.

Dottie had short black hair and a tight, anxious face. Her body was slight and tense, and whenever she moved, she moved fast, preferring to trot rather than walk, even when going from room to room in her own house. Her tongue was equally active: Silence appalled her, so she gave it no quarter, talking relentlessly from the moment she woke in the morning until her eyes finally closed at night in bed. Ronnie blamed his wife's "jitters" and "verbal diarrhea" on the ten or more cups of black coffee she drank each day, but even without caffeine in her system she couldn't sit still or refrain from commenting on anything and everything that passed through her mind.

"Whenever you're the teensiest bit sleepy, you just go right on and say so," Dottie said quietly to Julianna as *The Dupont Show* was interrupted by a commercial. "I've got the guest bed all made up and ready to go in Stevie's old room, and Ronnie and I will only be ten feet away and can be there in a jiffy if you need anything at all. You don't have to worry a bit about those hooligans down in the jail. They'll never hurt you again. Bonnor's down there with them, and he'll watch those filthy jackals like a hawk and shoot them dead if they so much as make a peep, I promise you that."

She leaned in closer and dropped her voice even lower. "Between you and me, I don't really like Bonnor. I tell Ronnie all the time that Bonnor Tucker is as mean as a snake and as dumb as a toadstool, but Ronnie won't fire him because he thinks Bonnor is a lot better than his last deputy. I'm not so sure of that at all, though, because like I was just saying to Ronnie the other night, Jared Jones may have been lazy and dishonest but at least he was nice and didn't ignore people like Bonnor does every time somebody tries to talk to him. Ronnie didn't like Jared mostly because he never shaved the back of his neck or changed his socks, but I keep saying that good hygiene isn't half as important as good manners, though I suppose intelligent people can disagree about things like that. Ronnie can be awfully pig-headed sometimes, but most of the time he's the sweetest man who ever lived. Anyway, I swear Bonnor Tucker sometimes sees me coming and turns around and walks the other way just to avoid saying hello. Can you imagine? Last week I went right up to him and . . ."

Julianna had no idea who the woman was who had been sitting on the couch next to her for the past three hours, but she certainly knew a chatterbox when she met one, and she'd quickly adopted Sheriff Buckley's obvious strategy of dealing with his wife's never-ending soliloquies: Namely, nodding and smiling kindly at Dottie every few minutes without paying the slightest bit of attention to her. It was all the acknowledgment the short, hungry-looking woman seemed to require, and it left Julianna's thoughts free to roam. Dottie's voice was like the hum of the two fans in the room, and Julianna didn't really mind it one way or the other, except for the fact that it made it difficult to listen for sounds from the basement, where her friends were being held.

Every so often that evening, she thought she'd heard suspicious noises drifting up from the jail, but the concrete floors of the building were too thick and solid to allow sound to carry very well, and she hadn't been able to determine if she was imagining things or not. She was almost sure she'd heard Jon yell something once, for instance, but between the television, the fans, and Dottie's patter, she'd eventually decided that her over-stimulated ears were deceiving her.

She gazed at the wall clock above Ronnie's chair and bit her lip when she saw that it was 9:32 p.m. She was terribly frustrated to have gotten so close to home, only to be stopped by such a silly misunderstanding; she knew her mother and father would be worried sick about her, and Ben's parents would be beside themselves.

I could just strangle Jon, she thought, nodding placidly at Dottie but seething inside. *If he hadn't broken Günter's lock, we'd all be back in Pawnee right this very minute!*

"What kind of a stupid name is 'Bonnor'?" Jon Tate whispered to Elijah. The hallway separating their cells was only a few feet wide, but Elijah didn't move on his bed and Jon wasn't sure the younger boy had heard him. He pressed his face against the bars of his own cell door and whispered again as loudly as he dared. "I guess I'd be a huge asshole, too, if I had such a dumb name."

Elijah remained still.

Jon was worried about his friend. They hadn't spoken all evening because Bonnor Tucker had forbidden it, but while Jon had spent much of the time pacing, Elijah had only risen once from the metal cot in his cell, to pee in the toilet. During the evening, he'd lifted his head from the mattress now and then to glance over at Jon (as if reassuring himself that the older boy hadn't somehow been spirited away), but other than this, he hadn't moved at all. Jon could see he was awake and staring at the ceiling, and something about this wide-eyed, cadaver-like stillness was making Jon fear for him. It would no doubt anger Bonnor if he caught them talking, but for some reason it seemed crucial to know what Elijah was thinking right then and there.

Both boys were still handcuffed, but ever since their supper several hours earlier the cuffs were now in front of their bodies instead of behind them. Deputy Tucker had intended to cuff them behind their backs again when they were done eating, but Sheriff Buckley, before retiring for the night, had said, "Are you gonna wipe their asses when they need to take a crap, Bonnor?" and the deputy had been obliged to reevaluate his plan.

This minor aggravation aside, however, Bonnor Tucker had been enjoying himself immensely that Sunday evening. The instant the sheriff had gone upstairs, Bonnor had begun doing everything he could think of to make this experience a memorable one for his prisoners, and he was 100 percent certain he had already achieved this goal. Granted, the first few minutes had been by far the best part, but even so he wouldn't have missed a single second he'd spent with Elijah and Jon that night for, in his words, "all the pussy in China."

"What are you saying in there, you piece of shit?" Bonnor now barked at Jon from the open door of the tiny office at the front of the building. The jailhouse office—with barely enough room for a desk, a phone, a cot, and a trash can—was at the opposite end of the hall from the steel door that led to the Buckleys' residence. "Don't make me come in there and teach you little buttwipes another lesson!"

Bonnor had given each of the boys what he drolly referred to as "a lesson in manners" soon after Buckley had collected their dishes and disappeared upstairs for the final time. Elijah had been the first to receive Bonnor's instruction; he now had a swollen jaw and an ugly, livid bruise on his right cheek to go along with the puffy lower lip he had gotten during the arrest itself. He was also in considerable pain from having a knee driven into his groin, and there was a walnut-sized welt on his left bicep from Bonnor's nightstick. Jon's private tutorial had been somewhat less harsh—three vicious, surgical jabs to the stomach, followed by an uppercut to the chin—but only because the deputy was out of breath by then and decided he needed to pace himself.

All these punitive measures, or so the boys were informed at the time, were merely "a down payment" on what they had coming, yet after this initial assault Bonnor was content to sit in the office and verbally abuse Jon and Elijah from there every few minutes. These harangues served as a palate cleanser of sorts between the dozens of phone calls he was making to everybody he could think of; the calls themselves were to ensure that all the people he considered important in the "whole goddamn dipshit county" (he was currently speaking to Ardell Watley, his retired third-grade teacher) knew just who Deputy Bonnor Tucker had in his charge. Every hour or so he wandered down the hall to taunt his prisoners at close range, but a belated realization that he might have a little explaining to do the next day to "some candy-ass, stuck-up, hairless, nut-suckin' mama's boy FBI agent" concerning the physical condition of Hunter and Tate had thus far restrained him from entering their cells again.

"The fuckin' feds always ruin everything," he kept saying mournfully to the boys.

Meanwhile, down the hall in the jail cells, Jon's whispered remarks about the deputy's name had taken several seconds to penetrate Elijah's consciousness. The brutal beating earlier that had left him gasping for air and cradling his crotch on the floor of his cell had also stopped his mind; he had no memory of crawling on his bed afterward, nor could he recall what he'd been thinking or feeling as he stared up at the ceiling for the better part of four hours. As Jon's hushed voice now brought him back to their grim surroundings, despair beyond anything he'd ever known threatened to overwhelm him, and he immediately tried to sink back into the oblivious, restful state he'd been in before Jon disturbed him.

"Go away, Jon," he murmured, turning on his side. Every muscle in his body burned with pain, and he almost hated his friend for trying to rouse him. "Just let me be, okay?"

He continued staring into space for a little bit, but he could feel Jon watching him, and he began to feel bad for making the other boy fret. He stirred at last on his bed, sighing, then rose gingerly from his mattress and shuffled over to the cell door, wincing with every step. Jon was directly across from him as he came to a halt, and the two gazed at each other for a long time, both leaning against the bars of their cells.

Elijah was shocked by Jon's appearance. The harsh glare of the single fluorescent bulb on the hallway ceiling didn't extend all the way into the cells, but now that they were closer to each other Elijah could see the other boy's injuries in lurid detail. Jon's left eye—swollen shut and circled by a hideous raccoon-like black ring—was especially gruesome, but his entire face was a patchwork of cuts and bruises that were nearly as bad, and his chest and shoulders were scraped raw in places from being

thrown on the gravel during the arrest. Elijah's wounds, however, looked equally bad to Jon: A sickly yellowish bruise on the
younger boy's jaw was the worst of it, but there was also matted, dried blood under his nose and on his chin, and the welt on
his left arm looked like some kind of ghastly, plague-related
boil.

Neither boy knew what to say; the bleakness of their situation had stricken them both dumb. Elijah finally cleared his
throat—after making sure the deputy had resumed speaking on
the phone in the office—and gave voice to the only thing that
seemed worth talking about.

"Yeah, Bonnor *is* a dumb name," he whispered. His jaw was
throbbing and he was having difficulty standing upright because
of the pain in his groin, but he could see Jon was hurting, too, so
he tried to grin for the other boy's sake. "Wanna bet everybody
called him 'Boner' when he was a kid?"

Jon attempted to smile, too, even though the hopelessness in
Elijah's face made his own heart ache. "Yeah, I bet you're
right," he answered.

"I mean it!" howled Bonnor Tucker, slamming the receiver
down on a semi-senile Ardell Watley in midsentence. Bonnor
couldn't hear what his captives were saying, but he didn't care
for their whispered conversation one little bit. "I swear to God
I'll break your goddamn heads open if you don't shut the fuck
up right now and sit your asses back down on your beds!"

Jon and Elijah grimaced at each other, wanting to keep talking but knowing it would be foolish to do so. The unfairness of
their plight became unbearable for Elijah, and his dark eyes
filled with tears. Jon's throat tightened, and without thinking he
reached through the bars of his cell door, awkwardly twisting
his upper body and stretching his handcuffed wrists toward the
younger boy as far as he could, wanting to offer comfort but not
knowing how. Elijah understood what Jon was trying to do, and
began to cry harder. He put his own arms out in the hall a second later, trying to grasp Jon's hands in his own. Both boys
strained as hard as they could, but the metal bars of their cages
made it impossible to extend their arms into the hallway much

past their elbows. Jon cursed under his breath in frustration and Elijah bit back a sob when their fingertips remained several inches apart in spite of all their effort.

"Ahhh, if that ain't the sweetest thing I've ever seen, I'll eat my own fuckin' jockstrap," Bonnor Tucker mocked. "But what part of 'sitting your asses down on your beds' did you two little fudge-packers not understand?"

The two boys talking was bad enough, to Bonnor's way of thinking, but actually reaching across the hall and trying to hold hands like a couple of lovesick fairies was an unforgivable breach of jailhouse etiquette. He picked up his nightstick and lumbered down the hall, relishing the effect each heavy footfall he took had on the boys' faces as he approached them. Even from fifteen feet away he could smell their fear; the reek of their sweat permeated the whole first floor of the building.

I can only give them a couple of love taps this time, he reminded himself. *The fuckin' feds always ruin EVERYTHING.*

Jon and Elijah quickly backed away from their cell doors, looking at each other in dismay as Bonnor drew even with them, reaching for the key ring on his belt. He inserted a large skeleton key in Elijah's door, and the teenager stumbled backward, his eyes huge.

"Jesus Christ, man, he's sitting down, okay?" Jon pleaded from behind Bonnor.

"Shut your goddamn mouth," Bonnor snapped over his shoulder. On impulse he withdrew the key from Elijah's cell door and turned around. "On second thought, maybe I'll start with you this time, pecker-breath."

He unlocked Jon's cell door and it swung open on its hinges, creaking. Jon backed away from the hallway until he could go no farther, holding his hands up.

"But we haven't done anything wrong!" he cried out. His desperation turned to rage as Bonnor kept moving forward. "Why are you being such a fucking ASSHOLE?"

Bonnor's blood rose immediately; he didn't appreciate being called names. "It looks like you need another lesson in manners,

fucknuts," he said, reattaching the keys to his belt. "Calling me
a bad name like that is gonna cost you a few teeth."

Bonnor figured he could always tell the feds that Jon had
tried to grab him as he was walking by the cell.

With an almost casual motion, he knocked Jon's arms out of
the way and half turned the younger man, exposing his bare
back. The nightstick came down instantly, striking Jon just
above the left kidney. As Jon screamed and fell against the wall,
Bonnor struck him twice more on the left flank, and then spun
him around again and popped him in the mouth with a glancing
blow of his fist. The poorly aimed jab didn't have as much force
as Bonnor had intended, but Jon's head still snapped back and
hit the concrete wall; he sprawled on the floor, dizzy with pain.
He tried to crawl away from the deputy, but Bonnor bent down
and flipped him on his back as easily as if he were a turtle.

"Just think of me as your friendly neighborhood dentist,"
Bonnor said amiably, taking careful aim at Jon's mouth with the
tip of his nightstick.

"HEY, YOU FAT FUCKING PILE OF SHIT!"

The shout that came from behind Bonnor was stupefyingly
loud, as if someone had put a megaphone over his entire head
and bellowed into it. Bonnor jerked upright and spun around,
forgetting all about his desire to deprive Jon of his teeth.

"THAT'S RIGHT, *BONER,* YOU PISS-DRINKING COCK-
SUCKER, I'M TALKING TO YOU!" Elijah continued wailing
at the top of his lungs. "WHY DON'T YOU GET YOUR FAT
ASS OVER HERE RIGHT NOW? I'VE GOT A NICE HOT
STEAMING PILE OF NIGGER SHIT FOR YOU TO EAT,
YOU BUTT-UGLY, RETARDED SON OF A BITCH!"

Elijah Hunter had never been more afraid in his entire life.

What am I DOING? he thought in astonishment. There wasn't
a flicker of doubt in his mind that he was signing his own death
warrant, yet he couldn't seem to make himself stop.

What the FUCK am I DOING?

Courage, Elijah had always believed, was a character trait he
had been born without. And as much as he might despise him-

self for what he saw as a lack of spine, he had long since accepted that being a hero was simply not part of his makeup. Yet as he had watched Bonnor Tucker beat Jon without mercy, something unprecedented had occurred: He had found himself willing to do anything, anything at all, to protect somebody he cared about.

Even if it meant getting himself killed.

"WHAT'S IT LIKE TO HAVE THE STUPIDEST FUCKING NAME IN THE WHOLE GALAXY, *BONER?*" he bellowed, giddy with recklessness. "DID YOUR MOM CALL YOU THAT ON PURPOSE, OR WAS SHE EVEN MORE RETARDED THAN YOU ARE?"

Bonnor Tucker was no longer enjoying himself in the slightest. The sense of having Jon and Elijah in his power was completely gone, lost in the mind-numbing effrontery of Elijah's taunts.

"YOU'RE DEAD, NIGGER!" he screamed, belatedly lurching into motion. He charged out of Jon's cell and flung himself at Elijah's door, grappling for his keys with one hand and banging the nightstick on the iron bars with the other.

Elijah knew he couldn't last two seconds against Bonnor, but the wrathful elixir coursing through his veins had stolen every ounce of his reason. Now that he'd gotten Bonnor away from Jon, the only thing he cared about was having the opportunity to try to dig Bonnor's eyes out of their sockets with his thumbs before the deputy killed him.

"SPEAKING OF YOUR MOM, I HEAR SHE KNOWS MORE ABOUT BONERS THAN ANY WOMAN ALIVE!" he raged, ramming his handcuffed fists through the bars straight at the deputy's large head. Bonnor dodged aside and attempted to grab Elijah's arms, but Elijah leapt away. "JESUS CHRIST, BONER, I'M FROM MAINE, AND EVEN I'VE HEARD ALL ABOUT YOUR OLD LADY! SHE'S A GODDAMN LEGEND!"

"SHUT THE FUCK UP!" Bonnor howled. He couldn't get the key in the lock; his hand was shaking too badly from the overmastering need to kill Elijah right *now*. He ducked another two-fisted attack from Elijah and aimed a kick through the bars at the teenager's shins; the kick missed and the toe of his boot clanged into a bar instead.

"GODDAMMIT!" he yelped, dancing in agony. "YOU'RE GONNA PAY FOR THAT!"

Jon Tate stirred on the floor of his cell, shaking his head woozily. He felt as if he were hallucinating: Elijah was standing behind his own cell door, laughing like a madman at the enraged Bonnor Tucker, who was hopping around the hallway on one foot. The younger boy seemed oblivious to the danger he was in, but one glimpse at the side of the deputy's murderous face was all it took for Jon to grasp just how far the man was willing to go to exact vengeance.

Jon forced himself to sit up, looking around wildly for a weapon. Bonnor had left Jon's own cell door wide open in the rush to get to Elijah, but Jon was in no shape to take him on unarmed; the simple act of sitting up had almost made him pass out. Yet Bonnor was already back at Elijah's cell, and this time when Elijah tried to strike him, Bonnor was finally able to land a blow, jabbing the boy in the sternum with his nightstick and sending him reeling. Bonnor got the key in the lock and began to turn it, and Jon, frantic and weaponless, did the only thing he could think of.

"HEY, BONER-BITER!" he shrieked. "WHY DON'T YOU COME ON BACK OVER HERE?"

Bonnor's head spun around. He seemed amazed to see Jon's cell door standing wide open and Jon rising slowly to his feet; he stared back down at the skeleton key he was using to open Elijah's lock, as if he could no longer remember what it was for.

"THAT'S RIGHT, YOU MORON!" Jon resumed, trying not to let his face give away how frightened he was. "I'M GETTING READY TO WALTZ OUT THE DOOR WHILE YOU JUST STAND THERE LIKE THE DUMBEST GODDAMN DOUCHE BAG THAT'S EVER LIVED!"

Bonnor took a step toward Jon, then froze and looked over at Elijah once more before swinging his head back to Jon. The deputy was apoplectic by this point, but the inability to choose who to kill first had briefly rendered him incapable of action.

Elijah reentered the fray immediately, fearing for Jon's safety yet again.

"HEY, BONER! DID YOU FORGET ABOUT ME? I'M RIGHT IN HERE, YOU GOAT-FUCKER! COME ON IN HERE AND EAT MY—"

"NO WAY, BONER!" Jon interrupted. "COME OVER HERE SO WE CAN TALK ABOUT GIVING YOU A NICER NAME! HOW ABOUT BUNGHOLE TICKLER? DO YOU LIKE THAT? HOW ABOUT BUTTLICK TURDMUNCH? HOW ABOUT ..."

The stereophonic abuse proved too much for Bonnor Tucker. His self-control utterly gone, he dropped his keys and seized the handle of the revolver on his belt, ripping it free of its holster and pointing the gun straight at Jon's head. The young man shut up with gratifying speed, and Elijah, too, fell silent behind Bonnor, his breath deserting him as he watched the deputy cock the hammer of the weapon.

"Say something else, shithead," Bonnor whispered to Jon. "I dare you."

Jesus Christ, Jon thought dumbly. *This guy is even crazier than Julianna.*

"You can't kill us," he said unsteadily. "We're both handcuffed, and in our cells. There's no way you could justify shooting us like this."

Bonnor's finger whitened on the trigger of the revolver. "Let me tell you a little story, asshole. Once upon a time, you and the nigger tried to escape, so I blew your fuckin' heads off and everybody else lived happily for fuckin' ever. The End."

Elijah's heart was racing. The deputy was within his reach, but grabbing him at this point would almost certainly get Jon killed. Yet doing nothing seemed an equally terrible option: Bonnor was likely to pull the trigger at any second, and Jon would be just as dead. He stared with feverish intensity at an inflamed pimple on the back of Bonnor's neck, right above the starched shirt collar of the man's uniform, and he began to pray harder than he ever had in his life.

Across the hall, Jon Tate's eyes grew enormous as he watched

Elijah's long, handcuffed arms snake through the bars of his cell and hover in the air just behind Bonnor's crewcut head.

"Not so smart now, are you, fucknuts?" Bonnor goaded, attributing the anxiety in Jon's face to his last remarks. "Your brains are gonna look real pretty on that goddamn wall behind you, boy."

The room was absolutely silent, and the silence became more strained with each passing second. Jon remained motionless, not daring to breathe, and Bonnor, oblivious to Elijah's fingers floating near the base of his skull, let nearly a minute tick by, gradually regaining enough of his wits to realize that if he were to go ahead and kill both boys, he would have no time to come up with a plausible explanation for their deaths before Ronnie Buckley heard the shots and came running downstairs.

It's a wonder Ronnie ain't already been down here to see what all the fuckin' screamin' was about, anyway, Bonnor told himself, tardily noticing his supervisor's absence. It was hard to hear anything in the jail from the upstairs apartment, he knew, but the ungodly commotion the boys had been making in the cells before he drew his gun had surely been enough to get Ronnie's attention, even through the concrete ceiling. *It ain't like him to miss a chance to bawl me out for every goddamn thing he thinks I ain't doin' right.*

Thus pondering the mystery of Sheriff Buckley's truancy, Bonnor tilted his head ever so slightly from side to side in an effort to relieve the tension in his shoulders without lowering his gun. It was a far more benign motion than any he had made recently, yet the tiny movement of his square head proved to be too much for the overwrought fifteen-year-old boy in the jail cell behind him. Elijah threw himself in a panic against the bars and seized the back of Bonnor's collar, desperate to save Jon's life.

"NO!" Jon wailed, flinging his hands up.

And the Colt went off.

At 10:17 p.m.—exactly seven minutes before all hell broke loose in the jail cells—Julianna Dapper, upstairs with Ronnie and Dottie Buckley, found herself becoming restless. The sudden urge to go home was making her fidget on the sofa; she kept thinking about her mother and father, and how they would likely ground her for staying out so late without telling them where she was.

The late-night news had replaced *The Dupont Show* on television. Julianna was seated midway between the Buckleys, with Ronnie to her right in his armchair and Dottie to her left on the sofa. Sheriff Buckley was still fast asleep, with a half-full popcorn bowl balanced on top of his mountainous stomach; his mouth was open and he was snoring lightly. Dottie, on the other hand, was alert as always, twitching her head from side to side like a guinea hen hunting for deer ticks in the grass.

"Do you need something, honey?" Dottie asked, resisting the impulse to stroke Julianna's freckled wrist.

Julianna nodded and smiled. "I'd like to have my dress back, please," she said politely. "I've had a lovely time this evening, but I really do need to be going."

Dottie's mouth twisted with compassion. "Oh, you poor thing." She could no longer restrain herself from touching Julianna; she reached over the seat cushion separating them and rested her hand lightly on the other woman's vulnerable-looking knee. "I know it's hard for you to understand, but you'll just have to stay with us tonight."

Julianna's smile became fixed. "Don't be silly. If Jon is still willing to drive us, Ben and I can be home in less than half an hour, safe in our own beds."

Dottie blinked. Her own uninterrupted monologue that evening had prevented her from truly crediting the extent of Julianna's mental illness, even though Ronnie had told her while Julianna was showering that he believed the woman was "nuttier than a whole goddam peanut farm."

"That's impossible, dear," she said soothingly. "You're from Bangor, Maine, and that's, well, goodness, that's at least a thousand miles from here."

Julianna's huge green eyes became even larger. "Who on earth told you I'm from Maine?" she asked, feeling strangely uneasy. "I've lived my whole life in Pawnee, Missouri. Surely you've heard of Pawnee? We're practically neighbors!"

Dottie blinked again. "Oh, honey," she said, hating to argue but afraid to indulge the other woman's delusions, either. "I'm really sorry, but I can't say as that does ring any bells. But I can be such a silly-billy sometimes and maybe I just . . . well, now, wait, hold your horses just a gosh darn minute, now that I think about it I do seem to recall hearing a few old stories about a little town called Pawnee that used to be down by Eagleville in Missouri ages and ages ago, but I can't for the life of me remember what happened to it. I'm pretty sure it isn't there anymore, though, because Ronnie and I go down that way all the time on Saturday mornings to have breakfast at a little hole-in-the-wall diner in Eagleville. It's really only a truck stop coffee shop, but they've got the best doggone cinnamon rolls in the world, as big as your head and freshly baked every day! Anyway, I've never heard anybody say a word about Pawnee in I don't know how many years and you'd think if it was still around I'd have met somebody from there by now. I may be wrong, of course, which would be just like me, I'm such a goose, but we should wake up Ronnie and ask him, just to be sure. He might know more than I do, but it seems to me that maybe there was a big fire or a tornado or something like that way back in the twenties and . . ."

Dottie had not been watching her guest's face for the past few moments—she was admiring the other woman's long, graceful fingers, instead—and so she hadn't noticed anything amiss. But when she raised her eyes again she was stricken dumb by Julianna's expression; the woman's previously serene features were now twisted almost beyond recognition by alarm. Dottie gasped in dismay and reached out instinctively to offer comfort, but Julianna evaded her touch and surged to her feet, ripping the blue bathrobe from her shoulders as if it were scalding her skin.

"I need my dress back now, please!" she demanded stridently, fairly dancing with agitation in Dottie's night slip.

Ronnie Buckley woke up mid-snore as Dottie sprang to her feet, as well; the sheriff gazed with bleary incomprehension at the two disturbed women standing over him.

"What's wrong, Dottie?" he grunted.

"I don't really know!" Dottie moaned, wringing her hands. "We were having the nicest little chat but I think I must have said something to upset her!"

She extended her arms again in a soothing gesture but Julianna backed away from her and looked around the room in distress. She saw the doorway to the hall and instantly made a beeline for it, nearly running.

"Is my dress down here?" she barked over her shoulder as she disappeared from view.

Ronnie rubbed his eyes, still trying to wake up. "Why does she want her dress back?" he asked, struggling to rise from his chair without upending the bowl of popcorn on his gut. "What's going on?"

Dottie flipped off the television set and trotted over to the doorway to monitor Julianna's whereabouts. "I don't have the faintest notion!" she blurted, biting her lip. "I was just telling her about the cinnamon rolls at the Eagleville diner and she got all riled up and now she says she wants to . . . OH my Lord, the poor thing, she's just taken off her nightie and is running around the house naked as a jaybird!"

She darted after Julianna, still wringing her hands.

"We can't let her go anyplace tonight, Dot," Ronnie called after her, galvanized by the notion of seeing Julianna naked but having undue difficulty getting to his feet. The stress and excitement of the big arrest earlier that night seemed to have taken more of a toll on him than he'd expected. "We're supposed to keep her here until Social Services comes to get her in the morning."

Julianna, who had indeed torn off Dottie's night slip with no regard for modesty, had found the laundry room by this point. Her green evening dress (or rather, Nurse Gable's evening dress, looking rather the worse for wear with a shredded, blood-stained right sleeve) was hanging neatly in the corner, and her underthings were folded neatly on top of the washer. She quickly slipped the dress over her shoulders, in far too much of a hurry to bother with her underclothes. Dottie came into the room before the dress was completely on; she stopped still and gaped at Julianna's exposed buttocks.

"Oh, dear," she said, feeling herself flush but unable to look away from the other woman's smooth, shapely thighs. "You really should put on your panties first, honey. It isn't proper to go about like that."

Even though Jayne Meadows would be lucky to have a bottom half as nice as yours, she added silently, her flush turning crimson. Dottie had always believed her own thighs were too slim and boyish, and she wished that she, too, could have such a softly rounded backside.

"Have you seen my shoes?" Julianna responded, tugging the dress down to cover herself and then reaching up behind her back to grapple with the zipper.

Ronnie showed up in the doorway of the laundry room, looking disappointed and out of breath. *If I wasn't so damn fat I could have gotten here fast enough to see something,* he chastised himself.

"You better come on back into the living room with Dottie and me and sit down again, sweetheart," he rasped. "Everything's going to be just fine in the morning, you'll see."

"She's not even wearing her underwear!" Dottie hissed at her husband. "We have to do something!"

Julianna spotted Nurse Gable's black pumps on the floor by the dryer; she finished zipping up her dress and bent down to retrieve them. Her skin was pale and she was unsteady on her feet, but as she straightened again a pronounced change came over her. The worry lines in her face vanished and her hands ceased to shake; the bewildered look in her eyes was displaced by a keen, startling intelligence that unnerved Ronnie and Dottie as they gazed at her.

"You've been very sweet to me tonight, but I really must be going," Julianna said. Her tone was gracious but left little doubt she intended to do exactly as she pleased. "My friends and I have a few miles yet to go tonight, and we have no time to waste."

Straight across the hall from the laundry room was the kitchen, and on the other side of the kitchen was the door to the downstairs. Julianna's eyes drifted toward the kitchen, then back to the Buckleys. Dottie was standing by the washer, but Ronnie was still planted firmly in the doorway, blocking access to the hall. Julianna studied the stocky sheriff for a moment longer, then smoothed the front of her dress and walked straight up to him with no outward sign of misgiving.

"Well, then!" she said brightly. "Thanks ever so much, but I really must say good-bye for now."

She was almost as tall as Ronnie, and the expectation in her eyes that he would let her pass without a fuss made him feel like an adolescent bully for not immediately moving aside.

"I can't let you leave here, sweetheart," he murmured, shaking his head in a reflexive, nervous imitation of Ernest Borgnine. Ever since seeing *Marty,* Ronnie had practiced, in front of the bathroom mirror, many of his favorite Oscar-winner's distinctive hangdog mannerisms, and he often mimicked them unconsciously whenever he felt unsure of himself. "I wish I could, but I just can't."

Borgnine's ability to appear both resolute and lovable at the same time was what Ronnie most admired about the pug-faced actor; he now tried to convey these same qualities to Julianna, hoping this might convince her to listen to him. Regrettably, though, Julianna did not appear to be a fan of Ernest Borgnine.

"I beg your pardon?" she asked. She tried to edge around Ronnie but he put a hand on the door frame, barring her way. She glared down at his arm with indignation and raised her eyebrows. "You're not behaving in a gentlemanly fashion, and I'll thank you to let me be on my way."

"Now, honey," Dottie coaxed. "Ronnie's just trying to help you. He's the sheriff, you know, and that means he always knows best." She took a tentative step toward the other woman.

"How about I help you out of that dress again and into another nightie?"

Julianna opened her mouth to respond, but whatever she'd intended to say was lost in a high-pitched scream erupting from the jail cells below them.

Ronnie blinked in surprise, knowing full well how impossible it usually was to hear anything at all from downstairs once the thick steel door at the base of the stairs was shut. Yet for all the concrete flooring between them—not to mention Dottie's plush rugs and several dozen handcrafted, sound-absorbing wall plaques—Elijah Hunter's voice, though too muffled to hear distinct words, was coming through loud and clear.

Dammit, Bonnor, Ronnie thought, grimacing as Elijah screamed a second time. *What in God's name are you doing to those two boys?*

"That's Ben!" Julianna cried, her self-possession gone as abruptly as it had surfaced. "Oh my Lord, something awful must have happened!"

Elijah's third scream seemed to ricochet around the laundry room, and Julianna, frantic to go to the aid of her friend, launched herself at Ronnie without warning. Dottie began to hyperventilate as Ronnie, knocked off balance by Julianna's onslaught, flung his arms around the tall woman and attempted to restrain her without causing injury. From down below Elijah kept screaming, and each of his shrieks spurred Julianna to greater efforts to free herself; she started clawing at Ronnie in an attempt to weaken his hold on her.

"OW!" Ronnie yelped as one of Julianna's fingernails dug a deep trough across his forehead.

"Oh, please, Julianna," Dottie wheezed almost inaudibly, seizing her own breast with both hands and fighting for oxygen as a line of blood appeared above her husband's eyebrows. "Please please please stop!"

"Let me go!" Julianna snapped, sinking her teeth into Ronnie's flabby shoulder.

"OW!" Ronnie yelped again.

Deputy Bonnor Tucker's howls of outrage now mingled with Elijah's in the jail cells, and a moment later Jon Tate joined in, as well. Julianna—yanking ruthlessly on Ronnie's left earlobe—finally managed to escape the sheriff's clutches and squeeze around him; she dashed for the kitchen with Ronnie at her heels, cupping his ear with his hand and swearing. Dottie staggered after them but only made it as far as the hallway before losing her balance and overturning a small shelf of knickknacks by the kitchen entrance. A vase full of plastic purple flowers shattered on the floor in front of her; she stepped on broken glass in her bare feet and fell to the floor, wailing. A macramé-framed table plaque (inscribed in delicate gilt letters with *JESUS LOVES US, ONE AND ALL: THIN AND FAT, SHORT AND TALL!*) snapped into splinters beneath Dottie's boyish thighs.

"I'm coming, Ben!" Julianna sang out from the far side of the kitchen, tearing open the heavy oak door at the top of the staircase.

"Gotcha!" Ronnie panted, catching her from behind and lifting her off her feet before she could exit the apartment.

The three young men below inexplicably stopped yelling, and Julianna and Ronnie likewise fell silent, too winded to do anything but breathe harshly as they lumbered around the stairwell door in a violent, exhausting dance of some duration, both red-faced and sweating from exertion. Dottie watched numbly from the hallway as Ronnie—wearing pajama bottoms and a T-shirt, and looking oddly underdressed compared to Julianna in her formal evening gown—began turning purple from the neck up. Dottie's feet were bleeding heavily but she was too worried about her husband at the moment to tend them.

"Just let her go, Ronnie," she begged. Her heart went out to him, knowing he was doing all he could to keep from hurting Julianna, even though the woman was still scratching and biting him every chance she got. "You're going to throw out your back again if you aren't careful!"

She's probably right, Ronnie grudgingly admitted to himself as sweat and blood ran into his eyes, blurring his vision. The zipper on the back of Julianna's dress had come partly unzipped again and the soapy smell of her skin at the nape of her neck seemed to be making him dizzy. *Maybe I should just lock this hellcat up in a cell until she . . .*

His left arm went numb all at once, followed by a lancing pain in his chest. Unaccountably losing control of his limbs, he staggered toward the open door at the top of the steps again, still holding Julianna off the ground even though she was writhing in his arms.

"Ronnie!" Dottie gasped in horror.

The marriage of Ronnie and Dottie Buckley may not have had much romance remaining in it, but as Ronnie teetered on the top step of a dark, steep staircase, Dottie teetered, too, on the brink of a life without Ronnie in it. In a harrowing flash of self-discovery, she understood that romance was no longer important to her, nor was the chronic discontent she had felt for years. The man she had shared her life with for decades was in mortal jeopardy, and losing him was unthinkable: These two simple facts were all that mattered to her now.

"Ronnie!" she cried again, fighting to rise but unable to get her legs under her. "Just put her down!"

"Let . . . me . . . go!" Julianna squeaked out, unable to catch her wind because of how tightly Ronnie was clasping her around the ribcage.

Unlike Dottie, Ronnie Buckley had never faulted his spouse for any dissatisfaction he had with his life. His unfulfilled Academy Award aspirations aside, in fact, he considered himself to be a lucky man, and he looked forward every night to coming home to Dottie. He loved listening to her talk just as he loved listening to the news on the radio as they lay in bed together on Sunday mornings; he loved watching her buzz around their apartment, chattering harmlessly, just as he loved watching the sunlight gleam on the clean countertops in their kitchen as they ate their breakfast and drank their coffee together, each day before he went to work. She comforted him, and she needed him, and he had always believed that marrying her was the smartest thing he had ever done.

"I'm . . . okay . . . Dot . . ." Ronnie puffed, aware of her distress and hating to worry her. His bare feet were slippery with perspiration on the linoleum. "Just need to sit down . . . and maybe have a little . . ."

This unfinished sentence was not what Ronnie Buckley would have chosen as the last thing he would ever say, but even if he'd had the gift of foresight and could have come up with something more fitting, Dottie wouldn't have heard him. Blood loss and terror had done their work by then, and she had slumped over in the hallway in a dead faint seconds before he spoke. She would regret this ill-timed swoon of hers for the rest of her life, but in truth it was a blessing: Blacked out as she was, she missed the pivotal moment when Deputy Bonnor Tucker, grabbed from behind by Elijah in the jail cells below them, frantically pulled the trigger on the Colt revolver aimed at Jon Tate.

The mercy of unconsciousness should never be underrated.

At the sound of the gunshot beneath them, Julianna went berserk, flailing her arms and legs like a drowning child. Ronnie—who had finally understood he was in the throes of a major heart attack—released her all at once; she collapsed in surprise on the top step at his feet, almost tumbling down the stairs before managing to save herself at the last second by seizing the bannister.

The Oscar-worshipping sheriff of Creighton County, Iowa, however, was not so lucky.

Clutching his chest in a spasm of agony, Ronnie accidentally tripped over Julianna's torso and plunged headfirst down the long concrete staircase, unable to break his fall or slow it in any way. His heavy body bounced off the steps several times before landing with bone-jarring force on the concrete floor at the bottom, yet even this wasn't enough to stop him; his momentum was such that he rolled over once more in an almost graceful somersault at the base of the steps and banged his skull on the steel door leading to the jail cells. The door chimed like a gong, low and mournful, and Ronnie Buckley crumpled to the ground at last, already dead before his limbs ceased moving.

Chapter 12

Deputy Bonnor Tucker gripped the bars of his jail cell and began screaming at the middle-aged black couple and the older white man the instant they stepped into the hallway of the Maddox, Iowa, jailhouse at 10:49 p.m. that Sunday night.

"It's about FUCKING time!" he raged, rattling the iron bars but otherwise having no effect. "Get me the FUCK out of here!"

Bonnor had only been conscious for five minutes, but being alone in a silent building with the corpse of his former employer a few feet away had made the time stretch for what seemed an eternity. The absence of windows in that part of the building made him feel as if he'd been buried alive in a mausoleum; his cries for assistance had been swallowed by the shadows beneath the cots and in the corners of the room, and he'd known that no one passing by on the sidewalk outside would ever hear him, even if it were the middle of the day.

The black man and woman were slender and neatly dressed; the older gentleman was rumpled and bald. Bonnor had never seen any of them before but was too distraught to even hazard a guess as to who they might be. All three froze in place as they saw Ronnie Buckley's body by the open steel door at the opposite end of the hallway. The older man staggered a little in shock, and the black man reached out to steady him.

"Yeah, that's right!" Bonnor's voice broke a little. "Those murdering cocksuckers killed Sheriff Buckley!"

For all his grumbling about Ronnie Buckley, Bonnor had

liked the man very much, and found himself wanting to cry every time he looked over at the base of the stairs. Ronnie may have talked to him every now and then like he was a naughty three-year-old, but the majority of Bonnor's memories of the sheriff were good: Ronnie hiring him fresh out of high school and teaching him to shoot a gun, Ronnie belting out a painfully tone-deaf rendition of "Over the Rainbow" one night in the jail cells when he thought Bonnor had already left the building, Ronnie allowing car after car to go speeding past him on the highway because he was too busy woolgathering about the Academy Awards to care. (Bonnor had learned of Ronnie's Oscar aspirations years earlier, during a heart-to-heart conversation the two men had over a beer after work.) The truth was that Ronnie Buckley had been a good man, and a kind one— never making fun of Bonnor's name—and Bonnor couldn't seem to come to terms with the fact that he was gone, just like that.

Things like this ain't supposed to happen, he thought, grieving.

It never occurred to Bonnor to wonder why Elijah Hunter and Jon Tate would have left him alive if they had indeed killed the sheriff. All he knew was somebody he cared about was dead, and the two boys he held responsible for this atrocity needed to pay for it, as well as for everything else they had done. He glared at the strangers watching him from the doorway of the sheriff's office and tried to mask his sorrow with another burst of fury.

"For shit's sake, don't just stand there!" he roared. "Find the goddamn keys and let me the fuck out of here!"

Bonnor's head was throbbing; there were two olive-sized bumps on the crown of his skull. One was from where he had struck it on the bars of Elijah's cell after the teenager had seized his collar and pulled him backward, causing him to fall, and the other was from being clubbed with his own nightstick, ripped from his fist by Elijah when he, Bonnor, was lying on the ground in front of the cell, too stunned by the first blow to protect himself from another. He had lost consciousness after Elijah hit him, and when he came to, both boys were gone—along with his gun and his nightstick—and he was locked in the very cell Elijah had been in less than twenty minutes before. He could still smell the black boy's sour sweat in the air, mingling with his own.

The first thing Bonnor had seen when he regained consciousness was Ronnie Buckley's body. Bonnor had immediately begun bleating for help but nobody had heard him. Maddox was a ghost town on Sunday nights, and the jailhouse was surrounded by stores and offices that wouldn't be open until the following morning. His relief at the timely arrival of his rescuers was enormous, but in spite of his impatience to be let out none of them seemed in any hurry to follow his orders.

"Jesus Christ, will you hurry up?" he railed at them. It was obvious from his uniform he was no criminal, and he couldn't understand why they were just standing there staring at him as if he were a goddamn monkey in a zoo. "I have to call the state police right now so we can catch those little bastards before they get too far away!"

The older white man finally took a step toward Bonnor's cell but he stopped abruptly when the small woman held up a restraining hand.

"Please examine the sheriff's body, Dr. Reilly, just in case he's still alive and needs your help." The woman's voice was calm, but had an underlying edge. "You should also have a look around upstairs after you're finished, to see if anyone else is hurt."

The man identified as "Dr. Reilly" slid what appeared to be an M&M into his mouth and winced apologetically at Bonnor. "Shouldn't we let the officer out first?" he asked.

"I'll see to the officer," the woman responded. "Please do as I ask."

Dr. Reilly jumped as if he'd been prodded with a branding iron and trotted down the hall, averting his eyes as he passed Bonnor. The black couple followed him, but more slowly, scanning as much as they could see of the jailhouse in the light cast by the single bare bulb dangling from the hallway ceiling. To Bonnor's displeasure, the woman ignored him when they drew even with him, choosing instead to step into the empty cell across the hall.

"Hey, get the hell out of there!" Bonnor demanded, glancing at the black man but quickly focusing on the woman again after intuitively realizing she was the one who required his attention. "This is a goddamn crime scene, lady, and I'm the goddamn county deputy! Who do you think you are?"

The black man joined the woman in the cell, and both of them stared at the back wall. The wall was concrete and painted white, but five feet or so above the floor there was a small gouge in the paint, surrounded by a sparse constellation of dark red dots, visible even in the shadows at the rear of the cell. Some of the red had run down the wall in streaks; it looked as if an artist with a taste for the abstract had dipped his hand in red paint and flicked it once or twice, lightly spraying the concrete around the gouge.

Mary Hunter groped for Sam's hand.

"Even if that's Elijah's blood, he's still alive," she whispered to Sam. "The deputy just said as much." She managed to control her trembling, but only barely. The gore on the wall was a bad sign, yet surely there wasn't enough blood to suggest anything besides a superficial wound.

Based on the deputy's comments and the evidence of her own eyes, her son had somehow escaped the Maddox jail, hurt or not. Everything else was less obvious, however, and the presence of the dead body at the end of the hall both terrified and confounded her. Her first concern, however, was ascertaining if Elijah had indeed been injured; the rest of the details could wait.

She schooled her features and turned around again to face Bonnor Tucker.

This is not a smart man, she thought, sizing up the hostile, uniformed officer before her in a single glance. Boneheaded bullies like Bonnor Tucker—she could always spot them—were child's play to her, and under other circumstances it would have afforded her a great deal of amusement to slowly demolish the man's blustering persona bit by bit. But there was nothing funny whatsoever in the blood on the wall behind her, or in the dead sheriff on the floor, and she had no time to spare for anything but a blunt interrogation.

"Where's my son?" she asked quietly.

The woman was half his size, and Bonnor could barely hear her. But something in her taut, pretty face—as well as her now obvious connection to Elijah Hunter—made him lose any inclination to scream at her again.

He studied her through the bars before beginning to speak hesitantly. "So you're the nigg . . ."

He stopped. He had been about to ask for confirmation that she was indeed "the nigger's mom," but on further reflection he realized she'd already told him the answer. He also had an unusually sage notion that referring to Elijah as a "nigger" in front of his mother and father might be a bad idea. He was unarmed and trapped in a jail cell, and for all he knew they might be just as dangerous as their sneaky, vicious child. There was certainly something in the woman's manner that he found frightening, in spite of her diminutive size.

"I don't know," he muttered. "They knocked me out, and both him and his friend were gone when I woke up."

"I see." Her eyes, glacial and unwavering, appeared to treble in size as they bored into him. She gestured at the stains on the wall behind her without turning her head. "And whose blood is that?"

Braver men than Bonnor Tucker had buckled under the force of Mary Hunter's personality, and none of these unfortunate souls had been subjected to the pitiless psychogenic battery she now brought to bear on the Creighton County deputy. The barometric pressure in the room seemed to drop in the same way it did when a tornado was nearby, and Bonnor was suddenly, and unreasonably, terrified. The menace emanating from Mary's small frame made him feel like she had probed all the hidden recesses of his mind and had seen each and every blow he'd inflicted on her child that evening.

"Not *his!*" he blurted, stricken by a nearly uncontrollable urge to pee. "It's the white kid's, I swear!"

Bonnor wondered how much the woman knew about the mischief her son had been up to, but her face was unreadable, and so he kept on talking, praying that the rush of words tum-

bling from his mouth would somehow appease her. "I was aim-
ing my gun at Tate, the white kid, when the ni— when your son
grabbed me from behind and made me fall. I got off a shot on
the way down and must have hit Tate somewhere, but your boy
took my nightstick and knocked me the fuck out before I could
see for sure what happened. I swear to God the blood is Tate's,
though. Your kid was behind me the whole time."

Even under the intense pressure he was feeling, Bonnor was
unwilling to share just how badly he'd screwed up. Like Mary,
he, too, knew that there wasn't enough blood on the wall to in-
dicate a mortal injury, leading him to conclude that he'd obviously missed his intended target. If he'd succeeded, there'd be
one less asshole in the world, and Jon Tate's corpse would be on
the floor of the other cell, sporting a nice big hole in the middle
of his forehead. Bonnor guessed the bullet had caught Tate in
the shoulder, however, or maybe the bicep. It had apparently
passed clear through him, as well, taking a chunk out of the
wall afterward; the bullet was still probably somewhere in the
jail cell. Wherever Tate had been hit, though, the little shit-for-
brains was plainly still mobile—which meant, of course, that
Bonnor had also failed to do any real damage to him, or even
slow him down much.

I bet it hurt like a bitch, though, he told himself, trying without success to find a glimmer of consolation. Ronnie Buckley
was dead, after all, the two murderers were once again free, and
the women upstairs were either dead themselves or had been
taken hostage. And all Bonnor had managed to do was wing
one of the little pricks before they went on yet another killing
spree.

Well, fuckin' hurray for me, he thought with remorse. *Maybe
I'll get a fuckin' merit badge from the Boy Scouts.*

The black man spoke up for the first time. "How long ago
did this happen?"

Samuel Hunter was in little better shape emotionally than
Bonnor Tucker. The stress and fatigue of the long trip from New
England had worn him to a frazzle, and this alone made it

nearly impossible to keep his feet under him. But to finally arrive where he had believed Elijah was being held, only to discover that his son was missing again—and yet another person was dead—was more than his fragile spirit could handle. He wanted to sob with frustration; he could feel his heart turning to dust in his chest.

Bonnor Tucker had shifted his attention to Elijah's father, and the spell of obedience he'd been under while talking to the woman was broken. He realized he'd been revealing things he probably shouldn't have, and he was still caged up and chattering like a mynah bird when he was the one who should be in charge.

"I'm done answering questions, mister," he said, straightening to his full height and glowering down at the much smaller man. "I'm an officer of the law and you fuckin' people had better let me out of here right now if you know what's good for you."

Mary Hunter stepped across the hallway and stood less than a foot away from the massive deputy. "Answer my husband," she ordered.

Bonnor blinked, then swallowed hard and dropped his eyes to the floor.

"I don't know," he mumbled, shocked by the meekness in his voice but unable to speak normally. It was all he could do to keep from calling her "ma'am" and bowing to her like a footman. "Not very long, I don't think, but I don't have a watch, and like I said I was out cold when they got away." He paused. "Can I *please* be let out, now?"

Dr. Reilly cleared his throat over by Ronnie Buckley's body. "This man is dead, I'm afraid." His chin was quivering. "He's got several broken bones and some trauma to his head, too, but there's no way to tell for sure what killed him without an autopsy."

Bonnor swore, crushed by this official confirmation of Ronnie's death. He had already known what Edgar was going to say before he said it, but some part of him had still hoped that the sheriff had just been knocked unconscious, like him, and would soon revive and start putting things to rights again. He stared woodenly at Edgar, noting the sweat on the man's bald head and his trembling jowls.

Guy looks like a fuckin' walrus, Bonnor noted, unaware of the tears coursing down his own face, one after another.

Mary didn't allow her face to soften as she watched the deputy weep in front of her; she had a strong hunch the man had treated her son cruelly that night, and in light of that she had no intention of showing him more mercy than he deserved.

"Sam, you better go upstairs with Dr. Reilly and take a look around," she suggested. "I need to stay down here and ask the deputy a few more questions."

Sam nodded and started moving toward the staircase, but then stopped again, frowning. "What about Gabriel?"

Mary started; Gabriel Dapper had slipped her mind entirely. It was funny, really; the man had been foremost on her mind when they'd entered the jailhouse just a few minutes ago, but ever since she'd seen what awaited them inside the building she'd actually forgotten there was at least as much to worry about *outside.* Her face turned suddenly still as she glanced down at the jailhouse office, thinking.

"I've got an idea," she said at last, sighing. "You won't like it, but I don't think we have any other choice at this point. You and Dr. Reilly better hurry upstairs, Sam, and I'll join you as quickly as I can."

Who the fuck is Gabriel? Bonnor Tucker wondered.

This can't be happening, Dr. Edgar Reilly kept repeating to himself as he and Samuel Hunter knelt beside the unconscious body of Dottie Buckley in the hallway of the Buckleys' upstairs apartment. Edgar was beginning to believe he was hallucinating. The deranged woman he had unleashed on the world was leaving a trail of casualties behind her, strewn about like bloody bread crumbs, and God only knew how many more innocent souls would be killed or hurt before Julianna could be recaptured.

A dozen or so plastic purple flowers and the fragments of a

glass flower vase were scattered about on the wooden floor-boards around them, along with the chipped remains of several ceramic figurines, all apparently having been dislodged from a shelf beside the kitchen doorway. One of the figurines was a cherubic Bavarian boy, dressed in lederhosen and a bright green vest; the boy had been cleanly split in two at the waistline, as if sawed in half during a failed magic trick. The figurine's cheerful, big-toothed smile struck Edgar as obscene, and he turned it face-down to avoid its gaze while he tended to the injured woman.

"Does she need an ambulance, Doc?" Sam asked him. "She doesn't look so good."

Dottie Buckley had lost a fair amount of blood from the multiple lacerations in her feet, and thus far Edgar hadn't been able to revive her. Her skin was pale, and the nightie she was wearing was soaking with sweat from the heat in the apartment. Using a first aid kit Sam had found for him in the bathroom, Edgar had done what he could to tend to her cuts, but one of them was still seeping blood in spite of his ministrations.

He nodded, mopping the perspiration off his forehead with his sleeve. "She's not in any real danger, but she's likely very de-hydrated, and she's going to need a lot of stitches," he mur-mured, trying to pick glass from a cut on Dottie's right elbow with a pair of tweezers. "I hope they have a hospital in this god-forsaken town."

Sam rose to his feet to begin to look around for a phone, but as he stepped from the hallway into the living room Dottie at last stirred and opened her eyes.

"Oh, my," she gasped up at Edgar. "Who on earth are you?"

Edgar attempted a reassuring smile but could only manage a twitch of his lips. "My name is Dr. Reilly," he said. "You've been injured, but you're going to be fine. We're getting you an ambulance right now."

Dottie felt dizzy and confused; she couldn't seem to recall for the life of her what she was doing on the floor or what she had been doing before she had fainted. She studied Edgar's tired-looking face for clues, but saw nothing there to help her.

He looks like a walrus, she thought.

"Are you new in town, Dr. Reilly?" she asked, suddenly aware she was only wearing a nightgown and feeling embarrassed to be so underdressed in the presence of a stranger. "It's very nice of you to make a house call like this, but my normal doctor is Andy Hyden. Are you filling in for him tonight or something? I'm Dorothy Buckley, by the way, but everybody calls me Dottie."

Edgar began to explain what he was doing there but Dottie cut him off.

"Oh, my goodness!" she exclaimed, catching sight of Sam standing by the phone table in her living room. Dottie had little experience with non-Caucasians, and in her current condition it seemed inexplicable to her why a black man would be in her home. Her breathing quickened and her nostrils flared with alarm. "There's a Negro over there!" she whispered to Edgar.

Sam glanced over his shoulder and raised his eyebrows before lifting the receiver from the cradle to dial the operator.

"Yes, indeed," Edgar agreed absently, finally managing to extract the glass shard from her arm. He indicated the broken knickknacks on the floor around them as well as the cuts he had just bandaged on her feet. "Can you tell us what happened, Dottie? We know Julianna Dapper was here tonight, and we're looking for her and the two boys who were downstairs in the jail."

Dottie's face darkened at the mention of Julianna's name, and her memory came rushing back.

"Ronnie!" she cried out. "Where's Ronnie?"

Edgar's gaze darted involuntarily toward the stairwell on the other side of the kitchen as he realized who she was calling for. He swabbed the wound on her elbow with alcohol and cleared his throat, forcing himself to speak. "He's . . . downstairs."

In the living room, Sam had frozen with his finger in the O slot on the phone dial. From the moment he and Edgar had entered the apartment he'd assumed the injured woman had to be the wife of the dead sheriff at the bottom of the steps, but the panic in her voice as she cried her husband's name told him she was about to suffer a far greater injury than anything that had been done to her body. He was stricken with sadness at the sight of a bowl of popcorn sitting on the brown shag carpet by an armchair; the homey ordinariness of the sight felt like a mockery to him.

"Why isn't my Ronnie up here with me?" Dottie demanded. "Is he hurt?"

There was a long pause, and Sam could hear Edgar's fingers fumbling about in the first aid kit.

"I'm very sorry," Edgar said quietly. "I'm afraid I have some terrible news for you."

Sam's eyes stung at the gentleness in Edgar's voice. There was silence in the room, and then Dottie Buckley began to keen.

Gabriel Dapper stood beside his Cadillac, gazing at the two-story brick building with a sign above the front door that read "Creighton County Jail." Lights were on in both floors of the jailhouse and the windows on the second floor were open, but he couldn't see much of the interior of either floor. The brooding look on his face didn't alter as he swatted at a mosquito on his forearm; he leaned on his car and chewed on a thumbnail, still attempting to sort through the conversation that had occurred between himself and Mary Hunter when they had pulled up in front of the jail ten minutes before.

"Why are we stopping here?" Gabriel had demanded as they all stepped out of their vehicles. "What's going on?" The last time he'd spoken to the Hunters and Edgar Reilly had been at a gas station a hundred miles or so behind them, and no one had said a word about planning to visit a jailhouse in a sleepy Iowa town late on a Sunday night.

The twenty-two-hour trip from New England to Iowa had taken a toll on each of them. Gabriel, Sam, and Edgar were rumpled, sweaty, and unshaved; Mary's face was drawn and her blue dress was wrinkled. All four were exhausted, but Gabriel was by far the worst, having had no sleep whatsoever.

Mary Hunter had glanced at Sam first, then walked over to Gabriel, looking uncharacteristically subdued. She'd met his eyes and taken a deep breath before answering his question.

"Your mother and Elijah are here," she said quietly.

The hum of a streetlight over their heads was the only sound for several seconds as Gabriel had gaped down at her, floundering for words.

"Here?" He couldn't believe he'd heard correctly. "Mom is *here?"*

"Yes," Mary answered. "Or at least that's what Sam was told when he talked to the police earlier tonight on the phone."

"I don't understand." Gabriel had stared at her, nonplussed. "Why didn't you say something sooner?" Panic flickered over his face. "Is Mom hurt?"

He turned quickly toward the jailhouse door, but Mary caught his arm before he'd gone two steps. He stopped walking but he didn't bother to hide the impatience in his voice. "What do you want, Mary? I need to see my mother."

"She's fine, Gabriel," Mary had said. "The sheriff and his wife are taking care of her." She paused, releasing his arm again as he relaxed ever so slightly. "There's something you should know, though, before we go in there."

Gabriel's eyes had flicked over at Sam and Edgar, standing side by side in silence a few feet away, then he studied Mary again darkly.

"What's going on?" he asked again. Anger had begun to rise in him. "Why the hell did the three of you keep this from me all this time? What didn't you want me to know?"

Mary had sighed. "We would have told you sooner, but we had to make sure you didn't get here before us if you took the news badly." She hesitated for a fraction of a second before continuing. "It's absolute nonsense, Gabriel, but the police are claiming that your mother was sexually assaulted by Elijah. I don't know what the other boy is capable of, of course, but I swear on my life that Elijah would never, *ever* do such a thing."

The blood had drained entirely from Gabriel's face; under the streetlight his skin was the color of bleached flour. He stared at Mary in silence for a long time as the light hummed an endless nasal note to the darkness surrounding them.

"Sweet Jesus," he'd breathed at last. "My mother has been

raped, and you're standing here telling me I should just ignore the police when they say your son was the one who did it. Jesus Christ, lady, what's the matter with you? Why should I believe anything you say?"

"Because I know my son," Mary had answered simply. "And I can tell you he'd cut off his own private parts before he'd lay a finger on your poor mother, no matter what anybody else is saying about him. All I'm asking is that you give him a chance to tell his side of the story. Please, Gabriel. If you'll just listen to him, you'll see what I'm telling you is true."

"Do you really think the cops haven't already heard everything he has to say?" Gabriel snapped. "Elijah didn't get tossed in a jail cell just for the hell of it, Mary. What will it take to get you to admit that your little angel might not be exactly who you think he is?"

Mary's lips had thinned. "A little proof, for starters," she said wearily. "Look, Gabriel. Can you be fair to our son or not? I'm not asking you for special favors, but because Julianna is your mother everything you say will carry a lot of weight with the sheriff. So if you go in howling for Elijah's blood you're going to make . . ."

Gabriel interrupted, his temper snapping. "You want me to be fair? Sure, no problem! I can do that. How about I take Elijah out for an ice cream cone, too, while I'm at it? I'll even buy him a pony later, if he wants one! He only kidnapped and raped my *mother,* for Christ's sake, and dragged her clear across the goddamn country, but we wouldn't want to treat him *unfairly,* now, would we?"

Mary's expression didn't alter in the slightest, but something in her eyes had nonetheless told Gabriel that their uneasy alliance had just come to an abrupt end. If he had been feeling less outraged he might have regretted this development, but as it was he couldn't seem to make himself care.

"Very well," Mary had answered coldly, stepping around him at once and moving toward the door. "I'm truly sorry you feel that way."

Sam had fallen into step at her side with only a quick, appraising glance at Gabriel, but Edgar Reilly had paused for several seconds before hurrying after the Hunters with a troubled look on his face.

And Gabriel had been standing outside ever since, thinking.

As anxious as he was to see his mother, he couldn't seem to make himself walk toward the jailhouse entrance. Something else was preying on his mind, something he couldn't ignore or put off any longer. He turned at last and stepped back to his Cadillac, opening the driver's door and leaning down to grope under the seat.

"Hello?" Bonnor Tucker called out softly from his locked jail cell. He stared at the staircase on the other side of Ronnie Buckley's corpse, wondering if it was safe to begin screaming for help again, or if the awful Hunter woman would reappear the instant he opened his mouth. "Is anybody there?"

His voice died in the shadows of the jailhouse.

Bonnor didn't know what was going on, but as much as he wanted to scream out his rage and frustration—and rattle the bars of his cage until the whole building fell down on top of him—he didn't dare. The last thing the Hunter woman had said to him before she vanished up the staircase was "I won't be happy at *all* if you start yelling your fool head off again while I'm still in this building. Understand?"

And just thinking about the look she had given him made Bonnor shudder.

Mary Hunter was easily the most frightening human being Bonnor had ever met in his life. He couldn't have said why, exactly; she was so tiny he could have picked her up with one arm and held her several feet above the floor without even breaking a sweat. But something about her eyes when she looked at him—something unearthly and unspeakable—chilled him to the core. Now that she was no longer standing in front of him, however, he began to feel a bit ridiculous; surely she hadn't been all *that* scary.

"Hello?" he called again, slightly louder. "Are you still up there?"

A deep, angry voice answered him. "What the hell is going on in here?"

Bonnor whipped around in his cell and gaped down at the open office door. A man even bigger than Bonnor had suddenly materialized, filling the door frame. The stranger had enormous shoulders and thick, heavy thighs; he was wearing slacks and a button-down white shirt, and he'd wadded up his suit coat into an awkward-looking bundle beneath an arm.

"Who the fuck are you?" Bonnor challenged cautiously, still not wanting to bring Mary's wrath down on him. "Find a key and let me the fuck out of here!"

The man saw Ronnie Buckley's body at the far end of the hall and almost dropped his bundle. "What happened?" he demanded, hurrying forward. "Where's my mother? Where are the Hunters, and Doc Reilly?"

Bonnor blinked, perplexed. "Who the *fuck* are you?" he repeated. "And how the hell should I know where your mother is?"

"I'm Gabriel Dapper," the man snapped. There were deep lines of exhaustion around his big green eyes and at the corners of his mouth; he looked as if he could barely stay on his feet as he paused in front of Bonnor. "My mother is Julianna Dapper, and I was told she's supposed to be here! Is she upstairs? What happened to that man over there? Where are the little bastards who kidnapped Mom?"

Bonnor swallowed hard; the bundle under the man's arm had come partly undone, and he could see the handle of a gun next to what looked like some kind of wooden rod.

"Just let me out of here, mister," he said timidly, "and we'll get this all sorted out, okay?"

Gabriel looked at Ronnie Buckley's body again, then sprinted for the stairs without a backward glance at Bonnor.

Five minutes before Gabriel began speaking to Bonnor, Mary Hunter had entered the Buckleys' cozy upstairs apartment and found Sam standing over Edgar Reilly and a weeping Dottie Buckley. Broken ceramic figurines and shattered picture frames circled Dottie on the floor; the grieving sheriff's widow reminded Mary of a cruelly mistreated child, surrounded by broken toys.

"Julianna's not here?" Mary had asked Sam quietly.

Sam shook his head. "Mrs. Buckley doesn't know what happened to her, but . . ."

"But she must have gone with Elijah and the Tate boy," Mary had finished. She sighed. "That's what I was afraid of."

"Me too," Sam said. He paused. "Gabriel's not going to like this at all."

Mary nodded, reaching down to touch Dottie Buckley's shoulder. "I am so, so sorry, honey," she murmured.

Dottie, still cradled in Edgar's arms, wept harder. Edgar patted her on the back with a helpless look on his face and whispered in her ear that the paramedics would be there soon to take care of her.

Mary had looked back up at Sam, disregarding the tears in her own eyes. "We have to get as far away as we can before Gabriel sees all this," she said. "We *have* to find Elijah before he does."

"How?" Sam asked brusquely. "Even if he hasn't come inside yet, he'll be standing by our truck when we try to leave. There's no way he'll let us out of his sight once he knows what happened in here."

"We're not taking our truck." Mary dug into her purse and showed him a set of car keys, attached to a miniature key ring in the shape of a nude woman with massive breasts.

Sam raised his eyebrows. "What in the—"

"These belong to Deputy Tucker," Mary interrupted. "His station wagon is parked in the alley in back of the building, and he tells me there's a fire escape through one of the rooms up here that will take us right down to it."

Sam's eyebrows rose higher, and Edgar lifted his head to stare at her.

"He actually gave you the keys to his car?" Sam asked, almost grinning in spite of himself. "Just how did you pull *that* off?"

Mary's eyes flickered. "Deputy Tucker is the biggest sissy-pants I've ever met, that's how." She leaned down to Dottie

again and spoke softly to her. "Ma'am, I know this has probably been the very, very worst night of your life, and the last thing
I want to do is trouble you for anything. But if it's all right with
you, I need to ask you one quick question before we leave you in
peace."

Dottie gave a small, tentative nod and Mary touched her
head gratefully.

"Can you tell us where we might be able to find a little town
in Missouri called Pawnee?" she asked.

Interlude

Sunday night, June 24, 1923, 11:47 p.m.

Ben Taylor grabbed Julianna's arm as soon as she reached the bottom of the ladder and dragged her into the shadows by her father's tractor, avoiding a patch of moonlight by the barn's open doorway.

"Over there," he hissed in her ear, pointing across the lawn at the Larson house. His breath was hot on Julianna's cheek and she could hear the fear in his voice. "Rufus just did something to your back door!"

The rear of the house was thirty yards from the barn and Julianna had only the light of the night sky to see by, but she immediately spotted the mammoth shadow of Rufus Tarwater standing in the darkness on the steps to the back porch. She could only make out his general shape and size, but after their confrontation the day before she would have recognized his over-large head and hulking shoulders anywhere. Rufus had his back to her now, and all his attention seemed to be on the house. He appeared to be looking up at the open windows on the second floor, as if searching for signs of life in her brothers' bedrooms.

Julianna began to cry out, but Ben clapped a hand over her mouth. "Don't!" he whispered frantically. "He's got a gun!"

Julianna's eyes grew enormous as he released her. "Are you

sure?" she whispered back. She searched Tarwater's silhouette but saw no sign of a weapon.

Ben nodded. "Yeah. He put some stuff down by the well a minute ago."

As if on cue, Rufus vacated the steps and moved over to the well, leaning down by the pump handle. When he straightened again he was holding a rifle in his right hand and what looked like a maul in his left.

"Oh, God!" Julianna moaned, stricken with horror. "Oh dear God in heaven!"

There was no doubt in her mind about what Rufus was up to. The look on his face the previous morning as he'd sat on his horse in front of their house came back to her full force, and she couldn't believe she'd managed to convince herself he wouldn't try anything for a while, or that if he did her mother would be able to handle him with something as inconsequential as a revolver. If Rufus went inside now while her parents and brothers were all sleeping, he could do anything he wanted and they wouldn't stand a chance. The doors to the Larson house were never locked, and if he were quiet he could be standing over their beds before they were even aware he was there.

"We have to wake them up right now," she gasped, readying herself to scream as loudly as she could. The windows were all open, so she knew her family would hear her. Her heart felt as if it was going to burst from her chest; it was all she could do to keep from charging straight at Rufus like a madwoman, just as she had done yesterday. The memory of how *that* particular assault had ended, however, was temporarily making her more circumspect. "Get ready to run, Ben."

Ben shook his head fiercely and seized her arm again to hold her still.

"What are you plannin' to do, Julianna?" he asked in a murmur. "Rufus'll shoot you for sure once he knows you're here."

Julianna's blood ran cold at the grim certainty in Ben's voice, but she pulled away from him. "I don't have a choice," she said, trembling. "You didn't see him yesterday, Ben. He'll *kill* them if I don't do something!"

Ben knew better than to argue with her, but he wasn't sure at all any of the Larsons would live to see the morning, regardless of what Julianna did. Ben had heard every story there was to hear about Rufus Tarwater's violent temper—including rumors that some of the people who ran afoul of the man in his moonshine business were never seen or heard from again—and he'd always been warned by his parents to stay as far away from Tarwater as possible.

"He beat his own daddy half to death with his bare hands," Ben reminded her, almost vomiting in fear. "And he would've killed his own brothers for sure if they hadn't run off."

Across the yard, Rufus stepped away from the well and made his way toward the west side of the house. Julianna and Ben stared after him in confusion; both had been expecting him to enter the back door, but it now appeared this wasn't what he had in mind. From where the two teenagers stood, they had a good view of everything but the front of the house, so the big man was still in their line of vision as he moved around to the west. He lumbered toward the front porch, but stopped well before he reached the corner. From this distance his body was indistinguishable from the rifle and whatever else he was carrying; he looked like a large black bear standing on its hind legs.

"What's he up to?" Ben demanded, straining his eyes to see in the dark. "I can't see what he's doing."

A glimmer of light on the back of the house distracted Julianna's attention for a moment, until she realized it was just a reflection of the crescent moon on one of Seth's window panes. It was possible Seth might still be awake, she supposed, but she doubted it very much. He and Michael had just left the barn a few minutes ago on their way to bed, but both her brothers had been blessed from birth with the ability to fall asleep the second their heads hit the pillow, and she didn't know why tonight should be any different. They'd be hard to wake, too, but Eben and Emma were both light sleepers and could be counted on to quickly rouse their sons if Julianna's screams didn't suffice.

The skin on Julianna's arms and neck began to crawl as a macabre thought stole her breath away. Her brothers would have gone in the back door of the house tonight, like always, and it seemed impossible for them to have missed running into Rufus. What if Rufus had seen them coming and had somehow gotten the jump on them? What if Seth and Michael were already dead, and her mother and father were next?

That Rufus Tarwater may have already begun killing her family was more than she could bear. Disregarding everything but the overpowering urge to make sure Seth and Michael were still alive, she leapt into the moonlight and sprinted across the lawn with Ben right behind her—loving her too much to let her face Rufus alone, even though he already guessed how this was going to end. Julianna's first scream tore from her throat at the exact moment Rufus lit a torch and tossed it through the window of her father's study.

Rufus Tarwater believed he had outdone himself in his plan to "get even" with the Larson family for the way they had treated him.

Amazin' what you can do with a few fuckin' pennies, he thought, jamming a fifth coin into the space between the bottom of the Larsons' back porch screen door and the door frame. The door was solid maple on the bottom, but with only a flimsy screen on the top half.

The front porch door had taken eleven pennies before it felt like it wouldn't open without actually ripping the thing from its hinges, but the back door wasn't going to need quite as many to make it equally unusable. The idea of the crippled Eben and his chunky wife having to crawl through a door screen or out a window was particularly appealing.

Rufus wanted the Larsons' deaths to look like an accident, however, so as much as he would enjoy such a sight, he was hoping they wouldn't wake up until it was too late to even make it down the stairs. No neighbors lived close enough to interfere—except for Clyde Rayburn, who was deaf as a stone and so afflicted with gout that it would take him forever to get there—

and when other people started showing up Rufus would be long gone.

As would Eben Larson and his whole goddamn snooty family.

It was an ingenious plan, in Rufus's opinion, but if worse came to worse and some of the Larsons actually got out and tried to run, he wouldn't hesitate to shoot them. Using his gun would throw a fatal cog in his whole "accident" scenario and set the law to sniffing around his door, but he figured he'd have to hightail it out of the state anyway if any of the Larson family lived to implicate him, so he might as well gun them down and worry about the fallout later.

The eighth penny did the trick on the back door; he tugged on the handle and could feel that nothing short of a sledgehammer would budge the thing. He admired his handiwork for a minute, then searched the windows on the rear of the house to make sure he was still unobserved. He froze when he caught a glimpse of movement in one of the second-floor windows, but then realized it was just the corner of a curtain, fluttering in the breeze. Satisfied, he made his way over to the well to reclaim his rifle and the ax handle he'd presoaked in gasoline, then proceeded over to the west side of the house.

Fuckin' uppity bastards, he thought, drawing even with the window of Eben's study and remembering all the books and papers he had seen in there. Those very same books were going to make one helluva fire.

He reached into his shirt pocket and pulled out a match, but before striking it he paused, unsettled by a rare flicker of conscience. He had indeed killed people before, of course—with far less provocation than Eben Larson and his family had given him—but not while they were sleeping in their beds, oblivious and helpless. The thought that some people might perceive this sort of thing as an act of cowardice vaguely troubled him, but then he recalled Seth's talk about tying him up the day before, and how the young bitch had attacked him, and how Eben had threatened to sic the sheriff on him, and how Emma Larson had actually gone ahead and done just that, calling Sheriff Burns and sending him out to give Rufus a talking-to. Lastly, Rufus remembered how the two boys had held him at bay on their front porch with a pitchfork and a fence post, and how mouthy they'd been. The veins in his head began to throb again as he thought about each of these indignities, and in one quick blur of motion he ignited the match with his thumbnail and lit the ax handle. The makeshift torch was so saturated with gas that it caught fire instantly and singed his face.

"Son of a bitch!" he hissed in pain, jamming the burning brand through the screen of the open window.

Emma Larson opened her eyes in the darkness of her bedroom and stared at Eben's perspiring back in the bed beside her. The night air was hot and still, and through the open windows she could hear a bullfrog croaking down by the pond. The air was fragrant, too; she could smell lilacs and roses, and Eben's sweat and her own, and the pleasant, pervasive aroma of wild clover, overlying everything else like an invisible canopy. Emma lightly ran a finger down Eben's spine and wondered what had awakened her. She wondered if her children were all in their beds or still out in the barn together; she wondered if Ben was still with them or had returned home.

Something isn't right, she thought. She suddenly lifted her head from the pillow. A sense of foreboding was growing stronger in her breast with each passing second, and she abruptly sat up, her heart pounding. *Something isn't right at all.*

And Julianna's first scream shattered the silence of the night.

Emma was out of bed in an instant, but even as her feet hit the floor she heard three gunshots in quick succession, and then Ben Taylor began screaming, as well.

"Julianna!" Emma cried out, seizing her glasses from the nightstand. She knew without question that Rufus Tarwater was trying to kill her daughter at that very moment; she was terrified that Julianna may already have been shot.

"It's Rufus!" she yelled unnecessarily at Eben, who was on his feet by that time, too, naked and struggling to get into his pants. "Where are the boys?"

Eben shouted for Seth and Michael and then stumbled to the

door with his pants still unbuttoned, cursing his useless foot for slowing him down. Emma, in a night slip, tore open the top drawer of her dresser and grabbed her new revolver, then barreled after her husband. Michael—undressed, too, save for a pair of white boxer shorts—intercepted them in the darkness of the hallway between their rooms, still half asleep but yelling for Seth. Two more gunshots sounded from outside and the screams of Julianna and Ben were cut off.

Seth burst from his room at the end of the hall, bellowing Julianna's name and racing for the staircase. He was only clad in his boxers, as well, but he was carrying the old .22 rifle he and Michael used for squirrels and rabbits, and he had a look of unbridled fury on his face. From his bedroom window he had just seen Ben Taylor—distinguishable even in the dim light by his wild mop of hair—fall to the ground halfway between the barn and the house.

"I think Rufus just shot Ben!" he howled, hurtling down the stairs. "He's trying to shoot Julianna, too!"

"Wait, Seth!" Emma cried, torn by the ferocious need to save her daughter and the equally primal imperative to protect her sons. "Don't go out there until we know where Rufus is!"

Seth called from the bottom of the steps as two more shots sounded outdoors. "I think he's by the study!"

"Where's the other revolver, Daddy?" Michael demanded, chasing down the stairs after his older brother.

"In my desk in the study, but don't go in there!" Eben snapped, hobbling down the steps as fast as he could manage with his lame leg. "Don't do anything without me!"

"The house is on fire!" Seth screamed from the living room. "That son of a bitch set our house on fire!"

Emma Larson could not run as fast as her family—not even Eben—but her mind was working far more efficiently than any of theirs. The only windows in the house besides the one in Eben's study that faced west were in Julianna's room at the top of the stairs, and her sons and husband had just sailed right by Julianna's doorway without realizing there might be a clear shot at Rufus from there.

"Please, God!" Emma panted, tearing into Julianna's room. "Don't let anything happen to my children!"

Julianna's first scream almost made Rufus drop his rifle. He spun away from the study window and gaped across the back-yard, unable to see who was making such a rumpus. The wild flare of fire on the ax handle before he'd thrown it into the house had briefly blinded him. He raised the rifle anyway—a bolt-action Enfield he'd traded a couple of gallons of moonshine for in Kansas City earlier that year—and pointed it toward the sound of the girl's screams, then fired off three bullets as fast as he could.

More people began screaming, both inside and outside the house.

"Son of a bitch!" Rufus muttered, blinking rapidly and trying to distance himself from the bright light of the house fire. His night vision was coming back, but he still couldn't see much of anything. He thought he could make out the girl crouched on the lawn over somebody else, but he wasn't sure. There were definitely two voices, though, and both of them were yelling their lungs out. He pulled the bolt on the Enfield and fired off another two shots.

"It won't open!" Seth gave up kicking at the bottom of the front door with his bare feet and began ripping at the screen as Michael caught up to him. "Rufus must've done something to it."

Smoke was pouring down the hall from Eben's study, and the two boys recoiled in horror as flames leapt out of the study door and began climbing the walls of the hallway. Rufus's homemade torch had done its work all too well; it had landed squarely on a stack of papers on the floor by Eben's desk and turned the entire room into a furnace in a matter of seconds.

"We need to put out the fire before it's too late!" Michael coughed, his eyes watering from the smoke. "We have to get to the well!"

Seth shook his head and kept tearing at the screen with his hands and the barrel of the .22. "There's no time! We've got to stop Rufus before he kills Julianna, then get Momma and Daddy out of here!"

They both jumped at the sound of Eben tripping down the last four steps of the staircase and sprawling onto the kitchen floor on the other side of the living room. He clambered to his feet again and limped into the living room, swearing.

"Get away from the door, boys!" he ordered. "You'll get yourselves shot."

Eben Larson couldn't see the study from where he was standing, but he could see the faces of his sons in the light from the blaze, and he knew the fire was bad.

My revolver was in there, he realized in despair. *Sweet Jesus, now what?*

"He's going to shoot Julianna, Daddy!" Seth argued, turning back to the screen and yanking out the last of it with a grunt. He grabbed a chair and hopped up on it, preparing to climb through the opening he'd made.

"Give me the twenty-two," Michael said to Seth. "I'll guard you while you're getting out, then I'll follow you."

"No, you won't," Seth snapped. "You get Momma and Daddy out of here, okay?"

Michael started to argue, but then above the growing din of the fire they heard the distinct crack of a revolver shot, and then another, coming from upstairs.

"Momma must be shooting at Rufus!" Seth crowed, elated.

"Get down from there, Seth!" Eben barked, finally reaching them. The louder report from Tarwater's rifle reached their ears and Eben's heart almost stopped as he realized Rufus was shooting back at Emma. Everything was happening much too fast, and he didn't know what to do about any of it. "I'll take care of Rufus, and you boys go help your mother!"

Eben knew what his own chances against Rufus Tarwater were, but all he really had to do, he hoped, was distract him a little, and give Emma a chance to kill the son of a bitch.

Seth looked at Eben for a second as if getting ready to comply, but then handed Michael the squirrel gun and scrambled through the door frame instead, eluding Eben's hands as his father tried to stop him. He dropped neatly onto the porch and spun around to reclaim the .22 from Michael.

"It's got to be me, Dad," he said. Seth would never have dreamed of defying his father under normal circumstances, but he wasn't about to let Eben go up against Rufus with a crippled foot and a .22 rifle that didn't always work. "You aren't fast enough anymore."

Emma's revolver fired again, as did Rufus's rifle, and after that all they heard was Rufus screaming obscenities. There was no response from Emma.

Eben's face trembled and Seth suddenly felt like crying, but there was no time to say anything else. He glanced at Michael, who *was* crying, then darted from sight, sprinting for the west side of the house.

Rufus could see the shape of a body on the grass in the backyard, but the one in a dress he'd been pretty sure was Julianna Larson was nowhere in sight. Behind him the fire was going like gangbusters inside the Larson home and he knew he needed to make sure no one else got outside, too, but he didn't want to give up his search for the girl yet.

Maybe I ain't got to worry about her, he thought, remembering how Julianna had come after him with a candlestick the day before just because she found out he'd killed her pooch. *A spunky little cooze like that ain't gonna run away and leave her whole family to burn.*

He just had to make sure to keep his eyes open, and let her come to him.

His left shoulder exploded with pain as a revolver shot sounded above his head. A second later the lobe of his left ear was blown off as he struggled to raise the Enfield, and even after he'd returned fire several times at the anonymous assailant in the second-floor window, a third bullet embedded itself in his right thigh.

"FUCK YOU!" Rufus howled in agony, shaking his rifle at the window. "YOU FUCKING SON OF A WHORE!" His enemy was no longer there, however; Rufus must have finally killed or at least wounded the treacherous prick. He couldn't believe he hadn't heard the screen being raised before the gunfight started; the rumble of the fire had almost cost him his life. He staggered toward the back lawn, barely able to stay on his feet but in a towering rage.

I am going to end this BULLSHIT right NOW, he thought, wanting to get into a position where he could cover most of the house and gun down anybody he could find. He didn't get far, however; yet *another* gun cracked in the night and Rufus bleated in shock as a .22 bullet entered his back at the base of his right shoulder. Nearly falling, he spun around like a wild boar, maddened with pain and fury, and found Seth Larson less than ten feet away, grappling frantically with the firing mechanism of a jammed squirrel gun.

Rufus squeezed his own trigger again and again. The first two bullets from Rufus's Enfield hit the boy in the chest, and the third caught him right above the navel. As Seth fell to the ground, the skin of his naked torso was already covered in blood.

Rufus's opening salvo of the evening had shattered Ben Taylor's left knee. Julianna wasn't aware of this at first, of course; all she knew was that one moment Ben was at her heels, screaming as loudly as she was to wake her family, and the next she was running by herself. Ben was still screaming, but his screams had become unbearably strident.

Acting on instinct, Julianna dropped to the grass and looked over her shoulder. Ben was about fifteen feet behind her, on his side and thrashing in pain.

"Oh God, Ben!" she cried, crawling back to him as fast as she could.

Ben saw her coming and even through his suffering understood that she was going to get shot herself if she tried to save him.

"Look out, Julianna!" he wailed, his voice cracking. "Get behind something!"

She ignored him and kept on crawling until she was beside

him. She knew it wasn't safe to move him without finding out how badly he was injured, but she also knew she had to get him out of the line of fire. She grabbed him under the arms and started dragging him toward the outhouse, less than eight feet behind them.

"Oh GOD it hurts!" Ben bawled, unable to help himself.

"Shush, Ben!" Julianna pleaded. Ben's hair was in her face and she was weeping in terror and pity. Her feet slipped and she fell with Ben on top of her; she cried out an apology and started to rise again.

A bullet from Rufus's gun ricocheted harmlessly off the outhouse above them, but the next one hit Ben directly in the left temple, killing him instantly and spattering Julianna's dress with blood. He sagged in Julianna's arms, nothing but dead weight, and she fell again, her wail of fury and loss silenced as her air got knocked out of her.

The enormity of what was happening was paralyzing, but the part of her that had earned her the nickname of "Amazon" was screaming at her to *MOVE RIGHT NOW OR DIE.* She could no longer do anything for Ben, but her family was still alive, as far as she knew, and she *had* to stay alive long enough to find a way to save them. She rolled from under her dearest friend's body and crawled behind the outhouse, panting and sobbing.

The noise of the fire was growing—flames were now licking out of the study window and greedily sampling the siding above its frame—and she could hear her brothers and father yelling inside the house. A second later a revolver shot rang out in the night, and then another, and her heart filled with a savage joy as she realized her mother must have entered the fray at last. Julianna looked around the outhouse in time to see Rufus, now clearly visible in the bright light from the fire, raise his rifle and shoot back at Julianna's bedroom window.

"Momma!" Julianna whispered, putting a hand to her mouth as she glimpsed Emma's stocky body leaning out the window frame.

The revolver cracked again, and so did Rufus's gun, and then Rufus was cursing like a madman on the lawn and shaking his rifle at the empty window where Julianna's mother had been not a moment before. Julianna reeled away from the outhouse in horror and fell to her knees on the ground. She rose momentarily and then fell again, unable to control her limbs.

"Momma," she whispered again. "Oh, Momma."

Seth hurtled around the corner of the house in his underwear, armed with the squirrel gun and looking like an avenging angel. Rufus was lurching toward the backyard and didn't see Seth coming, and Julianna's heart stopped beating as she saw her brother raise his gun and fire it at Rufus. Rufus shrieked and spun around, stumbling, and Julianna prayed with all her might for Seth to shoot him again.

Her prayer went unanswered.

She saw Seth struggle with his rifle. She saw Rufus return fire three times, and she saw Seth fall to his knees, dropping the squirrel gun on the grass beside him.

"SETH!" Julianna howled. "SETH!"

And twenty seconds later, Michael came sprinting around the corner of the house, too, armed with nothing but one of their father's canes. Julianna was not aware of this, however, for she was no longer in the backyard.

"We've got to get your mother!" Eben cried, after Emma's revolver had fallen silent upstairs.

Michael nodded, coughing in the smoke, and started running back toward the stairs in the kitchen. He had only gone a few steps, however, when both he and Eben heard the sharp report of Seth's .22 outside, followed seconds later by three shots from Rufus's gun.

"Seth!" Michael screamed, reversing direction and launching himself back at the front door.

Eben caught his younger son in his arms for a moment but couldn't hold him; they were both slick with sweat, and Michael was too strong and wild. He freed himself from his father's grip and seized one of Eben's canes by the entrance, then bounded onto the chair and dove awkwardly out the top half of the screen door. Eben stood frozen for a moment, torn between his children and his wife, then turned and limped as quickly as he could toward the stairs. Flames from the fire danced into the empty living room behind him and began feeding on the sofa.

Seth was on the ground when Michael flew around the side of the house. Rufus Tarwater was still pointing the Enfield down at Seth but had finished firing; Rufus—looking none too steady on his feet—seemed to be waiting for Seth to do something else. Michael charged straight at Rufus without slowing, the sound of his footsteps masked by the roar of the fire. He nearly reached Rufus before the big man was even aware of his presence.

Nearly.

A bullet ripped through Michael's belly at the same moment Michael swung the cane like a baseball bat at Rufus's head. The cane snapped in two and both Michael and Rufus fell to the ground. Michael landed beside Seth and curled into a ball, shrieking in agony, and Rufus lay still, knocked senseless and bleeding heavily from half a dozen injuries.

"Michael," Seth gasped.

The older boy was still alive, but barely. He somehow managed to roll onto his side and reach out for his brother. Michael quieted a little and whimpered as Seth's fingers touched his hair, but he began to wail again when Seth's hand stopped moving.

And behind Michael's back, Rufus was slowly climbing to his feet again.

Eben fell twice on the steps before he reached Julianna's room at the top of the staircase. The whole house was full of smoke, making it hard to see, and he was in too much of a hurry for a man with a bum foot and a heart twisted by grief and rage. He tripped into Julianna's bedroom, crying for Emma, and found his wife on the floor by the window. She was still alive but sorely wounded; Rufus's last shot at her had caught her in her left breast and punctured a lung, yet she had still managed to squeeze off another round before falling to the floor.

"Emma!" Eben dropped beside her and tried to put his arms

around her. "Oh God, Emma!" Her short brown hair was wet with sweat, and the front of her night slip was sticky with blood.

"Eb," she whispered, fighting to breathe. She pushed him away with an effort and shoved the revolver into his hands, then nodded emphatically at the window closest to her. Another gunshot rang out in the night on the lawn and Eben heaved himself over to the window to look down at the yard on the west side of the house. In the glow from the fire that was destroying their home he could see the bodies of both his sons lying on the ground, side by side, not far from the prostrate body of Rufus Tarwater. Seth wasn't moving and Michael was crying his brother's name.

Eben made a low moan of denial, deep in his throat. He felt Emma's eyes on his back, watching him, and he began to sob.

Outside, Rufus was rising slowly to his feet. He looked hideous, hunched over with pain and bloody from head to foot, but he was still alive. He pointed his rifle at the back of Michael's head.

Eben brought the revolver up and fired, again and again, weeping uncontrollably and trying his damnedest to kill the man who was responsible for destroying his family. There were only three bullets left, however, and he missed all three times.

Julianna was on the other side of the burning house, in the driveway, when she heard another gunshot and Michael's screams. Her hands did not pause in what they were doing, however, even as her tears blinded her. She knew from the screams that Michael was probably dying now, too, soon to join Seth and Ben and very likely Emma; she didn't know where her father was, but she knew that if Eben were still alive she only had seconds to save him before Rufus took his life, as well.

"I'm coming, Daddy," she whispered. "I'll be right there."

The fire in the house had taken over the entire first floor. Through the windows of the kitchen and living room, all vomiting smoke, she could see flames on the walls and the ceilings;

her home, too, was dying, crying out in the night just like
Michael.

I'm coming, Michael, Julianna promised in silence, almost
ready to return to the battlefront on the other side of her home,
and praying with her whole soul that the only weapon she had
at her disposal would be a match for Rufus Tarwater and his
rifle.

This time her prayer would be answered.

Rufus was preparing to put a bullet through Michael Larson's blond head when somebody began shooting at him again
from the second-floor window. Forgetting all about the boy,
Rufus gawped up at the window after the first shot and tripped
over his own feet as he tried to dodge the two shots that followed the first in quick succession. Whoever was shooting at
him this time, however, was clearly nowhere near as proficient
with a revolver as the son of a bitch who had managed to hit
him three times in a row earlier; the revolver fell silent once
more and Rufus was blessedly no more damaged than he already had been.

*The one who got me before musta been Larson, but now it's
his goddamn wife,* he thought.

"NICE SHOOTIN', SWEETIE-PIE!" he bellowed in mockery. "HOW ABOUT I SHOW YOU HOW IT'S DONE?"

He pointed his rifle at the window and saw that he'd been
wrong about the order of shooters; it was Eben Larson himself—making no attempt to duck or save himself—who was
gazing down at him with hatred and anguish. Rufus smiled and
took careful aim, pleased at this opportunity to kill the man
face-to-face, but before he could squeeze the trigger the distinctive, nasal bleat of a car horn sounded on the lawn directly behind him. He spun around just in time to make out the grille of
a Model T Ford less than ten feet away.

Rufus made a desperate lunge to get out of the way, but the
Larson family had not been the least bit kind to his body that
night, and he could no longer move fast enough to save himself.
Eben Larson's Model T Ford gobbled up the last inch of lawn

between itself and its prey, and the body of Rufus Tarwater sailed through the air like a rolled-up newspaper and landed close to Emma Larson's rose bushes, thirteen feet away. Rufus was still marginally alive when he finally stopped moving, but the Model T soon took care of that, bounding across the lawn and running over him twice more.

Julianna Larson was not in a forgiving mood.

"Tarwater's dead," Eben told Emma as he struggled to raise her from the floor. The smoke in Julianna's bedroom was so thick he could hardly breathe, and there were flames on the staircase outside the door. "Julianna just ran over the son of a bitch with the car."

Julianna's still alive! Emma thought, feeling tears of joy well up in her eyes. During her own gunfight with Rufus, she'd thought she'd seen her daughter on the back lawn, but she hadn't been sure at all that Julianna would survive. Emma was unable to speak because of all the fluid in her lungs, but she squeezed Eben's shoulder hard and gazed up into his face with a look that was more clear than speech. *What about Seth and Michael?*

Eben's throat closed completely. He shook his head, and she closed her eyes.

My boys, Emma mourned. Nothing in her life had ever hurt as much, nor ever would again. *Oh, my sweet boys.*

Eben somehow got her to her feet, but all her weight was on him. Her face was against his naked chest and his arms were wrapped around her middle, and he staggered toward the door, eyeing the fire as it crept into the room. He was hurrying as much as he could, but it was taking all his strength just to keep them both upright and balanced.

"We've only got one good leg between us, now, Em," he gasped in her ear. "I'm afraid those stairs aren't going to be any fun at all."

She didn't answer.

Julianna dropped to her knees beside Michael on the lawn and put his head in her lap. He had stopped screaming at last but he was now humming under his breath and didn't seem to notice her.

"Michael, can you hear me?" Julianna begged, frantic to get to the house and save their parents but unwilling to leave her brother alone. "I've got to get Momma and Daddy, okay? But I'll be right back and we'll get you fixed up good as new."

He stopped humming. "Julianna." His eyes, green and huge just like hers, sought her face and he smiled up at her. "Baby girl," he murmured.

She tried to smile back at him through her tears. "That's me."

He coughed up a mouthful of blood on his chest and swiped weakly at it with the heel of his hand. "I think I must be coming down"—he grimaced as another violent spasm wracked his body—"with a cold or something."

She choked on her tears and glanced at the house, knowing Michael probably only had seconds to live but also knowing that she was going to need every one of those seconds to rescue Eben and Emma. The top-floor windows were now filled with flames, and the roof was on fire, too.

"I'll be right back," she promised, her voice breaking as she lowered his head to the ground.

Michael reached up as she tried to rise and touched her face. "Is he dead?" he whispered.

"Rufus? Yes."

He shook his head. "Seth."

Julianna flinched and involuntarily looked over at Seth's body.

Michael's face contorted and tears spilled from his eyes. "Ben too?"

Julianna put her finger on his lips. "I'll be right back, Michael," she sobbed, leaping to her feet and sprinting for the back door.

Eben knew Emma was dead before he started down the steps with her body, but he wasn't going to leave his wife to burn in the house, and that was that. The stairs were on fire, but he thought if he hurried he might still be able to get safely down them; there seemed to be a narrow path on one side that would allow him to reach the kitchen. The heat was making breathing difficult; his lungs felt as if they were full of cinders.

"DADDY? MOMMA?"

Eben faintly heard Julianna's screams, but he couldn't tell where they were coming from; the din from the fire made it impossible to guess.

"DON'T COME INSIDE, JULIANNA!" Eben bawled as loudly as he could, praying she wasn't already in the house. "STAY WHERE YOU ARE!"

He knew his daughter would ignore this order completely, of course, even if she had heard him, so he plunged down the stairs at a mad clip for a lame man, more to forestall Julianna's entry into the inferno their home had become than to get out himself with Emma's body. His bare feet started to blister immediately as he hopped from one sizzling, steaming step to the next without pause, and he cried out in excruciating pain as he nearly lost his balance on the fourth step down. Emma flopped against him lifelessly, her head lolling from side to side as if shaking her head at the folly of such an enterprise.

"DADDY?"

Julianna's voice was louder this time; it sounded as if she were in the kitchen. Eben didn't know how such a thing could be possible, though; what he could see of the kitchen at the bottom of the steps was an image from hell itself; floor-to-ceiling flames of red, orange, blue, yellow, and white, flames so high and bright they could cook the soul out of a person in less time than it took to incinerate an ant in a wood stove.

"GET OUT, SWEETHEART!" Eben shrieked, not knowing where Julianna was, but knowing she was going to die if she were still in the house. "GET OUT NOW!"

Emma's night slip caught fire, and then Eben's pants. Eben howled in terror but continued hopping down the steps, having no alternative but to keep going. He made it down three more stairs before tumbling down the rest of the staircase; he landed on top of Emma on the kitchen floor and the wood beneath their bodies groaned as they slammed into it.

"DADDY!"

The last thing Eben saw before his hair caught fire and he lost all awareness of his surroundings was his daughter, standing on the outside steps of the back porch and clawing wildly at the red-hot door screen that was preventing her from reaching him. She had never made it inside the house; the pennies Rufus Tarwater had so artfully jammed into the door frame were now serving to safeguard the sole surviving Larson, who otherwise would have joined the rest of her family in their fate that night.

Eben Larson did not know of Rufus's pennies, nor was he capable of any thought whatsoever by this point. He was more fire than man now, and the only feeling left to him before his consciousness fled was pain. Pain past bearing, pain without limits. Yet before the end he *had* seen his daughter, alive and safely outside the house; he *had* known she loved him and was doing all she could to save him. Whatever torments of the damned he suffered afterward, surely he was at least granted that much in the way of comfort before everything became meaningless to him.

Or so Julianna told herself for years to come, to keep from going mad.

The tragedy at the Larson farm was not the only game in town that night.

Fewer than three minutes after Rufus Tarwater tossed a burning torch through Eben Larson's study window, Dr. Wilbur Colby's cat, Zeke (short for Ezekiel), knocked a candle and a half-full bottle of whiskey off the nightstand in Colby's bedroom, while the good doctor—a widower who lived alone—was squatting in the outhouse behind his home in downtown Pawnee. The flame on the candle ignited the spilled whiskey, and the bedspread and mattress quickly caught fire, as did a dog-eared copy of the Bible, open and facedown, that Colby had left beside his pillow. By the time Colby returned from the outhouse, the entire top floor of his residence was ablaze.

Colby's cramped living quarters were on the floor above his office, right next to the general goods store. The doctor's initial attempts to extinguish the fire were severely hampered by

inebriation; the half-full bottle of whiskey that had been shattered by Zeke (real Scotch whiskey from a grateful Scottish
patient who had smuggled a case of the illegal stuff into the
country) had been completely full earlier in the evening, and
Colby, normally a teetotaler, had declined to share a drop of the
precious liquor with anyone. As a result, no one else became
aware of the fire until more than a few stray flames had traveled
down the side of Colby's office and scurried over to the general
goods store. One of these bright, overeager flames spied a shelf
with several gallon jugs of kerosene on it, and—rather more
generous than Dr. Colby had been with his Scotch—graciously
invited a few of its friends to join it in a toast.

And that was all it took.

Three-quarters of Pawnee's 137 residents lived on farms outside of town and were in no danger whatsoever, but those closer
in were not so lucky. The general goods store was next to the
bakery and the smithy; the smithy abutted a shed that held,
among other things, a twenty-gallon tank of gasoline. All the
buildings in Pawnee were made of wood, and it had been a dry
spring in northern Missouri. The post office, the school, the tele-
phone/telegraph office, the bakery, half a dozen private homes—
in short, every single structure on Pawnee's only street—was
either leveled or already beyond saving in less than an hour, and
all the attempts to prevent the fire from spreading from one
place to another proved to be futile, especially because Pawnee
had no fire department, and nowhere near the manpower to
deal with such a fierce conflagration.

Hence the reason the glow from the Larson farm, a mile and
a half to the north, went virtually unnoticed, though some people the next day would recall hearing gunshots in the distance.
And while the Larson family and Ben Taylor would certainly be
mourned a great deal, they were not the only casualties on that
Sunday night in June. Seventeen people died in the Pawnee fire
of 1923, more than half of whom were trying to help their
friends and neighbors escape the devastation. One of these was
Doc Colby, who was crushed by a falling roof beam while attempting to rescue the family of Lars Olson, the blacksmith; an-

other was Tom Putnam (a janitor at Julianna's school in Hat-field), who tried to save Zeke the cat, and was last seen carrying the terrified creature in his arms and running for the back door of the doctor's office when the ceiling above them collapsed.

The oddest death of the night, however, belonged to Clyde Rayburn, the next-door neighbor of the Larsons. Clyde—yet another bachelor—awoke at midnight in his bed. A childhood illness had left him mostly deaf, and thus he'd heard nothing of the gunshots over at the Larsons' house. What had awakened him had been the smell of smoke on the night breeze. He stuck his head out the window to track down the source of the smell, and was shocked to see *two* major fires at work, one to the north and one to the south. He ran as fast as his gouty feet would allow, threw a saddle on his horse, Celeste, and galloped toward the Larsons' home. He had almost reached the Larsons' driveway when a fragment of still-burning ash drifted from the sky and extinguished itself in one of Celeste's eyes, causing the beast to buck wildly. Clyde tumbled from the saddle, catching his foot in the stirrups, and a frenzied Celeste dragged her owner for a quarter of a mile on the gravel road, well past the Larsons' house and out into their cornfield before at last subsiding. Clyde ended up on his back with his foot still snared in the stirrup; he bled to death in the field, gazing up at the smoke-filled sky.

Coincidence loves playing with fire.

Chapter 13

Julianna Dapper lifted the bloody bandages on Jon Tate's chest as gently as she could and bit her lip as his face tightened in pain.

"Don't be such a baby," she chided, hiding her concern. She inspected the small, evil-looking hole by his left armpit first, then made him twist around on the backseat of the squad car so she could get a better look at the larger exit wound an inch or so away from his shoulder blade. She was on her knees in the driver's seat, facing the rear of the car; she had to duck her head to avoid hitting it on the feeble dome light that was their only illumination. She relaxed after a moment and released Jon with a satisfied smile. His bleeding had slowed significantly since they had fled the Creighton County jailhouse twenty minutes ago, and she felt certain he'd be fine until they reached Pawnee.

"It looks much better," she said. "You're in no danger."

He grimaced and muttered thanks, slumping against the seat behind him with a groan.

"Momma can stitch you up when we get home." Julianna faced front again, her knees popping as she straightened her legs under the steering wheel. She caught Jon's eye in the rearview mirror before turning off the dome light. "But I surely hope you've learned your lesson."

Julianna, Jon Tate, and Elijah Hunter were parked out of sight behind the boarded-up Dairy Queen in Mullwein, Iowa, right around the corner from where Sheriff Buckley and Bonnor Tucker had trapped them earlier that evening. Chuck Stockton's lime-green Volkswagen was still where Bonnor had left it to be towed the following morning, beside a faded sign advertising nineteen-cent hamburgers and twelve-cent Dilly bars. The night air was sticky and still; a swarm of moths was besieging a street-light in the distance.

"What are you talking about?" Jon demanded. He didn't mean to snap at Julianna, but he was exhausted, on edge, and in a fair amount of pain.

"Günter's lock, silly," she said mildly. "If you hadn't broken Günter's lock yesterday, none of this would have happened."

Jon put his face in his hands. "Oh, for God's sake."

"Are you sure this is a good idea, Jon?" Elijah broke in from the passenger seat. He was looking over at the rear bumper of the Volkswagen, which was all that could be seen of it from their hiding place. "Maybe we should just keep this car instead and leave the Beetle here."

"We can't do that, Ben." Julianna opened her door and the dome light flickered back on again. She stifled a yawn as a bone-deep fatigue suddenly hit her; she couldn't wait to get back to Pawnee and put this long day behind them. "That would be stealing."

"Yeah, Elijah," Jon mumbled. "God forbid we do anything illegal." He dropped his hands again to answer Elijah's question. "I still say we need to ditch this car. The cops are looking for it right now, and I think we're safer in the Bug."

The dead sheriff's squad car was far too conspicuous of a get-away vehicle, but the Volkswagen was much slower, and nearly as conspicuous. Jon's only hope was that the police might assume he and the others wouldn't return to the Beetle tonight, and hence wouldn't bother checking on it for a while. He supposed stealing yet *another* vehicle was an option, but at this point such a venture seemed worse than pointless. He didn't know how to hotwire a car any more than Elijah or Julianna did, and finding one with its keys already in the ignition—as they'd found the Volkswagen at the dairy farm—would take a lot of luck, even in a town like Mullwein, where people probably left their cars unlocked all the time.

Elijah had turned around and was studying him. In the muted glow of the dome light, the bruises and cuts on the younger boy's face looked worse than ever, but he was no longer the terrified little kid he had been a mere six hours before. The confrontation with Bonnor Tucker had clearly changed him, somehow, and Jon wasn't sure at all that this was a good thing.

"Okay," Elijah said, nodding reluctantly. "Let's make the switch, then. But I'm taking the radio with us. We need to keep track of what's going on."

The police radio in Buckley's squad car was on, but so far they'd heard nothing on it that had anything to do with them.

Jon shook his head. "It's bolted to the dash."

"Oh, for goodness sake, you two," Julianna scolded, unsettled by all this talk of thievery. "You're acting like a pair of gangsters. Can we just go home, please?"

She lifted Ronnie Buckley's Colt .45 from the seat beside her and got out of the car. She'd found the holstered weapon hanging on a coat rack at the bottom of the stairs of the Buckleys' residence, right above the body of Ronnie Buckley. She had no faith in her ability to shoot the thing, of course, but she was glad to have it anyway; the way their night had gone so far made her wonder what else might happen to them before they made it back home.

Half an hour earlier, Ronnie Buckley's head had struck the steel door at the base of the steps less than five seconds after Bonnor Tucker's skull first collided with the bars of Elijah's jail cell. In the hallway of the jailhouse, the effect was like two bells being rung at a monastery, summoning the monks to matins. A percussive thud followed immediately as Elijah brained Bonnor with the deputy's own nightstick, and then the steel door at the end of the hall swung open, revealing Julianna Dapper with a gun in her hand, standing over an ominously motionless Ronnie

Buckley. Julianna's face was wild at first, but the instant she saw Elijah gawking back at her, her expression had changed to joy.

"Oh, thank God!" she cried. "You're alive!"

Elijah would wonder at himself later when it occurred to him that seeing the sheriff's body at Julianna's feet hadn't made much of an impression. His relief at Julianna's return and his fear for Jon had taken precedence over everything else; all that mattered to him at that moment was that Julianna was back with them, and Jon was in urgent need of her help.

"Julianna!" Elijah pressed against the bars of his cell, temporarily forgetting that Bonnor had left the keys in the cell door during their confrontation and he could now let himself out. He was still in a crouch after wrestling Bonnor's nightstick away from the man. "Jon's been shot!"

"No, I haven't," Jon said in an odd, detached voice. He was on his feet, but he was staring down in shock at the hole in the far left side of his chest. There was a line of blood running from the bullet wound all the way to the waistband of his shorts, and he suddenly seemed to become aware of what this actually meant.

"Jesus Christ," he said, raising his head to gape across the hall at Elijah. His eyes were the size of quarters. "I've been shot!"

He fell to his knees as the room spun around him.

Julianna was at his side in an instant, followed a few seconds later by Elijah, with Bonnor's revolver and nightstick securely in his possession. Julianna set the sheriff's gun down on the floor and examined Jon's injuries, then placed her hands directly on the bullet holes, ignoring Jon's moan of protest as she pressed hard to slow the bleeding. Elijah knelt on Jon's other side and looked on anxiously.

"How bad is it?" Jon asked, clenching his teeth. "It hurts like hell."

"You were very, very lucky," Julianna murmured, adopting her mother's reassuring manner with people who were sick. "I don't think the bullet hit anything too important. We'll get you fixed up in a jiffy." She looked at Elijah to tell him to find some clean cloth or bandages, but the moment she saw all his bruises and lacerations close up she recoiled.

"Dear God in heaven!" she gasped. "What on earth happened to you?"

Elijah tried to smile through swollen lips. "Things got a little rough down here."

He glanced over his shoulder at the unconscious Bonnor with a sense of unreality bordering on stupefaction. Everything had been so chaotic in the past few minutes that he had only begun to process exactly what it was that he'd done.

I'll be goddamned, he marveled. His chest felt as if it were going to burst with pride; it was the first time in his life he'd ever experienced such a glorious sense of self-satisfaction. *I actually KO'd that dumb son of a bitch!*

Julianna followed his gaze and her eyes narrowed as she studied Bonnor Tucker's prostrate form. Bonnor was breathing normally and his color was good, and Julianna froze as her highly developed instinct for survival stirred in her breast.

"There's not much time," she whispered. "We have to go home right now."

She glanced down the hall at Sheriff Buckley's body at the base of the staircase and knew without checking that the man who had been her host that night was now dead; his neck was at an awkward angle, and one of his beefy arms was twisted under his back in what looked like a contortionist's trick. Julianna couldn't recall exactly what had transpired upstairs—she had only a vague memory of two people in a laundry room pleading with her to calm down—but she somehow knew she was to blame for the sheriff's death, and likely more than this, as well. She closed her eyes in grief, but quickly opened them again, forcing herself to concentrate.

"Ben, we have to move fast." Her voice was calm, and both Elijah and Jon began to breathe a little easier as she spoke, responding unconsciously to the steadiness of her tone. "Help me drag the deputy into one of the cells before he wakes up."

Elijah stared down at her, then hopped to obey, surrendering the revolver and the nightstick to Jon. Julianna released Jon's shoulder and stepped into the hallway, stooping to wipe the blood from her hands on Bonnor's uniform before seizing one of the deputy's booted feet and ordering Elijah to grab the other one. Puffing and straining together, they heaved Bonnor into the cell Elijah had recently vacated, then they returned to the hall and locked the cell door behind them.

"Good," Julianna said with a dismissive sniff. She removed Elijah's handcuffs with Bonnor's keys and stepped back into Jon's cell to do the same for him. "Now stay here with Jon while I find something to bind his wounds. Put your hands on him like this, right on the bullet holes," she demonstrated on Elijah's chest and back. "Push hard, even if he complains. Understand?"

She waited for his nod, then nudged him toward Jon as he hesitated. "There's no need to be squeamish, Benjamin. It's just blood."

The top part of her dress was unzipped in back and she reached back to correct this oversight before trotting down the hall to the office, leaving the two boys by themselves. Jon was now seated on the cot in his cell, feeling lightheaded, and Elijah joined him, sitting down on the cot beside him. The younger boy swallowed hard, fighting a wave of nausea as he looked at the bean-sized hole on Jon's chest, about an inch away from his armpit. The exit wound on Jon's back was messier and larger than the one on his front, but both were oozing blood at the same slow, steady rate, like sap trickling down the bark of a maple tree.

"Pretty gross, huh?" Jon grimaced, cupping the hole on his chest with his right hand in an attempt to staunch the flow.

Elijah shoved Jon's hand out of the way and covered the wounds with his own palms, pressing on each side of Jon's body just as Julianna had instructed.

"Shit!" Jon gasped. He looked away as blood ran between Elijah's fingers. "I think I'm gonna puke."

Elijah's throat burned with bile and he had to look away, too.

"I think Julianna must be some kind of nurse or something," he mumbled, trying to distract both of them. "She seems to know a lot about this kind of stuff."

"Maybe," Jon grunted, not paying attention. He nodded his head toward Buckley's body at the base of the stairwell. "The sheriff's dead."

Elijah's chin trembled a little but his voice stayed even. "I know." He looked over at the dark staircase ascending to the second floor. "What do you think happened to his wife?"

Jon shook his head. "Dunno."

The possibility that yet another dead body was in the building with them was too much for both boys; neither could bear to dwell on it. Jon glanced at Elijah and purposely changed the subject, remembering something else. "What got into you tonight?"

Elijah frowned. "What do you mean?"

"When you started screaming all that stuff at Boner."

Elijah shrugged. "I just got mad, I guess." He stared at the rear wall of the cell; the bullet that had pierced Jon's shoulder had left a gruesome smattering of red dots that reminded him of a Rorschach test. "He was really hurting you, and I couldn't take it anymore."

Jon studied Elijah's face. He had the feeling this was not the sort of thing Elijah would ever dream of saying to anybody else, and the offhanded honesty of it moved him.

"Well, you definitely got his attention, man," he said. He paused for a moment and the corners of his mouth quirked up. "Especially when you started in on his mom."

Elijah grinned back at him, flushing. "Yeah." He glanced over at Bonnor again. "I almost peed my pants when he started coming after me instead of you."

"I thought you'd gone nuts." Jon shook his head. "Seriously. I thought you and Julianna were twins, or something."

Elijah giggled. "You were just as bad, man," he retorted. Elijah had never called anybody "man" in his life, but Jon's speech patterns were beginning to rub off on him. "You were the one who called him 'Buttlick Turdmunch,' remember?"

"No shit?" Jon scratched at the stubble on his face, leaving a dab of blood on his chin. "I was too scared to know what I was saying." He paused and laughed aloud. "I guess maybe that explains why he got so pissed at me."

"Yeah," Elijah agreed, chortling. "I don't think he liked you very much."

Their laughter had a touch of hysteria in it and they both sobered at once. Even if the body at the base of the stairwell hadn't been there to reproach them, everything else that had happened in the past two days would have been enough to stifle their levity—the trooper Julianna had run over, Bebe Stockton's accidental death, the burning of the dairy farmhouse, Bonnor Tucker's cruelty. There wasn't much to laugh about, and they both knew it.

Elijah peeked down at Jon's injuries but quickly looked away, his stomach lurching at the sight of all the blood on his hands.

You better get used to it, Elijah told himself bitterly. He couldn't believe he'd almost forgotten his role in Bebe Stockton's death the previous day. Who else was going to get killed before this was all over?

"What are we going to do?" Jon muttered, wincing as Elijah applied more pressure to his wounds. "After we get out of here, I mean?"

The combination of blood and sweat was making Jon's skin slick, and Elijah was finding it difficult to maintain his grip. He apologized as he shifted his hands again, then he pondered the older boy's question. He sensed Jon would want to get as far away as possible from the jailhouse, and he sighed before answering, anticipating an argument.

"I think we should help Julianna get where she needs to go," he said at last.

Jon looked at him blankly. "To Pawnee, you mean?" He raised his eyebrows. "You *are* crazy, Elijah. You know that, right? I doubt the place even exists."

"I know." Elijah tilted his head to wipe his nose on the sleeve of his shirt (*Jon's shirt,* he reminded himself belatedly). "But what else are we going to do? We can't leave her alone, and she won't go anyplace else unless we take her there first."

Jon knew better than to try to talk Elijah into abandoning Julianna—and in truth, Jon no longer wanted to leave her behind, either. For better or worse, it seemed, the three of them were in this nightmare together, and he also knew there was no chance whatsoever of convincing Julianna to give up or even to delay her quest. Still, a gnawing feeling in his gut was telling him that Pawnee was the last place on earth they should go; he was almost certain that whatever was waiting for them there was far worse than anything they had already gone through.

He lowered his voice to a whisper. "Listen to me for a minute, okay?" He waited for Elijah's nod, then pressed on. "Look, I want to help Julianna, too. I really do. But there's no point in going to Pawnee, is there? We both know that even if it's still there, which is a HUGE *if* by the way, then it's not going to be the same place Julianna thinks it is. It's probably only going to upset her to see it, and every second we waste chasing down the messed-up picture she has in her head is a second we should be using to get someplace safe."

Jon could hear the desperation creeping into his own voice but he didn't care.

"What if we head for Canada instead?" he urged, locking eyes with the younger boy. "All three of us, I mean. We can tell Julianna we'll bring her back here in a couple of months, when things have cooled down. She might actually listen to you, if you just ask. *Please,* man. I know she might not go for it, but can't we at least *try* to talk her out of this? We're not going to get another chance to get away, and I've got a really, really bad feeling about where she's taking us."

Jon's fear was palpable, and Elijah couldn't help but be unnerved. He chewed on his lip, considering the possibility of reasoning with Julianna, but then sighed again, knowing full well what the outcome of such a discussion would be.

"It's no good," he said. "She won't listen."

The courage that was Elijah Hunter's birthright as Mary Hunter's son had been awakened in him that night, and it wasn't going back to sleep anytime soon. Risky or not, Julianna was headed to Pawnee, and Elijah was going with her. He didn't understand why, exactly, but he knew it had something to do with the look on her face when she'd come back to them a few minutes ago. He couldn't turn his back on her now, especially when she was so close to the end of her journey.

He hesitated, looking away as tears sprang to his eyes.

"You should take off after Julianna gets you patched up, man," he said softly. He made himself go on, even though the words caught in his throat. "I'd miss you like hell, but I'd understand."

There was a short, strained silence. He could feel Jon glaring at the back of his head, and a few seconds later the older boy began to swear under his breath. Elijah couldn't hear most of what he said, but "dumbass" and "fucktard" came through several times, more clearly than the rest. Elijah wiped his eyes on his sleeve and gripped Jon's shoulder tightly, unable to keep from smiling a little at each muttered curse. He knew what the oaths really meant, and that Jon was just frightened, and letting off steam.

Julianna bustled back down the hall with her arms full. In addition to a first aid kit, she was also carrying all the things that Bonnor and the sheriff had confiscated from the boys during their arrest—belts, wallets, Jon's money and books, the keys to the Volkswagen. She was inordinately pleased with herself for unearthing all these treasures in the sheriff's desk and file cabinet, but dangling from the index finger of her right hand was the find she was most proud of:

A spare set of keys to Sheriff Buckley's squad car.

"Only thirteen miles to go!" Julianna rejoiced, easing the Volkswagen into first gear and pulling out of the Dairy Queen parking lot in Mullwein. Ronnie Buckley's squad car was in back of the Dairy Queen, its exposed rear bumper concealed behind an overturned garbage can and a picnic table.

Yippee, thought Jon Tate, slumping against the passenger door of the Beetle's front seat. He felt as if he were on the way to his own funeral, and he couldn't believe he was doing something so stupid of his own free will—even getting Becky Westman pregnant had been smarter than this.

"It's nice to be back in the Bug again," Elijah said from the backseat, enjoying the feel of the warm night air blowing through the open windows as they drove south on Highway 69, toward the Missouri border. He leaned forward to talk to Julianna and Jon. "When I buy my first car I'm going to get one just like it."

Elijah was suddenly acting almost as jubilant as Julianna, and Jon scowled, not understanding how the younger boy could so easily shake off the sense of doom that was consuming Jon. Still, he supposed, it *did* feel better to be out of the dead sheriff's car and on the road again; they had the highway to themselves, and the stars and the moon were out, and the only sounds were the hum of their tires on the pavement and the familiar purr of the Volkswagen's small engine. It was peaceful and comforting, and he could almost convince himself everything was going to be okay.

Almost.

The Beetle's high beams lit up the asphalt road in front of them, but everything else was in darkness save for an occasional porch light they passed on their way out of Mullwein. Jon rested his head against the door frame and closed his eyes, trying to ignore the throbbing pain in his shoulder. There'd been some aspirin in the first aid kit at the jailhouse, but Julianna had only allowed him to take two of the caplets for fear of thinning his blood too much while he was still bleeding.

Remembering how deftly Julianna had dressed his wounds in the jail cell made Jon believe that Elijah may have been right about her being a nurse. She had told him the bullet had only damaged muscle tissue, miraculously missing his lungs, bones, and arteries; she'd also told him he was fortunate he hadn't been wearing a shirt when Bonnor shot him, because otherwise the bullet might have left some cloth in his body on its way through, increasing his risk of infection.

Yeah, I'm one lucky son of a gun, he thought wearily, opening his eyes again. He'd impregnated a fourteen-year-old girl; he was wanted for murder, arson, and rape by the FBI; he'd been beaten and shot by a redneck deputy; he was being chauffeured around by a woman with more loose screws than a lumberyard, and he was most likely going to be dead before the night was over.

Just call him Lucky Jon.

Julianna seemed to sense his disquiet. She turned her head and smiled at him, shifting the Volkswagen into high gear as they left the town limits and passed into the countryside.

"You don't have to be one bit nervous about meeting my family, Jon," she said, raising her voice to carry over the wind. "You'll feel right at home the second you walk through the door."

Jon tried to smile back at her, touched by the genuine sweetness in her expression. "Thanks," he said awkwardly, ignoring Elijah's grin. "I'm really looking forward to meeting them."

"There are only five of us you have to deal with," Julianna continued. "Momma and Daddy, my two older brothers—Seth and Michael, who are both about your age—and me. We live on a farm just north of town, in a big old house Daddy and some of our neighbors built right before Daddy and Momma got married. Anyway, I can't wait for you to see it. I think it's the best farm in Pawnee." She laughed. "Momma tells me I'm biased when I say things like that, but I swear it's true. We live on top of a hill, and the sky is so pretty at night it makes you cry to look at it. When I was little I used to think I could reach up with my bare hands and touch the moon and the stars." She laughed again. "Seth and Michael both tease me about that all the time, don't they, Ben?"

"Yep," Elijah agreed, still grinning. "They sure do."

Jon raised an eyebrow at Elijah, then turned back to Julianna. "So what are your brothers like?" he asked, surrendering to the absurdity of the conversation.

Julianna snorted. "Like little boys in big men's bodies." A rabbit darted across the road in front of the Volkswagen and she gasped, barely missing it. "They like to think of themselves as all grown up, just because they've gotten so tall, but they still act like two-year-olds. They show each other the food in their mouths when we're eating, and the other day when we went swimming in our pond they got in a fight about whose turn it was to use the inner tube." She pinched the bridge of her nose as if warding off a headache, then dropped her hand to the steering wheel again. "But they're also very sweet. For Momma's birthday this year they made a chocolate cake for her and decorated it with marshmallows and whipped cream, and they carried Momma around the kitchen in her chair while Daddy and I sang *God Save the Queen.*"

Jon and Elijah had stopped smiling. Julianna's eyes were glistening, and in the scant illumination from the moon and the Beetle's headlights the tears on her face looked like ghostly war paint.

"Julianna?" Elijah touched her shoulder. "What's wrong?"

She attempted to laugh. "I'm not really sure." She blinked a few times and bit her lip to keep it from trembling. "I'm just homesick, I suppose. This is the longest I've ever been away from my family."

Elijah squeezed her shoulder. He wanted to tell her they'd be in Pawnee in just a few minutes, but the feeling of certainty he'd had at the jailhouse about this being the right course of action was weakening. Maybe Jon had been right.

He sighed, leaving his hand on Julianna's shoulder as he stared out the window at a scarecrow in the middle of a cornfield. Right or wrong, it was too late to turn back now; Julianna was driving, and Elijah had learned his lesson about trying to take the wheel from her when she didn't want to relinquish it. Besides, if Julianna was right about how close they were to where she'd grown up, they'd be there in fifteen minutes, and surely the police wouldn't be able to find them once they were off the main roads—at least not without a great deal of luck.

Julianna was already smiling again as if nothing had upset her, and a few seconds later she began to hum. Elijah blinked as he recognized the tune: It was something his mother had sung as a lullaby many times when he was little. He no longer knew the words, but he seemed to remember it was called "Goin' Home."

The hot night air suddenly felt cold to him and he shivered, recalling something else. He'd asked his mother to stop singing that song after he'd gotten old enough to understand what it was about.

Death, he thought. *It's about death.*

Chapter 14

Goin' home, goin' home, I'm a goin' home
Quiet like, still some day, I'm just goin' home

As Julianna Dapper steered the Volkswagen toward Pawnee on that late Sunday night in June 1962, the words to an old spiritual she had learned from Ben Taylor's mother some forty years before kept repeating in her mind, though she didn't sing them aloud. She was too preoccupied with the moonlit countryside around her to do anything but hum the simple melody as her eyes flitted over each tree, sign post, and farm pond they passed, taking everything in and trying to quell a growing feeling of unease in the pit of her stomach.

The late-night sky of northern Missouri was just as dark as it should have been, and the smells of dirt, cows, pigs, and wild flowers were no less pungent than what she expected. Something wasn't right, though—she couldn't put her finger on what it was exactly, yet she couldn't shake the feeling that she wasn't where she was supposed to be. As they passed a radio tower and a massive grain silo she stopped humming for a moment, perplexed.

"Where on earth did *those* come from?" she asked, frowning.

Ben Taylor's presence in the backseat reassured her, as did a familiar intersection at the crest of a hill, followed by the welcome sight of Günter and Polly Miller's dairy farm in the distance.

But we already passed the Millers' farm, she reminded herself, shying away from the disturbing images that came with this recollection. How had the dairy farm gotten in front of them again? Her eyes widened as they drew closer; she could make out half a dozen new buildings that didn't belong on the property.

What in heaven's name was happening?

Jon Tate said something to Elijah that Julianna didn't hear, and she glanced over at the wounded boy in the passenger seat next to her. She remembered picking Jon up recently in her father's car, yet she couldn't recall exactly where or when, nor could she remember what they had done with Eben Larson's Model T. Her eyes took in Jon's naked chest and flat stomach and she flushed a little, grateful for the darkness in the car. His bruised knee was only an inch or so from the gearshift, and she found herself wanting to touch him.

Shame on me, she thought with a rueful smile.

She resumed her humming, using her voice as a sort of sonar to navigate through all the anomalies of time continuously confronting her: a road that was much straighter and smoother than it should have been, hundreds of telephone poles that weren't supposed to be there, a face in the rearview mirror that sometimes belonged to her dear friend Ben Taylor, and sometimes to a taller, more handsome boy named Elijah Hunter, whom she had met only the day before.

> *Morning star lights the way*
> *Restless dreaming done*
> *Shadows gone, break of day*
> *Real life just begun*

Even her own voice was a conundrum. To her ears, her humming sounded richer and deeper than it should have. She'd always been able to sing, but this was different, somehow, darker and more nuanced. It was the resonant, mature voice of a middle-aged woman, and it both thrilled and appalled her. She didn't really sound like herself at all, she realized; she sounded more like her mother.

Julianna reflexively turned west onto Route 46. The hills grew far more pronounced and the road narrowed and roughened, changing from pavement to asphalt, and then at last to gravel. Potholes the size of washtubs forced her to slow down, and she gritted her teeth at each delay. The boys could feel her growing anxiety and they remained quiet, peering through the windows at the hayfields surrounding them.

"Almost there," Julianna whispered after a few long minutes of silence. The large hill they were approaching sent a thrill of recognition through her, and she gunned the Volkswagen to make sure they'd have enough momentum to reach the summit of this last obstacle between herself and Pawnee. She had to downshift before they reached the top, but once there she eagerly looked for lights in any of the stores in the valley at the base of the hill, but she could see nothing, not even the stores themselves.

"Everybody must be in bed," she muttered. "I suppose I shouldn't be surprised, though, as late as it is."

Elijah and Jon looked at each other grimly. Aside from another gravel road that headed north at the foot of the hill where Julianna's attention was focused, there was nothing except hayfields and an occasional tree. Julianna proceeded down the hill and turned onto the northbound road when they reached the bottom; the Beetle's headlights allowed them to see a sign that read "County Road YY."

"There's the post office where Momma works!" Julianna told Jon, coming to a stop and pointing out his window as she allowed the Beetle to idle in neutral. "And there's the bakery right over there. Tomorrow morning we can come back to town and buy a loaf of Nellie's sourdough bread to have with breakfast. It's so good you'll think you've died and gone to heaven!"

For all of Julianna's enthusiasm, every time she turned her head the familiar structures of Pawnee seemed to vanish before her eyes, replaced by shadows in the moonlight. Doc Colby's porch could have been a patch of brush by the roadside, Lars Olson's smithy a stand of Scotch pine trees.

"Julianna," Elijah murmured. "I don't see anything."

She swallowed hard and eased the car into gear. "Benjamin Taylor," she responded wearily. She was so tired she could hardly keep her eyes open. "The second we get home, I swear I'm going to slap you silly for giving me such a hard time today."

"Where's your house, Julianna?" Jon asked carefully, sensing just how fragile Julianna was becoming.

"Right down this road, about a mile and a half from here," she answered. The Volkswagen was picking up speed as they headed north. "We always tell visitors to go to the top of the third big hill north of town and turn left at the mailbox. You'd have to be blind to miss it."

After a few hundred yards, they passed a lonely farmhouse with a mobile home parked in its driveway. There were no lights on at the house and Julianna didn't even spare it a glance. She was now staring straight ahead, refusing to look at anything except the road itself. It had no shoulders and was barely wide enough for one car; it wound up and down the steep hills just as it should, and she began to breathe freely again, reassured by the tractor ruts in the mud next to the gravel and the smell of wild roses and juniper bushes in the air.

The third hill north of Pawnee appeared in the headlights. She smiled joyfully as the Beetle struggled toward the crest and she began honking the horn to let her family know she was finally home. As they reached the summit she cranked the wheel to the left to pull into their driveway, still honking the horn.

"What on *earth?*" she cried, slamming on the brakes and stalling the engine.

The front wheels of the Volkswagen slid to a stop a few inches from a shallow ditch lining the edge of the road. On the other side of the ditch—looking like a military cemetery in the moonlight—was a cornfield.

Julianna's skin was the color of wax as she gaped through the windshield of the Beetle at the knee-high rows of cornstalks revealed in the headlights. Her hands fell limply from the steering wheel into her lap and her breathing was the only sound in the car. Elijah reached out to touch her again, putting his hand on the back of her neck and murmuring her name.

Home sweet home, Jon Tate thought bleakly.

* * *

The speed limit was twenty-five miles per hour, but Samuel Hunter—driving the "borrowed" 1959 Ford Country Sedan station wagon owned by Bonnor Tucker—barreled through the town of Mullwein, Iowa, at more than three times that speed, praying nobody else would be on the road at eleven thirty on a Sunday night. Sam knew he'd never forgive himself if he plowed into another car, or God forbid a pedestrian, but it was a risk he had to take if he, Mary, and Edgar were to have any chance at all of catching up to Elijah and his companions ahead of Gabriel and the police.

Mary was in the passenger seat, holding herself as still as possible by clutching the door handle with her right hand and bracing her left palm against the dash. Sam could sense the tension in his wife's body as the public library and the Mullwein State Bank blurred past their windows, but he knew she wanted him to do exactly what he was doing, in spite of the peril to themselves and others. On the highway between the jailhouse and Mullwein, she had urged him to push the station wagon to its limit, but a series of hills and sharp curves had seldom allowed them to go full out for more than a few hundred yards at a time. The constant acceleration and frenzied braking had made for a stomach-churning ride, and Sam feared the rest of the journey would be no less harrowing.

"Oh God Oh God Oh God," Edgar Reilly moaned in the backseat. To Sam's surprise, the tightly wound psychiatrist had not suggested slowing down, but the roller coaster–like ride was clearly not agreeing with the older man at all. He had unwrapped at least a dozen lemon drops in the past ten miles, yet even with his cheeks packed like a squirrel's he seemed unable to refrain from moaning under his breath every few seconds.

They sped violently over a set of railroad tracks, the headlights of the station wagon bouncing crazily on the asphalt road in front of them, and then shot down a steep hill; Mary gasped out a warning when she noticed how the highway veered to the left on the other side of a Dairy Queen at the bottom of the hill.

"I see it!" Sam said, stamping on the brakes and grappling

with the steering wheel to control the turn. The tires of Bonnor's car squealed in protest and the tail end slid madly on the road, but Sam held on with a death grip and a second later they were headed south, toward Missouri—going much too fast to notice the empty squad car tucked away behind the Dairy Queen.

"Oh God Oh God Oh God," Edgar ground out through clenched teeth. The scent of lemons wafted over the front seat.

The highway before them was blessedly straight and devoid of other travelers, permitting Sam a quick glance at Mary. "She said another ten miles after we get out of Mullwein, right?" he asked. "And then look for Highway 46?"

Mary nodded. Dottie Buckley had told them she was only guessing where Pawnee might be found, and Mary knew Sam remembered everything Dottie had said as well as Mary herself did. The numbered roads and the distances between them were a kind of mantra for him, though, and she understood he was only repeating them to calm his nerves.

"We'll find it, Sam," she said.

"After that, though," he continued, "I'm guessing we'll probably have to stop and ask somebody who lives in the area for specifics."

"We'll find it," Mary repeated.

Mary wasn't just saying this to comfort Sam; she believed it to be true. If she had to, she would wake every farmer in the county until somebody told her what she needed to know. She was not about to get this close to her son, only to fail because the place they were looking for was apparently as elusive as El Dorado. Mary had grown up in farm country—though in the Deep South—and she knew what folks were like in such places: They stayed put forever, and they had long memories. With any luck at all, she and Sam wouldn't need to knock on too many doors before they found somebody who knew exactly where Pawnee was. Or at least where it *used* to be.

We're coming, Elijah, she thought as Sam floored the accelerator and the speedometer crept over a hundred miles per hour. *We're coming just as fast as we can.*

* * *

Gabriel Dapper was driving even more recklessly than Samuel Hunter, but he was still five minutes behind Elijah Hunter's parents and Edgar Reilly. Gabriel had no idea why Mary Hunter and the others were still so sure that Pawnee, Missouri, was where Elijah Hunter and Jon Tate were taking Julianna, yet he wasn't about to lose track of the only hope he had of finding his mother.

"I'm coming, Mom," he murmured aloud in his Cadillac. "Just hang on a little longer."

The chase after the Hunters and Edgar Reilly had acted like an analeptic in Gabriel Dapper's bloodstream. His fatigue was entirely gone; he felt like he could stay awake for eternity. The sound of his tires on the road's surface changed pitch as the asphalt highway gave way to concrete, and the Cadillac whipped past darkened houses and lonely streetlights. He paid no attention to his surroundings, however; he was too busy trying to make sense of the senseless.

The depth of his ignorance appalled him. He didn't understand why the two little shitheads who had kidnapped and raped his mother had now taken her with them yet again; he didn't understand what these same two shitheads would have to gain by taking her back to her hometown. As the Cadillac blew through downtown Mullwein, rumbling like thunder over a two-block stretch of cobblestone, Gabriel asked himself the same questions over and over:

Why Pawnee? What were the kidnappers up to? What did they know that he didn't?

He screeched around the sharp turn at the bottom of the hill by the Dairy Queen. The right rear tire of the Cadillac slammed into the curb with enough force to pop off its hubcap and send the bundle beside him on the passenger seat flying to the floor. Gabriel didn't really notice the collision; he simply stamped on the accelerator again and resumed his pursuit, leaving two burned-rubber marks on the highway behind him.

He'd never even heard the name of "Pawnee, Missouri,"

until his mother got sick and started talking about it all the time. Why had she never said anything about it when she was sane? Why hadn't he ever pushed her harder about her past? It was *his* past, too, by extension; surely he had a right to know more about it than he did.

On his visits to the Maine State Mental Hospital in Bangor, Julianna had mentioned "Momma and Daddy" and two brothers named Seth and Michael, but that was the extent of what Gabriel knew about the people who were apparently *his* family, as well. He thought back to his own childhood, and to the few times he had attempted to ask Julianna about her parents and siblings. Her answers had always been either evasive or monosyllabic, but it seemed to him now there had also been something in her voice he had missed each time, an undercurrent of emotion he would have noticed right away if he'd only been paying closer attention. He'd heard the same undertone again when she was hallucinating in the hospital, but he was only now beginning to get a glimmer of what it might be:

Enormous love, and an equally powerful grief. Perhaps the knowledge that the best part of her life was over, and things would never be as good again. The end of hope, the end of childhood, the end of faith in a just and moral universe. All of these and more, bound together and spun into a dark, haunting melody, a threnody of loss for anybody who knew how to listen for it.

Gabriel was suddenly blinded by tears. There was no way he could possibly know what had happened to Julianna, yet something was telling him it was a wonder her mind had not broken decades before, split into a million pieces by memory and loss. And now she was apparently being dragged back to where her life had been ruined, the hostage of two criminals who had done unspeakable things to her and had some hidden purpose for taking her there.

Gabriel glanced at the bundle on the floor of the passenger seat. Wrapped up in his suit coat were three souvenirs he'd brought home with him at the end of World War II. One was a

Mauser pistol; the other two were German hand grenades (nick-named "potato mashers" for their long wooden cylinders and brutal-looking metal caps). Until the previous day, all three weapons had been locked up in a trunk in his attic for nearly seventeen years; he had actually forgotten all about them before Edgar Reilly called to tell him that his mother had been kidnapped. Gabriel was not a violent man by nature, but the boys who had taken his mother were no doubt armed, and he would not be caught with his pants down. He would do whatever it took to get Julianna back; he would somehow find a way to make things right for her again, and give her some peace.

"I'm coming, Mom," Gabriel mourned, accidentally running over a rabbit on the road without feeling the bump.

Julianna wandered in the moonlight through the foot-high rows of corn, looking for her home. To all outward appearances, she could have been out for a midnight stroll in the country, stopping every few steps to enjoy the play of shadows on the ground as a light breeze tugged this way and that at the cornstalks surrounding her.

"Julianna?" Elijah was following her at a respectful distance, not wanting to intrude but too worried to stay silent any longer. "Are you all right?"

She nodded her head, swaying from side to side like a little girl and breaking up a clod of dirt with the toe of her shoe.

Julianna had stepped out of the Beetle a few minutes before, leaving it parked with its headlights pointing at the cornfield and its rear end jutting into the middle of the road. Elijah had chased after her at once, leaving Jon to park the car in a more conventional manner. Elijah heard Jon coming now through the field, walking as fast as his injuries would allow, and he half turned to wait for the older boy.

"I tried to find a place to hide the Bug but there's no place close by that will work," Jon muttered to Elijah, catching up. "I couldn't even put it in the cornfield because there's no way it would make it through the ditch."

Elijah glanced back at the road, some fifteen yards behind them. The moonlight was bright enough for him to make out the Volkswagen's rounded roof with no difficulty. "We'll see anybody coming from up here a long time before they get here," he said. "We can always make a run for it if we have to."

Jon nodded wearily. "What about the guns? You and Julianna left them in the car and I couldn't decide if I should bring them or not. I thought Julianna might be weird about it."

Elijah blinked, surprised by Jon's apparent willingness to follow whatever course he, Elijah, believed to be best. "I guess we can leave them for now," he said, trying to sound more sure than he felt. "Like I said, no one can sneak up on us here."

Julianna turned around and motioned for them to join her. The boys obeyed at once, both feeling oddly diffident as they drew closer. She searched their faces when they drew even with her, then gestured at the ground by her feet. "The front porch was right about here," she said matter-of-factly, sounding like a distracted tour guide at a museum. "Our barn was over there, and a little north of that was Daddy's tool shed." She smiled a little. "Seth and Michael always called it 'The Mouse House.' "

Elijah and Jon stared at her. Her voice gave them no clue as to her mental state; she was still speaking in the light manner they associated with her teenager persona, yet it was clear from what she was saying that she was no longer hallucinating, at least for the moment. She didn't seem to need them to say anything; she simply kept looking around the hilltop.

"Momma's garden was just over there," she continued, turning in a slow circle. "About ten feet away from where that fence is. We used to tease her that she loved her garden more than she loved us, because she spent so much time in it." She bent down to finger a leaf on a cornstalk. "She'd be so mad if she knew they'd plowed it under."

Jon slapped at a mosquito on his bicep and the quick movement caused a twinge in his shoulder. That he'd been shot earlier that night still felt unreal to him. He kept staring at the bandage taped to the left side of his chest as if it had been put there by mistake, thinking about how easily the bullet had torn through his flesh.

"What happened to your family, Julianna?" Elijah asked quietly, pulling Jon's attention back to the hilltop. "Do you remember?"

Julianna looked up at the stars in the sky, and then back at the earth. For an instant she thought she heard gunfire and screaming, and the roar of an enormous fire. Her knees began to buckle but then the night went mercifully still again.

"Ben," she whispered, looking at Elijah as if she were just noticing his presence. "I don't feel very well."

Coincidence was setting the table for a lavish feast.

Samuel Hunter pulled into the driveway of the first house he saw after Highway 46 changed from asphalt to gravel, to ask for better directions to Pawnee than a traumatized Dottie Buckley had been able to provide. The house was a small one-story home with a flat roof and a yard more dirt than grass; there was an empty chicken coop on the property and an old Chevy Bel Air parked beside it.

"Looks like they're already asleep," Sam said, reaching for his door handle. "I'll go knock."

Mary shook her head and put a hand on his arm to stop him. "Seeing a black man on the porch at this hour may frighten the poor things to death. I'll do it." She turned her head to look at Edgar in the backseat. "It might be best if you come with me, Dr. Reilly. Some folks may not want to talk to me, either, but you're not as likely to give them the willies."

The thought of waking potentially hostile strangers in the middle of the night on a deserted country road was not appealing to Edgar, but he nodded in agreement and cleared his throat nervously.

"Whatever you think best, Mary," he said.

The two of them got out of the car and walked to the door together, listening to the sound of their shoes on the gravel and the hooting of an owl in a nearby tree. The headlights from Bonnor Tucker's station wagon allowed Mary to note that the house was old and badly in need of a paint job, but there was a stunning flower garden circling the foundation—she saw poppies, mimosas, cockscombs, African lilies, Bells of Ireland, and several other blossoms she wasn't familiar with—and she smiled to herself as she knocked on the door. In her experience, people who cared more about their flower gardens than the houses they lived in were not likely to be overly hostile.

"Should we knock again?" Edgar asked, looking back with longing at the station wagon.

Mary shook her head. "Somebody's already coming."

The porch light flickered on over their heads a moment later, and Mary, who had not expected to see another dark-skinned face in this part of the world, blinked in surprise when the door opened and an elderly black woman in a pink bathrobe peered out at them. She appeared to be in her mid-seventies, with short white hair and a heavily lined face, but her shoulders were straight and her eyes were more curious than wary.

"We're very sorry to wake you, ma'am," Mary said. "But it's an emergency, and we need directions."

"I wasn't sleeping, honey," the woman answered. She was taller and heavier than Mary, though not by much, and there was no hint of the South in her voice, as there was in Mary's. "I was just staring up at the ceiling in my bedroom. What are you looking for?"

For some reason, Mary's spine began to tingle. "We're trying to find a town that's not on the map," she answered. "It's called Pawnee. Have you heard of it?"

The older woman had been fussing with the waist-tie on her robe but her hands now froze in front of her and she stared hard at Mary for several long seconds before responding.

"Who on earth have you been talking to?" she asked. "Is this some kind of a joke?"

Mary assured her that she was acting on her own behalf, and quite serious.

"I'll be doggoned," the woman said, looking dumbfounded. She resumed cinching up her robe but couldn't seem to make a proper knot. "My husband and I used to have a farm in Pawnee, but the whole town burned to the ground back in twenty-three, and nobody ever took the trouble to rebuild it. How did you ever hear of such a pitiful little place?"

The mysterious tingling in Mary's spine became a shiver she couldn't suppress. She wasn't surprised to learn that Julianna Dapper's hometown was no longer in existence, but if it had indeed vanished so many years before, it seemed a huge stroke of luck that the first house Sam had stopped at that night just happened to be owned by somebody who not only knew of Pawnee, but was actually a former resident.

"It's a long story, and we don't have much time," she said quietly. "Can you tell us where it was? It's very important."

The old woman was clearly baffled; she looked from Mary to Edgar and then back again at Mary before responding.

"Just get back on Route 46 there right behind you," she pointed past them at the gravel road, "and head west for about two miles. Soon as you see a road going north, hang a right and you'll be smack in the middle of Pawnee. Nothing's there now but corn, though." She paused, still studying Mary's face with incomprehension. "Were you looking for somebody in particular, honey? I knew every soul in town, and as far as I know I'm the only one left alive these days who can say that."

Mary glanced at Edgar, who was staring at the old woman with a fascination that equaled her own.

Jung called this sort of thing synchronicity, Edgar Reilly was reminding himself, taking refuge in psychological theory to calm the goose pimples on the back of his neck. The odds of immediately knocking on the door of perhaps the only living survivor, aside from Julianna, of a town that had ceased to exist four decades ago seemed to be a whopper of a coincidence to Edgar, too, and Edgar did not care for such things—especially late at night on a deserted country road.

Mary looked over her shoulder at Sam in the station wagon, then faced front again. "We're looking for a woman named Julianna Dapper, who supposedly grew up around here."

The old woman's brow wrinkled and she shook her head. "There was only one girl in Pawnee named Julianna, but her last name wasn't Dapper. It was Larson."

Edgar started. "But that's her! Julianna's maiden name was Larson!" He reached for a cigarette and dropped the whole pack on the porch in excitement. "Did you know her?"

The woman smiled sadly. "My youngest boy and her were thick as thieves their whole lives. But there's no way in the world we're talking about the same person. The Julianna Larson I knew died the night of the fire."

Mary raised her eyebrows. "I beg your pardon? Are you certain?"

Sudden grief twisted the woman's features. "I'm afraid so. My son was with her, and he died, too."

Edgar knelt in the heavy silence to retrieve his cigarettes. "I don't understand," he murmured. "They *have* to be the same person."

Mary reached out to touch the other woman's wrist. "I'm very sorry to upset you," she said. "I don't understand this, either, but the person we're looking for is named Julianna, and her last name used to be Larson when she lived here." *And she's with my son instead of yours, now,* she added silently. "She's been living in Bangor, Maine, for a long time, but according to Dr. Reilly," she indicated Edgar, "she knows all about Pawnee."

The older woman caught Mary's hand in her own and held it. "Julianna Larson burned to death with her family, and my"—her voice cracked—"and my boy Ben, too. The sheriff and the coroner identified all the bodies in *both* fires. There's a tombstone with Julianna's name on it up at the Lone Rock cemetery."

Mary Hunter frowned. "There was more than one fire?"

The woman struggled to explain. "The Larson farm burned down, too, that same night, a mile or so north of town. But the fire at their farm wasn't an accident, like the one in town was. My son and all the Larsons were murdered by a man named Rufus Tarwater, who shot them all and then tossed their bodies in the fire." Her face twisted. "Tarwater got away, and was never caught."

Something else clicked in Edgar Reilly's head. "Ben!" he

blurted. "You said your son's name was Ben! Was his last name Taylor, by any chance? Are you Mary Taylor?"

Mary Taylor's grip tightened painfully on Mary Hunter's hand as she gaped at Edgar.

"How could you possibly know that?" she breathed.

Mary Hunter sighed, glancing over her shoulder toward Sam in the station wagon. They couldn't stay there any longer to sort this out; she was certain Gabriel would be coming any time now.

"Can you please come with us, Mrs. Taylor?" she asked abruptly. "I have a feeling we might need your help."

The blacktop on Route 46 ran out but Gabriel Dapper didn't slow down as his Cadillac's tires hit the gravel. He was just in time to see the taillights of Bonnor Tucker's station wagon disappear over a hill directly ahead of him. Dottie Buckley had given Gabriel the same vague directions she had given the Hunters and Edgar Reilly, but they'd gotten a three or four mile head start on him and he'd begun to fear he wouldn't catch up.

"There you are," he breathed, hurtling down the road.

Thanks to the resourcefulness of the nightshift dispatcher for the Missouri State Patrol, Bonnor Tucker knew exactly where to look for his fugitives, as did the Iowa *and* Missouri State Patrols. The dispatcher had located a fifty-year-old map listing Pawnee, Missouri, as an unincorporated town in Harrison County, right at the junction of Route 46 and County Road YY. Even so, only four officers—Bonnor Tucker, an Iowa State Patrolman, and two Missouri troopers—were en route to Pawnee on that late Sunday night in June; the Iowa patrolman was about one minute behind Bonnor, both headed southwest, and the the two Missouri troopers were approaching Pawnee from the east in separate vehicles. No one else on duty at that hour was close enough to offer assistance.

And that was just fine with Bonnor Tucker.

"The less fuckin' dumbass troopers the better," he muttered, crossing the state line between Iowa and Missouri with the bubble light flashing on top of his squad car.

One of the Missouri troopers had already given Bonnor flack

over the radio about intruding on their jurisdiction, and the last thing Bonnor was in the mood for that night was a pissing contest over who had the right to track down and deal with Elijah Hunter and Jon Tate. It was a moot point, as far as Bonnor was concerned, because Gabriel Dapper would beat them all to Pawnee, anyway, and if the look on Gabriel's face when he had charged out of the jailhouse was any indication, Bonnor doubted the two little shitheads who had killed Ronnie would still be alive by the time Bonnor and his colleagues caught up.

"I just wish I could be there to see it," Bonnor said sadly.

"I don't feel very well," Julianna Dapper whispered to Elijah.

She continued to spin in a slow circle, searching the fertile earth around her for any sign of human habitation, and was finally given a reward for her diligence: Thirty feet south of where she and the boys were standing she glimpsed what appeared to be a small wooden raft in the middle of a lake of corn. It took her a moment, however, to recognize this anomaly for what it was; with everything gone it was hard to keep the hilltop in perspective.

"That was our well," she murmured. "It looks like they've boarded it over to keep people from falling in, but I bet that's it."

In her mind's eye, Julianna saw hundreds of ashes floating through the air above her head. Some of them were still burning, and the wind carried them toward the barn, and the toolshed, and the outhouse. One eventually landed in a stack of hay bales inside the open barn door, and soon the entire hill was alight with fire. Smoke billowed around her, and the horses in the corral behind the barn screamed in terror, and the night air was distorted from the heat, making everything she saw look like a reflection in a funhouse mirror. It was hell on earth, and Julianna was the only one left alive to witness it, standing in the middle of her backyard.

Except it seemed she wasn't alone after all: Ben Taylor was there with her, and Jon Tate, too.

But Ben is dead, she protested silently. *He was the first one Rufus killed.*

For thirty-nine years, the youngest child of Eben and Emma Larson had managed to elude the memories of her last night in Pawnee. She had also sidestepped the monstrous images that haunted her dreams, banishing them from her thoughts the instant she awakened. Every now and then, however, she'd find herself shaking for no reason, and she quite often felt like screaming—but she always ignored these physical and emotional quirks, or dismissed them as the by-products of fatigue, or a migraine headache. But on a sunny afternoon a few weeks before that Sunday night in the cornfield, Julianna Dapper had come home from teaching in Bangor and read a story in the newspaper about a fire on a family farm in Maine. The people in the newspaper article were unknown to her, but the similarities between their fate and that of her own family, decades earlier and half a continent away, were impossible to ignore. The Maine fire was the result of arson, and those who had lived on the farm—a mother, a father, and three children—had all died. Worse yet, the autopsy revealed that each of the victims had been shot in their beds before the blaze was set.

And Julianna Dapper, née Julianna Larson, confronted by nothing more than an ugly coincidence, had finally lost her grip on sanity.

"Momma was next," she now whispered, standing on the hill where her family had been slaughtered a generation ago. Julianna had never known for sure if Emma had already been dead by the time Eben tumbled into the inferno of the burning kitchen with her mother's body in his arms, but she had prayed for this to be the case, unable to bear the idea of Emma suffering—as Eben had—when the flames engulfed them.

"Rufus shot Momma, and then he shot Seth," she informed Elijah and Jon in an eerily calm voice. "Then he shot Michael, too."

"Sweet Jesus," Elijah murmured. "Jesus God Almighty."

"Daddy died in the fire, though," Julianna continued, staring past the boys at her memories. "I couldn't get the back door open and he burned to death in the kitchen. He was holding Momma but I think she was already dead."

Elijah felt tears running down his face, one after another. He watched Julianna fall to her knees, and he rushed to her side and held her tightly to his chest. Jon Tate was there a second later, kneeling beside them. The older boy looked as miserable as Elijah felt, and Elijah reached out to him, as well, taking one of Jon's hands in his own.

"I ran back to Michael," Julianna murmured in Elijah's ear. "But he'd already died."

She lifted her head and studied Elijah's wet face in the moonlight as if his features were unfamiliar to her. "You really don't look like Ben very much," she said quietly. "But you're just as sweet." Her eyes drifted away to the well once more and she half turned in his arms. "Ben died right over there. I was trying to drag him out of danger but I wasn't fast enough. Rufus shot him in the head."

As if the boarded-up well held all her memories and was now releasing them one by one, Julianna began to share everything that passed in front of her eyes. She spoke in a steady murmur, without hurry or inflection, and Elijah held her, and Jon Tate sat close by, and the young men were as silent as children listening to a ghost story beside a campfire. She started by telling them how

. . . *how after watching her father die she had gone back to Michael and found him dead, too, his head resting on Seth's arm and his eyes open, staring sightlessly at the stars he had adored . . . how the blood on his bare stomach had looked like a garish tattoo in the flickering light . . . how she had sat motionless beside him and Seth as the house fire raged unopposed, flinging burning ash into the sky . . . how she had stumbled to the backyard to sit with Ben, too, after remembering she'd left him there . . .*

. . . how she had eventually spotted the orange-reddish glow in the sky above Pawnee, and realized her town was as dead as her family and her dearest friend . . . how she had begun screaming as the barn and the other buildings on the property also caught fire . . . how she had regained her senses sometime later and knew she would never have the strength to endure another day on that godforsaken farm or in that godforsaken town . . .

   . . . how in her desperation to flee from so much horror she had somehow dragged the remains of the three dead boys she had loved onto what was left of the front porch of the burning house, to be cremated along with her parents . . . how while doing this she had glimpsed Rufus Tarwater's crumpled body on the lawn and raced to save a ten-gallon drum of gasoline from under a lean-to by the tool shed before the lean-to also caught fire . . . how she had rolled the drum back across the yard . . . how in the extremity of her grief she had saturated the dead man's clothes with gasoline, then set a flaming brand to his shirt . . . how she had continued pouring gas on the carcass until there was nothing left of Rufus Tarwater but a charred mound of flesh . . . how she had ignited the drum itself, and flung Rufus's rifle in the farm pond . . .

   . . . how before daylight she had gotten in her father's Model T at last, as the fires around her began to dwindle . . . how she had driven away from Pawnee forever, or so she then believed, turning north at the end of the gravel driveway instead of south toward town, not wishing to encounter any fellow survivors or speak to anyone who would ask her what had become of her family and Ben . . . how she had driven until the Model T had run out of fuel, and then rolled the car into a ditch somewhere in eastern Iowa . . . how she had hitchhiked from town to town and state to state until she reached Veteran, Maine, four days later, where a distant cousin of Emma's took her in and Julianna's future husband, William Dapper, owned a farm . . .

   . . . how she had somehow started a new life, rising from the ashes of her former self . . . how she had married William Dapper and given birth to their son, Gabriel . . . how William had been kicked in the head and killed by a horse three years after Gabriel was born . . . how her heart fell apart once more, almost as badly as it had in Pawnee . . .

   . . . how she and Gabriel had moved to Bangor to escape yet another set of memories . . . how she had evaded and denied her past for almost forty years until it caught up to her at last on her own front porch, breaching her defenses in an unguarded mo-

*ment and swamping her mind . . . how she had set fire to her
neighbor's garage in Bangor because she'd somehow mistaken it
for her father's tool shed and couldn't bear to have her memories reawakened . . . how the police*

". . . came and took me to the hospital."

The stillness on the hilltop was so abrupt that Elijah and
Jon—who had been listening to Julianna for nearly twenty minutes without moving or speaking—both started a little, as if
awakened from a trance. Julianna seemed to be listening to
something, yet all the boys could hear was the sound of their
own breathing, and the rustle of the breeze in the corn around
them. They waited uneasily to see if she'd resume her narrative,
but she remained silent, her head cocked to the side in the darkness. Elijah cleared his throat and this caused her to stir at last;
she glanced at him for the first time in a long while.

"I'd forgotten everything," she whispered. "Absolutely
everything."

She dropped her forehead in exhaustion on Elijah's shoulder
and began to hum again, apparently not expecting an answer.

Elijah rested his chin on the crown of Julianna's head. He had
stopped crying some time ago but he felt completely wrung out
and fragile; he didn't trust his voice to work correctly even if he
could have thought of something more to say. He noticed with
surprise that his fingers were still interlaced with Jon's, and he
was reminded again how much had changed in the past two
days: Julianna was cradled against his chest and Jon was holding his hand, and he had no desire to break away from either of
them. Jon tried and failed to say something; Elijah clutched his
hand tighter and closed his eyes.

Please, Lord, he prayed, feeling the older boy's pulse beating
in his fingers and Julianna's tears soaking through his shirt.
Please help this poor woman, and keep my friend safe.

The night air was calling to Julianna, distracting her with familiar, evocative smells: the black, rich dirt she was sitting on, a
patch of wildflowers on the other side of a nearby fence, the perspiration of her companions.

"Whew," she whispered, suddenly wrinkling her nose. "Momma won't let you boys in the house smelling like *that*. You can wash up by the well."

Momma's dead, she corrected herself at once, recalling with an effort where she was—or more accurately, *when* she was. Elijah/Ben spoke her name; she could feel his throat moving against the side of her face. She was too tired to talk, but her well-ingrained manners wouldn't allow her to just ignore him.

"Mmm?" she replied.

He paused. "Are you okay?"

She shook her head on his shoulder and hoped that would suffice for an answer.

Jon Tate spoke softly to Elijah. He was saying something about needing to get back to the car, but Julianna paid him no heed. She had no intention of going anyplace else tonight, no matter what Jon said; it was late, and her parents and her brothers were waiting for her and Ben just inside the house.

They're all dead, Julianna Dapper whispered. *There is no house.*

Don't be ridiculous, Julianna Larson snapped back. *Ben is right here with me, and everybody else is waiting up for us in the living room.*

She felt Ben's arm go rigid around her.

"Shit!" he gasped.

Jon Tate swore, too, and she forced herself to open her eyes. Both boys were staring south, toward Pawnee; from their current position on the hill, it was possible to see most of the gravel road between the Larson farm and the town. The headlights of two cars almost a mile away seemed to be what had alarmed the others, but Julianna didn't understand why this should be the case. She was mildly curious about who might be out and about at this hour of the night in Pawnee—only a few people in town owned cars, after all—yet the boys were scrambling to their feet as if somebody had lit a fire in their pants.

"You're a bad influence on Ben, Jon," Julianna complained. "He never used to curse before he met you."

She didn't notice the grimness of her friends' expressions as they gazed at her, because she was now watching the approaching cars with more interest. The headlights were getting closer very quickly; she hadn't known it was possible for automobiles to move at such speeds.

"Whoever they are, they're certainly in a hurry, aren't they?" she asked.

Chapter 15

"This is insane!" Mary Taylor protested, glancing nervously over her shoulder at the headlights of the car that was gaining on them even though Sam Hunter was driving at a suicidal speed on the bumpy county road. "I don't have any idea how this crazy woman you're trying to find knows the name of my son—or anything at all about Pawnee—but whoever she is, she is *not* Julianna Larson, and that man behind us is *not* Julianna Larson's son. Julianna Larson died when she was *fifteen*, and I promise you she never had a child!"

The two Marys were in the backseat of Bonnor Tucker's "borrowed" station wagon, gripping their respective door handles to keep from being tossed around in the seat as Sam floored the accelerator and swerved madly left and right in a futile attempt to avoid the biggest potholes in the gravel beneath their wheels. Edgar Reilly was in the front passenger seat, clutching his own door handle and moaning to himself.

Mary Hunter—who had spent the past two minutes or so filling in the older woman on why Gabriel Dapper was pursuing them—spoke calmly over the rumble of the station wagon's engine. "Did you ever learn what happened to the man who killed your son and the Larson family? I know you said he was never caught, but did you ever hear anything else about him?"

Mary Taylor shook her head, marveling that the younger woman could remain so poised while being flung about like a rag doll.

"The Larsons' car was abandoned up in Iowa someplace, but the police never found a trace of Rufus," she answered. "I've prayed every day of my life for news of that man, because if there was ever a soul on this earth who deserved to hang for what he's done, it's Rufus Tarwater. Nobody ever proved he did all the killing, but he disappeared the night of the fire, and everybody knew how much he hated Eben Larson."

"What if he kidnapped Julianna instead of killing her?" Mary Hunter asked, forcing herself to concentrate. She was steeling herself for a showdown with Gabriel Dapper and had little energy to spare for a decades-old murder mystery. "What if he took her somewhere else and she managed to get away from him?"

Mary Taylor shook her head and stole another glance through the rear window.

"They found the remains of all five of the Larsons, along with my boy," she said. "The coroner had an awful time because the bodies were so badly burned, but there were definitely six of them. Ben was . . ." Her voice thickened and she paused to swallow. "The three bodies they found at the front of the house were Ben and the Larson boys. The fire didn't get quite as hot there and you could still see enough to . . . to guess who they'd been. But there was almost nothing left of Eben and the two women. The coroner said the one on the lawn was most likely a man, so he figured it was Eben—which meant that the two in the kitchen *had* to be Julianna and her mama. But the kitchen was where the fire was hottest, and the body on the lawn had been . . ."

She fell silent, staring at nothing.

Edgar Reilly's curiosity temporarily overrode his fear for his life, and he turned around in the front seat. "Julianna's father didn't die in the house with the others?"

"No." Bitter lines formed at the corners of Mary Taylor's mouth. "Rufus singled Eben out for special treatment, or at least that's what the sheriff guessed. There was an empty barrel of gasoline next to Eben's body, and the coroner said Rufus must have used every drop of it on Eben." She looked down at her lap. "I'll give Rufus Tarwater one thing: That man sure knew how to hate."

Sam spoke over his shoulder. "How much farther until we're there, Mrs. Taylor?"

She peered over the seat through the windshield. "The Larson farm was right on top of that hill yonder." Wonder was slowly dawning on her face, warring with her doubt and sadness. "If by some miracle it turns out that Julianna Larson really *is* this person you're looking for, I would dearly, *dearly* love to see her again."

Edgar Reilly cleared his throat. "I'm afraid she might not recognize you," he cautioned. "Julianna's memory is highly selective, and quite unreliable."

Mary Taylor nodded. "I'd still like to see her." A glimmer of a smile touched her face. "She and my Ben thought the world of each other, and even if she can't answer questions about how he died, it would be good just to hear somebody else say his name. I thought I was the only one left on this earth who even knew a boy named Ben Taylor once existed."

The third large hill north of Pawnee loomed in front of them, and Sam floored the accelerator of the station wagon to make the ascent. Gabriel's Cadillac was less than a hundred yards behind them and closing the gap by the second, and the younger Mary in the backseat leaned forward anxiously, searching the darkness ahead of their own headlights for any sign of Elijah and the others. If Elijah was indeed on top of the hill, she was somehow going to have to find a way to keep him away from Gabriel until they got everything sorted out. She and Sam had no weapons, and if Gabriel wanted to hurt their son, she didn't know how she could prevent it.

"It will be all right, Mary," Edgar Reilly said, surprising her. "It will all work out."

She glanced over at him and managed a tense smile. Julianna's overtly neurotic psychiatrist was trembling with anxiety about the coming conflict, yet there was a resolve in his voice she hadn't heard before.

"Yes," she murmured, oddly reassured. "Yes, it will. Thank you, Edgar."

Edgar smiled back, resisting an impulse to offer her an M&M.

The headlights of the station wagon suddenly revealed the rear bumper of a lime-green Volkswagen on the right side of the road, fifty or sixty feet ahead of them.

"There!" Mary Hunter cried out, reaching over the front seat to seize her husband's shoulder.

Sam shot a quick look at the rearview mirror to gauge how soon Gabriel would catch up to them. The Cadillac was barreling up the hill toward them and was almost on their bumper.

"Gabriel's right behind us!" Sam snapped. "What should I do?"

Mary Hunter didn't have time to respond. The instant she opened her mouth, she saw a thin white boy leap from the cornfield on the left side of the road up ahead, running for the Volkswagen. He was wearing khaki shorts and a pair of sneakers; there were white bandages on his chest and back.

"There's someone!" Edgar squealed. "Is that the Tate boy?"

"Don't let Gabriel get around us, Sam!" Mary Hunter yelled, flinging an arm out in an attempt to prevent Mary Taylor from being injured. "Block the road!"

Obeying, Sam slammed on the brakes and spun the steering wheel to the left, causing the station wagon to skid to a dramatic halt twenty feet away from the green Beetle. The Cadillac behind them veered for the left side of the road and bounced violently across the cornfield ditch in a flanking maneuver, but it stalled out and came to a full stop seconds later, its high beams pointing west into the cornfield at the top of the hill.

The same cornfield where Elijah and Julianna were standing side by side, shielding their eyes from the glare of the lights.

Exactly thirty-nine years before the moment when Gabriel Dapper saw his mother and Elijah standing together in a Missouri cornfield, Mary Taylor had awakened her husband, Silas, from a deep sleep to tell him she wanted to bring their son, Ben, home from the Larsons' farm, on the other side of Pawnee. She and Silas loved the Larson family dearly, but after hearing about Rufus Tarwater's assault on Julianna Larson the day before, Mary knew she wouldn't be able to get any sleep herself until Ben was home safe and sound in the room next to hers. Silas tried to reassure her that Ben had probably just lost track of time and would be back soon, but she had been adamant, and Silas had at last gotten out of bed to hitch their horse to a buggy.

They didn't get far.

As they were leaving their home they smelled smoke in the air and saw the glow of an enormous fire over downtown Pawnee. Silas urged the horse into a gallop and they raced into town, where they spent the next several hours doing what little they could to help fight the conflagration. They were both still worried about their son, of course—especially when none of the Larsons showed up to assist with the fire—but they reasoned that the distance between town and the Larsons' farm had probably prevented Ben and the others from even knowing what was happening. Mary was still determined to bring her boy home later that night, however. But since Ben was far safer with his friends than he would be in Pawnee itself, she was willing to wait until she and Silas were no longer needed by those trying to contain the blaze.

This being the case, the Taylors didn't turn into the driveway of the Larsons' farm until nearly sunrise. By then there was nothing left on the hilltop but smoking ruins and dying coals; even the grass was black with soot and ash. Silas had to physically restrain Mary from doing harm to herself, and counted himself lucky when the force of her grief finally caused her to pass out in his arms. He drove the buggy back into town to get the sheriff, who was still investigating the town fire, and it would be several hours before the county coroner arrived and the remains of Ben Taylor and all of the Larsons could be dealt with.

Thus ended the first act of the tragedy that was Pawnee.

* * *

It's over, Elijah thought in despair as he, Jon, and Julianna all watched the cars drawing closer to the hill. Elijah assumed, as did Jon, that the vehicles belonged to the police; the absence of flashing lights and sirens was no doubt only an attempt to escape detection until the last possible moment.

"We can't outrun them," he said quietly. His heart was beating fast and his stomach had a knot in it, but the sheer terror that had plagued him all his life whenever anything bad happened was remarkably absent. "Even if we got into the Bug right now, they'd catch us in a mile or two."

Jon Tate heard the hopelessness in Elijah's voice and felt the same way himself.

"So what do we do?" he asked, fighting a nearly irresistible urge to flee on foot into the cornfields. He had no idea how the police had found them so quickly; it was as if they knew precisely where to look. "Should I get the guns?"

Julianna was frowning. "It's much, *much* too late for visitors. Momma's going to be mad as a hornet if they wake her up at this hour."

Elijah swallowed past a lump in his throat as he gazed into Julianna's confused face. "I've never fired a gun in my life," he said, turning to Jon. "And I don't think I can shoot anybody."

Elijah had guessed things were going to end like this eventually, but now that the actual moment was there he didn't care for his choices. Back at the jailhouse, things had seemed easier; Julianna had needed to get to the end of her journey, and that was that. But the circumstances had changed, and Elijah was no longer sure what was best for her—or for himself and Jon, either. Maybe it would be okay to let the cops take her back to the hospital now; maybe he and Jon had done all they could.

Jon was looking at the younger boy with desperation. "We've gotta do *something,* man," he pleaded. Jon hated the idea of shooting somebody as much as Elijah did, but he couldn't just stand around and wait for the police to haul them all off again. "Shouldn't we at least try to bargain with them or something?"

Elijah had no illusions about the outcome of any sort of standoff with the police involving guns: He and Jon would end up dead within minutes. Yet if Jon wanted to try for a better outcome he wasn't going to argue with him; a life in prison—or the hangman's noose—was all they had to gain by letting themselves be caught and led away like a pair of sheep.

He met the other boy's gaze with a bleak nod and swallowed hard.

Jon bolted for the car at once, not needing any other encouragement. "Stay here with Julianna!" he ordered over his shoulder. "I'll be right back!"

Elijah and Julianna watched him sprint through the cornfield, moving very fast in spite of his wounds. The cars were on their way up the hill now, and Elijah almost yelled out for Jon to come back, not sure at all that the older boy would be able to beat the police to the Volkswagen, even though the Beetle was only fifteen yards away from where he and Julianna were standing.

Julianna stirred. "You boys don't know how lucky you are to run around all summer long without having to wear a shirt," she murmured. "It's so unfair."

Gabriel Dapper saw Jon Tate leap into the road at the same moment the Hunters did, but his elation at finally spotting one of the boys who had taken his mother was short-lived.

"Shit!"

The station wagon he'd been chasing suddenly skidded to a halt and effectively blocked the road in front of him. Gabriel shot out into the cornfield, trying to go around the other vehicle, but his Cadillac bottomed out in the ditch and the engine stalled as Gabriel bashed his forehead against the steering wheel, opening a cut over his left eyebrow.

He rocked back in his seat, cursing, but then froze as he gazed through his windshield. His mother was only a few yards away, standing next to Elijah Hunter on the hilltop. The boy was holding Julianna's arm with one hand and shielding his eyes with the other.

"MOM!" Gabriel howled, fumbling for the weapons on the floor of the passenger seat. "MOM!"

* . * . *

Mary Hunter was the first one out of the station wagon. She saw the Tate boy yank open the driver's door to the Volkswagen on the side of the road but paid him no mind; all she cared about was reaching her son ahead of Gabriel Dapper. The dome light in Gabriel's Cadillac popped on as Gabriel threw his own door open in the cornfield; the big man was yelling for his mother as he clambered out of his vehicle.

"NO, GABRIEL!" Mary screamed, running into the cornfield. She could hear Sam right at her heels. "GET DOWN ON THE GROUND, ELIJAH! HE'S GOT A GUN!"

Blinded by the headlights of the car facing them in the cornfield, Julianna stumbled a little and Elijah took hold of her arm to steady her. They could hear car doors opening and a man roaring, "MOM!" over and over again.

"I think I know that voice," Julianna muttered, puzzled. "But I can't quite place it, can you?"

"NO, GABRIEL!"

A woman's cries sliced through the man's, and the sense of unreality Elijah was already feeling increased a thousandfold.

"Mom?" he whispered, shielding his eyes with his free hand in an attempt to see what was going on. "MOM!"

"GET DOWN ON THE GROUND, ELIJAH! HE'S GOT A GUN!"

Who the hell ARE all these people? Jon Tate wondered, clawing his way back out of the Volkswagen with Ronnie Buckley's and Bonnor Tucker's revolvers in his hands. *Where are the cops?*

Elijah and Julianna were standing in the glare of a car's high beams, and a small black woman and a thin black man were running through the cornfield toward them. An elderly, paunchy white man and an old black woman—both of whom seemed uncertain what to do—were getting out of the station wagon on the road beside the Volkswagen. And standing by the car in the cornfield was a huge shadow of a man, matching scream for scream with the running black woman. Elijah dragged Julianna to the ground as Jon watched, and the big man inexplicably spun around to face Jon and raised his right arm over his head a moment later. Jon—thinking he saw a gun in the man's other hand—brought up one of his own revolvers in a panic just as his opponent in the cornfield made an exaggerated throwing motion.

Jon froze as something came flying through the air, straight at him. *What the hell is THAT?*

Mary Hunter screamed a warning to her son, and Elijah instantly seized Julianna and dragged her to the ground.

"LET GO OF MY MOTHER!" Gabriel bellowed, threatening the boy with a pistol. "GODDAMMIT! LET HER GO RIGHT NOW!"

A sixth sense warned him to look back at the road, and in the glow of the station wagon's taillights he could see Jon Tate standing by the Volkswagen. The young man had a gun in each hand, and it didn't take a lot of imagination to guess what he intended to do with them. Gabriel instinctively pulled the cord on one of the German potato masher grenades and heaved it across the field at Jon, praying it would buy him enough time to save Julianna.

Julianna Dapper was more than a bit confused.

"Get off me, Ben!" she demanded, struggling to get out from under her friend's weight on the ground. "I can't breathe!"

"He's got a gun, Julianna!" Elijah snapped. "Please stop fighting me!"

Julianna froze at the word "gun," incapacitated by a flash of memory. *Rufus has a gun!* she thought in terror. *He's going to kill us all!*

Jon heard the dark projectile whiz by him, missing by just a few inches. It sailed into the open door of Chuck Stockton's beloved Volkswagen Beetle, ten feet behind him, and Jon gasped in shock, not knowing what had nearly taken his head off but assuming it was a large rock.

Jesus, that had some serious torque on it! he thought, belatedly dropping into a crouch in case the man threw something else.

Squinting through the high beams, Elijah saw the big man in the cornfield throw something at Jon Tate, saw Jon duck into a protective crouch after the missile rocketed past his head. There was an instant to wonder why the man hadn't just used his gun on Jon instead, but then the interior of the Volkswagen erupted in a ball of fire. Elijah watched in horror as a second, almost simultaneous explosion from the gas tank flung Jon facedown on the road, his arms and legs spread wide like a skydiver. The older man and woman who were farther away from the blast than Jon both reeled backward in terror, covering their ears with their hands as the Beetle was engulfed in hellish flames.

"JON!" Elijah wailed. "JON!"

Unthinking, he leapt to his feet, staring numbly across the field at the unmoving body of Jon Tate.

"No, Ben!" Julianna cried, scrambling to her feet, too. "Rufus will kill you!"

Mary and Sam Hunter had nearly reached their son when the Volkswagen blew up behind them. Both of the Hunters spun around in shock at the explosion, not believing what they were seeing.

"Dear God in heaven!" Mary cried, clutching at Sam as they gaped at the twenty-foot-high plume of flame in the road above the wreckage of the Beetle.

The glitter of broken glass was all over the road, surrounding the still body of Jon Tate, and shrapnel had shattered the windshield of the station wagon. Mary Hunter shook herself, recovering, and twirled around again, just in time to see Gabriel Dapper bringing the Mauser to bear on her son.

"NO, GABRIEL!" she shrieked, already knowing she was too late to make any difference.

*   *   *

Julianna heard someone scream "NO, GABRIEL!" and her past and present collided with the force of two atoms in her psyche. The man in front of her who had been Rufus Tarwater suddenly became her own son, Gabriel, and his well-loved face set her mind spinning dizzily, like a poorly designed top. Her body, however, still moved without hesitation—as if it didn't care whether it was the property of a teenaged girl or a middle-aged woman; as if it knew exactly what it was doing and the price it was being asked to pay; as if it belonged to a single united soul named Julianna, who wasn't about to let someone else pay that price for her.

Not this time.

"NO, SON!" she screamed aloud, instantly hurling herself between the man and the boy.

Elijah saw the barrel of the gun pointed at his own heart, saw Julianna dart between him and the man with the gun. He shoved her out of the line of fire but she sprang in front of him again, and he grabbed at her desperately, trying to shield her with his own body.

"LET HER GO!" Gabriel roared. "GODDAMN YOU, LET HER GO!"

Julianna broke free of Elijah's grip just as a gunshot rang out on the hilltop. Julianna staggered backward and fell at his feet like a drunkard.

"Julianna!" Elijah cried. There was a small, neat hole in her green dress, right beneath her breasts. He cried her name once again before dropping beside her.

"GET AWAY FROM HER!" Gabriel bellowed in rage and horror. "GET AWAY FROM MY MOTHER!"

He was still holding the Mauser in his hand but he didn't seem to realize it was no longer pointed at Elijah. The second potato masher was in his other hand, but it, too, was forgotten.

"Sweet Christ," he whispered, staring blankly at the scene before him.

"Oh, Jesus," Elijah sobbed as Julianna convulsed in pain. Julianna, gasping, reached out and clutched Elijah's hands, and in the light from Gabriel's high beams both Elijah and Gabriel could see the front of her dress had turned red.

"Is Jon okay?" she panted. "Is he alive?"

Elijah glanced over at Jon's body on the road and shook his head, choking on his tears. "I don't think so."

The bullet Gabriel had fired into his mother's body was somehow inside of Gabriel himself now; he could feel it working its way toward his heart. The anguish on Elijah Hunter's face and the desperation with which Julianna was holding Elijah's hands told him more clearly than anything else could have that the boy he had just tried to shoot was not a killer and a kidnapper after all, but only a boy.

"Oh, Jesus," Gabriel panted, running forward and falling on his knees beside his mother. He dropped his gun and the grenade on the ground and gathered Julianna's head into his lap.

Mary and Sam Hunter were struck dumb by the sight before them. The man who had just attempted to kill their son had discarded his weapons and was now seated less than a foot away from his intended victim; Gabriel's left knee was actually in contact with Elijah's right thigh. Mary's first impulse was to grab Elijah by the shoulders and drag him away from this bizarre tableau, but the vivid grief etched into his face stopped her. Mary's breath caught in her throat as her son's eyes met her own and she had to bite her lip to keep from crying out his name again.

"How badly is Julianna hurt?" Edgar Reilly yelled from across the cornfield, where he was hovering over the motionless body of Jon Tate. "I'm coming as quickly as I can!"

Mary didn't know if there was anything Edgar could do for the Tate boy, but it was obvious to her that nobody on earth was going to be able to save the woman on the ground at her feet. Julianna Dapper herself was apparently of the same opinion; she shook her head in Gabriel's lap.

"Tell him to stay with Jon," Julianna murmured to Gabriel. Gabriel—who knew a mortal wound, too, when he saw one—was beyond responding. He wanted to do what his mother had asked of him, but all he could manage was to raise his head and look toward the road in mute misery. Mary pressed Sam's hand and Sam left at once to relay Julianna's message to Edgar. There were sirens in the distance as Sam passed Mary Taylor in the cornfield. Gabriel pressed his forehead against Julianna's, and then broke down completely.

"Hush, son," Julianna whispered. "It's all right. It's all my fault." She blinked, gazing up at the sky. "The stars are so pretty tonight, aren't they, Ben? We should wake up Michael and Seth."

Gabriel made a bewildered noise and Elijah tried to explain.

"She means me," Elijah murmured. "She thinks my name is Ben."

Julianna sighed. "Your name *is* Ben, you ninny," she breathed. "Honestly, you may need psychiatric help."

Mary Taylor, her elderly knees popping, was suddenly kneeling at Julianna's other side. "Julianna? Oh, honey, I can't believe it's really you! It's me, Mary Taylor, Ben Taylor's mama. Do you remember me?"

Julianna searched the older woman's face for a long moment and then smiled in delighted recognition. "Hi, Mrs. Taylor!" she said. "Look, I've . . . brought Ben back . . . home, good as new!"

Tears spilled down Mary Taylor's wrinkled face. "Thank you so much, honey," she rasped, caressing Julianna's cheek. She glanced across Julianna's body at Elijah and her lips trembled as their eyes met. "I've been missing him something awful."

"It took us . . . took us forever to . . . to get here," Julianna gasped. "I'm sorry we're late." She turned her head and blinked again, and the timbre of her voice shifted abruptly. "Look, Elijah."

The grieving boy followed her gaze, barely noticing she'd called him by his correct name. A second later he cried out with immense relief: Jon Tate was on his feet and headed their way, supported by Sam and the older man Elijah had noticed earlier. The revolvers Jon had retrieved from the Volkswagen were now tucked awkwardly in Sam's belt, leaving his hands free to help Jon walk.

"Is that . . . your daddy . . . with Jon?" Julianna asked Elijah. "You're the . . . spitting image of him." She loosened one of her hands and reached up to stroke Gabriel's face; he blubbered uncontrollably as she ran her hand over the stubble on his jaw.

"My sweet Gabriel," she murmured. "You look awful."

Jon Tate, Edgar, and Sam joined the loose circle around Julianna. Edgar knelt beside Julianna and shook his head sadly as he pressed his hands to her wound; Jon sank down beside Elijah with a groan. The Volkswagen had borne the brunt of the explosion, but even so he was coated with dirt and blood; shrapnel from the blast had lacerated his back and his legs in several places and the bullet wound on his chest was bleeding again, saturating his bandages. He was trembling from shock and he put a hand on Elijah's shoulder to steady himself.

"Hi, stranger," Julianna greeted him sweetly.

"Hi, Julianna," Jon husked.

He tried to say more, but he couldn't seem to get the words out. The sound of sirens was getting much closer, and Julianna winced as she became aware of them. She looked at Mary Taylor once again and her brilliant green eyes filled as she studied the older woman more closely.

"I am . . . so sorry, Mary!" she cried. "I tried to . . . save Ben . . . but I couldn't . . . couldn't save . . . I killed Rufus . . . but . . . it was . . . I was too late."

Mary Taylor made shushing noises but she herself was no longer able to speak. Her hand continued stroking Julianna's face, however, never faltering, her slender, wrinkled fingers occasionally drifting into Julianna's short hair. Julianna's mouth filled with blood and she struggled to speak again; Elijah guessed what she was trying to say and said it for her:

"She loved your son very much," he rasped. "She told us he died trying to stop Rufus from killing her family."

Mary Taylor's chin quivered and she bent down to kiss Julianna on the cheek before turning away. Julianna looked at Elijah gratefully, and her eyes then moved to include Jon as she fought to say something else. The boys leaned closer to hear her, their heads touching.

"Thank you, boys," Julianna whispered. "Thank you for . . . bringing me home." She looked up at Gabriel again and smiled, thinking she was seeing Lars Olsen, the town blacksmith.

"What . . . are you . . . doing here . . . Lars?" she asked.

As Julianna fell silent and stopped breathing, Elijah put his arms around Jon Tate and cried into the older boy's shoulder. Jon rocked him back and forth, crying now, as well, and Mary and Sam Hunter watched in baffled sadness, feeling useless and more than a little taken aback by the extent of their son's distress over the death of a woman who had kidnapped him and dragged him halfway across the country. Elijah's weeping didn't sound like the child who had been stolen from them less than two days before; there was something in his grief they had never before heard from him, something wholehearted and terrible that made them feel as if they were watching a stranger. Equally disconcerting was that Elijah had turned for comfort to Jon Tate instead of to them; the Elijah they had always known would sooner pet a rabid dog than reach out to someone who wasn't family.

Mary felt a pang of jealousy she was immediately ashamed of. She told herself she should be glad her son had found other people to love; she reminded herself that after everything that had happened to Elijah it was only natural for him to seek solace from someone who had lived through the ordeal with him. But it was still a very hard thing to stand back and allow the Tate boy to hold him when he was suffering. All she wanted to do was take Elijah in her arms and whisper reassurances in his ear; all she wanted to do was feel his heart beating against hers and his breath against her neck as she had done a thousand times since the moment of his birth. Surely she had more right to be with him and help him through this than Jon Tate did?

No, Mary told herself sternly. *No, you don't. Stop acting like a fool, and just be glad he has someone to care for him.* She felt Sam take her hand, and with an aching heart she watched their son grieve without them.

Edgar Reilly, kneeling next to Mary Taylor, was startled to find that his own cheeks were wet. He hadn't cried in years and had almost forgotten what the sensation felt like. He wanted to speak to Gabriel, but he knew there was nothing he could say that would matter; the other man was in the kind of hell where words have no meaning. Edgar looked over at Elijah Hunter and Jon Tate, envying the innocence of their tears; his own felt contaminated with remorse for having played a part in all that had happened.

Gabriel Dapper raised his head and stared over at the road. Four police cars—two from the south and two from the north— were speeding toward them and would be there shortly; the fire from the Volkswagen on the top of the hill was as bright as a lighthouse beacon, drawing them to it.

Gabriel bent down once more and kissed Julianna's forehead, then carefully lifted her head out of his lap and slid from beneath her. He reclaimed his pistol and the grenade from the ground and stood up again. He didn't even glance at the two boys he had nearly killed that night, nor did he make any sign of recognition as his eyes flitted over Edgar Reilly and the Hunters. He turned and walked back toward his Cadillac, ten yards away; the two Marys, Sam, and Edgar all watched in stricken compassion as he got behind the driver's wheel once again and closed the door behind him.

The headlights on the Cadillac flicked off and left the hilltop in relative darkness, and Julianna Dapper's son stared through the window of the Cadillac at the moonlit silhouettes of the people circling his mother's body. His big hands were moving of their own accord as he sat there, and he was almost surprised to find that he had put the Mauser pistol down in the passenger seat. He was still clutching the grenade, however, and he glanced down at it as if he had never seen it before. In one smooth motion he pulled its cord and dropped it in his lap. The five-second fuse on the grenade permitted him just enough time to begin to sob before the inside of the Cadillac turned into a crematorium.

Chapter 16

Speeding toward the top of the hill in a squad car, Bonnor Tucker swore aloud as he saw his stolen station wagon blocking the road in front of the burning carcass of a Volkswagen Beetle.

"What the hell is this?" he muttered.

An enormous explosion in the cornfield to his left nearly caused him to drive into the ditch. He fought to bring his car back onto the gravel and he gaped at the inferno engulfing Gabriel Dapper's Cadillac. Twenty feet away from the explosion was a cluster of people all standing or crouching beside somebody lying on the ground; Bonnor immediately spotted Mary and Sam Hunter, and the fat doctor, and an old black woman he didn't recognize.

It took him another second, though, to notice who else was there, partially hidden behind the old black woman and the fat doctor.

Bonnor slammed on his brakes so fast that the state trooper who was following him up the hill almost rear-ended him. As Bonnor skidded sideways and came to a halt with his headlights pointed at the group in the cornfield, two Missouri squad cars flew over the top of the hill from the other direction and screeched to a stop, too, a dozen yards from the burning Beetle. Bonnor scrambled for his shotgun and threw open his door, praying that Elijah Hunter and Jon Tate would give him the chance to avenge Ronnie Buckley's death—and his own humiliation.

"Please, please, PLEASE do something stupid," he muttered, taking cover behind his door. The trooper who had followed him was doing the same thing, as were the others by the Volkswagen.

Samuel Hunter dragged his wife to the ground as Gabriel's Cadillac erupted in fire. Fragments of the car's windshield rained down in the cornfield all around them; Sam heard Edgar Reilly and Mary Taylor both cry out but was too astonished to do anything except stare at the wall of flame in front of him. An instant later he saw Gabriel Dapper's body inside the car, burning like a torch, and he recoiled in horror.

"Mother of God!" he gasped. Bile rose in his throat at the sudden, sickly sweet smell of roasted meat.

Mary spoke Samuel's name, jarring him back to awareness; they got to their knees together and turned as one to check on their son. Elijah was goggling at the fire with Jon Tate but neither of the boys seemed to have sustained any additional injuries. Edgar Reilly was tending to Mary Taylor, using his tie as a tourniquet for her forearm. Edgar himself was bleeding freely from a cut in his cheek, yet he was apparently more concerned with the older woman's injury.

A harsh, booming voice sounded above the crackle of the fire. "GET DOWN ON THE GROUND AND PUT YOUR HANDS WHERE WE CAN SEE THEM!"

Across the cornfield four police cars had lined up on the road, one after another; the blaze from the wreckage of the Cadillac was brighter than all their high beams combined. The shouted order came from one of the Missouri state troopers by the Volkswagen, but it was quickly followed by Bonnor Tucker's equally loud, equally hostile voice, a little farther down the hill.

"BACK THE FUCK OFF, ASSHOLES, THIS IS *MY* GODDAMN ARREST!"

There was a short pause, then the Missouri trooper responded.

"THE HELL IT IS! IN CASE YOU HAVEN'T NOTICED, ASS-WIPE, THIS IS *MISSOURI*, NOT FUCKING *IOWA!*"

Sam glanced down at the revolvers in his belt, deeply regretting having picked them up on the road earlier when he was helping Jon Tate to his feet. Jon had asked him to bring the guns along and Sam had agreed, thinking it might be wise to have them just in case Gabriel Dapper lost his head again. But now that Gabriel was dead and the police had arrived, Sam didn't want the revolvers anywhere near his family.

"WHO GIVES A RAT'S ASS WHERE WE ARE?" Bonnor Tucker roared back at the trooper. "THE TWO LITTLE ASS-HOLES OUT THERE KILLED RONNIE BUCKLEY, SO DON'T PULL ANY JURISDICTION BULLSHIT ON ME! THEY FUCKING BELONG IN *MY* JAIL!"

Mary Hunter's lips were thin as she sized up the situation.

"I will *not* permit that vile man to take the boys," she whispered to Sam, tilting her head in Bonnor Tucker's direction. "If he gets them alone again their lives won't be worth a plug nickel."

Her eyes were glinting in the firelight from the Cadillac, and for the first time that evening Sam felt hope stir inside him. He didn't know if Mary's mojo could do any good for Elijah at this point, but the menace exuding from her was a welcome sight nonetheless.

Please, Lord, Sam prayed. *Please don't let anybody start shooting until she's had her say.*

"MAYBE YOU SHOULDN'T HAVE LET THEM OUT OF YOUR JAIL IN THE FIRST PLACE, DIPSTICK!" retorted the Missouri trooper, out-shouting Bonnor. "NOW WILL YOU PLEASE SHUT THE HELL UP AND LET ME DO MY JOB?"

Elijah Hunter and Jon Tate had released each other but were still sitting side by side near Julianna's body. Neither of them was particularly interested in the heated exchange between the two policemen; the shock of Julianna's death and everything else that had happened on the hilltop had left both boys numb to anything so tame as a shouting match. Elijah took one of Julianna Dapper's limp hands again in his own and held it against his cheek. Her fingers were already growing cold.

"I'm so sorry, Julianna," he whispered, looking down at her still, pale face. He couldn't believe how much it hurt to lose her; he felt like he might cry for days. He glanced at Jon and saw tear tracks running through the grime on the older boy's face; Jon met his eyes, then bowed his head and ran a hand through his hair, sighing. Elijah's throat constricted and he shut his eyes, wishing he could just as easily shut his ears, too, against all the noise surrounding them.

Bonnor Tucker and the other lawmen ceased bickering at last; Bonnor had apparently lost the battle of wills because it was the first Missouri trooper's voice that now addressed them across the field.

"ALL OF YOU LAY FACEDOWN ON THE GROUND! I'M GONNA COUNT TO THREE AND WHOEVER ISN'T KISSING THE FUCKING DIRT WHEN I GET TO THREE IS GONNA GET SHOT, SO YOU BETTER LAY THE FUCK DOWN RIGHT NOW!"

"Great," Elijah Hunter murmured wearily to Jon. "Another cop that likes to count to three."

"Everybody do what he says," Mary Hunter said calmly, taking charge. "Elijah and Jon, move as slowly as you can. Make absolutely sure to keep your hands in plain sight, every single second, understand?"

"ONE!"

Elijah let go of Julianna's hand with an effort and sighed. It no longer felt wrong to surrender; if he and Jon tried to put up a fight or run away at this point, it would only get more people hurt. Besides this, he knew his mother's tone all too well and he wasn't about to argue with her. (He may have become braver in the last two days than he'd once imagined possible, but he doubted he'd ever be brave enough for *that*.) He began to stretch out on the ground beside Jon, but as the trooper yelled "TWO," Bonnor Tucker's distinctive voice interrupted the proceedings yet again:

"THE NIGGER'S GOT A GUN IN HIS BELT!"

Elijah froze on all fours, suddenly terrified not for himself but for his father, who did indeed have both of the revolvers Jon and Elijah had stolen earlier from the jailhouse. But Samuel was already facedown on the ground with the revolvers tucked securely beneath him; his empty hands were raised high above his head. Why was Bonnor just now making a stink about the weapons if he had seen them before Sam laid down?

"WHICH ONE OF THEM?" demanded the first Missouri trooper.

"WHICH ONE WHAT?" Bonnor roared back.

"WHICH ONE HAS THE *GUN,* DUMBASS?"

"THE KID, YOU STUPID SHIT! THE NIGGER KID!" Bonnor raged. "HE'S GOT IT UNDER HIS SHIRT!"

Elijah's jaw dropped, not understanding, but beside him Jon Tate began to swear.

After Bonnor Tucker had lost the war of words with his colleagues, things had become painfully clear. The two teenagers who had made a fool of him and killed Ronnie Buckley were slipping away from him, and if he didn't act quickly he would soon be sent back to the Maddox jailhouse with nothing but his own dick in his hands as a consolation prize. He'd be the permanent laughingstock of Creighton County; he'd be called "Boner Toucher" until the day he died.

"HE'S GONNA TRY SOMETHING!" he now screamed, determined to prevent such a fate, no matter the cost. "HE PULLED THIS SAME SHIT WHEN RONNIE AND ME ARRESTED HIM!"

No, I didn't, Elijah thought numbly, unsure as to whether he should continue lying down or stay where he was.

"YOU'RE A LYING SACK OF SHIT, *BONER!*" Jon Tate yelled. Jon, like Samuel, was facedown on the ground with his hands in the air, but his head was raised and he was glaring with hatred at the headlights of Bonnor Tucker's car. "ELIJAH DOESN'T HAVE A GUN, AND YOU KNOW IT!"

"FUCK YOU!" Bonnor screamed back. "WHAT I *KNOW* IS THAT YOU TWO LITTLE COCKSUCKERS LIKE TO KILL PEOPLE THE SECOND THEIR BACKS ARE TURNED!"

"Hush, Jon!" admonished Mary Hunter, also from a prone position. "Elijah, don't move an inch! Don't even blink till I tell you!"

Elijah was the only one by Julianna's body who wasn't stretched out on the ground; he wanted to lie down with the rest of them so he wouldn't feel quite as vulnerable. Emotional and physical exhaustion was making it impossible to think, and he glanced down at Julianna again, envying the peaceful expression on her face. The flickering firelight on her dress almost made it look as if she were still breathing. He hoped it was quieter wherever she was than on that hilltop; he desperately wanted to go to sleep himself, but everybody kept yelling at him.

"MY SON IS UNARMED, AND HE'S GOING TO LAY DOWN JUST LIKE YOU TOLD HIM!" Mary hollered to the first Missouri trooper. "PLEASE, *PLEASE* DON'T LET THAT *STUPID* MAN SHOOT HIM!"

"Can you tell if the kid has a gun?" This same Missouri trooper called softly to his compatriot by the Volkswagen. "I don't think he's got one."

The second trooper shook his head. "I think Boner's full of shit," he called back, snorting.

"ARE YOU SURE YOU SAW A GUN, BONNOR?" yelled Walling, the Iowa trooper on Bonnor's other side. "I DON'T SEE ANYTHING!"

"ARE YOU ALL RETARDED?" Bonnor yelled back. "I ALREADY TOLD YOU IT'S UNDER HIS SHIRT! YOU CAN'T SEE IT, BUT TRUST ME, THE FUCKING THING IS THERE!"

The Missouri trooper's temper was beginning to fray.

"I DON'T CARE IF HE'S GOT A GODDAMN ATOM BOMB TIED TO HIS SHORT HAIRS!" he bellowed at Bonnor. "AS LONG AS HE LAYS DOWN ON THE GROUND AND KEEPS HIS HANDS UP, WHAT THE *FUCK* DOES IT MAT-

TER?" He waited for a response but Bonnor remained gratifyingly silent. The trooper took a few deep breaths to regain his equilibrium, then turned back to Mary Hunter.

"NOBODY'S GONNA SHOOT YOUR KID, LADY! JUST HAVE HIM LAY DOWN NICE AND SLOW, AND EVERYTHING'S GONNA BE PEACHY, OKAY?"

Mary glanced at Sam for a moment and waited for him to nod, then she whispered to their son to do as he'd been told. Elijah obeyed immediately and started to lower himself into a spread-eagled position, keeping his hands as far from his waist as he could. Jon Tate hissed at him to slow down, and Mary nearly smiled in spite of herself. Elijah was already moving like a turtle; if he moved any slower he'd be at a standstill.

"HE'S REACHING FOR HIS GUN!" Bonnor roared.

Jon Tate had listened to Bonnor's accusations about Elijah with growing distress, not believing what he was hearing. That the trollish deputy from Creighton County was mean enough to pull the trigger was a given, of course, but that he'd actually think he could get away with committing murder in front of an audience boggled the mind. Jon heard the Missouri trooper who was in charge tell Elijah's mother that no one was going to shoot her son; he then heard Mary Hunter tell Elijah to lie down. The younger boy began to obey, moving too quickly for Jon's liking; Jon snapped at him to slow down, unable to remain silent.

"HE'S REACHING FOR HIS GUN!" Bonnor bawled as Elijah lowered himself to the ground incrementally.

Jon couldn't bear it any longer: Julianna's death was bad enough but losing Elijah was unthinkable; he felt certain Bonnor was going to pull the trigger any second. He sprung up and flung himself on top of Elijah, dragging him to the ground and shielding him with his own body.

And Bonnor Tucker, who had been praying for just this kind of precipitous, foolish move, pulled the trigger.

Coincidence had saved some of Its best material for last.

The daughter of one of Bonnor Tucker's neighbors in Maddox was a seven-year-old tomboy called Candace Perona-Schonhorst who loved to play with toy soldiers. She was especially fond of the tiny green riflemen, and owned hundreds of them; she liked to line them all up on the porch railing of her home and shoot them down one after another with rubber bands, often engaging in this activity for hours at a time until the skin of her right index finger was bloody from the friction of the rubber skimming across it.

Candace Perona-Schonhorst was equally enthralled by real guns.

The day before Bonnor fired his shotgun in that Missouri cornfield, he was sitting on his front porch during his lunch break, cleaning his weapons—which he did as ostentatiously as possible, savoring the wary looks from passersby. Candace was out playing in her own yard at the time, and she skipped across the grass to watch Bonnor oil and fondle both his shotgun and his revolver. Bonnor pretended to ignore her, of course, but he enjoyed having the small girl as a spectator for this almost daily ritual of his, mistakenly believing she was admiring him and not only his weapons.

He had just set the shotgun down after cleaning it and was moving on to the revolver when a cheeky carful of Maddox's teenagers drove past the house and screamed "BONER TOUCHER!" through their open windows. Bonnor instantly leapt to his feet and raced to the road with his revolver to put the fear of God in the disrespectful miscreants, but they had the good sense to not stick around and wait for his arrival. He was gone from the porch for just forty seconds or so, and his back was only turned away from his home for no more than twenty of these.

Twenty seconds, however, was more than long enough for Candace Perona-Schonhorst to discover a perfect hiding place for three of her tiny plastic riflemen.

Bonnor was a very good shot, and by all rights the large, lethal buckshot in the shells *should* have ripped through Jon Tate's back and burrowed straight into Elijah Hunter afterward.

But sadly—at least from Bonnor's perspective—it was not to be: The small, clever fingers of seven-year-old Candace had done their work well, and the three tiny toy rifleman she had jammed deep into the barrel of the shotgun caused the weapon to explode in Bonnor's face instead.

"FUCK!!" Bonnor wailed, dropping the ruined weapon and clutching his face in agony. The stock of the shotgun had slammed into his cheek with enough force to fracture the bone beneath his right eye, and he was blinded in that same eye by a microscopic bit of shrapnel. He reeled away from his squad car and fell into the ditch, still howling.

"FUCK!!" he shrieked again.

"HOLD YOUR FIRE!" roared the first Missouri trooper. "NO ONE ELSE DO A GODDAMN THING UNTIL I SAY SO!"

"Are you all right, Bonnor?" Iowa Trooper Walling called.

"NO, I'M NOT FUCKING ALL RIGHT!" Bonnor squealed, spitting out a broken molar.

"What just happened?" Jon Tate whispered to Elijah, who was still beneath him. From where they were, Jon could see Bonnor thrashing around in the ditch, but he didn't dare raise his head to investigate further. He was in no hurry to move, anyway; the side of his face was pressed against Elijah's back, and each and every inhalation Elijah took felt to Jon like a holy blessing, as did the frantic pounding of his own heart.

"Beats me," Elijah murmured in answer to Jon's question, resting his head on the earth and feeling strangely at peace. "But I don't think Boner liked it very much."

"Yeah," Jon agreed. "He sounds kinda upset."

"FUCK!" cried Bonnor Tucker.

Epilogue

Julianna Dapper and her son, Gabriel, were buried in the Lone Rock Cemetery in Hatfield, Missouri, right next to the graves of Eben, Emma, Seth, and Michael Larson—and just a few yards away from Ben Taylor. There was already a headstone there for Julianna, of course, but rather than attempt to sort out precisely whose remains were buried beneath each of the old stones, it was determined by a county judge that none of the Larsons' graves should be disturbed, and a new stone should be made for Julianna, as well as Gabriel. No one who had been made privy to Julianna's account of what had really taken place at the Larson farm on the night of the Pawnee fire was thrilled by this ruling, however, and Mary Taylor even went so far as to threaten to dig up Rufus Tarwater with her bare hands from beneath Eben Larson's weathered tombstone and toss his "filthy, murdering bones in the trash." After being informed that very little of Rufus would still be "tossable" after thirty-nine years in the earth, Mary was only slightly mollified.

"His damn dust is as bad as the rest of him," she had snapped at the judge before at last giving up. "No part of that man has any business being left next to those good people."

The graveside funeral for Julianna and Gabriel was attended by Elijah Hunter, Jon Tate, Mary Taylor, Sam and Mary Hunter, Dr. Edgar Reilly, and Jon Tate's parents, Earl and Marline, who had flown out to Missouri to be with their son through all the legal proceedings. The sky was cloudless, and the aromas of freshly dug earth and roses mingled with the less pleasant bouquet of cow dung from a pasture bordering the cemetery. The minister of the Lone Rock Church asked if anyone would like to say a few words about either Julianna or Gabriel, and Elijah tried to say something about Julianna but was unable to speak. Jon tried to come to his rescue but fell mute himself after only a sentence or two, so in the end it was Edgar Reilly who felt called upon to offer a short eulogy.

"I never knew Julianna when she was sane," Edgar said, furtively removing a lemon drop from beneath his tongue so he could speak clearly. "And I only really knew Gabriel when he was under a terrific strain. I'm sure neither of them would have chosen to be remembered in this manner, and I'm sorry I didn't know them when they were . . . more themselves. But regardless of their mental states at the end, their deaths are a terrible tragedy."

Edgar's voice abruptly roughened and he paused. It was another blistering summer morning and he was perspiring heavily, though not nearly as much from the heat as from his smarting conscience. He glanced over at the iron fence surrounding the cemetery, and at the small, whitewashed Lone Rock church nearby, where Julianna and her family had once been parishioners. Edgar's gaze at last fell on the two sad boys standing by Julianna's open grave, and he spoke directly to them when he resumed.

"There are many, many things I wish I had handled differently in all of this," he said quietly. "I am sorrier than I can say for everything you boys have gone through, and as I told the authorities, you are not to blame for *any* of the awful things that happened. My only consolation is that if Julianna hadn't escaped from my care, she may never have found the peace she so desperately needed. Nor would she have met the two of you, and I believe she was very lucky to have you with her on her strange odyssey. It comforts me to know she spent her last days on earth with people who were kind to her, and cared for her, and did everything in their power to keep her safe. Thank God for you boys."

"Amen," Mary Taylor murmured, and Mary Hunter reached out and briefly took Edgar's hand in her own as he fell silent again.

Over the past few days Elijah and Jon had gotten to know Edgar a little. At first they'd found him a little pompous, and overfond of giving unsolicited advice, but they'd gradually warmed to him, especially after learning everything he had done to get them out of trouble. The FBI had completed its investigation, and Edgar's testimony had proven crucial in proving their innocence. He had insisted that everything that had happened was Julianna's doing, and consistent with her pathology. That Lloyd Eagleton had finally awakened from his coma and confirmed that Julianna had indeed been driving the Edsel when it had run over him was also pivotal, as was Mary Taylor's account of what had passed between Julianna and her supposed "captors" after Julianna was shot.

Moreover, Cecil and Sarah Towpath—the elderly couple who had first reported Julianna's kidnapping—were sought out, and soon confessed to exaggerating their account of the incident. The FBI also had an equally fruitful telephone conversation with Sal Cavetti, the perpetually stoned poet who had accused the boys of raping Julianna, in which Sal was told by the lead investigator to "Cut the bullshit, freak, or I'll drive out there myself and kick you in the ass so hard your goddamn balls will pop off." The hastily updated testimonies of the Towpaths and Sal in hand, there remained only one felony indictment against the boys: The assault on Deputy Bonnor Tucker at the Maddox jailhouse. Mary Hunter paid the stubborn deputy a short visit, and thirty minutes later—after the district attorney received an urgent phone call from a gibbering Bonnor Tucker—the FBI's two most wanted criminals were no longer wanted for much of anything. Jon still faced prosecution for stealing cash from his employer, but as Jon's parents promised to take him back to Tipton to make amends (and, unknown to the police, to tend to Becky Westman's pregnancy), both boys were free to attend the funeral for Julianna and Gabriel on the following morning.

And after that, to part company and go home.

They stood side by side as Julianna's casket was lowered into the earth. As they listened to the minister's benediction the reality of what was going to happen in the next few minutes began to sink in. Jon would get into his parents' rental car—along with Edgar Reilly, who was hitching a ride—and head south to the Kansas City airport, and Elijah would join Sam and Mary in their pickup and depart immediately for the east.

I can't believe this, Elijah thought, with a tight knot in his stomach. He had known the separation with Jon was coming, of course, but until that moment he'd managed to put it out of his mind. *First Julianna, now Jon.*

Hold your shit together, Jon Tate ordered himself sternly as he felt his eyes beginning to burn. *Don't be a baby.*

"In the name of the Father, the Son, and the Holy Spirit," the minister intoned, "amen."

Mary Hunter looked at her son and Jon, and without a word spoken she herded Jon's parents and the rest of the adults away from Julianna's grave, allowing the boys some privacy to say their good-byes. Elijah and Jon stood in awkward silence until the others were out of earshot, and then Jon knelt slowly beside Julianna's grave and tossed a handful of earth onto her casket. Elijah knelt beside him and stared with dismay at an earthworm wriggling around in the wall of dirt an inch or so above the lid of the coffin.

"So," Jon muttered. "That's everything, I guess."

"Yeah," Elijah whispered. "I guess so."

Jon glanced over at him and cleared his throat. "You clean up good," he said. "I can't get used to seeing you in a suit."

Elijah was wearing a new dark blue suit his mother had bought him for the funeral. The bruises on his face were beginning to fade and the bags under his eyes had vanished. Jon was also wearing a suit; his parents had brought the brown three-piece Jon had last worn to his senior prom in high school. It was a little too short in the arms now, but it still fit reasonably well and made him appear older than usual.

"You look okay, too," Elijah answered, wiping his nose on his sleeve. "You shaved."

Jon grimaced. "Mom made me."

"My mother made me shave, too." Elijah paused. "I don't really know why, though. I've only got about four hairs on my whole face."

They fell silent again and listened to the wind blowing through the stones of the graveyard. They could hear the adults talking softly over in the small gravel driveway beside the church; Edgar Reilly was holding forth about something or other and it sounded as if Mary Taylor was teasing him.

Elijah cleared his throat. "So are your folks still mad?"

Jon shrugged. "They've stopped chewing me out for taking the money and running away, but Mom keeps going on and on about Becky Westman and the baby. She stopped yelling at me for a few minutes this morning, though, so I think she's starting to run out of steam."

Elijah bit his lip. "Will they make you get married?"

"I dunno." Jon broke apart a dirt clod and let the loose earth run through his fingers. "Before I ran away, Becky's parents said they'd call the cops if we didn't get hitched, but maybe they've calmed down by now." He paused and sighed. "I doubt it, though. They were mad as hell."

Elijah untied a shoe and then retied it. "Maybe they'll just let you pay child support or something."

"Maybe." Jon resisted scratching at the wound in his chest; it was itching a lot as it healed. "But either way I'm going to have to get a real job now, I guess." He tried to smile. "I'm not too worried about it, though. Know what I mean? After everything you and me have gone through, Becky and her folks don't seem so scary."

Elijah smiled back. "Yeah. At least they're not shooting at you."

"Yeah, that's a plus." Jon sighed, smile fading. "I almost wish they would, though. It might make things easier."

Jon's dad called out to tell them they had to leave soon if they were going to be on time for their flight. Jon waved to acknowledge he'd heard.

"Listen . . ." he started, turning back to Elijah, but his voice stopped cooperating before he got any further.

Elijah nodded and his eyes brimmed over. "You better get going."

Jon's chin trembled and he struggled to swallow. "I'll come visit as soon as I get things straightened out a little," he said. "That's a promise, man. Okay?"

Elijah nodded again and wiped his eyes. "I'd like that. I can show you around our farm."

Talking about getting together helped, but not a lot.

He'll probably forget all about me, Elijah thought.

Once he gets home I'll probably never hear from him again, Jon told himself.

Elijah rose to his feet and helped Jon get up, too. They stood beside Julianna's grave for another long moment, then Jon reached out and pulled the younger boy into a fierce embrace. Elijah squeezed back just as tightly, feeling Jon's ear against his own ear, feeling his friend's tears on his own cheek.

"Seeya, man," Jon murmured at last.

"Seeya," Elijah said.

Deputy Bonnor Tucker would wear an eye patch for the rest of his days. To his endless torment, this did not lessen the taunts about his name; in fact, it worsened them. The scamps of Creighton County found demonic inspiration in Bonnor's misfortune, and came up with a fresh batch of nicknames—including "Long John Nutsack" and "Bonerbeard"—to add to the old standbys.

Dottie Buckley had a terrible time dealing with the death of her husband, Ronnie. She moved out of the apartment above the Maddox jailhouse and rented a small house a few blocks away, but her loneliness grew with each passing day, and she tried to take her own life just four short months after Ronnie's funeral. What pushed her over the edge was the premiere broadcast of *McHale's Navy* on television. Seeing Ernest Borgnine on the small screen was too much for her; she couldn't bear remembering how well Ronnie had imitated Borgnine, and how much pleasure it would have given him to watch his Oscar-winning hero each and every week, in the privacy and comfort of their own living room. Dottie, never a drinker, promptly ran out to the liquor store and purchased a bottle of rum, which she then slugged down in its entirety, along with a quantity of sleeping pills her doctor had prescribed the week before. She had been having trouble sleeping in spite of the pills, but on this night she almost found eternal rest, curled up in Ronnie's old armchair. One of her sons dropped by for a visit, however, and discovered her in the nick of time; the same son came to the hospital the following day to get her after she had recovered, and insisted she come live with him and his wife. Dottie became a grandmother soon thereafter, and found a great deal of joy late in life helping to take care of little Ronnie, her grandson, who looked a great deal like Ernest Borgnine.

Orville Horvath, the fire-worshipping marshal from New Hampshire, nearly burned to death in an accidental blaze at his own home, but was saved at the last minute by Lucy the Rottweiler. The diminutive marshal had decorated his Christmas tree with multiple candles (in the Scandinavian fashion) and had fallen asleep on the floor while admiring his handiwork. The tree caught fire, and Lucy—who had been confined to the basement earlier in punishment for eating one of the candles—clawed her way through the basement door and physically dragged Orville from the living room after he had passed out from smoke inhalation. Lucy's frantic barking alerted a neighbor who summoned the fire department, and both Orville and Lucy escaped from the fire unscathed, save for the bite marks on Orville's ankle from where Lucy had clamped on to him. Unfortunately, Orville suffered extreme humiliation after waking up on his own front lawn: The tree-lighting ritual he had been engaged in (decidedly un-Scandinavian in origin) had required him to be naked, and even after being wrapped in a blanket by the firemen, he was unable to conceal the excitement he felt as he gazed at the flames ravaging his home. His superiors dismissed him from active duty shortly thereafter, and he and Lucy moved out of the state, never to be heard from again.

Mary Taylor lived another seven years after the deaths of Julianna and Gabriel Dapper. She passed quietly in her bed one night, dreaming of her husband, Silas, and her son, Ben, and of their years together in Pawnee. Edgar Reilly wept when he heard of her death; the two of them had become unlikely pen pals and he found himself missing her letters terribly after she was gone. She was buried in the Lone Rock Cemetery with her family, and because she had outlived almost everyone with whom she had shared her life, there was almost no one at her funeral. Her passing marked the true end of Pawnee, as well, for she was the last soul on earth who had once lived there, and could still picture the little town in her mind's eye.

Dr. Edgar Reilly was forced to retire at age eighty-two from the Bangor State Mental Hospital, because he himself was exhibiting signs of dementia. The hospital staff members who had been most closely linked to Julianna—Helen Gable, Jeptha Morgan, and Connor Lipkin—were all long gone by then, but Edgar had begun to address all his nurses and orderlies by the names of their vanished predecessors. By the time he was released from his responsibilities, his desk drawers were crammed to overflowing with M&M's and lemon drops, and he was whistling the tune of *I'm a Little Teapot* nearly nonstop each and every day. Edgar died of a heart attack on the same afternoon he was scheduled to be admitted to a nursing home; the paramedics found him on his sofa, surrounded by hundreds of Tootsie Roll wrappers and the collected works of Carl Jung. It took six strong men, grunting and cursing, to carry his substantial body from the house.

June 24, 2012

At the top of the third hill north of town, a purple Volkswagen Beetle with Maine license plates sat by itself on the side of the gravel road, basking in the hot sun. The Beetle was bug-spattered and muddy from a long journey; its windows were open and its backseat was littered with Pepsi cans and empty wrappers from various fast-food restaurants. Next to the gravel road were rows and rows of knee-high cornstalks, blanketing the hill and reaching down into the valleys on either side: an entire army of corn, standing at rigid attention and awaiting inspection.

In the middle of the cornfield, right at the crest of the hill, stood Elijah Hunter, watching Jon Tate wander around the cornfield, looking for the boarded-up well that had once been the last trace of the Larson farmstead.

"I guess they filled it in," Jon called out. "But it was right around here."

Elijah nodded. "That's what I remember, too," he called back. "Or maybe a little behind you."

Jon walked back toward him and Elijah watched him come. The half century that had passed since the last time they had visited this hilltop had been kind to Jon; he was turning seventy in another month but he might have passed for a man in his mid-fifties. He was still slender and handsome, with a full head of salt-and-pepper hair; his face was relatively unlined and he moved easily across the field. The only sounds on the hill were of the breeze moving through the corn, and the hum and chirp of insects.

Jon stopped in front of him and sighed. "Pretty weird, huh?"

Elijah smiled. "Which part do you mean?"

Jon grinned back. "All of it." He looked around the field. "Fifty years ago it was a war zone up here, and a long time before that, Julianna's whole family got wiped out on this exact spot. Now it just looks like a great place for a picnic, and we're the only ones left alive who know what happened here. Us and your folks." He turned back to Elijah and raised his eyebrows. "And then there's us: Two retired old geezers on a road trip, paying our respects to the lady who almost got us both killed— oh, and by the way, she had schizophrenia, and her son blew up two cars with grenades."

Elijah laughed. "Yeah, okay, it's a little weird."

He squatted and put his arms around his knees, and his face slowly sobered as he studied the field. The memories of that long-ago night on the hilltop were still vivid; he knew if he closed his eyes it would be waiting for him, ready to play itself out like a movie in his head.

Jon knelt beside him. "So if the well was over there, then . . ."

"Then this is about where Julianna died," Elijah finished. He put a hand on the dark Missouri soil, dug his fingers into the earth. "Yeah. I guess it probably would be."

Jon was right about the strangeness of everything; Elijah felt a surprising ache of sadness as he remembered the feel of Julianna's hand in his and the sound of her voice.

Since that frantic weekend in 1962, five decades had passed, and the boys they had been were just as dead as Julianna. Elijah and Jon had both lived full, busy lives: For Elijah there had been college, two tours in Vietnam, law school, a successful law practice, marriage and kids, grandkids, and now a great-grandkid; for Jon there had been marriage to Becky, kids, college, divorce, grad school, remarriage, a college teaching job, more kids, and now grandkids, as well. Their friendship had never faltered through any of it; they still lived in separate towns in Maine but they saw each other all the time; Jon's kids worshipped Elijah and Elijah's kids adored Jon; Jon was also a second son to Samuel and Mary Hunter, who were now in their nineties but healthy and happy, and still very much in love. Mary kept herself busy by terrorizing the staff at an assisted living facility in Elijah's hometown, and Sam spent his days playing cribbage with ex-Sheriff Red Kiley, who lived next door to them in the same facility. Elijah and Jon went to visit the elder Hunters often, separately and together, and never left without a kiss on the lips from Mary and a bear hug from Sam.

In short, Elijah had a very good life, and he knew it. But until that moment he had not realized how much he still missed Julianna Dapper.

He brushed the dirt from his hand and looked up to find Jon watching him.

"What?" Jon asked.

Elijah shrugged. "I was just thinking about what our lives might have been like without Julianna. I'd probably still be wetting my pants every time I had to leave my house, and we never would have met. And you'd probably be . . ."

". . . I'd probably still be on the run from the law." Jon paused, considering all the years that had passed since he had gotten into an Edsel on a rainy day in June, when he was nineteen, and far from home, and hating his life.

He studied Elijah Hunter's well-known and much-loved face, remembering the first time they'd met. Elijah was mostly bald now, with a fringe of short white hair above his ears, but his eyes were the same, brown and sensitive, and his smile was the same, too, warm and generous. There was no denying the deep wrinkles around his eyes and at the corners of his mouth, though; he was starting to look like a grandfather, and a man with a far longer road behind him than the one he still had to travel.

"She took us on one hell of a ride, didn't she?" Jon asked quietly, unable to keep from grieving a little bit for everything that had been lost to time, and all the loss still to come. "Do you think she's waiting for us someplace?"

Elijah read the shift in Jon's mood and reached out with a gentleness that had always been his, putting a hand on the other man's shoulder. He didn't say what he was thinking, though; it was too hard to put into words. Yet if their time with Julianna Dapper had taught him anything, it was that the world was an arbitrary and ridiculous place, where all things were possible. Coincidence and human stupidity held sway much of the time, but not always: There was love, too, of course, and companionship, and now and then even a measure of grace.

At least for those who were wise enough to have faith in the ridiculous.

The very last thing that passed through Julianna Dapper's mind before she died, oddly enough, was a memory of two boys, running side by side down an alley in a small, nameless

Midwestern town. It was early morning, and there was a stripe of green grass in the middle of the alley, and a puddle of water that shimmered in the sunlight as the boys skirted it and came back together on the other side. Julianna was standing next to a lime-green Volkswagen Beetle in a gas station parking lot, and she was waiting for her friends to come back to her. She could hear the sound of their shoes on the gravel and see the glint of perspiration on their skin; she could smell freshly cut grass from a nearby lawn. She watched the boys run together, and she thought how beautiful they were—like a pair of mismatched colts, one black, one white—and she wished the alley were longer so she could keep on watching them for a while. But even as she wished this they were at her side again, and talking about stopping someplace for breakfast soon, and wondering how much farther it was to Pawnee.

"Not far," she told them, thinking what a fine thing it was to have such good company on the road home. "We'll be there before you know it!"

As last images go, it was a good one.

Please turn the page for a very special
Q&A with Noah Bly!

Where did you get the idea for this novel?

My grandmother, Nellie Nixson, was born and raised in Pawnee, Missouri, a tiny little town in northern Missouri that burned to the ground sometime around the Great Depression. When I was a kid, she used to take my family and me around the area where Pawnee stood, showing us where her house was, where the blacksmith's shop was, etc., but everywhere she pointed there was nothing left to see but cornfields and weeds. This made a big impression on me, knowing that a thriving little community had come and gone without leaving a trace behind, and I always wondered what this must have been like for Grandma looking at all that nothingness through the lens of her childhood memories. The book is completely fictional, of course—save for the actual name of the town and the fact that it was destroyed in a fire—but I like to think my grandmother would have been tickled to see Pawnee briefly resurrected, even if only on paper.

You've said that this book is in the picaresque tradition. What do you mean by that?

I think it can be seen as a more modern take on Don Quixote: a crazy person on a quest, aided by sane friends—kind of a "rogues on the road" sort of thing. The cross-country journey and the oddball friendship between Elijah Hunter and Jon Tate both remind me somewhat of Huckleberry Finn, too, though the similarities didn't dawn on me until I was most of the way through my first draft.

What research did you have to do?

Lots and lots of stuff on Wikipedia, mainly about 1962 and 1923, but also about everything in between, too. What the inside of an Edsel looked like, the eccentricities of a 1957 Volkswagen Bug, how a German potato masher worked, etc. I also had to harass, relentlessly, a couple of older cops (mostly

Sergeant Jeff Yates of the Bettendorf, Iowa, Police Department—a man of seemingly infinite patience) about small-town sheriffs and deputies in the 1960s and what their job was like, the equipment they used, the kind of guns they trained on—you name it, I asked about it. Fortunately, neither time period I was writing about was in the far distant past, so I was able to find most of what I needed without much trouble.

Did you revisit the site where Pawnee used to be?

Three times. The first two were intentional—just poking around the cornfields to get the feel of the landscape—but the third was a bizarre coincidence. I went to a high school reunion one summer weekend last year in my hometown, which is thirteen miles or so away from where Pawnee was, and ended up visiting a classmate's farm for dinner and having drinks with some old friends. It turned out that the farm we'd been invited to was located smack in the middle of where Pawnee used to stand. Pawnee has been gone for seventy-five years or more, and there are only a handful of people left alive who even know it was ever there, so it seemed pretty weird to find myself, by complete chance, sitting on a back porch looking out at the same remote hills and fields I'd been writing about for the past three years, and only a few hundred yards from where my grandmother grew up. The book is largely about coincidences just like this one, though, so I guess maybe I shouldn't have been so surprised.

What's your writing process?

For this book I found myself napping a lot. Sad but true. I'd write for a bit, get stuck on something, then have myself a fifteen-minute nap to recharge my imagination. In general, though, I try to write a page a day. Sometimes I'm lucky if I get a usable sentence, other days I dash off two or three pages in a couple of hours. There doesn't seem to be any real pattern to it, other than sitting down to write each day. If I don't write every day, I lose the momentum of whatever story I'm trying to tell.

Who are the authors you admire the most? What books inspired you to be a writer?

Oh, God, there are so many. I'm a big fantasy and science fiction fan, so I love Tolkien, Ursula K. Le Guin, Patricia McKillip, Guy Kay, Steven Erikson—just to name a few people I wish I could write like. I also love Michael Cunningham, Annie Proulx, Michael Chabon, E. B. White, Chaim Potok, and John Irving, but if I had to pick my overall favorite author I'd probably have to say it's Charles Dickens. The man had so much talent—and so much heart—it's unbelievable. *David Copperfield* is an absolute masterpiece, cover to cover. Another one of the main books that made me want to be a writer is a collection of essays by E. B. White called *One Man's Meat*. The writing in those essays is nothing short of gorgeous—gorgeous without being showy, witty without being overly clever, sweet without being cloying, sad without being sentimental, wise without being pompous and all-knowing. I can remember reading those essays for the first time and thinking: "Jesus, I want to do that." I've never even gotten close, of course, but maybe someday . . .

THE THIRD HILL NORTH OF TOWN

Noah Bly

About This Guide

The suggested questions are included
to enhance your group's reading of
Noah Bly's *The Third Hill North of Town*!

DISCUSSION QUESTIONS

1. Does *The Third Hill North of Town* fit into a specific genre? Is it a crime novel? A tragedy? A dark comedy? An action-adventure story? What best describes it?

2. Which of the three main characters—Julianna Dapper, Elijah Hunter, or Jon Tate—is the strongest? The most vulnerable? The easiest to care about? Of all the minor characters, is there one that is particularly appealing (or repelling)?

3. Is there a discernible theme to this novel? If so, what would it be?

4. Throughout the story, Coincidence is referred to many times as a type of deity, almost like the trickster character Coyote in various Native American mythologies. What does this contribute to the overall narrative?

5. Edgar Reilly's Edsel Ranger and Chuck Stockton's Volkswagen Beetle are very much part of this novel, possessing distinct "personalities" of their own. Why do you think the author chose these particular automobiles for this story?

6. The interludes all take place in 1923, as opposed to the rest of the book, which is set in 1962. How does the author weave these separate timelines together to tell Julianna's story? Why are the interludes interspersed throughout the novel instead of just having the 1923 story be told all at once?

7. Julianna, Jon, and Elijah—a trio of misfits—become very close over the course of the novel, though in reality they are only together for two days. Why do you think they bond the way they do? What does each of them gain from the others?

8. In a sense, every character in this book can be seen as emotionally damaged. Who is the least damaged? The most?

9. As the story progresses, several characters noticeably change, for either good or bad. What are some examples of this? Which character changes the most?

10. Much that happens in this book is bittersweet, including the ending. What do you think the author is trying to convey about the nature of friendship and the passage of time?